The
Romance
Novel

Erika Ramson

♥ - Chapter 1 - ♥

Harley Millsboone had taken a year off before going to college. Being nineteen and entering higher education did not sound strange to her. She did have her own concerns, but she was sure they were no different than anyone of any age once they entered into the process of a degree.

Her family was with her, carrying her belongings into her dorm. Between the four of them, Harley had barely done any carrying at all. Her father and brother insisted that they take care of it, giving her the chance to fully enjoy her moving in without heavy lifting. There was also very little lifting from her mother, and Harley knew well enough that she never really stepped in on this territory anyway. Her father was stronger, he didn't want his wife to concern herself. Harley never saw her mother complain or even think much about this, she must have seen it as a good deal.

It would be an interesting few years. She knew the plan was four, and she was hoping that would be the exact amount of time. She had a major, she'd spent part of the year off deciding on it, thinking it over long enough that she could no longer doubt it was what she wanted.

She looked down at her right hand. She still wore her high school ring on that ring finger. It glistened slightly from the sunlight, and like with any bored person wearing finger rings, she gave it a quick spin with her other hand.

It was white gold, with a pink stone. Some people preferred to have the color of their birth stone, but Harley always saw this as narcissistic, she simply chose a color scheme that she thought was cute. This was the attitude she normally had when it came to dressing herself.

Today she wore blue jeans, with a pink flower design stitched on her left leg. White shoes, no heel, she rarely ever felt daring enough to walk around like a dizzy giant. Her top was light grey, and she had another cloth shirt over it, open like a jacket. Today was not one of the days she chose to wear something low-cut. She felt no need to bare her goods today, and had no interest in using the tactic to grab someone's attention. This was her first day of college, she could bother attracting men at a later time.

On the subject, her last boyfriend had been perfectly fine for a high school love affair. They had broken up shortly after high school had ended. Her soul searching led her to realize that he wasn't as big a part of her life as she had once believed, not unlike many people with their first love.

He took it surprisingly well, apparently he was growing tired as well. She considered keeping in contact with him, but it was best to wait at least another year. She heard too many stories of young women keeping in such close contact so soon after a break-up that they ran right back to him, married him, and had the most bitter divorce you could imagine the year after. Being friends with him did not necessarily mean she would jump back into his arms, but she may as well wait until she was sure every romantic feeling towards him was in fact dead.

Granted, perhaps she never had too romantic of feelings in the first place. She had dated him the full four years, no other boy had gotten her attention. They'd gone to prom together, but only in their senior year as neither of them felt junior prom meant anything.

They'd never slept together. Harley was never a prude, she knew it was mostly hypocritical to be one, that nothing was wrong with the act of love if you were consenting and knew what you were doing.

And yet here she was, a virgin. She was comfortable with her body, she'd gone to a school that taught her exactly how to safely practice, she had parents who gave her the talk after her first period. She simply didn't love the guy enough to ever even talk about it to him.

He'd never brought it up either, perhaps the most damning sign they would end, neither discussing the subject. Sure, the act of sex had been a subject they talked about, just never involving the two of them. Only hypotheticals.

Whilst in the middle of her reminiscing, her father walked over to her.

"Hon, we've got everything out for you."

"Thanks dad."

He walked her into her dorm, the first of hopefully only four that she would be living in for the next four years.

It had been cleaned up quite nicely. Her side was quite lovely, if she said so herself. Girly if she was being kind to stereotypes, but maybe more mature than many others would decorate once they gained their first living space outside of their parent's house. Maybe not, she would have to find out later.

She hadn't chosen her side on her own, the roommate she had yet to meet had arrived the day before and already unpacked. Harley knew this roommate was a year younger, but she clearly had everything put together up top, which hopefully meant they would get along just fine.

She just now noticed a note left on the roommate's bed. At first she ignored the other side of the room, but the little slip of paper finally caught her eye.

Hey roomie. Lol.
I'm Anne Shaman, hope you like me.
I'll be here the day after you.
I unpacked but I need to stay home for a bit.
Maybe I'll explain, depends how much I like you.
Lolz.
Sorry if I sound dumb, don't have much time to write this.
Kisses.

With a letter like that, Anne's likability could go either way, Harley figured. She folded the note back up, and simply put it back on her roommate's bed. She could throw it out for herself, or at least Harley could do it later if there was nothing else to do.

Harley turned back to her father.

"Alright kiddo. I guess you say goodbye to all of us now."

"Yeah. I guess I do."

Harley returned down to the front of her dorm building. She noticed her father seemed very reserved, he was good at keeping harder emotions in when he knew to. He never subscribed to the theory that men always need to hide their emotions, but ever since she was a little girl he told her that he felt it was always useful to know exactly when to emote what you are really thinking.

As her mother was a wreck, clearly her father didn't want to make the situation last longer by joining her in the sorrow.

"I'm not dying mom I'm just living here now."

"You're my little baby girl and I don't want to say goodbye to you."

"It's not all that far away. I'll still see you when I can."

"I know but it's not the same."

"Mom. Please. You knew I was going here, I rather you just said you're proud of me and let me be."

"I am proud of you but I don't want to say goodbye."

Her mother held her, and proceeded to cry all over her shoulder. There was enough moisture to start trickling down her shirt. Thankfully her mother let go before it was bad enough she'd have to change.

"Okay." Her mother said "I know. You have you go. I love you. Be careful."

Her father walked up to her next.

"See you kiddo."

Her father hugged her as well. Harley was not entirely sure if she was surprised that her father ended up shedding a tear as well.

"Tell anyone I ended up crying and I tell them about the time you were nine and you slept with us because of the thunderstorm." He whispered to her.

"I'll keep that in mind." She whispered back.

The last one was her brother.

"Um. I. Huh. I need to talk with you alone I guess." He said

"Alright?"

Harley and her older brother took a few steps around the corner of the building. To respect their privacy, their parents had left to the car.

"Look, I, I'm your big brother so I guess I'm supposed to give you advice."

"Okay then. Say what you want."

"Harl. Sorry if I trip up I only just thought of this." He took a second. "While you're here, no matter what, do whatever the hell you want to do. Don't, don't get scared of what people think of you or, fuckin', don't do something to get friends unless you'd like to actually do it, or. Fuck. Look. People will judge you your whole life because people are like that, so fuck what they think and just do what you feel like you'd like to do. You'll find people who don't give a shit, who'll love you. Alright? Do I, do I make sense, or?" He stopped, his thought had ended.

Harley gave him a smile. "Yeah. You make sense. I'll bang and I'll drink or I'll skydive because I fucking feel like it. I can be an adult and handle the consequences, no matter what anyone says."

He ruffled her hair. "I love you little sis. I'd say be good, but, fuck it. Come back alive and I'll be happy."

"I love you too. I'll come see you all soon."

Harley watched as her family drove away. Quietly, she walked back up to her room. Without a roommate, she was completely alone, so she fashioned her trashcan, and proceeded to open her tissues.

She only needed two, but she'd always been the kind of person to use just enough, or less, than she needed.

Around the start of the evening hours, which being fall meant it was already dark, there was a knock on her door. Harley figured that most likely, her roommate Anne had come back earlier than the two of them first believed. Instead, she was face to face with a young man in a button-up shirt, acid-washed jeans, brown shoes, and a nametag.

"Hi!" The nametagged boy said "My name is Josh!"

Harley counted her blessings that he didn't actually point at the nametag when he had said that.

"Yeah, hi." She said

"I'm one of the many RA's in your building! I'm just letting you know about the floor meeting we have in about twenty minutes!"

"Do I have to go?"

"It's highly recommended that every person in the building come down to meet and greet everyone! There'll be games and food for everyone."

Harley thoughts were ranging from "Get out of my face." And "Shoot me now."

"If it's all the same to you I'm sure I'll meet everyone else later."

Harley noticed a tiny twinge in Josh's face after her answer.

"I think it'd be really good if you came downstairs with all of us," He searched for her name on the door "Anne."

"Anne's gone, I'm Harley."

"I'm sorry, I'll be sure to get it from now on. Now why don't you think more about heading downstairs for the floor meeting?"

"Fine, I'll think about it."

"Then I'll see you there!"

Harley closed the door, whilst not slamming it, to ensure Josh would leave as soon as possible.

She turned back to lay in bed when she realized how crafty he'd been.

She'd only said she'd think about it, knowing he'd go away, but by saying he'd see her there....

"He'll fucking come back if I don't show." She felt so stupid she had to say it aloud. "Next time one of these is about to pop up I'll head out of here before he can get me."

Harley instead went to her fridge and grabbed a soda. She could at least try to be on the same level of insane energy as Josh had been. Maybe it would make him more tolerable, and maybe it would simply make it easier to talk back to him.

After her quick drink, she walked her way down. Being early could be an easy way to see if anyone was actually going to come.

There was hardly anyone in the stairwell who wasn't bringing in their stuff. Maybe this is what an extra year had taught her, that it was smart to go early to avoid getting trapped by everyone who came in the middle of the night.

And while the stairwell was not barren, the room for the floor meeting was close to such. There was still ten minutes until the actual event, and Harley's guess was that everyone else was going to be late. Or that the majority of the dorm's residents had every intention of not coming at all. She'd find out the answer if she waited long enough.

Josh had tried talking to her a few times while she waited. His interest went beyond her, he had tried talking to everyone else who was there. Harley noticed a few of the RA's were like Josh, and a few others couldn't muster the ability to give a crap.

In around ten minutes, the others arrived. It turned out that several of them did in fact decide to show up. From the look of it, most of the people present were first year students like her. Something about they way they introduced themselves to everyone, making it obvious they didn't know anybody yet and were ready to make an impression.

Harley was not beside herself. She was hating every single moment of this boredom atrocity.

"Alright!" Josh said, practically screaming with joy "We'll throw this ball around, and every time someone catches it, they say their names, their hobbies, and their major. It's an old theatre trick I learned in high school, great fun!"

Harley thought, "Staring at a fucking wall could probably be something you would find fun." And she was close to saying it to him as well.

The ball was thrown around the room. Harley was forcefully introduced to several people. A couple of Mirandas, an Amanda, a Keith, some Jims and Bills, all names she was going to forget by tomorrow, and maybe within the hour.

After the game, everyone either chatted with each other, or went directly to the food. Harley was the latter, but they ended up not being anything she wanted after all. Fruit punch and cookies were fine on occasion, but she hadn't eaten dinner and this would not help her out tonight.

She decided to stare out the window, hoping maybe some other, much more interesting activity, would show itself.

She couldn't believe it when said event actually did happen.

"Oh shit it's a barbeque." One of the others said, maybe one of the Jims or Bills.

"Oh right." One of the bored RA's said "There's a bigger meet and greet for the whole campus tonight. Couldn't remember if it was tonight or tomorrow."

Everyone seemed happy at this new plan. Harley was more so eager to actually eat something that could count as her dinner. The only one not happy about the event, was Josh.

"Yeah, well." Josh said, slower than usual. "A barbeque sounds fine but we're already all here, we might as well wait a little bit."

Most everyone else, including RA's, had already left.

"Hey. HEY!" Josh said "Come on! We were getting to know each other."

Harley felt no pity for the guy, but it was beneficial to speak nicely to him right now. "You can meet everybody if you go with us Josh. It's not like it'll be too different from what we were doing."

Josh began getting slightly huffy. "Yeah. I'll go. You get on ahead then, I'll just clean all of this up I guess."

Harley was given permission to leave him alone, and she immediately took it.

The smell of cooking meat filled a lot of the outside air. It had gotten late, so the typical smells of nighttime were also around. The crisp grass being cooled by the moon, the air gently blowing the trees, and dirt being kicked up by everyone around her. Yet nothing was as strong as the barbeque grills themselves.

Toasted buns, some of which slightly burned, barbeque sauce, hot dogs, all the condiments needed to make one perfect, and burgers. Harley never liked burgers, but she did like the smell. There was something about beef patties sizzling, something that made her envious of those who did enjoy them. The crunch could even be detected just by how well they smelled, how well they had been cooked through. From raw to well-done, and everything in between.

Harley, however, did like hot dogs. She received one from the people handing them out. The grill outline on hers was a light brown, enough to give the dog a pleasant taste and still hold all of its meaty juices. The bun had been buttered before it was cooked, giving it a golden outside that looked incredibly crispy.

Harley chose her condiment, which was only a little bit of mustard, and walked over to a tree to begin eating. Her first bite proved everything she suspected about it to be correct. This was a well-cooked hotdog, and the mustard had been kept cold enough to both compliment and contrast it.

She leaned up against a tree to keep eating. She didn't really care about being around anybody, it wouldn't have been a burden if someone came over to talk to her either.

And someone did come up, but it was clear he only was looking for a quieter place to eat as well. He was a well-dressed young man, smart in the fashionable sense. He wore blue jeans, not faded like Harley's, these were quite possibly brand new, and one of the more vibrant blues she'd ever seen for pants. He had a black t-shirt with long sleeves, and over it he had both a dark purple vest and jacket. His shoes were white-and-black, and his black almost-curly hair was parted quite finely.

After she noticed his clothes, he noticed her existence.

"Oh, hey." He said "Sorry were you trying to be alone?"

"Nah." She said "You're welcome here or whatever. One person won't stop me from eating."

"Cool." He said "Glad to know."

They quietly continued eating. After Harley had finished her dog, the stranger decided to give her a formality.

"My name's Max Turtle, by the way. In case we get to know each other."

"Max, Turtle?"

"I know, weird name. I've had it long enough to kinda like it."

"No no, it's. I think I've heard it before."

She took a look at his face. It wasn't placeable, but the name was sticking out for some reason.

"Did you join the band in your high school?" She said

"Yeah, yeah. I was a trumpet player, very briefly."

"So was my brother, well, in the band I mean. I don't remember your school, but did you have a game against us and both our bands played? My name is Millsboone."

"Huh. That name kind of sounds familiar, but I didn't meet him. Can't even place his first name, either. Guess it sticks out less than Turtle.

Huh. Strange little world, we didn't meet until now."

"Yeah. Strange little world."

"So, how are things?"

"To be honest, I just got here. I'm going to wait and see how this turns about before I'll have an answer for you."

"At least I know you're smart."

Only their first conversation, and the young man already complimented her. No reason to, he was just speaking the honest truth as far as he could see it. Harley smiled, why not, this complete stranger made the effort to be nice and he was pulling it off.

They continued talking, with Harley allowing Max to finish eating when the chances came. They say first impressions are important, that you cannot take them back. So far, first impressions were almost stunning.

Max planned on being a fashion designer, which explained his unique but workable taste. The band did not work out for him like he thought, but he had no regrets.

"You know, you just seek out an avenue and see if it works." He said "If it doesn't, then you were made to do something else."

"That's why I took the year off." Harley said "You really gotta learn who you are sooner or later. Figured it was best to do that before homework wrapped the noose around my neck and tried pulling."

Max chuckled. "Hate to tell ya, but I think we'll both have to learn more about ourselves anyway. My dad kept saying that to me earlier. You don't stop learning until a good deal after your twenties, and then there's still some minor shit after you wished you knew before."

"Smart man from the sound of it."

"Has his moments, like most dads."

The moon began to creep it's face around from the clouds. The two of them stopped once they noticed it.

It was a nice night, maybe a beautiful one. Nights like this, the sky was a special kind of black, or sometimes simply dark blue. The moon was incredibly close to full, Harley's favorite. It lit up the night sky, and yet there could still be some mystery covered in the dark.

She caught Max out of the corner of her eye, looking at the sky and moon roughly the exact same way she was. The moon was kind to him, she could see him clearly and make out a lot of him.

He was more attractive than her original notice gave.

Huh.

"It's a really nice night." Max said

"Yeah. You know, I love when the moon is like this. You see everything, but there's just a little bit of moon still hidden in the shadows."

"Yeah. I think I get ya."

"I know what the moon looks like, but it's like some crappy mystery where I know the answer but I still want to find out."

Max laughed again. "You've convinced me, I like whatever this moon phase is called too."

Now, Harley had turned to him. A thought was running through her head. A daring thought, something crazy, something she'd only go through with if she could look him in the face and say it first.

"Hey?"

"Yeah?" He turned to her now.

"Can we go to my room?"

"For what?" Max wasn't an idiot in the situation, it was clear to Harley how much he was just making sure he hadn't read the situation wrong.

"For exactly what you think I'm asking." She said.

Max thought it over. His arms were crossed, his eyes closed, and his head hung low. There were a lot of reasons why he'd be thinking it over, and Harley was hoping it wasn't because she'd thrown him for too hard of a loop. Eventually, he opened his eyes back up to look back up at the sky. Before he answered he brought his gaze back to her.

"Alright. You win, I'm game."

She didn't take another step before realizing the flaw in the plan. "Fuck, um. Yeah I don't have any condoms."

"I guarantee we can buy them somewhere around here."

Max and Harley had walked together to the campus convenience store. The concept sounded a little silly to her, completely on the nose to have a tiny little shop directly on the campus. Still, even if

16

it was going to overcharge them, she was happy it was there tonight.

"Er, how about I go in alone?" Max said "You don't know my size and it's less people seeing us together and starting the rumors that turn out to be true."

"I don't give a fuck about rumors but hey, take the privacy if you need it."

Max headed off inside. This gave Harley the chance to look up at the moon again and reflect.

"Hmm." She thought. "So I spent what felt like forever with you, and when it came to my first time, I ended up giving it to a total stranger instead Is this irony? I don't even know if I need to know, but, it's kind of funny." She laughed to herself. "Ah, life is so fucking stupid. Thanks for the advice bro. I'd have probably done this without it but it's nice having someone else on your side for the stupid shit."

Max only took about five minutes, which was still enough time for Harley to have both noticed and cleaned out some dirt she found on her nails.

"So, get this." Max said "I literally found a brand called 'turtle shell'. I hope you love that, because I do."

Max and Harley were only a few steps away from her door. While neither of them would have cared, they'd managed to sneak away while no one else was in the hall or anywhere near them. She

17

may not have cared about getting caught, but the idea of sneaking past a full hallway did excite Harley now that she knew that wouldn't happen.

Harley turned her key in the door, and let the two of them in.

It took a lot for her to not say "Make yourself at home." It was too stupid to say but she was almost completely willing to say it.

Instead, she just closed the door, put her keys on the table, and walked to her side of the room. They faced each other, dead in the eye.

Harley always expected banter, something cute and romantic before they, for lack of better terminology, dived into each other.

Instead, they just smiled and stayed quiet.

There was no tearing of clothes, the two removed them all by themselves. They were now down to their underwear.

Harley didn't usually wear silk, but she was glad that she was tonight. As if some foresight had told her it would pay off, and it did. Her bra was white as well as her panties, and both of them had a light pink trim. For her bra, it was the outer lining of the straps, while her panties were pink on their lacey edges.

Max's boxer briefs seemed designer. There was a company name plastered all over the top band, and it was a decent shade of green.

Without another word, Harley went for her bra. Nothing more than a second later and it gently feel to the floor.

She broke the silence. "What do you think?"

"I like 'em. They're round, come to a nice point. Not really sure what you'll allow me to say."

"I think that's fine for now."

She was never big, but she was never small either. A classic B-cup is she ever knew them. Maybe another compliment would have been nice, but that would come in another form in only a few minutes.

They both reached for what little clothes remained on them. Max's cock was nothing to sneeze at; he was the typical size, happened to be circumcised, and was good enough to have his pubic hair trimmed down and in line.

Harley's vag was clean, and as regular as she could tell. Standing up, she couldn't see it, so she had to base how it looked right now on the way Max looked at it. He seemed very happy.

He walked over to her.

"Okay, so. This means I have permission to kiss you, right?"

"Permission granted."

He did. And he was not a bad kisser. His lips were soft and caring, and he knew how to work his tongue against hers. He'd managed to avoid their teeth touching, the one thing she had hated about her first kiss. They didn't take long enough to make out, but after this little taste, Harley was game.

The important thing at the moment was working with the condom. Max had been smart and bought two of them.

"I didn't exactly want to buy a box, but I didn't want to walk all the way back if we broke it."

Harley had had a decent enough education on rubbers, as had Max. They worked very slow, as careful as possible. Max held his cock as Harley helped roll the condom down. It was completely covered, and they went for another kiss.

They moved to the bed, him on top of her. They hadn't started just yet, instead Max continuing the kissing and had started to play with her short brown hair. It was becoming a turn-on for her.

A not too-familiar buzz had begun through Harley's head. Fuzzy, almost warm, sending a quick rush of blood down to her body. She could almost feel a wetness growing, but it hadn't been too strong just yet.

She was calm. Every sense in her was telling her not to worry about this guy, he was going to make her feel as good as he could.

"So." Max said "How do you want to do this?"

"I'm up for whatever you think will work. I've never actually done this before."

"Me neither. Who'da thought? Just you and me, without any history before that. I have some high hopes though."

"Tell me."

"I'm thinking, well, realistically. I'm thinking I can go in easy enough, just let my sweat drip down on you as we eventually see just how hard we can go? Does uh, does that sound good?"

Harley had spent her life speaking honestly, and the surprisingly honest response from Max was, enjoyable fine. She wasn't sure if it fully turned her on, and yet, she did find it adorable. And maybe that's all it needed to be.

"Yeah." They kissed again. "I'm up for whatever we feel like doing. Probably shouldn't keep waiting."

It had been a wonderful time. During her cooldown now, Harley had said goodnight to Max, and watched him, mostly his butt, go back to his room. Once again, everyone else seemed preoccupied, still at the barbeque.

According to Max, he was completely beat. Harley herself had loved it, but she had to admit to herself that there were a few things she knew could have been even better. She'd been building up for something the entire time, but what she got had still been very enjoyable.

In reality, they had been very clumsy in their love making. A few rough spots, not complete knowledge of how to move and just how awkward the process truly was. No pain, her hymen had been ripped long before from a soccer game, though of course the worry of first time pain still lingered just before they'd begun. She'd also had to redirect him more than once, and he'd had no problem taking direction. He seemed to quite like it, actually.

It had still been effective, and the surge of energy and blood was still a rush. She didn't keep track, but she knew they hadn't made love for very long. Perhaps over a minute, but that was her best guess. A few of her friends shared stories of men who only lasted a few seconds their first time, so Max's time was certainly okay by that standard. She'd also heard some men only lasting a seconds despite not being virgins, and there was no justification for those men.

Taking the moment to calm down, she smelled the residue from their night on her sheets.

"That's not the greatest." She said "Guess I'm seeing if I can do laundry."

She removed her bedding from the bed, and walked it over to the laundry room, key in pocket. It was not a long walk, and she thanked God that it wasn't. Bedding seemed heavier when you had to avoid a cold stain.

The room was open and usable as she had hoped. There were only a few washers, and less dryers, but they were all empty for the night. She discovered that laundry was free of charge, as long as you had your own detergent and the like.

She hadn't brought any, so regular water was going to have to be all she used. She set the washer, and watched it go. The time above stated half an hour, and with nothing to do, she stood up and played with her phone. She had no one she wanted to call or text, but just staring at her contacts felt like something.

As she stood, a small drip fell from her vagina and down her left leg. She figured this was more than likely her own discharge versus Max's semen. She'd personally disposed the spent condom in the trash, she knew there were no holes or ruptures. Any chance it was semen only meant it was semen that didn't make it far enough to matter anyway.

Around ten minutes rolled by, and according to the washer it had only been five. She was going to be waiting here longer than the half an hour, typical of most washing machines.

Eventually, Josh ended up walking into the laundry room.

"Oh, someone is in here." He said "Thought I heard something."

The barbeque had finally taken its complete toll on Josh. He'd dropped his overbearingly perky attitude, and instead was just a typical douche bag.

"Are you seriously washing your sheets on your first day?" He said

"Of course I am," Harley said, smiling "I just had sex."

He clearly didn't believe her and wasn't in the mood for what he thought was a joke. "Hey whatever, look just don't use these too late at night. It's hard to sleep and I won't be the only one pissed off."

Once Josh left, Harley checked the time on her phone.

It was only 8:15.

"Try all you want Josh, this is not the night you can ruin my mood."

♥ - *Chapter 2* - ♥

Harley awoke that morning feeling fine. Her pajamas were warm and cozy against her freshly washed sheets, and she had a lot of energy to burn. She walked to her closet, and grabbed her shower bag and towel.

Showering outside of her old home was not exactly anything new. It was something she'd gotten used to back in high school. She removed her pajama top and bottom, and looked around for her sandals. She'd heard from her brother that you needed sandals in the shower, unless you wanted to catch athlete's foot. She wondered how many people would either not know that little tidbit, or would be stupid enough to ignore it until it bit them.

She found her sandals, a simple pair of aqua-marine rubber flip-flops, placed them upon her feet and wrapped her towel around herself. She headed out her door into the hallway.

It would not take very long to reach the bathroom, which was lucky, it was a noticeable amount of effort to have to wear a towel and walk around. A shorter trip made it much easier.

Once she entered the bathroom, she discarded the towel as soon as she could. The chance of someone's boyfriend taking a peak was now out of the picture, and there was something comfortable being around other naked women. Solidity, understanding that no one cared, whether only a perceived notion or not.

A few other the women were still modest, wearing their bras and panties still before the shower curtain could cover them. One had discarded the bra but her panties remained, she clearly coveted one over the other in what strangers could see.

Many others were simply still in their towels. Everyone clearly felt differently.

Regardless, Harley had just spent the night with a man and she needed to scrub what remained of last night. She turned on the water, and proceeded to soap her body.

There were some areas she needed to scrub harder and more thoroughly than usual. Between her legs now seemed to be crust. It placed the memory back into her head, but maybe in the future she figured it would be best to just shower directly after.

With her body washed, she shampooed and conditioned her hair before finishing. Her hair was nothing she worried about, this only took a few minutes. Once she was done, she let the water wash everything away, and turned it off.

She toweled off briefly before wrapping it around herself. Her hair was short enough that she never bothered keeping a second one to wrap around her head. She felt dry enough, and headed back to her room in her towel and sandals.

She turned the key, and inside, she finally met her roommate.

"Hello." She said

"Hi." Harley closed the door and sat down at her desk. The two may as well talk for a brief moment before Harley dressed.

"So," Harley said "you're Anne."

"Oh, I prefer Annie. Guess I didn't write that."

"Alright then. Annie Shaman."

"Ah-ha, yeah, this one I should have spelled out too. It's pronounced 'shay-men' not 'shaw-min'."

"Uh huh."

"So what's your name?"

"Harley Millsboone."

Harley reached over for her discarded class ring on her desk. She tried to avoid wearing it to bed, afraid she would somehow scuff it when turning in her sleep, although that didn't always pan out. She slid it back onto the corresponding finger as the conversation continued.

Annie herself was wearing a cute light blouse with a few bows sew around it. She had a frilly skirt just down to her knees, and white and pink sneakers. On her right thumb was a pink plastic ring. Annie's style seemed to be "cute", part traditionally girly-girl, but more-so like she could style herself the same way you could an expensive doll.

She was only 18, the age Harley couldn't help but assume she would be. Although her fashion sense headed more towards something the age of 16 or 15, if Harley had it in her mind to be critical of how people dressed. Admittedly, even if it wasn't, it seemed to work for her. Maybe she should stick with it no matter her age.

"You still wear your class ring?" Annie said, more curious than judgmental.

"Yep." Harley said "Won't be able to wear it forever, so I'm getting the most I can out of it right now."

"Right on. So, uh, you like it here?"

"I just got here last night. Pretty alright so far."

"Right. Right, yeah."

"How come you had to leave yesterday?"

"It's a little complicated. My grandma lives just a little too far away from here and she wanted me to spend the night with her before I headed off."

"Ah."

"So ya wanna bone?"

Annie had an incredibly awkward smile the second her "joke" left her lips.

"I..." Annie said "probably should have phrased it like a joke, instead of just saying it like I meant it. It, was a joke if, you didn't. I'm sorry."

"I'm going to get dressed." Harley said

Harley looked into her closet, barely grasping her towel. She wanted to have it on until she picked out her outfit, the room had gotten a colder.

"It's freezing in here." She said aloud.

"It wasn't a second ago." Annie said "I mean yeah I agree with you don't worry about that, just, yeah whatever I don't know just thought that was useful."

"Uh-huh."

Harley picked a jean jacket, white t-shirt, punk boots, and jean shorts. She dropped her towel to the floor and started putting them on.

"Punk huh?" Annie said "Nice. I'm more of a-. Well. Okay I don't know what I'm more of."

Harley fully dressed and walked over to the refrigerator.

"Hey, you wanna get some breakfast? Get to know each other?" Annie said

"I have a cantaloupe I brought from home, was planning on eating that in all honesty. Sorry"

"Right. Yeah. Fruit don't last long. Um, I don't have a cantaloupe so I'm going to head out. Nice meeting you."

Annie headed out the door, her head tilted more towards her chest. Not every day you see someone fluster themselves over a bad joke and a breakfast rejection.

Harley figured they'd have plenty of time for second impressions, but right now, she was hungry.

♥ - Chapter 3 - ♥

Harley had been given one day to unpack and settle in, and then the day after that to get familiar with the entire area. Today was her first real college class. It was math, and a simple one at that, she didn't need anything above basic this semester.

She'd chosen trigonometry. Angles and triangles may not be important to many outside of mathematicians, but Harley's major required it. May as well grin and bear it, she didn't usually have trouble with math anyway.

She chose a seat, the second row at the far end. She placed her math book on the table and opened her notebook to the first empty page. The first few pages were only cardboard. She'd bought it from the school, and the school did it's best to give her a reliable notebook as much as it tried it's best to gain more of her money with less effort.

She tugged at her shirt after she sat down. Her choice today was a yellow blouse with a frilly bottom she'd never worn before. She also wore blue-green pants with no pocket, a floral-print purse, white shoes that let her see around half of her toes, and on top of her head was a pair of sunglasses with orange rims. She didn't realize the severe amount of color until she was about to leave, and by then, she didn't have the time or patience to change.

The class was full. There seemed to be an equal amount of men to women, and at this point in her college education, Harley had no recognizable faces to go off of. This was her first class, and it was a class full of strangers.

The professor walked into the classroom. He was older, Harley figured his mid-fifties at the most likely earlier. His hair had thinned, a minor combover had been attempted but it only did so much. He was dressed the way most professors would have dressed in the back of Harley's mind, according to movies she had seen. A business suit, black tie. He was nothing original nor did he need to be.

"Hello class." The professor said, and continued to introduce himself and the basics of the class.

He was dry, rather witless, but there were no signs he'd be bad at the job. Hopefully he'd be even better than that let on.

"I may as well see if everyone is familiar with the basics. Raise your hand if you're never heard of the Pythagorean theorem."

Harley was not one of the hands raised. In total, only about five of the students did so, and one seemed to only raise her hand because she wasn't entirely sure she knew.

"Majority says they know it, so I'll try to be quick as I can."

Pythagoras himself most likely would have been happy with how the professor covered the subject. For as dry as he was, and he was also slower than he'd initially promised, he explained everything just fine. Harley may have known this theory well, but she decided to start taking notes anyway. If she didn't start from the beginning, then she may skip out on the task in the future as well, and that would have hurt her grade. Something she didn't need in a required class.

"I see about," The professor paused briefly the survey the class "half of you have gotten the book. Raise your hands if it's on backorder for you."

About three students raised their hands. Harley lost a little bit of faith for new coming freshmen.

"Alright, fine. Be sure to get the book as soon as you can. You won't be cracking it open until next week, but I still want you to bring it every class, and once we start using it it'll be a large portion of the class.

"Now, let's take a quick look at each triangle type, and a few of the other shapes we'll be covering in the future."

Harley's next class, basic sketching, starting in around half an hour. She'd gotten her artbook and headed out to the area. As far as she was concerned, it payed to be early. The art building was near the end of the campus, entirely brick and with a few separate doors all leading to different studios. She had to do some asking around to figure out which room her class was set to be in.

With that out of the way, she figured she could kill ten or maybe twenty minutes leaning against the back wall. Maybe take in the scenery.

She hadn't been the only one to think of that. As Harley turned the corner, she saw a young woman about the same age as Annie.

She had shoulder length black hair, messily hanging down. She had a blue top, the left strap of which was hanging on for dear life over her shoulder. She had a tattered dark blue skirt, and her shoes were either brown or were so old they had turned brown. She had a cigarette dangling behind her left index and middle fingers, and upon noticing the cigarette, Harley also noticed this woman was wearing a black hair tie around her wrist like a bracelet. She may not have been fashionable, but she was sensible enough to have a plan of action if her hair got in her face.

"Hello." Harley said

The young woman looked over a Harley for a short while before answering. "….Hi?"

"Weren't you in my math class?" Harley had now recognized her as the young woman who was sitting in on of the back seats, one of the ones who didn't look like they were paying attention when the professor was asking the hand-raising questions.

"Trigonometry?" She said

"Yep."

"Oh, right." The young woman pointed at Harley's hair. "Sunglasses."

"So why are you back here? Waiting for an art class?"

"Yeah."

"Basic sketching?"

"....Yeah." The woman looked her in the eyes now, more inquisitive than anything else. "You're uh, saying we have two classes together?"

"Looks so, and maybe even more. Only the first day and all. I'm Harley."

"I'm, Jane."

"If we're going to be spending time together we might as well get to know each other. You think so?"

"...... I dunno. Guess that makes sense."

"Alright Jane, what's your major?"

"I don't technically have a fucking major, I'm just doing some basic art classes. I'm going to be a tattoo artist."

"Ah, nice. We might have a few more classes in common next year then, this year I only have basic sketch."

"Yeah and I'm only taking trig because the school needed me to take a math class. Fucking bullshit."

"I need it but yeah, sounds like bullshit for you, and I'm sure a lot of other people."

"I just need some fucking art lessons, I don't need more fucking high school math. Shit, I have to take a fucking history course tomorrow. Fucking history. I'm not even an art major, I'm un-fucking-declared and they're pulling this shit on me."

Harley let Janie complain for the next few minutes. It was the civil thing to do in this situation. Every once in a while, she would add in her thoughts. Usually to agree, in a much calmer fashion.

"I think we need to head in by this point." Harley said

"Right, yeah, sure the fucking teacher will be pissed if we're late." Janie snuffed her cigarette out on the ground.

The two walked in together, eventually sitting down near each other at a pair of easels. It seemed too early in the class to need them, but they could move if that was the case.

Around five more students had taken their seats. This was not going to be as crowded as the earlier math class, and the empty space felt comfortable after that. There would be enough room to get up and stretch, and given the class was three hours long, Harley would end up appreciating that fact several times.

And then, one person she should have expected.

Max. Turtle.

Max saw her as well, and he smiled at her. There wasn't time to say anything, so they all could do was smile.

Today he was wearing an awful lot of blue. Light blue dress pants, a regular black t-shirt, and gray shoes with blue highlights. Over his clothes was a blue painter's smooch. Even as briefly as she knew him two nights ago, she could tell he was the kind of man to really get into drawing and painting. It was no surprise he owned a painter's smooch, nor that he wore it today. On his left hand were two gold rings, on the index and middle. The one on his middle finger seemed to have some sort of stone, ruby from the look of it. The one on his index plain a simple, a little thin but still shiny and distracting.

A quick thought ran through her head. "Do I count my first time as a one-night stand and have nothing else to do with him? Or, do I make sure I'll stay in contact with him? Doesn't matter where it would go. Keep a part of my future life as well as my past?" The smiles had already given her the answer. "It won't hurt to be friendly with him, and probably better now than later."

Once Max took his seat, the professor started with a quiet head count.

"So that's everyone!" She said, getting up from her seat.

The professor was wearing solid brown pants, like those of a gardener. Her shirt was light green, and if shirts could cry, this one would. Harley had only heard of H-cups before now, but if she had to guess, they are exactly what the professor had.

Harley also noticed Jane give a quick resentful look towards the professor's chest. Jane had nothing to be ashamed of, like Harley she was a B-cup, but a slightly smaller size. It was a little hard for Harley to fully understand the idea of chest envy. She liked what she had, and that was all that mattered to her in the end.

The professor also seemed to be a huge fan of jewelry. She wore silver rings on both thumbs, her right index and ring finger, and her left middle finger and pinky. Each one had a different design, with the thumbs both being spirals. Her middle finger was two feathers, her pinky was a regular band, her index was a band with the shape of a shark tooth on top, and her ring finger had a detailed artist's palette, with little colored-in circles for the paint.

Harley was half-surprised she didn't have peace symbol earrings. She did have earrings, they were simply gold hoops, not even the big kind.

"I'm Professor Anghula." She said "Now, I hope at least most of you are ready for a little bit of art work today. I'm going to give a quick lecture for the first hour, but after that, I'm going to let everyone draw whatever they would like. I feel like it's the best way to get to see everyone's different talents and interests. You don't have to share them with everyone if you don't want, but I still have to see them, of course."

The professor went around the room asking for her student's names. The only information Harley found relevant from this was that Jane's last name was Olber. She wasn't opposed to making more friends out of these classmates, and as rough as Jane had already seemed, Harley's interest in befriending her did not falter.

Harley had finished just over half of her drawing. While the class was about sketching, the professor allowed them to let loose and draw whatever they liked with provided art pencils.

Harley had gone with a rabbit. Rabbits sounded easy enough to draw, before the more complicated aspects showed around. She had colored in some of it's fur with grey, and had detailed the eyes, ears, the complete head. What she had to do left was more detail for the appendages, the tail, and to define the fur more than just the light coloring she did.

"This is very nice Ms. Millsboone." Professor Anghula said "Did you have a pet rabbit?"

"No but I saw them all the time outside." Harley said "Basically ingrained in my skull by this point."

"It shows."

The professor walked over to Janie and her drawing. It was a flaming skull, not uncommon in the tattoo profession she claimed to aspire to. It had a septum nose ring, nails drilled into its empty eye sockets, and the mouth was perfectly closed, not a single gap or a hint of the tongue. It was much closer to done than Harley's drawing as well, Janie was doing the last of the shading.

"Well look at this." The professor said "This is lovely Ms. Olber. You should show this one off."

"Yeah." Janie said "I think it's good just staying here."

"Oh come now, the others will love this."

"It's not even colored in."

"Black-and-white can be very stunning Ms. Olber, and you've proved that."

"Yeah well I'd rather color it in before I showed it to anybody but you."

"Fine. Very well, you're free to take it home."

The professor walked to another group of students. Her departure caused Janie to sigh from the pent-up anger she'd been hiding back.

"You alright?" Harley said

"It's just a Goddamn drawing." Janie said

"Can I see it?"

"Nope."

"You're not going to junk it, are you?"

"'Course I am."

"Don't, it's good to keep all of your work. If it doesn't go in your portfolio you can still look back on it or whatever."

There was a short pause before Janie spoke.

"Fine I'll keep the fucking thing."

About ten more minutes passed, and the professor allowed the students to take a break. Janie turned to Harley, as if expecting a conversation.

"Hang on one second Janie." Harley said "I've uh, I've got someone I need to talk to."

She made a bee-line for him about as well as she could. First thing he did was give her another warm smile.

"Hey Max." She said

"Hey Harley." He said "Kind of surprised. For a while there I thought smiling was the only way we'd communicate."

"Eh, I like taking risks. You know that already. You know I really should have expected you to take a class like this."

"Well whattaya gonna do? Can't prove I can make a design unless I show people I can draw."

Max turned his drawing over to Harley. It was a lemon tree. Well detailed, around the same amount as with Janie. However, Janie's style was more dark and in-your-face, while Max had gone for subtle aspects that stood out when you noticed them. He also bothered to draw the ground and the sky, something neither Harley nor Janie had remotely bothered with.

"Nice." She said "I just drew a bunny."

"Can I see it?"

"Sure, but after class is over. Not done yet."

"Great. Hey?" Max took out his phone. "Should we be in contact with each other?"

"I was going to ask the exact same thing." Harley said

"The way I see it, what we did, that was nice. I hear, like, people do that as a one-off and never see each other again. But, I think there's no harm in us being friends."

"Yeah. Yeah, staying in contact sounds great to me."

They traded phone numbers, and shared a few more pleasantries before Harley decided to head back.

"Maybe we'll talk soon." She said

"Yeah, maybe." Max smiled at her again. "See ya."

"Yeah. I gotta go, rabbit can't finish drawing itself."

Harley put her phone away, and walked right back over to her seat.

"Sorry about that." Harley said "Complicated little thing I felt like taking care of."

"Friend of yours?" Jane said

"Well he is now."

"Huh. Alright." Jane tapped at her pack of cigarettes. It took here a few more seconds before she said anything else. "So, what's the plan for after class?"

"I dunno. I'm headed back to my room for a little bit before getting something to eat. Why did you want to do something?"

Jane stop tapping and looked Harley right in the eyes. She looked, slightly confused. "I wasn't really thinking about that, I. I dunno, not today but I guess if that means you want to do something we could do something."

"Alright. Give me your number."

Now Harley had exchanged numbers with a second person that day.

"You, uh. You can save me in that contact as Janie. .... If you want." She said

"Janie." Harley said. "Cute, I like it."

College was different from high school. Friends didn't force their way in just because of similar classes or being part of the group. Harley was not going to know even half of her class mates, only the ones she decided were worth being interested in.

And Max was good enough to know, he'd have been fine on his own. Janie could have a place as well, and Harley saw no reason to deny it from her.

The professor called a notice, four more minutes until class started back up.

Harley opened her door. The drawing had taken a lot out of her, and she needed a chance to relax just a little bit.

Annie was already in the room. She was at her desk, facing an open computer and eating noodles she'd made with the microwave.

Annie was wearing a shiny purple blouse with a butterfly embroiled on the back. She also had light gray low heels, and semi-tight blue-green pants. Her fingers today were bare, apparently unlike Harley, she did not set her hand jewelry to be exactly the same every day. Harley also noticed that Annie had the exact same hair color as Jane, except Annie preferred tying it back with a scrunchie. Today is was pink, but Harley couldn't remember what color the last one was. She needed to pay a little more attention to the young lady she was living with, she realized.

Annie looked up at the sound of the door, and shot Harley as peace sign with her right hand. An adequate hello as her mouth was full.

Harley went over to her desk, and sat down. The thought of pulling her phone out for a third time to register someone's number popped into her head. Looking over at Annie eating, she figured, well, maybe it wouldn't hurt to do that another time.

♥ - Chapter 4 - ♥

Harley was sitting at the steps of one of the bigger buildings on campus. On some days it would be the place she'd go for her math class, but today she had no classes at all.

Her reason was purely out of a simple interest. She'd bought a small cup of soup from inside the building, and she had chosen the stairs as the nicest place to eat it. With little to no classes, hardly anyone was walking about, but they kept the buildings and the mini-stores inside of them open. It wasn't a holiday, only a Saturday.

The weather was finally starting to get chilly, so today Harley had chosen a button-up brown sweater with long sleeves, over a plain white t-shirt. Her pants were blue jeans, and her shoes were a pair of worn sneakers.

The soup was nice in the cooler weather. It was chicken noodle, with large chunks of carrots and some smaller chunks of celery. It wasn't going to be too filling, practically more than a snack, so she would have to find something else to eat in an hour or so. But for right now, it was a nice warm bowl of surprisingly good soup.

She ate and watched, seeing if anyone else was up and about today. Hardly anyone was. In the span of five minutes, she only saw three people, and two of them had been together. From the look of them, they were trying to find a private place to make-out, possibly more, even though they for some reason could not bother to just stay in their own room to do so.

She glanced up at the clock. It was eleven, but her guess was that a strong majority of campus residents were sound asleep. Taking the extra hours they could get. They could sleep all they liked, the quiet was appreciated.

Without noticing it until she placed the empty spoon in her mouth, she'd finished her soup. Harley walked up to the trash and threw the plastic cup away. She had very little homework, so she turned to go for a quick walk around campus before heading back to her room.

The leaves were turning orange, and she didn't want this to be the first year where she couldn't be bothered to take a closer look.

Annie and Harley were silent. Staring at their individual laptops, the glow bouncing off of their faces. Harley was cataloguing internet videos she was planning on watching at some point, and she had absolutely no clue what Annie was doing.

They were minding their own business.

Quietly.

"You know what?" Annie moved her chair over to Harley, looking her directly in the face. "It's been four weeks and we don't know anything about each other."

"Well, yeah." Harley said "I guess so."

"That's stupid." Annie said "You and me, tonight. There's a bar and we're going."

"I don't have an issue with the idea of me drinking, but I'm sure the people who own the place will."

"Did I say go drinking? I did not remotely say go drinking. You and me get all dressed up to look pretty, we go down to the bar, order some food while being the best-looking ladies there. We chat with anyone, hopefully also each other. We just have a good night out and have a great time. Sound good?"

"I guess so."

"I'd like it if you sounded happier about this."

"Annie, sorry just, I don't know you at all. I hope I like you, I hope I like this idea. If you want me to say anything that's really all I can think of."

"Well. Then I guess tonight is the night I make you form an opinion of me."

Harley had not switched out of her earlier ensemble, with the exception of a pair of black low-heel boots. She put in an effort to fluff out her hair, but there was little to no difference in her appearance. She wasn't a stylist.

Annie had pulled out a dress from the back of her closet. It was cream-colored, and to Harley's surprised, there were images of full beers mugs printed all over the bottom. She had no clue if this dress was bought or given to her as a joke, but it was still a dress that her roommate consciously decided to wear. Around Annie's neck was a silver necklace of a skull and crossbones.

"You like it?" Annie said "I make the boys think I'm sweet and cute, but they come close and get just a little look of danger and intrigue."

"It's the beers that are grabbing my attention."

"I know. I fucking love this adorable stupid dress. My nana bought it for me. Told me to wear it until I can buy the drinks myself. If I make it obvious I wish I could drink, the boys feel pity. Get me?"

"Huh. Guessing you can work with that."

"You don't know me well enough, trust me, I can work with anything. Now let's get goin'."

Annie quickly slipped on a pair of white low-heel shoes that revealed part of her toes, and a large formal sun hat.

"Isn't it a little dark out to wear that?" Harley said

"The point is to look pretty." Annie said "It works better than when fucking losers put their sunglasses and leather jackets on at this time in the middle of the night."

"Solid point."

The two women stepped out of their room. Harley had her key shoved in her little red purse, which was useful, as it looked like Annie had completely forgotten about the locking door.

"Fuck I forgot-"

"I've got my key, we're good."

"Lifesaver. Replacing those apparently costs a lot of money."

The two headed out of their dorm building, and across half of the parking lot. Harley slowed down, but Annie continued at her regular speed towards the sidewalk.

"My car's over here." Harley said

"Shit you have a car? Thought we were going to walk."

"No, just point me in the right direction. Besides, we can't drink there anyway, might as well drive."

"Yeah, but, can we park a little bit aways from the bar?"

"Why?"

"I think it'd be nice to walk a little bit of the way there. Like it's an adventure, you know? We only made it so far and we have to trudge the rest of the way."

"Fine by me. Whole trip was your idea, only fair to go along with your suggestion."

Annie opened the passenger side door, and took her seat. Harley opened the driver's door, and poked her head in first to make sure nothing was going to get in her way. There was no trash or mess, so she simply got in and buckled up.

"This is a nice car." Annie said "It's very spacious."

"Yeah, well." Harley said "It's new, might be why. My dad swears these fucking things start to shrink when you've had them for three or four years."

"You could afford a new car?"

"I did mention I took a year off from high school, right? Saved a lot of money working odd jobs."

"So why a new car? Didn't you have one when you worked?"

"I did, but my brother and his girlfriend kind of shared it with me sometimes."

"I sure hope they gave you a lot of money, cars are horrifically expensive."

"Hey, this car may look really nice but it's only 'new' because the guy I bought it from never used it. He's a friend of my brother. Thankfully it's nicer than I was afraid of, I expected something caked with rust or missing a tire. Still, I guess cars really do lose their market value fast, even when you can convince yourself they're still new. Plus, my brother got to keep my old one and even floated me some cash as a thank you."

"How long have they been together?"

"Five years, and they are very serious."

"Shit. I can't imagine that. I'm uh, well I'm into serious relationships but mine don't tend to last all that long. You get me?"

"Whatever works for you."

"See, now you've gotten me to like you. Oh, shit, take a left here."

Annie narrated Harley the rest of the way to the bar. As requested, they parked around half a block away. Both the car and the bar were insight of each other, but they still had to walk for about ten minutes before reaching the front doors.

The place was full, being a Saturday night. There were a lot of people sitting right at the bar itself, all of them older than Annie and Harley.

"Let's sit at the bar." Annie said

"Yeah, they'll never let us get away with that. Let's just get a table."

The two had to wait for a member of the waiting staff to come over and help them to a table. Once she did, she handed them both a menu and headed back to take care of the other customers.

"Alright." Annie said "Now I'm the one who dragged you here, so I'll be nice and foot the bill."

"Works for me." Harley said

"One caveat. If you want dessert I get most of it. I'd say half but in this case I don't think that's actually fair."

"Only one dessert then. Still sounds good."

Harley looked over her menu. Normally, she would only concern herself with what looked appetizing and worry about the cost later. However, it wasn't her money to spend today, so she only looked at the entrees section.

"Huh." She said "Chili cheese fries."

"Oooh, those sound good." Annie said "Want to get a large and split it?"

"I've never eaten here before, I don't know if a large here is enough for the two of us."

"Or too small either, really."

"I'll just stick with a regular."

"Is that all you're getting?"

"Probably get a root beer, but that's it. I'm not really hungry."

"Cool. I'm getting, huh. There's a special for two salmon fillets. I'll get that and some onion rings, and you can have my other fish."

"Great." Salmon wasn't a favorite for Harley's choice of fish, but she was more than happy not to pass it up.

The waitress came back and took their orders. She left along with their menus.

"And now we get to know each other." Annie said "First things first, can I see your hand?"

Harley knew which hand she was talking about. "Sure."

Harley placed her right hand in Annie's open left palm. Annie leaned in slightly to get a closer look at Harley's class ring.

"It's so pretty." She said "You know I almost got one of these but I could never muster up."

"I had to pay for mine myself. Well, okay, half of it."

"It wasn't so much the money for me." Annie gave Harley her hand back. "You've probably figured this out by now but my rings are basically all costume jewelry."

"I kind of noticed that."

"Sue me, I like looking cute. Of course, I'm a grown ass woman now according to the law, so soon enough I'll be buying the real things. I'll still wear my old stuff, but hey, mixing and matching is always fun. You know, I'm getting my ears pierced winter break. Can you fucking believe it, eighteen years old and my ears aren't pierced?"

"It's a little weird I guess. I got mine done when I was nine."

"So did everyone else I know. Even some guy friends I have. How come you hardly wear them?"

"Sort of got bored with earrings. If you see me put any in by this point it's basically so the holes don't close up."

"When I get mine done, let's go jewelry shopping. Maybe it'll get you back into the habit."

"Not a bad idea."

At this point, a young man had shyly walked over to their table. He was facing Annie's direction.

"Um. Hi." He said "I'm sorry if I'm bothering you I just wanted to say hi."

"Hey." Annie said "How are you?"

"I'm uh, I'm good. How's life treating you?"

"I'd say life's been alright so far. Harley this is Andy, ex-boyfriend."

"Hi."

"Hello." Harley said

"I'll uh, I'll let you go." Andy said "I'd catch up with you but I'm sure it's not a good time."

"No." Annie said "But I'll text you later. It's good to see you."

Andy walked back to the bar where he had originally been.

"He's so adorable." Annie said "Sucks we didn't work out."

"How long were you two dating?" Harley said

"Two weeks." Annie said "Which for me, is enough time to figure out pretty much everything. You know?

"I get ya."

"I wouldn't mind having boyfriends for longer than that, but it just doesn't end up that way. It's rare they last longer than a handful of months. What about you?"

"Honestly I haven't dated all that much. I had one boyfriend in high school."

"We're very much opposites then." Annie leaned back in her seat. "My first boyfriend asked me out when we were fourteen. Only guy I ever went out with for over a year."

"How serious was it?"

"He's the guy I lost my virginity too, I was fifteen."

"How was that?"

"Good. Quick, reeeeeeeeeeeeeally hurt, but good. Well, I did give him a blowjob about a month before that, and I know that does count but I was talking about full-on virginity. It didn't help his time all that much but hey, he learned."

"Why'd you break up?"

"By the time we were sixteen we kind of just lost interest in each other. We weren't all that compatible anymore. He liked taking things slow, but I'm ready for all of it by a week and a half. Really that may have just been because he was a high school boy. I don't know what they say to each other but Christ, they get so scared at the thought of actually getting pussy so quick, it's all talk until they decide their mother called them and they bail on you before you even get the illusion of sex. Chickenshits. Thankfully college boys tend to have figured it out."

"I guess so." Harley somewhat smiled

"What about you?"

"When did I lose mine?"

"Yeah."

Harley full-on smiled. "Nineteen."

Annie motioned with her eyebrows. "You're nineteen now."

"Exactly."

"Well, this is a story you'll have to tell me later."

The waitress came back with their orders. Once she left, Annie slipped her second fish over to Harley's plate. The two started eating, occasionally chatting about their grades and classes. Classmates came up in conversation as well, but neither became too specific about anyone. Each mentioned person became explained away with either "You'll have to meet them" or "I don't have enough time, I'll tell you about them later."

Once their fish and entrees were done, and with their drinks still half full, the two looked at the dessert menu on the table.

"You in the mood for anything?" Harley said

"Well. Chocolate of some kind, I'm in the mood for some kind of pie I guess."

"Oh. Here we go. Look, chocolate cheese cake. It's not even that much money."

"Then I like your suggestion. I'm going to order another cola, think you need a refill?"

"Nah, I'll barely be eating."

Harley took one more sip of her root beer, while Annie finished her drink off. The waitress came over to take care of the empty dishes, and took the rest of their order.

"Hey, tell me." Annie said "You worried about any class?"

"Nope." Harley said "I was never the greatest student but I'm expecting a B in most everything, it's how I always did."

"Good. I mean, you did take a year off. I hear it can be weird to get back into the swing of things."

"Well, thanks for the concern. I think I've adjusted just fine though. What about you?"

"Eh. I have literally nothing to worry about. Well, I think I may have forgotten an assignment in one class, and if it's a big one, then my grade will not be stellar. It'd be the only one, so I guess I'll just grit my teeth about it."

The waitress arrived with their dessert. They both took a bite of it.

"Huh." Harley said

"Yeah." Annie said "It's certainly not great, but hey, I can't say that it's bad."

"Well, it fills a hole I guess. Least you didn't pay too much money for it."

"How much more of this do you want?"

"A couple bites, let's say the rest of this end here."

"Great."

Once dessert was done, Annie grabbed her money for the bill. Surprisingly, Annie had figured out the total before it had arrived, taking thirty-two dollars out for it. Harley offered to help with the tip, but Annie decided see could worry about it if there was a next time.

"Although I have to say I am starting to like you quite a bit." Annie said "You're a smart cookie, you know?"

"Thanks." Harley gave a smile.

"And I gotta admit. You know how to hold back on a good story. Here's hoping I actually get to hear it."

The two got up to leave, but a few steps after, Annie stopped.

"Hold on." She said "I wanna do something."

Annie walked over to the bar.

"The hell?" Harley said

Harley walked behind her. Her distance was kept before she could be questioned for her license.

"Hey fella." Annie said. It was not directly to any of the men at the bar in particular, just any who would answer her.

"Er, hi." One of them said

"Would you buy a girl a drink?" Annie said, flashing a huge cute smile and winking at him.

Harley stifled a laugh.

The man looked her all over, although at first his eyes only went as high as her cleavage.

"Alright. Want do you want?" He said

"Give me a shot and see what it gets ya." Annie said

The man paid for a shot, and quietly handed it to Annie. The man had no clue he just gave alcohol to a minor, or if he did, then Annie was good enough to promise him it was worth it with body language alone.

"Thanks buddy." She said "I hope I see you around here again."

Annie was about to turn to leave when-

"HEY!" A woman older than the two of them walked over. Harley noticed a wedding ring, and that made her look over to the man's hand. He had one too.

What the man also had was a look that more than suggested he was enjoying this spat by a great deal. Most likely, it was everything he'd expected and it made him very happy to do nothing but watch it unravel, as his wife basically forgot he had any fault in the matter.

"Oh shit...." Harley said

"The fuck are you doing with my husband?"

"Oh no!" Annie said. Jolting up and out of the character she was playing. "I'm so sorry! Please I wasn't going to, I was just pushing my luck."

"Yeah, you fuckin' were." The wife said "And give me a good reason to not kick your ass."

"Look please I'm just a slutty college girl fishing for free drinks, I'll be on my way."

Harley gently grabbed her by the arm. "You can say it or you could just do it."

"Back off bitch I'm talking to your shitty friend." The wife said

"Uh, point taken."

Harley tried to drag Annie out with her.

The added weight did not make her very fast.

The two roommates were walking back to Harley's car. Harley had a small scuff on her knee from tripping after the man's wife had pulled Annie away from her.

Annie herself had her hair all messed up, the scrunchie ripped and thrown off, her left dress strap was falling, and she was suffering a massive black eye.

They were halfway to the car, and, suddenly. The two burst out laughing.

"I just got the shit kicked out of me!" Annie said, barely stopping her laughter.

"And I fucking feel down and ate shit!" Harley said "I'm so sorry I let her get you."

"I'm sorry I flirted with a married man."

The two continued walking and laughing. Annie put her hand on her head to try and fix her hair.

"Aw shit." She said "I lost my floppy hat. I didn't love it or anything but that was a good fuckin' hat."

After a while, they couldn't keep walking, they had to stop in their tracks due to laughing too hard. In the back of Harley's head, this was it. This was the night the two became friends.

"Excuse me miss?" A cop car had pulled up from the noise they were making. "Are the two of you alright?"

"Just laughing." Harley said

"Yeah." Annie had a giant smile on her face.

Harley had a suspicion there was going to be something else. "What are you-"

"Hey copper check this out!"

Annie pulled down her dress and bra to flash the policeman.

Harley's instant response was to grab Annie by the arm again, and hold on to her much tighter than last time as she ran away with her. Despite the trouble she thought they were in, the cop did not give chase. He had just seen an of-age woman's breasts and he apparently felt no reason to do anything about it.

"The fuck was that?" At first Harley's tone was confusion, but once she calmed down, she began quietly laughing again.

"I'd love to say that was the shot." Annie said "But I think I just straight-up wanted to see what that cop would do if he saw my boobs."

"Well, whatever it was, at least he doesn't seem to be following us."

"It's too bad, because let's face it I've got some great boobs. How jealous are you? So jealous that, yeah you'd be jealous...."

"You know, I think I've figured you out since the day we first met."

"Really?"

"Yeah. You're not really funny, but you're fun. You could use some help with the jokes, but hanging out with you is a blast."

"Thanks. That's what I'm trying for. Well, okay I'm also trying to be funny, but at least I make the night fun. Let's hope the boys are saying that about me! Well. Okay actually a lot of them have told me that...... Yeah okay I see where you're coming from."

The two got back in Harley's car, and she drove them back home.

♥ - Chapter 5 - ♥

"Can I speak with you Professor Bills-Brooke?" Harley had just gotten a C- on her last test. It was not a grade to worry much about, however, it was the lowest grade she had gotten on a test, and that test happened to be worth thirty-five percent of her total grade.

"Oh, Millsboone. Sure, you'll have to follow me to my office."

The professor's office was only down the hall from the classroom. He opened the door for the two of them, placed his book and papers on his desk, and offered her a seat.

"So what is this about?" The Professor said

"I just want to know how my grade is looking so far. I wasn't worried until that last test."

"Ah, well I'll just pull up your grades so far."

The professor opened his folder listed "Trigonometry", and looked under her name.

"You've mostly been getting B's, and you got an A early on. Remind me, are you a math major?"

"No."

"Ah, okay. Then you would be able to pass with a D, and trust me, by this point, even if you completely bomb the last two tests you'll get higher than a D."

"Good. This one was worth a lot so I had to double-check."

"You did the smart thing Millsboone. You're not a bad student. You know, I have a very high pass rate, in an average class only two or three people tend to fail. It's only basic math, but besides, if a majority is failing than it speaks volumes about the kind of person who is teaching. Either way, if you want the grade to stay nice, just try to avoid another C- or lower. I can't speak for the end yet, but you are in the B range thus far."

"Thank you professor, I'll be on my way."

Harley left through the office door. As usual, she had plenty of time before her art class, and all she had to do was find something to occupy her time.

Harley, as usual before her art class, was leaning up against the wall with Janie. Today she leaned more carefully, she didn't want to mess up her new clothes.

It was a pink frilly halter-top, tied off behind her neck and showing off a lot of her back. Her pants were dark blue capris. Her shoes were low heel pink pumps with a splash of white on the toes. She also decided to try wearing earrings on a constant basis again, after her and Annie's night of fun, and she had studs shaped like little stars. The outside edges were yellow-gold, and the inside were a light orange.

"How can you wear that?" Janie said

Janie herself had been wearing a jacket for a week, and today was no exception. Her pants were full-length jeans, and from the look of them, were insulated on the inside. Her shoes were solid black sneakers, and like always she still had the elastic strapped on her wrist.

"It's only fall." Harley said "Hell the winter's not all that bad really. We don't get snow."

"Your fucking back's open. The most I've ever seen you wear was a sweater, how are you not cold?"

"Some days aren't bad at all. I grew up here, I'm used to it this time of year."

"Yeah well I don't care how far away I used to be, it's fucking cold out."

Janie shifted her weight against the wall. She'd spent so much of her focus on talking that she'd lost her position. After checking her phone for the time, she grabbed a fresh cigarette from her pocket.

"Cute earrings by the way." She said

"Thanks, I haven't wore them in a while."

Harley now noticed that Janie went with two simple black rings for her ears. Harley now felt a little embarrassed for never noticing them, as now that she had, she saw Janie's left ear had the earring in the typical bottom of the ear, whilst her right ear had it in the cartilage area. It seemed, fashionably asymmetric. Janie clearly didn't put much effort into her attire, so a small thing like this must have taken time.

"I love what you do by the way." Harley said "Just noticed it, it's cute. It makes both of your ears stand out." A burst of honesty in the also honest compliment, hopefully enough to make up for the lack of attention paid before.

"Thanks." Janie actually managed to crack a smile. Out of the side of her mouth, but a smile none the less. "Got 'em pierced that way. It took way too long to explain it to the guy. He did a good job but he was a fucking idiot."

"It's really cute. I like it."

"Yeah. …. Hey." Janie removed her cigarette to speak full on. "Look. I'm, in about two weeks I'm getting my first tattoos."

"Tattoo*s*?"

"Yeah, more than one, you heard me." Janie proceeded to tell Harley the exact time and date of the appointment. "You uh, you think you'd like to go with me?"

"Sure, I'm free then. I'd love to go."

Janie cracked another side-mouth smile, but this one she tried to hide. "Cool. Should be fun." Janie took a long drag. "Hey class starts in like five minutes, you may want to get in there before I'm done here."

"Will do. See you in a second."

Harley walked into the classroom. She caught a quick glance at Max, and took the chance to wave at him. He noticed and responded the same. Harley took her seat, and to her surprise, Professor Anghula headed over to her.

"Harley, have I told you about my tracing class?" The professor said

"Uh, no." Harley said "I don't think so."

"Oh, well I think you should think about it." She said "It's not until next Fall, but I think it will help you out. Considering what you want to do. I can e-mail you the details."

"Sounds good to me."

The professor today was wearing an orange floral shirt, low cut. She had to lean over to converse with Harley, and despite being straight, Harley admittedly had a hard time not wanting to look down, it was too big of an area that she had to go out of her way to ignore it. Once the professor stood back up, Harley noticed she was also wearing a long pink skirt, and purple open-toed strappy shoes. She wore the same rings as always wore, and this was something Harley found impressive. Her fingers must have been heavy, even if she was clearly used to it. And, today, she was wearing the peace sign earrings Harley was betting she owned.

Harley wondered if it was a breach of student-teacher etiquette to ask her where she shopped. The style was starting to grow on her, especially Anghula's hands.

Once professor Anghula headed back, Janie entered the classroom.

"Jane." The professor said, after taking a quick sniff. "I have to ask. I know that smell but I can't place it."

"I was smoking." Janie said, completely flat. "Cigarettes."

"Ah. Right." She said "It's been so long since anyone had the nerve to smoke around here. Don't get caught, it's a little breathtaking to smell the after effects after so long."

"Right."

Janie took her seat next to Harley.

"Fucking professor hippy boobs." Janie whispered in Harley's direction.

"Eh." Harley said "I like her."

Janie cocked her eyebrows. "Whatever you say, I guess. I didn't come here for her to talk to me more than needed."

The art class was on its usual break time. Which meant Harley was using her usual allotted free time to chat up with Max.

Today Max wore red. Damn, he looked good in every color.

It was a red vest and a red tie. His undershirt was black, and had long sleeves. Apparently he wasn't as good at handling the weather as Harley was. His pants were blue jeans, however, there were small red designs on the left, and the right leg had a streak from the top to bottom. Just like Janie, Max found a way to make asymmetry stand-out. He did an admittedly better job, but Harley would have been shocked if it was ever the other way around. His shoes were simply white sneakers.

Honestly, if they were anything but, he'd have over done it. Most likely, he knew this.

"You talk with the math professor yet?" Max said.

Harley had discussed her grade with him a night or so ago on the phone. He was in a similar situation.

"Just today. He says I literally have nothing to worry about. Which is what I figured."

"At least you care. I've forgotten to, and I'm not the only one."

They chuckled at this little remark. Afterwards, Harley noticed a small smile from Max, which turned bigger in a matter of seconds.

"You know what." Max said "Fuck it. Um, hey. I know we're, um-"

Janie walked over to the two of them, having little to no respect for the conversation.

"Yo Harley." Janie said "Sorry but I just broke my fucking paint brush."

"How?" Harley said

"I dropped it. It happens, they aren't made of metal. Help me get the professor to get another one."

"I guess so. Oh. I've never introduced you two. Sorry, I'm an idiot. Max this is my friend Janie."

"Yeah hi."

"And Janie this is my, very good friend, Max Turtle."

"Yo." Max said "I'll, let you two figure that problem out. See you soon Harls."

Max walked back to his seat.

"He calls you 'Harls'?" Janie said

"Yes, and you can too."

"Yeah no, I'm good with your regular name."

Janie decided to walk back to Harley's room with her. They chatted very little while doing this. Two of the male residents attempted to hit on Janie, and the two of them separately said more to her than Harley did.

Harley turned her key in the door, and the both of them found Annie applying lipstick while using her webcam as a mirror.

Annie was wearing a dark blue bucket hat, a white floral dress that showed half of her shoulders, and white flats with black heels.

"Hey Annie." Harley said "This is Janie. Friend of mine."

"Well hello then." Annie said

"I think I'm going to go, actually." Janie said "I'll see you soon."

"Alright then." Harley said "We still on for your tattoos?"

"Yeah, of course." Janie simply turned around and headed out.

Once she was out, Annie lowered her eyelids slightly. "She looked goth."

"She's not. Just a little, well, mean to the world if she feels like it. You know."

"Yeah, I pieced that together. I'm guessing there's some reason you like her though."

Annie stood up and wrinkled out her dress with her hands. "Well!" She said "I have a date. I really like this guy, so I have no idea if I'll be back."

"Have fun."

Annie left the room. With the complete privacy, Harley opened up her phone.

She'd been meaning to call her father.

"Hey sweetie." Her dad said

"Hi dad. How's everything at home?"

"Fine. Your brother brought his girlfriend over for a few days. Your mother is flipping out a little about it, I'm sure you're not surprised."

"No, but hey. She still loves us."

"She doesn't realize she also loves the very woman she's freaking out about. She's a member of this family now, even if your brother's still a little too gutless to make anything official."

Harley giggled. "She's patient. It'll pay off for them."

"So what about you?"

"A friend of mine just invited me to join her while she gets tattoos."

"Wait, say that again? You and your friend are getting tattoos?"

"No, sorry, I'll explain it again. My friend is getting some tattoos, and she wanted me to come with her for moral support. I think for moral support, he's a little too gruff to admit that."

"Oh. Okay." She heard her dad give a quick chuckle. "For a second I thought one of my children was going to show a wild side."

"Nope."

"Well, too bad I guess. It would have been interesting. You interesting in getting any at some point?"

"The craziest thing I'll ever do is dye my hair."

"Okay. Do what you want sweetie. Oh. Your mother asked me to ask you this. We want to plan our Christmas shopping. Is there anything you think you'll want?"

"Uhhhh. Off the top of my head. Oh. I'm going to need some new sketch books. I'm halfway through mine, and I'll be taking at least one other art class while I'm here."

"Practical. How many?"

"Er. Maybe two or three? I'll only need one for a class but I'll want some for personal time."

"I'll write it down. Anything else?"

"Not right now. I'll think of something."

"Alright sweetie. Well, I need to go. Call me again when you get the chance. I love you pumpkin."

"I love you too dad."

♥ - *Chapter 6* - ♥

Harley sat in an empty seat as Janie sat in the designated tattoo seat. Harley's outfit today was a pair of jean shorts, a green t-shirt, and brown flats. She figured Janie would've wanted her to underdress, so that is what she planned.

Janie herself wore a short black tank top. She also had black biking shorts, and a pair of black sneakers Harley was sure she'd seen before. Despite how cold she'd claimed to be, she needed to bare as much skin as she could to make it easier on the man about to carve ink into her flesh.

Said man was in his mid-twenties, had a fairly impressive physique, and noticeable stubble. It seemed orange, which matched his red hair. Although his side-swept bangs had been dyed black-and-white. The rest of his outfit was a gray t-shirt with a small breast pocket, gray cargo pants, and he wore gloves due to the equipment.

"Alright Jane." He showed her a section of his book. "These were your designs right?"

"Yep." Janie said

"Great. Anything you'd like to add?"

"No, they look good."

Janie had scheduled three tattoos. One on her right middle finger, one on her right shoulder, and one on her stomach. Harley hadn't looked at the designs when they were brought over. She wanted to be surprised at her friend's choices.

"You want the easy one first, or last?" The tattoo artist said

"Eh." Janie said "Do the small one first, I don't care if which one was supposed to be easy."

Janie stuck out her hand, parting the other fingers away. She did not clench them in a fist, and she did not simply flip the artist off. This tattoo was going near the knuckle, so he needed the space that both flipping him off or balling into a fist would have removed.

It was a barbed wire band. Harley had seen countless people have these tattooed on their forearm, seeing one on a finger was a very interesting take.

Slight drops of blood showed under the black ink. More would be coming. It only now stuck in Harley's mind exactly what the tattoo gun was doing, and she had a feeling most people getting their first tattoo or watching someone get a tattoo for the first time also had this revelation.

"Alright, we're good." The artist said "Now just turn to the left a little bit.

The tattoo gun started it's work on Janie's shoulder. It was a star, and the way it was done fascinated Harley, there would have been no way to do it without the tracing method that had been used. He only drew the outline, slowly and perfectly, without having any lines on the inside, unlike how most people would draw a star.

He then colored the star red, leaving the outline a thick black.

"Alright, lay back now." The artist said

Janie laid back, practically in sleeping position. The seat folded back, and the top of her head just barely reached over the end.

This one seemed to make her eyes twitch a little bit, which was unfortunate as this one proved massive. But not the most massive. Harley had been able to coax out of her that the one planned for her belly was her biggest and proudest of the three.

It was a massive cobra's head, fully detailed hood, done with time and research. Inside of its gaping mouth was a giant eye, serpentinely slit. This tattoo alone took over an hour of the session time, and it was worth it.

"Alright Jane." He said "I'll patch you up now and give you some ointment."

Gauze had been taped over her tattoos. Small drops of blood leaked through the bottom of the tape. She took a container of ointment, and handed the money over in payment.

"Alright." Harley said "You ready go get out of here?"

"Yeah." Janie's voice sounded a little winded.

Harley walked with her back to Janie's car. They opened their doors, and got comfortable in their seats.

Janie reached for the wheel, and then looked at her hand.

"Huh." She said

"What?" Harley said

"Well, my hand hurts and I don't know if driving will be easy."

"I'll take over then, I can drive."

Janie looked over at her, clearly not believing her. "Really?"

"Sure. It's no big deal. Where do you live on campus?"

"I don't."

"Hm. Well, is it okay if I come over then?"

Janie didn't answer.

"It'd be easier, from where I'm standing."

"Yeah." Janie said "Yeah, you have a point. Alright. I guess we'll hang out at my place."

Janie walked Harley up into her apartment. The complex itself was rather small, and from the look of it, this was not the high rent area. The building had a few cracks, paint had chipped in four or five places. It was a shame, because from the ride up, it looked like quite a nice neighborhood.

Janie's apartment was not barren, she had all the essential furniture. Granted, she also had a fair bit of open space, notably hidden with a large round area rug.

"Alright." Janie said "Make yourself at home."

Janie plopped down on the couch. Aside from a patch job on the right arm, it was a nice sofa. Harley sat on the other end and found it to be very comfortable.

"How come you don't life on campus?" Harley said

"This place is really cheap and I don't have to deal with the idiot freshmen."

Harley did not hate or even dislike the freshmen on her floor, but she could see where

Erika Ramson

Janie was coming from. Between the childish yelling in the middle of the night, to the repeated Internet-born jokes, and she was pretty sure she'd tripped over things they'd forgotten about in the hallway.

"What are the neighbors like?" Harley said

"Eh." Janie said "There's a small family on the second floor, they're nice enough. The guy who delivers the mail lives here on the third. I don't really know much else."

"So you're usually alone here?"

"Basically. This is the top floor so no one lives above me, and get this, no one's rented the apartment under me either. I don't have to worry about noise."

"Cool. So, what did you want to do?"

"We can just chill out. I didn't have anything in mind." Janie poked a little at her gauze. "Besides I have to make sure to cover these with ointment when I have to."

"Will they look the same as they did earlier?"

"Mostly. No blood and no red marks, but the ink will look exactly the same. Maybe better. Hey. You want a beer?"

"You sure?"

"I have plenty of beer, it's no problem."

"Eh. Sure. I haven't had beer since, oh God I don't actually know."

Janie went up to the refrigerator. True to her word, there was an ample supply of beer. From what Harley could see, there were no trances of anything stronger. She'd never tried anything stronger, so perhaps not being able to have the temptation was a good thing.

Janie came back with a six-pack. She gave Harley a bottle and took one for herself. She opened the both of them.

"I'm going to stay clear-headed." Janie said "So you want any more out of this pack go for it."

"Alright." Harley took a drink of the beer.

It was bitter, harsh, and rough.

But it was workable.

"I think." Harley said "The last beer I had was when I was, I think twelve. Yeah. Yeah I had a sip by accident. This is what I remember it tasting like."

"Beer's really only good for hanging out with friends or getting wasted." Janie said "If you want to get wasted, I am going to cut you off at some point. I'm not cleaning a mess."

"I've never been drunk before."

"Really?" Janie seemed to scoff when she said that. "Alright. You want to get drunk?"

Harley thought it over. "You know what. Sure. I want to remember tonight, and I don't want to throw up, but sure, I want to get drunk."

"Cool. I'll keep those in mind. Oh, speaking of puking." Janie pointed in the direction of one of her doors. "That is the bathroom. If you have to take a dump, you'll need to fill a bucket of water from the tub. The flush doesn't work."

"That sucks. How long has that been the case?"

"Last week. Landlord's trying to get a repairman, but whatever, I got used to it fast. If you have to piss, well, you can leave it if you want. It's what I do, until it starts to smell."

Janie and Harley began to talk about normal, everyday things. In all fairness, it was the only thing keeping Harley from stopping her drink. After a few moments, she was down one bottle.

Janie opened a second one. "Alright. I'd say," she blew out with her lips "three more might do it. It did not take me very long to get drunk my first time."

"How old are you?" Harley said "I don't think I asked."

"Eighteen." Janie said "Before you ask I get the beer from a friend of mine. He works at the grocery store so I can't tell you his name. Loose lips get people fired."

Harley felt courageous, and took a larger swig of her beer. This time, already feeling a slight buzz from the first beer, she liked the taste a lot more and it went done much easier.

She belched.

"There you go." Janie said "Now it's starting."

"Sorry." Harley said, and then belched again. "Goddammit. Sorry."

"Stop apologizing and just keep drinking. So, the guy who inked me." Janie looked away from Harley for a moment. "You think he took a peak at me?"

"Didn't look like it." Harley said, as blunt as anyone who'd been drinking. Not that she wasn't blunt beforehand.

Janie turned back, seemingly humorless and confused at this reaction. "Okay? Why do you think that?"

"Well, I mean, it's pretty obvious when a guy peaks at you. This guy was a professional and treated you like a client. You sound kind of upset, you're not worried about this are you?"

"It's not that. It's a little, you know. You sayin' I couldn't change his mind on that?"

"I'm saying the Mona fuckin' Lisa couldn't change his mind on that."

"So you're saying a fucking painting looks hotter than me?!"

"Look are you insecure of something because you're very pretty. You have nothing to worry about." Harley tipped the empty bottle right up against her mouth, trying to get whatever she could.

"I'm fine." Janie quickly grabbed another bottle, opened it, and handed it over to Harley. "Just keep drinking.

"Alright, that's what I'm here for." Harley took drink of her third beer. "Oh shit! How will I get back home?"

"You can bring yourself to school tomorrow. Just bring my car back as soon as possible."

"You're not going to school?"

"I already told the professors I needed that day to heal. I can't afford to take the others off but at least I got the day after the appointment."

"Cool. Right. You're very smart. You know I've seen you in math and you look like you don't pay attention but I never hear you complain about a bad grade."

"Because I'm passing. I pay enough attention to pass, and that's all that matters."

"See? You're smart and you're pretty. Boys like the goth thing. Or is it not boys?"

"No, it's boys. But I don't exactly date."

"Define the 'exactly' part."

"If he's cute, I'll talk to him. If he's nice, I'll spend time with him. If I find a good reason, I'll fuck him. I don't want to waste my time here having to be on someone's arm all the Goddamn time. If it can be quick, sure, I'll have some fun. I don't need an actual boyfriend."

"You do you. Well, I assume you do you when you don't do the boys."

"Yep. Gotta keep myself up. By the way, you and that Max guy?"

Harley grew a dumb, stupid, really big smile. "Yeah."

"Are the two of you banging?" Janie said

"Once. Huh. I didn't think about going back to him again. We want to be friends, but, well we survived the first time. Wait, no, we became friends because of the first time. Huh. By the way I'm out."

"Yeah, I saw." Janie cracked open Harley's last beer. "No more after this, unless you're heavier than I thought."

"And thank you. But yeah, Max and I did have sex, and after you've said it, I guess I could see it happening again. I really don't know, he's not here for me to ask him."

Harley, barely thinking, downed the entire fourth bottle of beer all at once.

"Woo!" Harley dropped the bottle on the floor, where it thankfully bounced without breaking.

She belched again, louder than before.

"And here we go." Janie said

"Hey Janie." Harley leaned over and hugged her. "You a good person."

Janie snorted "In what way?"

"A good person way."

"Yeah, cool. So when you crash I assume you'll take the couch."

"We can't sleep on your bed?"

"My bed works for one person, but it's way too lumpy for two people. Besides I sleep naked and you don't have to see me naked just to go to sleep."

"Are you forgetting I have a, a" Harley snapped her fingers trying to remember the word. "a roommate. Yeah, we couldn't count all the times we've seen each other's boobs if we tried. Or pussies. You know her pussy is kind of-"

"I don't fucking care!"

"Okay."

"So your roommate. Little miss pink. How do you put up with that?"

"You know 'little miss pink' could describe me too." Harley put her right hand, backwards, up against Janie's face. "See?"

"Whatever. She looked kinda bitchy."

"Nah. She's great. Maybe you caught her at a bad angle. Although I didn't like her at first either. She's not funny. Not like me. I'm hilarious."

"Yeah that's one word."

"You're my best friend Janie. I like you."

Janie paused a little bit. "Cool. You're drunk and don't mean it, but, cool.

"Let's do something."

"Stop hugging me and sure, we'll play a board game or watch TV."

"Oooh, let's watch porn."

"My Internet's really bad here."

"You don't have any on video?"

"I'm sorry what fucking year is this?! No one has porn on video except old farts with too much hair grease who never got married or had anything meaningful."

"You exaggerate a lot."

"I'm a millennial, that's our shtick."

Harley got up from the sofa, already starting to wobble.

"A'ight." She said "Let's play a board game."

She fell.

Jane and Harley had played for about two and a half hours. They'd played long enough for Harley to sober up, and by this point, they had gone to sleep.

Harley groggily woke up, and checked the time. 11:50 P.M. She hadn't been all that tired when she'd gone to bed, and now she felt roughly the same. There was nothing left to do but stand up for a bit walk around, maybe tire herself out from minimal exercise. It usually worked at this time of night.

Her foot touched her discarded clothes. To sleep easier, she'd stripped to her underwear and bra, both dark red and simple. She missed her pajamas, and wished she'd had the foresight to expect staying over.

In thinking this over, she noticed she'd left her ring on. She removed it, and stuck it on top of her clothes pile. She doubted she would forget about it when she awoke, and it was much better than any pressure it would have given her fingers while tossing and turning on the sofa.

She walked over to the kitchen portion of Janie's apartment. She had no interest in taking any of Janie's food of even if she would have been fine with it, Harley just felt like the light of the fridge would possibly remind her brain exactly how late it was and that her body needed the rest.

With the light on, Harley's eyes glanced around the room to try and not become blinded.

She saw a lot of things, none of them were family portraits. Or hints of love letters, or anything, special. Harley herself kept everything she valued from her family in a smart place, everything here was thrown around, and meant to be used without a care if it became broken or disgusting.

"She doesn't have loved ones." Harley said, now too tired to realize it was out loud.

She closed the fridge and headed back to the sofa. Face first, she planted herself down and fell back asleep.

♥ - Chapter 7 - ♥

Today was the end of the final week of school. For Harley, the first half of her starter year was almost over, and she was spending this exact part of it finishing a math test.

Professor Bills-Brooke decided to be nice to them as best he could. Trigonometry required the final to be a test, but there were no stated rules on the difficulty or the importance on the final grade. As such, the test was only two pages long, and it only affected five percent of the total grade.

Still, it wasn't anything Harley felt she should whizz through. The questions were not too hard, barring a few, it was just that they all took a good amount of time to use their needed formulas.

Harley finished the last question of the test, and walked up to hand it in to the professor.

"Thank you." He said "Have a good break."

Harley waited outside the door for Janie to finish. She was only waiting about a minute or two before Janie popped up out of her desk to hand in her own test.

"Thank y-" The professor started to say. "Miss Olber you left the second question blank."

"Eh, didn't care." Janie said "Look I didn't put much effort into this one, I just want to get out of here and go home."

The professor seemed to sigh, but the shrugged it off. "Well, you've been doing fine, I suppose nothing this test could do would hurt you. Have a good break."

Once Janie walked out, she seemed surprised to see Harley waiting outside the door.

"The hell are you doing?" Janie said

"We got out early, I figured we could do something. You know, instead of just hang out against the wall."

"I can't." Janie said "I going to go to lunch. The place I want to go is a ways away, you don't need to go there just because I'm going to."

"Alright, I'll see you in a couple of hours."

Fittingly enough, Harley and Janie exited the building in separate directions. This was normal, considering Janie often quickly drove back home whilst Harley walked back, but today was the first and only day Harley was able to notice this.

Harley turned her key to get back into her room.

She saw Annie, sound asleep in bed. Annie's right leg was over the edge, and both of her arms were at adjacent and bizarre angles. She often slept like this when she simply crashed instead of preparing for bedtime.

She was in her pajamas, but hadn't taken the time to remove her makeup, which left both her red lipstick and black eyeliner smeared across her face and on her pillow.

Being as it was impossible to not notice her right foot, Harley also noticed that Annie somehow managed to get her green nail polish smeared across her toes as well. From the look of her, this was a story she may not remember.

Harley closed the door, and this awoke her roommate.

"Hm what?" Annie said, jolting up with eyes half open. 'What are you? Pizza man?"

"Nope. Roommate." Harley said

"Oh. Your coat's pretty."

Harley's "coat" was a long sleeve button-up blue sweater. She also wore black pants with white decals on the knees, and the opening for her feet. Her shoes her dark red strappy heels, and she wore long gold strand earrings.

It was one of her last days of this semester, she wanted to put extra effort in.

"What'cha wake up me for?" Annie said, slipping her way out of bed.

"I didn't, you heard the door."

"Oh. I'm going back to bed then." Annie slipped back under her sheets.

"You sure?"

"Yeah. I got really drunk and really high last night and I need to sleep it off for a couple of hours."

"Shit. Where are you hiding this stuff?"

"I was at a party with this guy I just met. There's some weed left in my drawer, you can have it. I don't remember which drawer."

"I'm good. I'll save my first time getting high for a special occasion."

Annie practically leaped out of her bed.

"You've NEVER gotten high!?" She said "I've been getting high since I was twelve!"

"It never occurred to me."

"You've haven't lived!"

"I'll see for myself soon enough. Hey, are you up now or are you going back to sleep?"

"You sobered me up way more than sleeping could."

"You want to help me pack?"

"Fine, but you better help me too."

Neither Harley nor Annie had much to pack. They would both be heading back to this same room barely a month after the day they left. Still, Harley did not want to wait until the night before, or worse, the morning of. Annie seemed to be willing to wait, but Harley's decision to pack now nullified her chances of waiting.

What Harley wanted to pack was her laptop, a few books she'd finished reading, and a few movies she decided she wasn't going to watch after all. It was hard deciding what else needed to be packed away, a lot of it seemed like something that could wait for her in the room.

The little amount of food she had left would be eaten later today, and Annie said she planned the same. She planned on packing her sketchbook, but until her final, she needed to still bring it to class.

"What finals do you have left?"

Harley went through her mind to remember exactly what was in store. Everything was on a strange schedule, making it hard to know off the top of her head.

"My art class has a final today." She said "Well, it barely counts as a final. The professor is bringing in a model for us, and he'll be nude."

"Nude model?" Annie said "Nice."

"Maybe. I don't think the point is to be aroused, I think it's to study basic humanity or something. God I just read the point of nude paintings in a textbook and I've already forgotten exactly what it said."

"Did you sell it back yet?"

"I'm selling tomorrow. I hear they don't give you that much money."

"Yep. I sold all of mine yesterday and I got like fifty bucks total. I think that might buy me one textbook out of the five I need for next semester. Shit, my next semester is going to really be something."

"What do you have?"

"I need a lot of math classes, and they allowed me to take them all at once. Trig, Stats, Calc, oh, and I'm taking a Geography class because I felt like it."

"You sure that won't burden you?"

"Nope. Granted, I didn't think it through until I'd signed up for them already."

Annie had packed some spare clothes into a large box she'd hidden under her bed. Despite the roughness of a simple cardboard box, Annie was careful in folding and storing her clothes inside. She also had a bag of dirty clothes set aside it.

Harley figured to do the same, but found she had far less clothes than Annie, especially of the currently-clean variety.

"We need to go shopping." Annie said "Honey you barely do your nails or anything."

"I try." Harley said "I like doing it just not that often."

"Speaking of, I see you went out of your way to look gorgeous today. Remind me, isn't that Max guy in your art class?"

"Yes. Very much so."

"You never told me what he looks like. Which is good, I want to be surprised when I eventually bump into him or you introduce us."

"He's a sharp dresser. You should at least know that."

"Ah! And you're trying to do the same so he notices. That's adorable."

"Well, yeah. We're just friends, but once you go through that, well. He kinds of rubs off on you and makes you care about certain things more. And I'm sure he's appreciates that I care that much."

"Hang on."

Annie walked over to her make-up box. Harley did not own a make-up box, nor enough make-up to justify one. She did her best to apply lip gloss or lipliner some days, and eyeliner on special days, but never really branched out more than that.

"Here we go." Annie handed her a small container of blue gunk.

"Blue eyeshadow." Annie said "It goes with your sweater, and always goes with anybody's eyes."

"Thanks but I've never used-" Before Harley could finish, Annie took back the eyeshadow, opened it, and placed some on her thumb.

"Shouldn't you get a brush?" Harley said

"Already packed it away. Don't worry I've done it this way a thousand times. Close your left eye." Annie said

Annie carefully painted the shadow on Harley's left eyelid. Harley then closed her right eye so Annie could repeat the process. Harley opened her eyes, and Annie retrieved a mirror.

"Oh, also." Annie said "It's glittery."

Harley saw the tops of her eyes sparkles in a deep dark blue.

"Okay." Harley said "This works on me."

Harley and Janie had taken their seats, as usual.

"When did you fuck your eyes up?" Janie said

"A little bit ago." Harley said "Some days are just worth being pretty for."

"Hm. Alright." Janie herself was sporting a large orange t-shirt. It was her art shirt, it had already seen splotches of paint, graphite, and marker residue. She had more than one art class, and this move was very smart on her part. She also wore orange sneakers, and gray jeans.

One thing was certain. Starting next semester, Harley was going to take lessons in fashion from three people: Annie, Janie, and of course, from Max. She had a style, and she knew it could be helped by absorbing from three completely different looks.

Harley readied her easel and drawing paper for what was going to come next. She'd never drawn a full body before, with or without clothes. The model himself was currently in towel, and just sitting on a large wooden rock.

"Well, everyone's here." Professor Anghula said "Now class, the man before you is an experienced and talented nude model. He's also my boyfriend." She gave him a kiss on the cheek. "Yes I know it's a little unprofessional, but really, if I had tenure *I* would be the one about to model for you. I believe this is a close enough trade."

"Thank God I don't have to see them." Janie whispered. "I'm fucking jealous enough as it is."

"Now honey," Anghula said "you can get into position."

The model leaned back in a comfortable position, and quickly removed his towel.

His nonerect penis measured eleven inches.

"Never mind." Janie had gone practically white. "Shit."

"Hey." Harley said "You're just looking at it, it's not going anywhere near you."

"Yeah, but. God. I wasn't expecting a nightmare."

Harley, Janie, and the rest of the class began drawing their version of the model. Professor Anghula had instructed them to be as realistic and close as they could, but to also add minor things to stand out from everyone else. Now knowing this was her lover, most likely she wanted to retain the student's individuality, while still gaining a flattering image of her man.

In all honesty, it seemed fair enough. Harley focused currently on the model, and would think of something to add when she was closer to done.

Having Janie to her side meant she could roughly see what part she was on. They both arrived to the man's privates at around the exact same time.

"Does." Janie mumbled, barely enough for Harley to hear. "Does she want his fucking veins and shit too? Because I can totally see them."

And now Harley could make them out as well. Harley was not as taken-back as Janie, for while she found it intimidating, at least the bigger size meant it would be easier to draw. He was circumcised as well, so her schoolkid days of crude bathroom stall drawings would slightly help. Granted, she had to be far more realistic, but the thought still occurred to her.

Harley decided to draw hard angles across the our edges of her drawing. As it she was framing it without a real frame. Janie had a similar idea, but with lizards and skulls around the entire edges. Harley also drew a flower onto the rock, while Janie opted for giant spider legs, as if the model was in fact lying on top of a fantasy beast.

"Nice." Harley whispered

"Yeah, thanks. The flower's cute." Janie said, half looking. "I like the edges. Very sharp."

They were not going to go on break today, Anghula did not want to tire out the model. So the two continued sketching their version, and were close to adding the color.

Class had ended. All of the drawings were handed in, and professor Anghula let them know that they could pick up their drawings next semester if they wanted to, and would e-mail them their grades.

Max and Harley had been chatting for the last twenty minutes. Max had been out sick the last two classes, and they were doing their best to catch up.

"So is this your last class?" Max said "Because it's mine. I go home tomorrow morning."

"No. I have one left." Harley said "But I drive myself home right after."

"Oh, you drive. Cool. I've been working on my license in my spare time. Is it that hard?"

"At first, yes. There's a lot of stuff they also don't tell you, mostly because it's hypothetical. I could show you sometime."

"I'd like that." Max seemed to slow down a little bit, he even cleared his throat. "Hey, uh. You, you know that model we just had?"

"Yeah, wouldn't exactly forget it in half an hour you know what I'm saying."

"Right. Um. The thing is. It made me think, and, since you're the only one who's. Hrm. I wasn't. Disappointing in that regard, right?"

"I would much rather have you than him."

"But you know me. I mean, my. My dick isn't small but, well. Compared to that, I."

"Max you're the only one I've ever had, I'm the wrong person to ask about sizes. If I had to guess I doubt it would have made any difference for what I like."

"I mean I've heard that, but I just-"

"Max. You were amazing and have nothing to worry about."

"Well, actually I don't even know if you could say amazing. I've, looked a few things up since then and, I think maybe I was a lot clumsier than I would be now."

"Well. Good."

"……. So you're saying my dick is alright the way it is?"

"Yep. I liked it quite a bit to tell the honest truth."

"Okay. Yeah. I, guess you have a point." After taking the chance to breathe out, Max cocked his head and squinted his eyes. "Are you wearing eyeshadow?"

"I am."

"It's very beautiful. I always liked the glittery kind. Not on me you understand. I did experiment with eyeliner in my junior year of high school and that kind of turned me off make-up."

"Stab yourself in the eye?"

"No but I came very close and I could basically taste the stuff through my eyes, if that makes any sense."

"Trust me, I know exactly what you mean."

"Well, I have to pack. Call me sometime over break, okay?"

"Of course. I'll see you when I get back."

Max turned and left. Harley started walking back to her room, and out of the corner of her eye, she saw Janie trying to light a cigarette. Her lighter was not obeying her at the moment. She had also found the time to change back into a black goose-down jacket.

The thought occurred to her how long it would be before she saw her again. She walked over to her.

"Hey, Janie." Harley said

Janie did not remove the unlit cigarette out of her mouth. "Hey. Saw you with that guy again. I'm surprised at your will power. Most chicks with that kind of relationship would have been sucking his tongue down their throat for the world to see."

"Point taken, and admittedly a little tempting. Now, do you want to get lunch with me? Here on campus."

Janie raised an eyebrow to her. "Why?"

"I won't see you for a while. I thought it'd be a good idea."

"Alright. I guess so."

"Can I bring my roommate? I think you two should meet."

"We did."

"I mean officially, actually. Sit down and talk to her instead of just looking at her."

"Whatever. I don't care."

Harley walked Janie up to her room. As she had been unable to light it, Janie carried the cigarette in her mouth the entire way up the stairs.

Harley opened the door to her room, slightly surprised to see Annie had fully changed and was wide awake. She wore a nice red dress shirt with a small pocket, black pants that were light in color but not light enough to be gray, and black flats. On her right middle finger was a thin wavy silver ring.

Her eyes were red and puffy.

"I don't got weed no more." She said, slightly giggling afterwards.

"You want to come eat with us?" Harley said "Me and Janie?"

Annie had her eyes closed as she talked, smiling stupidly. "Sure. I'm starving. Guess why?"

The three ladies were checking in to the campus dining room. They each had to use the student IDs to register they were in fact paying for these meals.

Once they were allowed in, the three of them picked a table. It was open enough for others to join in, not that they would have been invited.

"Guess I'll leave my coat here." Janie removed her coat, revealing her large orange shirt. "Oh Goddammit I forgot to take this off!" She then removed the large shirt.

Underneath it, she'd been wearing an orange blouse with no straps. It was surprisingly frilly for her, and revealed her neckline, and parts of her belly.

"That's cute." Harley said

"I had nothing else." She said "I think I found it at a charity store."

Today the dining room had changed up the schedule a little, to make up for the confusion of finals. There were pizzas, waffles, fries, the majority was snack foods to add onto real meals.

For that regard, they were making battered chicken sandwiches, and the students could choose any vegetables or condiments.

Harley herself went with a chicken sandwich with lettuce, tomato, and sriracha mayonnaise. She also grabbed a basket of fries and two slices of pizza. She only realized now how hungry she was.

Annie had gotten two sandwiches, but only with the chicken and a slice of American cheese, and a lot more fries than Harley.

Janie had a slice of pizza and some fries.

They all got their drinks, which were flavored colas, and sat back down.

"This pizza kind of tastes like a flatbread pizza on top of a flatbread pizza." Harley said "But with dough to bind it together."

"Eh." Janie said "It's alright."

"Personally I've had it enough times to not like it anymore." Annie said, shoving fries into her mouth.

Harley started putting ketchup on her fries, before eating a bit of her chicken.

"You should have gotten the hollandaise." Janie said "You'd like it, goes good with these fries."

"Nah." Annie said "Ranch dude. Ranch is where it's at."

"I hate ranch." Janie said

"Well I'm not fond of hollandaise, but hey, you said something first I thought I would too. You know?"

"I'll get some." Harley said "Of both I mean. I'm sick of ketchup anyway."

Harley left the two of them alone to go grab more condiments. Grabbing a packet of hollandaise and ranch, she decided on another fry basket to test them out there.

She dared to try them both together.

"This is pretty good."

She walked back to them, and could notice the two apparently didn't even try to talk to each other while she was gone.

"So." Harley said "We're all almost done with this semester."

"I assume so." Janie said, rolling her eyes.

"It's kind of exciting." Annie said "Knowing how close we are to the next part of our college experiences."

"Yeah, sure." Janie said "Real big exciting fucking journey."

"Hey, well." Annie said "I thought so. Can't possibly see why you would be so angry about that."

"What classes are you guys taking next semester?" Harley said. She came very close to sweating.

Annie and Janie discussed their picked classes. Very different, Annie was more math heavy while Janie opted for arts.

"Well Janie," Annie said "I'm sure that'll be a fun time."

"Jane." Janie said "I'd much rather Jane. We don't know each other yet."

Harley saw a small twitch in Annie's left eyebrow.

"Cool then." Annie said "Jane. I get it. Why don't you call me Anne then? Hm?"

The rest of the lunch played out very similar.

Harley was happy she'd gotten more fries.

Harley and Annie were walking back to their room. Janie had started the drive back to her place a while ago.

"So what did you think?" Harley said

"I don't like her." Annie said

"I mean. She's a good friend of mine."

"Then I'll tolerate her, but I ain't gonna start fuckin' liking her."

On the way to their room, they came across the overly excited RA.

"Hey ladies!" Josh said "Have you started your packing yet?"

"About to get the last bits in." Harley said

"Eh, I'm working on it." Annie said

"Well I hope your finals have been going good!" Josh said "I'll be seeing you two very soon!"

Josh walked off in the other direction. Harley wondered whether or not she really did hear him sigh out like she thought she did.

The two entered their room, and sat down at their desks.

"I still think it's a fun little adventure." Annie said "You know, next semester."

"Yeah, I can see it." Harley said "It's good to know I've got you and Janie to come back to."

"Yeah." Annie said "But I'll tell you this, I cannot wait until you an' me get my ears pierced. We're going on a shopping spree, so bring yo' money."

♥ - Chapter 8 - ♥

It was Christmas morning. Harley had been enjoying the week or so she'd spent with her family, but this was the day she'd been waiting for from the beginning. Nobody had opened anything just yet, in their family they always waited until the exact day.

She was sitting on the floor, next to her brother and his girlfriend. They'd always gotten along, but never had been able to spend much time together. However, for this school break, the family was able to convince Harley's mother to let the girlfriend stay over.

Her mother still hadn't fully gotten used to it, but at least she'd let it happen in the first place. Speaking of her mother, she and Harley's father were sitting on the couch.

Harley had dressed up for the occasion. It was traditional for her to wear a white sweater with Santa and a reindeer sewn in, she'd owned one ever since she was a child. She had a red skirt with a green trim on the bottom, candy cane earrings, no shoes or socks, and a smile.

She was the most Christmassy out of everyone else, and that suited her just fine. She loved this time of year.

Granted, both her brother and mother wore red and green elf hats, and her father would have worn a Santa hat, had they not misplaced it two years ago.

Both her mother and father wore light brown coats, and blue jeans. Her brother was wearing a white button-up shirt, and his blue pajama pants.

The girlfriend was completely in her pajamas, and as usual for her, worn a dark green lip ring in the center of her bottom lip. Apparently, she didn't take it off to go to bed.

Harley's presents were the art books she asked for from her father, and her mother had bought her art pencils. These were not inexpensive, and she thanked her heavily for them.

One thing she always liked about her brother was that when he couldn't think of a gift, he would buy her a lot of chocolates and candy. Truth be told, she hadn't pigged out on sweets in a long time, and was very happy this is what he decided on.

"Okay." The girlfriend said, handing Harley her gift. "I didn't know what to get, but your father said this sounded like a good idea. If you don't like it tell me I can handle it."

Harley opened the gift, a pearl bracelet with little bits of gold keeping it together.

"It's imitation gold." The girlfriend said "But not the kind that'll make your arm green or anything."

"I like it." Harley said, slipping it on her left wrist. "I don't wear much arm stuff, you may have just given me a reason to."

"That's very lovely." Her mother said "Well, I wasn't expecting something so nice. With you being so, new to our Christmas time."

"I tried." The girlfriend said "Need to make a great impression, and you guys are, important, to me."

It was clear to everyone in the room besides her brother that she almost said "family".

Harley actually saw her mother want to smile, not that she did.

"Cookbooks?" Her mother said, opening her gift from the girlfriend. "Huh. I haven't had any cookbooks in a while."

"I tried that sort of theme." The girlfriend said "Stuff you may have not had in a while, so you'd be pleasantly surprised or wouldn't mind if I had to bring it back."

"Well." Her mother said "I guess it was past time I tried reading from these. I appreciate them."

Everyone continued opening presents for the next half an hour or so. When they were all done, the next part of the agenda was that her parents were going to cook them all a big Christmas breakfast. Traditionally this meant red and green pancakes, many Christmas sweets, and anything else they decided to add.

On her way to the kitchen, Harley's mother spied through one of her new books. Harley decided to listen in.

"Huh." She heard her mother said "This doesn't sound bad. Honey? Do you think you could do this?"

The father agreed, meaning Harley's mother found a way to use the present from her son's girlfriend, without having to use it herself.

Harley loved her mother, dearly, and this was one of the reasons. She never met anyone else who had the rougher edges of the close-minded, but would go out of her way to try and accommodate.

It was mostly the bizarre look of the girlfriend that upset her. The whole "my baby boy is dating *that?*" But she was clearly still trying to come around to it, as the evidence this was his true love was apparent to even her.

"It's nice that you guys get to spend your nights together here." Harley said "You get to stay really close."

"Yeah well we'd spend better times together if the walls weren't so thin." The girlfriend gave her a wink. "I have to use the bathroom."

Once the girlfriend was gone, her brother pulled her aside and whispered to her "Harley could I have a quick word with you?"

The two siblings pulled over to the corner of the room.

"So now let me tell you I've never been more scared in my entire life." He said

"Will it's alright. What's the matter?" It wasn't common to see her brother open up in this manner.

Their father had taught them there was nothing wrong with learning how to speak your mind, and how to do so effectively without having to force emotions you didn't truly feel, or force others to feel them either.

So they'd always talked like this, but Will had never been in this state of worry and smallness.

"I love the hell out of her." He said "It's way time to, ahem, but I can't do it."

"Will." Harley said "I'm sure it's scary, but, maybe you could just talk with her about it."

"She's tried to." Will said "God help her, she knows me enough to figure it out, and she's talked with me about it. I guess most serious couples to. But I get scared and she sees it. Christ, I love her but I can't do anything about it. I just. I don't know if it'll work out if it gets to that level."

"Will she's clearly in love with you."

"And if we take the next leap? So many other people thought they could, and then nothingness immediately followed."

"You've been dating for five years."

"Yeah and one of those years was high school. We were different people."

"And you changed at roughly the same time and still figured you were worth each other."

Harley put her arm around her brother and gave him a small hug.

"You guys'll be alright." Harley said "Just try your best and be happy with what comes regardless."

"Yeah." Will said "It's time I made this 'honest' though, whatever the hell you want to call it. Maybe in another two years."

They stayed silent for a few seconds, just chilling out in the corner. When the girlfriend came back out of the bathroom, she found the scene so adorable she had to snap a picture with her phone.

It was now Christmas night. Harley was removing her clothes to slip into pajamas. At this point, she was down to her bra and panties, which was her only secret in Christmas attire.

They were red and green striped, diagonally. She found no embarrassment in them, but they were naturally a part of her clothing her family had never seen her wear. She'd done this ever since she was sixteen, and she had dubbed the bra itself under the name "Christmas boobs".

She was going to change into her pajamas, however, she suddenly remember what Janie said about always sleeping naked. College was the time of trying new things, and it was Christmas, an incredibly special day for her.

She decided, screw it, she would try sleeping naked.

The covers against her bare skin felt, comforting. Her sheets were heavy and warm due to the weather, and they felt like one of her sweaters, except covering her neck, legs, and feet along with her chest and arms.

It felt very nice, although most likely something she wouldn't do very often.

There was a gentle knock on her wall.

"Hrm?" She said

"I wanted to see if you can hear that." A voice came from where the knock did, belonging to Will's girlfriend. "Can you hear me too?"

"Yes Mimi I can hear you." Harley said

"Can I come visit you?"

"Yes but I won't be getting out of bed, I'll tell you why when you get here."

In less than a minute, Mimi had found her way to Harley's bedroom.

"I'm commando." Harley said "I hope you don't mind just because I don't."

"I don't, just don't get up." She said "You're like a sister to me, and my own sister hates being seen naked, so, I dunno, that might be weird to me. I've done what you're doing though, isn't it exhilarating?"

"Uuum, sure. I guess so. I kind of get t."

"Hm, well, I guess it's not as exciting to you. Anyway, I just wanted to come in here to wish you good night."

"Thank you. Good night to you too."

"Oh, and am I right in guessing you and Will talked a little bit about me? Not me, I mean, Will looked like the way he always looks when we talk serious about the two of us."

"Yeah. No offense to you, but sometimes it's easier sharing it with your sister than your girlfriend, I'm guessing."

"Hm. Well, as long as you didn't try to tell him what to do. I'm happy. I mean don't get me wrong I wish he proposed every single fucking minute we're together, but if he's just going to get flustered I can wait until he clears his head out. I guess."

"Patience is a virtue of something."

"Yeah well he's made me way more virtuous than I ever thought I would be. At least he's worth it. Maybe he'll talk to me about it soon enough. Good night Harley."

"Good night Mimi."

"Have fun at college."

"Trust me, I've been."

♥ - Chapter 9 - ♥

School was going to start up in one more day. Harley had already unloaded her miscellaneous stuff back into her room. But, she was not on campus today.

"Alright Harls!" Annie said "How much money you got? 'Cause we goin' shopping!"

"I've set aside about five hundred bucks." Harley said

"And I've got six hundred. Now let's get my ears pierced and see what eleven hundred bucks'll get us."

Harley walked with Annie to the piercing store in the mall. Malls were an interesting thing, in the right town. Harley had been to this one many times, and it was the same size as you would expect a real mall. She'd also seen strip malls, and malls that were better off becoming strip malls.

She'd been to this stop in the mall before, this was the same place that did her ears all those years ago. Some of the staff was different, naturally, but not by much as it was family owned. As far as Harley know, the people who did her's may very well have died since then.

Annie sat down in the piercing chair. Her outfit today was, well, daring in a sense. She wanted to show off her new earrings more than anything else of her body, so she covered up more than usual. While still dressing exactly how she always did.

She wore a beige t-shirt with short sleeves, and on the chest area were fake gemstones that spelled out the word "hot". She also wore a jean skirt that went down to just above her ankles, and a small triangular cut on the right side. On her feet were black women's boots.

Annie had also changed her hair over the break. It was no longer black, nor was it long enough to be tied in any fashion. It only barely went halfway down her neck, and she was now a blonde.

Harley was far more reserved, she wore a light blue dress, with a cream bow across the middle. It had been a gift from her mother, and it fit like a glove. On her left wrist was her pearl bracelet, on her feet were pink strappy low heels, and simple gold studs were in her ears.

Annie clicked her feet together in excitement. Harley remembered acting roughly the same way. Although Annie's wide smile seemed much bigger than the one Harley would have been capable of.

The piercing lady came over to them. There was most likely an actual job title, but Harley had no clue what that would be.

This lady was, in lack of better words, metal. She had three bottom lip studs, every ear piercing in her left ear, two cartilage piercings in her right ear, and a septum ring. She wore a leather jacket and leather pants. It really wasn't a surprise for this department, though it might have been a bizarre and unique look for any other career.

"Alright doll." The lady said "Just ease yourself, these ones are just a pinch."

"I know!" Annie said "I'm so pumped!"

Apparently she was so pumped she didn't even noticed it had happened.

"Well that was quick." Annie said, looking at her piercing earrings in the mirror. "But hey, I wasn't here for the pain, I was looking for the aftermath."

Annie paid out the money, and she and Harley left to go explore the mall.

"So where do you want to go?" Annie said

Harley blew out with her lips. "No idea."

"How about a boutique?" Annie said, squishing her face with her hands. "Make ourselves super beautiful?"

"I could do that at home."

"Well, I don't know about you, but I could honestly use a wax and a tan."

"You know that fake tanning is really really bad for you right?"

"Yeah but that's why I've never done it before. Come oooon, we don't live forever."

"I'm out."

"How about the wax?"

"You've seen me, I take care of that just fine."

"Well I'm way overdue, so maybe I should just meet up with you later."

Even Harley needed to be intoxicated to admit how much she agreed with Annie on how hairy she'd gotten. So, she shut up, and let Annie know she'd come meet her the second she got a text message saying she was done.

They temporarily went their separate ways. Harley hadn't been to the mall in a short bit, and she figured this was the best time to reacquaint herself with every store and kiosk.

There were clothing stores, jewelry stores. Most of the kiosks were selling poorly made t-shirts, all of which made to either appeal to idiot teenagers or the simple minded. There was a shoe store almost directly next to a discount family clothes store.

Harley had to go to a different aisle, she was getting sick of seeing clothes.

She found the food court, and was more than happy to take a few moments to get a soft pretzel and cheese dip. She also bought a lemon-line soda. She sat down with her food, doing as much eating as wondering whether this counted as her lunch. The pretzel itself cost five dollars, and even though it was very good, it turned her off from buying any more food, if these were the prices she could expect.

Finishing her food and tossing what she needed to in the trash, she turned the corner to see the next section of the mall. This was where the video games and toys were. More specifically, the multi-media centers, still standing proud even in the digital age the best they could.

A little ways from the gaming store, she spotted a man sitting on the floor playing a guitar. He seemed friendly enough, just strumming away. He had dark brown hair, mostly well-kept, and a short-sleeved purple shirt. He also had yellow jeans, very thin rimmed glasses, and on his right index finger was a silver ring with an image of the Earth.

"Hey there." The man said, as Harley had now walked over to him to hear better. "What'cha think of my playing?"

"I like it." Harley said

Harley figured it was worth giving him money, and took a few dollars out of her purse and looked for an open cap or bucket. Eventually the man saw what she was doing.

"No no." He said "I'm not playing for money miss, I'm just bored."

"Are you sure?" Harley said "Because I don't mind."

"Nah. Don't worry about it. I can get something much better from you beside money." He kept playing for a little bit before speaking again. "Wow that came out wrong. I mean if you like this music than that's good enough for me."

"Alright. How long have you been playing for?"

"Like five years old? Hard to remember. I can play a lot of songs but I never really tried to play everything, you know?"

Harley's phone buzzed with a message. She replied back letting Annie know exactly where she was.

"Sounds like you really know what you're doing." Harley said, texting at the same time.

"Lady I could play this with my dick by this point, you know? My dad showed me." He said "…. Oh my God that came out wrong too. Way wronger than the first thig…."

Annie came walking down and the two found each other. Annie had become a surprisingly flattering caramel color. A real tan would have still looked a million times better, but she'd been smart enough to not overstay her time in the booth.

"Who's your friend?" Annie said

"Don't know, didn't ask his name yet." Harley said "But he's a good musician."

"Hey there fella." Annie said to him.

The musician took a few moments before he spoke. "Hello miss. I'm Glad to meet you. Anyway, I need to get going. I hope you and your friend get up to some fun here. ….. Was that okay or did I say something wrong a third time?"

"I don't get it." Annie said

"Then that's good enough for me."

The musician left, leaving the two alone.

"Got anything in mind now?" Harley said

"No, but." Annie said "I bought you a little something to make up for the wait."

Annie reached into a shopping bag she'd been carrying, and handed Harley a decently sized metal ring with a black heart detailed on it.

"They were selling these for five bucks, but I think it'll look cute on you." Annie said

Harley had little interest in extra jewelry, but she gave it a try. It was a little big, and mostly fit on her thumb. It was still slightly big there, but not enough to slide off, only enough to spin around without a problem.

"Huh." Harley said "If this is stainless than I may be able to wear this again. It's not bad."

"Hey you can never wear it again if you want, as long as you wear it today." Annie said "Oh! Let's go replace my hat I lost."

They had been in the hat store for over an hour.

"Goddammit can you shop Annie." Harley said

"Look that was a good hat." Annie said "I want to buy it again and if I don't get a replacement than I'm just going to fuck myself over like last time."

The problem with her argument was that she'd already bought two sun hats. And a bucket hat. And a beret. And, for whatever reason, a bowler hat.

"You could try something on you know." Annie said

"Alright, you have a point." Harley said

Harley walked over to the beanies and skull caps. She found a dark gray skull cap, and fit it on her head. She was pleased with how it looked in the mirror.

"That doesn't really go with your dress." Annie said

"I didn't say it would." Harley said "But I like it, so I'm buying it."

Harley left Annie alone for a second to also buy two gray t-shirts with small left breast pockets, and a pair of fingerless gray gloves.

"You're into the grunge look?" Annie lowered her eyelids.

"Yep." Harley said "May as well try to embrace it. I like grunge as much as I like girly."

"Then buy a poodle skirt or something."

"Eh, maybe not. Although I have wanted a vintage dress for a while."

"Well now we're talking!"

After the clothes stores, the two moved on to a blacklit store that sold household gags and oddities. Harley hadn't been in one of these stores since her early teens. It did not surprise her that Annie found this store to be a blast.

"Dude check it out." Annie brought over two white plastic rings. "They glow in the dark!"

"I thought you were going to buy less costume jewelry." Harley said

"I can't help who I am at heart." Annie said "I'mma buy these and immediately put them on. Hopefully they get enough sunlight to see something later."

Harley decided to see if the store had anything that could get her attention. She had little interest in posters or action figures, and from what she could see, they had an awful lot of those. Eventually she found a dark blue purse, on it a picture of a cartoon dog giving a piggyback ride to a cartoon cat. She looked around it to look for a brand name, seeing if this was some actual cartoon show. She found no name, and that was fine enough for her to purchase it. If it turned out to actually be a tie-in product, it would be easy to show she had no clue, and was only interested in the design itself.

"Dude!" Annie walked back over to Harley. Holding, perhaps, the weirdest thing Harley had ever seen.

"Booby headphones!" Annie said, holding the said item, a pair of over-ear headphones with a detailed drawing of a woman's breast.

"Booby headphones!" She said again "I am so buying these!"

The two ladies walked over to the cashier to purchase their overpriced but enjoyable items. Annie kept true to her word and placed the glow-in-the-dark rings on her left middle and index fingers.

"Oh, do the two of you know about our party tonight?" The cashier said

The cashier was your typical male teen trying to deal with a slight acne problem, and head to toe covered in all black clothes with pop culture pins and logos all over. He even had a few pins on his sneakers.

"No." Harley said

"What kind of party?" Annie said, eyes starting to widen.

"We rented out the center of the mall tonight at seven. We'll have strobe lights and will be selling glow sticks and beverages. We won't serve alcohol but we're planning on making it worth it. We have live music and it's a large dance party with neon lights and everything you'd like at a party."

"I'm in!" Annie said

"Sounds like a solid marketing campaign." Harley said "Sure, why not?"

Harley and Annie walked out of the store to find a way to pass the time until seven.

"Let me know when it's about six." Annie said "Because I'm going to have to change. I'm not partying in this."

Annie had completely changed her image for this party. She wore a punk rock black-and-dark pink skirt, and a black t-shirt with torn short sleeves. She stayed with the same shoes, and her glow-in-the-dark rings turned out to work quite well after all.

Harley also found out that Annie's bra was neon orange. She had not told her this, she found this out because Annie decided to let one of the straps become slightly visible.

"You see." Annie decided to explain her look. "I'm going to make sure these boys know they won't be getting anything from me tonight, but I'm also making sure they get the gist I don't often think that way."

"Alright." Harley said, whom had not changed her outfit in the slightest.

Harley also got stuck holding all of her friend's shopping bags and clothes. She wasn't that interested in dancing, and this was her punishment for not caring enough.

Harley sat, funnily enough in the corner, and watched Annie work her magic on the dance floor. She could move, both elegantly and clumsily. She was a massive tease, unless you had the balls to ask her to dance with you.

It was kind of, interesting.

To see someone, just, have no problem gaining the love and attention of whom she wanted.

Harley was not jealous of her friend, jealousy was beneath her in every sense of the word. All this did, watching her gain love and admiration, was paint the reminder in Harley's head.

It'd been months since she even thought about men. Maybe this was okay, but for someone who'd spent most of the love life being very happy with someone, and a night of passion with another, maybe she figured it didn't feel all that right.

And maybe she was overthinking it.

Annie came back over to her. "Okay. I'm having a blast, but you should keep a closer eye on me. A few more nice words and I don't know if I'll be able to help myself."

♥ - *Chapter 10* - ♥

It was another day on campus. It had been February for a short while now, Harley and the other students had gone back to the regular schedules of balancing classes and schoolwork, and for many, part-time jobs as well.

Unfortunately, it also wasn't just another day on campus. It was a day that Harley did her best not to hate, but could never be anything kinder than apathetic towards. Not for the reasons most did, for entirely personal ones, but still a day she was never looking forward to hearing people jabber on and on about all day long.

Valentine's day.

It was going to take a lot for her to even get out of her room. Granted, she was hungry, and more than likely that was the only reason she needed to step out.

She wore a yellow V-neck t-shirt, with a logo of a large shiny purple heart with several smaller hearts inside of it. She also had a jean skirt, and white sneakers. She forwent any make-up or jewelry outside of her class ring, this was not a day where she wanted anyone to pay her any attention.

And then her stomach rumbled, and she sighed. She grabbed her key and headed out to go get something for lunch.

The hallways seemed empty today, everyone was probably either in class or on a huge date. Most likely, a lot of those dates would all end with going back to one of the other's rooms, and Harley was aware not every one of those people would be waiting for the date to end. Or start. Or bother with the date in the first place and just get it all done with in the first place.

She passed by the room of her RA.

"You know I don't usually have a girlfriend on V-day." She heard Josh say. "It sure is nice to spend this one with you. You know?"

"Yeah." She heard a woman say. "Today should be good."

"Hey, well. I'm hoping so."

Harley had already walked too far away to hear anything further, and felt no need to walk back just to eavesdrop, not when it was Josh. She was getting hungrier, and she just wanted to get eating over with as soon as possible so she could effectively hide back in her room.

There were pink hearts and streamers all over the place. It may not have been obnoxious to some, but Harley was not in the mood to see it as anything but obnoxious. She headed over to pay for her meal.

"By yourself honey?" Said the lady taking her payment, whom had a voice that could only be described as "eats cigarettes".

"Yep." Harley said

"Ya know we're offering free meals for couples today."

"Cool. I don't need it."

"Ah come on honey, you can just get a friend of yours and pretend you're love birds."

"I'm good."

Harley headed in to eat her full.

"Dear God." She said aloud.

There was even more hearts and pink on the inside of the cafeteria. And far worse than that.

Harley found several lines of cheap poetry stapled up on every single wall. There were pictures of romantic movies and famous romance stories, as big as a poster could be. There were white angel wings on several of the cartoony hearts, and even more angel wings on all of the baby cupids.

Someone who clearly thought they were funny had put up a picture of a realistic human heart. Admittedly it would have been funny, if this image had not been in a place where people ate.

Harley then saw plates and plates of candies and sweets, and decided some God or deity of some form should be thanked for it.

She wanted to earn the sweets, not just pig out on chocolate due to being slightly miffed. Her answer was to grab a slice of rhubarb pie.

She took her pie slice, and sat down by herself to start eating it. It tasted fine, nothing very special about it, but at least nothing about it that could be counted as bad.

"Hey there." She recognized the voice without turning around to see him. "Mind if I sit down."

"Go ahead Max." She said "You I don't mind."

Max's attire was far more subdued than usual. He wore a thick gray shirt, similar to a sweater or turtleneck without actually being one, blue jeans, and brown sneakers.

"Not fond of the holiday I'm guessing." Max sat down next to her, having an apple he'd already taken a few bites out of.

"Yeah but it's more complicated than you'd expect. Trust me, I'm not just some petty jackass."

"No one who hates Valentine's day is petty. I may not hate this greeting card holiday but it's completely pointless."

"'Greeting card holiday'? Sounds like you do hate it."

"No it's just I'm describing it. This day was literally created by some greeting card company."

"Ah. You know that makes an awful lot of sense."

"Well, I hope your classes go good today."

"Technically I don't have any. You see I'm taking this philosophy class, but the professor doesn't have us meet in person."

"Oh?"

"Actually we don't meet at all. He says we take the two hours the class is supposed to take up, and just journal our feelings and our personal take on what it means. It's kind of bullshit but I also kind of get it. We don't even have to do it on the right days, as long and it's roughly two hour periods every week."

"Is this easy or hard?"

"Easy, and according to the professor, he only assigns A's and F's. Most or all of the times you were supposed to journal, an A grade. If you never write or only do it like three times or so, you get an F. He doesn't care how deep we get if we don't think we can get deep on the subject."

"Do you?"

"Yeah. I figure there's no harm in it, and I signed up expecting work anyway."

"It's fun catching up with you like this. I haven't seen you since our art class."

He flashed her a smile. This time, his mouth was open slightly, she was used to his closed-mouth smiles, which she already quite liked.

She wasn't sure if he used a whitener, but, she couldn't help but notice just how clean and almost shiny his teeth were. It felt strange to notice it, and to think it, but. God, he had such nice teeth.

Harley finished her pie, and was about to walk back to get some sweets.

"Hey." She said "Did you have more classes today?"

"Nope." He said

"Then how about we hang out? My roommate's on a long date so I have no one to keep me occupied as I hide from the couples and flowers."

"You bet. It's way more fun spending this day with a friend than nobody at all."

For the second time, Max Turtle was welcomed into Harley Millsboone's dorm room.

"Make yourself at home." Harley said "You can sit on Annie's bed if you want. It's clean in case you've heard about her."

"A little bit." Max did indeed take a seat on the edge of Annie's bed. "Sounds like a fun and care-free person."

"That's actually kind of perfect."

"Who's this guy she's on a date with today?"

"No idea, but I think she's seen him before. That's how it goes before the dates get longer. She likes building up. Although she has told me a few times she likes the idea of just jumping in with someone one day. The only thing I care about is when she has a guy here while I'm out. I've come way to close to walking in on something way too many times."

"Exactly why I spent the extra money getting a single room. It's a piece of shit but I don't have to worry about anybody's lifestyles but my own. I'll invite you there sometime, try and even this out."

"It's a deal."

Harley liked opening up to him. She had no clue why, nor did she even think about it until just now.

And if she could be open with this guy, she may as well get it off her chest.

"So." Harley said "You want to know why I'm not that happy about today?"

"Shoot." Max said "I'm sure it's interesting."

"Well. Here's the thing. I'll phrase it another way. Happy twentieth birthday Harley Millsboone."

Max paused for a bit. His eyes filled, he got every single aspect of what she meant.

"Oh God." Max said "That fucking sucks."

"You're telling me." Harley said "We practically banned the holiday in my house so I could have cake and presents without having to think about the stupid fucking cards and doves."

"What was school like?"

"I skipped."

'Wait, you said twentieth."

"Yeah, I'm twenty."

"Did not know you were a year older than me."

Harley gave a big goofy smile. "So you had some older pussy. You want a pat on the back?"

Max found that hysterical. Harley found it surprising she actually said it.

Max let his laughter ride out.

"So." He said "Since you have two special events today, tell me. Do you want anything?"

"Huh?"

"You're not back home so you can't really party with your family. But I'm here, and we're friends so, if you want anything, tell me. I don't mind getting you a birthday or Valentine's present."

"Really?"

"Of course. And if you could I'd rather you just ask for something instead of saying that again. I don't want to go on a big spiel about how important a person you are in my life. Unless that's what you want, in which case I'll be more than glad to."

Harley decided it was worth thinking about.

Max was, special. She hadn't just slept with him, he was her first time and a lovely individual without the fact. A lot of the normal feelings she had for personal space and privacy, she did not feel when around him.

She'd been daring with him already, nothing she said could take that back and she felt no reason to think that was a bad thing.

"You know." She said "There was one thing my ex-boyfriend did for me, well, he only did it once but I really liked it."

"Okay." Max said "What do you want me to do?"

Harley scooted her way closer to him, now sitting beside him on Annie's bed. She took the neck of her shirt and pulled it slightly away from her skin.

"Kiss my neck." Harley said "I really like it and I've only had it done once."

Max smiled. "Great. You know, the last time we did something like this I was inexperienced. But this, I've had a lot of experience."

Max leaned over and softly kissed her neck. He was not kidding. His lips were soft, and yet, the pressure he delivered was hard and impactful.

"Oh." Harley said

This was only a kiss, not even on the mouth, and she could feel her body flush.

"We should." She said, having trouble breathing. "Move to my bed. This is Annie's and that, that just. I shouldn't be doing this on someone's else's stuff."

"Fair enough." Max said

Part of her wanted to be carried. Part of her even want to try carrying him.

This was just a stupid kiss, she tried to say, tried to think.

Once they were on her bed, he asked "So, do we continue from where we left off."

"Yeah." She said "Go right ahead."

She let him kiss her for several minutes. He moved up and down, making sure she could not get tired, as she had not yet asked him to stop.

"Hey." Another daring idea was entering her head. "I want to check on something. Tell me if you don't like it."

Max looked her in the eyes and gave her a grin, as she moved her hands over to unbuckle his pants.

"So." She said "You are enjoying this as much as I am."

"Guilty." Good God his smile could keep getting brighter.

Max continued kissing her. Lacking pants and sporting an erection did not get in his way.

It was on her mind. It would not go away.

To her that meant it couldn't have been a bad idea.

"Hey." She said "I still have that other condom."

"You do?" Max said "I thought I threw it out."

"No. I've been holding onto it. I didn't know why, but, well. If we already have it."

Instead of saying anything further, the two of them leaned into each other's lips. Kisses on the neck were one thing, but tasting him back, she could now completely remember how much she liked it.

She reached into her drawer to grab the condom, and slowly they helped each other remove the rest of their clothes.

"Now before we fit that on." Max said, now on top of her. "I did say I learned a few thing about what I should have done."

His face began to disappear downward.

Harley was putting her shirt back on, trying to remove the wrinkles it had from being tossed onto the floor. She happened to look over at the clock, and saw they'd spent fifteen minutes in the act. A vast improvement in time over the previous encounter, and there was no denying this made it an inarguably better time.

Max had stayed without clothes on her bed. He'd asked what she preferred, and she chose him to leave his clothes off as long as it was comfortable for him to.

"You know," Harley said "it'd be weird to say this was the best birthday ever, but I can say this was the best Valentine's day I've ever had."

"Glad I could help." Max said, flashing her a beautiful smile.

"So uh, I don't know if you were just going to head out now or what, but if you want to stay for a while you can."

"I wasn't really thinking of going just yet, I really don't have any more plans for today."

"Cool. I can tell you right now we're not having an encore performance but at least I'll have someone to talk to today. Which was the last thing I thought I wanted, honestly. Hell I didn't put any make-up on today just to stay invisible."

"That's why I muted my outfit. Figured you might have been doing the same when I saw you."

"You could tell I wasn't wearing make-up?" Harley was impressed, most men seemingly lacked the ability to notice make-up's tricks.

His response was "I work in fashion design, of course I can tell when someone's eyelids or cheeks aren't the same color as their skin."

"Aaaaah, that makes sense."

"Hey, you want pizza?"

"Sure but not right now."

"Cool. When you want some, tell me what you want and I'll order it. I can't really call fucking you a birthday gift but I can buy you some pizza."

"Hey the fucking was a good gift in my opinion but I won't turn this offer down either."

Harley turned to her door.

"I have to piss really bad." She said "Mind waiting until I'm back before we call it in?"

"No." Max said "I'll have to pee right after you though."

"Guess that makes sense."

Harley headed out of her room and into the bathroom. There was a slight hop in her step, she hadn't completely calmed down from the build-up. Getting there in no time at all, she found the first open stall, closed it, and sat down to relieve herself.

She heard a few ladies walk into the bathroom as she peed. They gossiped, as women in the bathroom tended to do. A lot of them talked about their boyfriends and girlfriends lovely Valentine's ideas.

There were also a few cases of completely pissed off women whose significant others didn't do anything special, or anything at all.

Harley flushed, and stepped out from the stall, accidently running face to face with one of the angry disappointed ones.

"You smell like you just had sex." She said, and Harley was not sure if this was her stating a fact or just trying to annoy her.

If it was the latter, she failed.

"Yep." Harley said, and washed her hands and headed back to her room.

On the way, she passed Josh's room again.

"So that was great." She heard Josh say.

"Yeah....." She heard his girlfriend say.

Harley got back to her room, and used her key to get in. She noticed Max quietly hide his penis under a blanket while the door was open.

"If you ask me you've got nothing there to be concerned about." She said

"Yeah," Max said "I just. It's no big deal, whatever." He took the blanket off his privates again once the door was closed.

And the blanket went back over once the door received a knock.

Harley slowly opened the door, seeing her roommate on the other end.

Annie was wearing a black plaid skirt, a blue spaghetti-string top with the straps loose on her shoulder, a white beret, and pink sneakers with white bows on the side.

"Dammit you are home." She said "I was kind of hoping I could have some alone-time fun in my room for once."

"Sorry." Harley said "Also I have company."

"Ah, cool. You don't got nobody special so at least you're not completely alone. Anyway, I just got dumped and I kind of saw it coming so since I can't jill off in here I'm going to head home."

"You're going to go home just to jill off?"

"I will jill off but that's not why I'm leaving. I used to visit my grandma on Valentine's day and we thought it would be nice to do that again this year. I'll be back tomorrow, so I guess you have the room to jill off."

"Eh, I think I'll be good."

"Buh-bye."

Annie practically skipped down the hall. Harley closed the door, letting Max go back to hanging loose everything he had.

"You want to stay here?" Harley said, who after being daring early had no reason to tone anything down. "You can sleep with me or on the floor or whatever."

"Why?"

"I've gotten a little too used to hearing someone else snore."

"Maybe. Oh. Before any of that, can I have your permission to do one thing?"

"How big a thing?"

"Super small."

"Alright, shoot."

Max got out from the bed. He walked over to her, looking her in the eye for a short bit, then leaning forward to give her a soft kiss on her nose.

"I always wanted to see what that was like." Max said

"It's cute." Harley said, giving him a smile. "Anyway, you said we'd get pizza. I think I know what kind I want."

♥ - *Chapter 11* - ♥

Harley was writing a few sections into her psychology journal. No major emotions had hit her today, it was just a calm morning without classes or anything much to do.

Annie was jamming out with her "booby headphones", slightly loud enough for Harley to make out that she was listening to pop. This did not annoy her, and as such, it did not go into the journal.

There was then a knock on the door, and somehow, Annie had heard it and decided to get up and answer it.

It was Janie.

"You're not the one I want to see." Janie said, as flat as she could have said it.

"Yeah." Annie said, trying to match the rudeness as best she could. "I kind of figured that."

Annie turned over to Harley, and pointed her thumb hard towards Janie. "*Your* friend."

Harley got up and over to the door. "Hey. What'cha want Janie?"

"I'm going to the beach." Janie said "You want to go to the beach with me?"

"Fuck yeah, sounds great. Just let me pack a few things."

"I'll be waiting in the parking lot."

Janie turned back down the hall to await her. Harley closed her door and checked through her closet for whatever could help her.

Immediately she changed into a swimsuit, practically dumping her old clothes onto the floor.

For the past two years she'd owned a cute little two-piece she'd been dying to finally wear out in public, and she lacked the shame in her body to prevent her from wearing it on the way instead of changing in the stall.

Both the bottom and top were divided by two color palettes. On the upper half of both pieces, they were yellow, and both bottom halves were pink. The top separated these colors with a red frill, and the bottom had red strings to tie it all together. On her feet she quickly slipped on a pair of blue flip-flops.

"Oh that's so cute." Annie said

"Thanks. I've been meaning to try it out." Harley said

"Hey uh, you should wear that ring I bought you. Might help you get some attention."

"Thanks but I'll just stick with this." Harley said, flashing her class ring

"I dunno." Annie said "I think it'd look great with what you're wearing."

"You're not just getting jealous of me spending time with Janie, are you?"

Annie simply shrugged. It looked as if the idea had not occurred to her, but she had no reason to act as if she was offended by the suggestion.

"Want me to get you anything?" Harley said "An ice cream or something?"

"Nah." Annie said "You go have fun with goth girl."

Harley found a small bag to shove her beach supplies into, and filled it with a towel and some sunscreen. She could not think of anything else she needed, and didn't want to keep Janie waiting.

She headed out the door, and started walking down the hall. She almost regretted her footwear after the sounds started reverberating through the halls, but she knew it would die down when against the sand.

It took her little to no time to get to the parking lot, and found Janie sitting on the hood of her car enjoying a cigarette.

"It's uh." Janie said "Nice swimsuit."

"Thanks." Harley said "Bet yours is good too."

"It'll serve its purpose. Anyway, get in."

Janie and Harley opened their respective doors. Harley buckled herself up, and once Janie had done the same, her cigaretted hand motioned its way towards Harley, gently dangling it in an offer.

"Drag?" She said

"Eh, sure." Harley said

Harley took the cigarette, and took a slow but small puff. She breathed it out, eyes closed, and ended with the word "Ugh".

"Yeah, not everyone likes them." Janie took back her cigarette. "Think that wouldn't happen but it's more common than you think."

Janie inhaled the rest of the cigarette and snuffed out the remains in the ashtray built into the car door.

"How long have you been smoking?" Harley said

"Six months."

"Really? Wow, normally you hear like 'since I was eight' and shit like that."

"Parents didn't just leave them around for me to smoke up or anything. Hell, they hated these things. I just got bored one day and didn't feel like my curiosity needed to be thrown out. For the record, yes I know I'll have to quit, but hey, it's only been a few months, I can wait to see how bad this gets."

"As long as you know what you're doing. When the time comes I can try to help."

"…..Thanks. Maybe I'll think about it."

Janie turned her car on, and started the drive to the beach.

"You want to turn on the radio and sing?" Harley said

"It's all shitty DJs who think they're funny and talk show hosts who think they're God."

"We might find something."

"If you want to sing there's a CD stuck in-between your seat. Don't know how far deep but it's there."

Harley took three whole minutes digging around until she came across it.

"It's uh, kid's songs." Harley said

"Right." Janie said "That's what it was, couldn't remember. I got it at a used store when I was hungover and wasn't thinking. It was fifty cents."

"Whelp, might as well see if it's worth singing along to."

Harley had been coaxed by Janie into the same stall after she had changed. Originally, she'd been alone so she could change into her black two-piece, but now she seemed to want Harley's help.

Tying her hair back into a short ponytail, she said "Look. Could you, help me with something."

"Of course, dude." Harley said "What'cha want?"

"It's, uh." Janie sighed.

Janie grabbed her small clothes bag, and reached in. She pulled out two wads of tissue paper and padding.

When she talked, it was out the side of her mouth. "I'm going to stuff my bikini top. Tell me if it looks good."

"You want help with the stuffing, I don't mind."

"Look, between you and me, I'm a little sensitive if you couldn't already figure it out. You're not seeing nothing okay, and helping the stuffing will only make that worse."

"Want me to close my eyes then?"

"No. If I start fucking up I want you to tell me, so, just, be careful what you're seeing."

Janie starting shoving the padding into her top. There was little resistance in the start, however, the padding was doing very little.

"How's that?" Janie said, completely flat, already knowing the answer.

"You're getting somewhere but you still look the same." Harley said

Janie became more frustrated, practically fighting her top as she shoved. On three occasions, it tried to slip off, and on two occasions, she'd accidently flashed part of her left nipple.

"Goddammit." Janie said, clearly wishing she could shout instead of whisper.

"For what it's worth." Harley said "Your boobs look perfectly fine."

"Are you straight?"

"Yes."

"Then why would I care what someone who doesn't like women thinks? I'm not stuffing my bikini to make straight women jealous of me, I'm stuffing it so straight men will think I look better."

"You look pretty Janie, you don't need the extra effort."

"It's the beach. You think they'll notice my make-up or my hair or anything else other than how well I fit in my swimsuit?"

"Alright, point taken."

The string on the back came loose, forcing her to hold it up. She grumbled, but it contained no actual words.

"Turn around." She said "I'll have to take it off and put it on with the shit inside it."

Harley did as requested. After a bit, Harley was tapped on the shoulder, and she turned to be her friend quite convincingly have an entire cup-size larger than only a few moments ago.

Harley let out an impressed whistle.

"I did this a lot in high school." Janie said

"Hey I did it before too but not as well as this. Mine looked all lumpy and I never did it again.

…. Granted I did it for with my boyfriend who I'd been dating for a year at that point. Should have figured a teenaged boy could tell his teenaged girlfriend had new dimensions out of the blue."

Janie ended up cracking a smile, and even chuckled a little bit. "Alright, was worth it to hear the story. Now let's go turn some heads."

Harley and Janie stepped out of the changing booths, and headed over to the beach itself. There were a good deal of people spending their afternoon in the sand, from women their own age, to families, even a few elderly couples. Janie picked out a good spot, and planted her beach umbrella to mark it.

"Nice umbrella." Harley said "Didn't think to bring anything like that."

"I go to the beach a lot." Janie said, a smile almost forming. "It's a quiet place to get away from everything, I like the smell of the air, and, well, it's a good spot to draw."

"Aw, damn. I didn't bring my art supplies. That sounds like a great idea."

"I can loan you a sheet of paper, but I can't do much more than that. Shit's expensive."

"Yeah I know. Anyway, want to go swimming?"

Janie looked down at her top. "Um, I know the pads are waterproof but the tissues aren't. How bad do you want to swim?"

"A lot, but if you want to stay here it's okay."

"No I'll go with you, just won't do more than get my feet wet."

The ladies headed down to the luscious white water. Harley practically dived into the ocean, while Janie stayed on the edge, letting the waves gently rush the warm water over her bare feet. Harley had swum out far enough that she was covered up to her neck. She could almost feel the temptation of falling asleep from how the water felt against her skin.

She'd been accidently splashed in the face a few times by children playing with a beach ball a few feet away from her. They weren't a nuisance, so she stayed in place, but they made her decide to look around at everyone else around her.

There were plenty of attractive young men, all without a shirt. Janie's idea hadn't sounded silly to her for this exact reason. While she wasn't going to talk to any of them, nor did she want them to come over and suddenly flirt with her, it was nice to be in an area where it was socially acceptable to only pay attention to physical attributes. For once it was comforting instead of creepy.

She looked back over at Janie, who'd move forward enough to let her knees get wet as well. Having no sense of time, Harley decided to swim back to her, it had probably been long enough.

They headed back to the umbrella, and placed their respective towels onto the ground. They started putting sunscreen onto their faces when Janie started to speak.

"So, could you. Do me a favor?"

"Shoot."

"I've uh. I've never asked anyone to model for me. Since uh. You're here."

"Can I keep my clothes on?"

"You're in public of course you keep your clothes on!"

"Relax I'm joking. Sure, I'd love to."

"Thanks. Just uh, lay down on the towel like you would have anyway."

Harley laid her back against her soft beach towel, staring up at the deep blue sky. There were only two entire clouds, both of them clear white and fluffy. Out of the corner of her ear she could hear Janie scratching away on her drawing pad.

For about fifteen minutes Harley simply enjoying the sun on her face. She was glad she didn't bother with sunglasses. She'd been able to avoid looking directly at the sun, and the sky was too beautiful to see with obscured vision.

"Hey, uh." Janie said. "Could you take your right hand and kind of, brush your hair out of your face? Hand facing me."

Harley simply did as instructed, no need to word a reply.

"Ah." Janie said "Don't move now. I'll be quick, but I want that position."

Harley's hand was already getting tired. However, in a few short minutes, Janie said she was done. Harley sat up to take a look at the finished sketch.

She whistled. "This is nice. You are very good at details."

"I need to be." Janie said "Or else my career is already over."

"Can I have this?"

"No but I'll make a copy when I get home, I have a scanner."

Harley stood up, stretching out her back.

"I'm hungry, how about you?"

"Nope." Janie said

"Well, guess I'm on my own then."

"There's a hotdog vender over there somewhere." Janie flapped her hand in a direction. "They do weird shit but hey a hotdog is a hotdog."

Harley took a short breath to grow a small tender smile. "Hotdogs have a bit of a special meaning to me. Don't care how weird they have."

"This story isn't going to go 'when I was about thirteen' is it?"

"Oh God no. Anyway, I'm out."

"I'm heading to the tide pool. I'll leave this sheet here if you get back before I do."

The two headed in their separate directions.

The familiar smell of hotdogs perfumed the air around her. And as she found out, Janie was not kidding, the vendor had very much gotten weird with everything.

There was a hotdog that had a side order of fries shoved into the bun with it, ketchup lightly dashed over as well as a slight hint of salt to top the entire thing off.

Another dog had tomato slices on one side and pickle slices on the other. The dog itself was vegan, the idea being this was how to pretend to eat healthy while still enjoying something that tasted exactly like a hotdog.

Yet another dog had been cut up into hotdog slices, and placed in the bun with copious amounts of cheese and yellow mustard to fill up the gaps. As if it was a surgery gone wrong.

Finally, there was a hotdog wrapped in a piece of French toast. Both a small bit of maple syrup and powdered sugar was on the dog, and cinnamon was clearly on the French toast bun.

There were, in reality, several more of these creations. But they were the four that Harley purchased.

Harley had been sketching the ocean front. She used hard lines to draw the rocks and the cliff sides in the far distance. She tried to capture the splendor of the crashing waves, but had only been able to render about two of them on the actual drawing, plus the build-up of another larger wave in the background.

She was halfway through the last of her hotdogs, and was careful to not spill any of the contents onto Janie's art pad.

Harley was almost done with her drawing by the time Janie had walked back.

"Hey." Harley said "See anything cool?"

"I saw a sick-ass dead jellyfish." Janie said "And a huge water spider."

"One of uh, the ones that live in bubbles?"

"Yeah. Those ones."

Janie scooched over to see the drawing. "You draw a lot more hard lines than I do."

"Of course I do, wouldn't make sense if I couldn't considering what I want to do."

Janie looked over at her phone she'd tucked into her beach bag. She had a message.

"Huh, I have a text." She said.

She scrolled through it while Harley finished up her drawing, tore it out of the pad, and folded it up.

"That was a friend of mine." She said "The guy who, you know, grocery store."

"Ah."

"He's over at my place, wanted me to know."

"He has a key?"

"We've been friends for a while and he brings me shit, so yeah, he has a key. Good guy if you ever get to meet him."

Harley finished off the rest of her hotdog. The entire time, Janie had seemingly tried to close her mouth with the edge of her hand.

"Okay look." Janie said, turning her phone towards Harley to use like a mirror. "You have mustard all over your face."

Harley looked into the phone, and what Janie said was true.

"….Oh." Harley said

"Here." Janie reached into her bikini top and ripped out one of the tissues for Harley to clean her face.

The ladies packed back into Janie's car. Janie had changed back into her attire from before they arrived, a black button-up shirt, grey jeans, and black sneakers. She kept her hair back.

"You forgot your tail." Harley said

"Nah I'm just keeping it in 'till later." Janie said "Either before I go to bed or when I wake up in the morning, whenever I remember."

"Fair enough. You don't have all that much hair to tie back though, it might just fall apart on its own."

"Then gravity will do the work for me."

Janie started driving away. Harley had cracked her window down to feel the breeze, happy that she wasn't driving. Normally she would have been concerned with the wind blowing her hair in her face, but even without the ponytail Janie would most likely have not had that problem.

"You want to get a slushy?" Harley said "I'll buy."

Janie made an "ick" sound. "No thanks, I can't stand those things."

"Oh. Well, uh. Can we stop anyway? Please?"

Janie looked over at her gas meter. "I'm running past half. You willing to split the bill?"

"Of course I am, you were nice enough to drive me here. You sure you don't want anything to drink?"

"We'll see, but probably not. Those fucking things taste like syrupy shit, and then you just have an ass load of ice."

"Eh, I kind of like the ice. It still tastes a little sweet."

Janie drove until they reached the gas station, and pulled over to the pumps. A young lady walked over to them for gas services.

"Full 'er up." Janie said

"Aye aye." The lady had a tiny lisp

Janie and Harley walked inside of the gas station to see loads of cheap junk food, old but still hot pizza slices, and the slushy machines Harley was hoping for. As per usual, any size was only a dollar, so Harley went for a large.

"You don't happen to want lottery tickets, do you?" Janie said

"Nope." Harley said

"Well, good to know. I'll just get cigarettes then."

"How about some donuts for you?"

"You're buying donuts?"

"There's a pack of them for two dollars."

"Oh, those kind. Fuck it, I'll share 'em with you I guess."

Harley stacked up on sugary snacks. Ever since she'd gotten to college, she noticed her sweet tooth becoming larger, and her stomach becoming laxer. She could worry about this later.

The two of them walked up to the cashier; Harley with her treats and Janie with a small coffee. Janie pointed out the cigarette brand she wanted, and the young man behind the counter grabbed them.

"That'll be uh," The man's eye shifted between the two of them. "ten bucks. So, what were the two of you up to?"

Harley fiddled through her purse. "We went to the beach."

"And no." Janie left her money on the counter "You don't get to help us wash the sand off."

A twitch appeared on the man's mouth, and a beat of sweat followed.

"Er. Got it." He said "You uh. It sure was a nice day for lovely ladies like you to head out though. You know, that's an awful nice swimsuit you have on. How come you uh, didn't also wear yours?"

"You can keep talking," Janie said "or we can decide to actually come back here someday. Which would your manager like to hear?"

"Hey I'm just making conver-"

Janie had already walked away with her purchases. Harley followed suit instead of hearing how the man would "recover".

The lady who pumped their gas had finished, and was bouncing on the back of her heels.

"What do I owe you?" Janie said

"Uh, fourtee-, fiftee-, oh, yeah, fifteen dollars." The lady said

Harley gave some money to Janie, and Janie combined that with her own to pay the service girl.

The service woman looked at the money and said "Is this the right amount?"

"Little extra." Janie said, getting in her car. "Don't let the vulture take it from you."

The service woman cocked her head, and Janie drove away.

"So back home?" Janie said

"I guess so." Harley said "I assume Annie's waiting for me."

"……. Hey."

"What?"

"It's just. You remember when I told you that I, I don't so much date I just kind of, do whatever?"

"Yeah, I remember."

"I kind of wanted to. Just so you knew. That doesn't mean I, I get out much or anything. I don't date because, you know, I'm trying to focus on not fucking up in school. I may be up for fun, but, not all the time or all that much."

"Nothing wrong with either way."

"Cool, cool. Glad to hear that. I mean, it's that, the most I get from guys is basically what we got just now."

"That happens to all of us."

"I fucking know. Just, whatever you get me."

Harley was walking up her hallway, heading back to her room. As much as she liked her swimsuit, it would be nice to change back into her normal clothes. As she approached the door, and was about to put in her key, she heard something through it.

"Oh. Yes. Yes." It was Annie's voice. "Yes yes yes, oh don't stop. Oh my God."

Harley realized she shouldn't have been surprised this is what Annie got up to when the room was all hers.

Harley pulled out her phone, walked back down the hall about halfway, and called up Janie.

"Er, hi." Janie said

"Sorry to bother you, but have you left yet?"

"Well, yes but I only made it about five feet before I had to pull over for this phone call."

"Would you mind coming back? Annie is having sex with, uh, whatever his name was. I don't think she'll hear me knock."

"Uh. I. Pfft. Sure, why not? Just let me tell Matt first."

"Who's Matt? Wait, this is the friend you mentioned. He's still at your place?"

"We don't see each other much, he wanted to see me in person. Guess I'll have to introduce you."

Janie walked Harley back up to her apartment. Everything seemed the same as it was last time. Janie opened her door, and said friend Matt was standing near the counter.

Matt was wearing a dark red t-shirt, and his brown hair did not have any sort of parting in his bangs. His jeans were gray, his sneakers were gray and white, and he had punk jewelry. A skull ring on both his right middle finger and thumb, a belt with a chain on the front of it, and as an added accessory he wore a black and white bandana around his neck, which bore skulls and bones.

His hair caught Harley's eye more than anything else. It was brown on the left side, and blonde on the right. His bangs were dangerously close to covering his eyes. Harley also noticed he had a were scraggly bits of fur over his chin. Not enough for a soul patch, but it was the closest comparison.

"Hello." Matt said "I'm guessing your Harley."

"And you must be Matt." Harley said

"By the way before you ask, no I don't normally dress like this. It's for a gig I have later."

"Matt's a DJ now, well, again." Janie said "It's this grunge and goth place. Used to go there when I first moved. Angsty as fuck and no self-awareness."

"That's why I came over." Matt said "Because you might get to work as one too."

"Really?" Janie said "That would be a nice surprise."

"Remember the other club I used to work at? They had an opening and asked my advice. I figure a place like that would look good on your kind of resume, and they're perfectly okay knowing they would have to replace you the second you get an apprenticeship."

"Fucking thank you!" Janie said "I have my second inking in a week and the money will be helpful."

"Be sure to tell them. The place fucking loves inked chicks. Honestly I was lucky to stay as long as I did even with how good I am."

Matt looked over at Harley, and after a few seconds, immediately looked away, and even closed his eyes. "Oh my God you're almost naked."

"Oh." Harley said "Whoops."

"I think we're the same size." Janie said "If you want to head in my room and change."

"Nah, I'd have to remember to bring them back. Look, Matt, you seem nice enough. Just don't stare me down, and if you happen to take a peak by accident just make sure it's no longer than a second or two."

"Deal." Matt did not open his eyes.

Janie led Harley just outside her room, the door open just a crack so Harley could see despite not being invited in. She decided to check out Janie's art while they were there, the best she could.

"I'll make the scan since you're here." Janie said "In the meantime, hey, feedback is always nice."

Harley looked over the art pieces she saw. It was hard to give any feedback when Janie's art style was considerably better than her own.

She found a long drawing of a detailed spider, similar to the venomous kinds that appeared in the deep woods of the state.

"This one's cool." Harley said

Janie peaked over to see which one it was. "That one's going on my wrist next week." She slapped her left wrist with her opposite hand.

"Anything else?"

"Nope. Had to be more careful with money than the first time. Hopefully this DJ gig will help me out."

Janie began scanning the drawing she made of Harley. As the machine began to whir and buzz, Janie headed under her bed.

"Hey, look." Janie appeared again, holding a brown paper bag holding a bottle inside. "I bored you with a stupid car story, so. Here. You can have this."

"What is it?" Harley said

"Whiskey. Matt got this from a friend of his, and he gave it to me, but, maybe you should have it. You should age it about two more years, and then it'll be really good."

"You don't have to give this to me."

"Look, you deserve something nice for being nice. Besides, I don't have the patience to age it but I think you do."

"Okay. I can see how little arguing will change your mind on it."

Harley took her friend's gift happily in her arms.

Harley was headed back up her hall once again. The sound of bed springs and fake orgasms was not heard this time, so Harley simply opened the door and let herself in.

"Hey Harls." Annie said, her hair a mess and her clothes the same. "How was the beach?"

"Lovely." Harley said

Harley instantly hung her portrait on the wall with some tape.

"Oh you look so pretty!" Annie said "Look, you even got a little shiny lines on your ring. Who drew this?"

"Janie."

"Really?! Alright, don't like her but she's a good artist."

"That reminds me."

Harley took her bottle on not-yet-fully-aged whiskey out of its bag.

"This was also a gift from her. I'm waiting for it to age. You're great and all, but do not, do not, ever open this. This is from her and I want it treated the way she asked me to treat it."

"Fair enough."

Annie reached over and found an empty box.

"Keep it in this box" Annie said "and I will always remember it as the 'Annie do not ever touch' box."

Harley placed the liquor in the box, and slid it under her bed for safe keeping.

♥ - *Chapter 12* - ♥

It was a special day for Harley. Her brother and his girlfriend had come over to visit her, and she could not wait to show them around.

She half dressed up for the occasion. Her shirt has a gray t-shirt with a pocket, and a white tub top underneath. Her pants were a pair of dark blue cargo pants, one of the few she owned. Her shoes were a pair of black flats, and she'd borrowed a white scarf with pink stitching from Annie. In her ears were little ruby hearts.

She'd spent the early afternoon having brunch with said guests, at a diner a few miles down from the college. Her brother paid for everything, and this was the first time Harley ever took advantage of the fact. It was also the first time this year she could afford a large meal.

For whatever reason, both her brother and his girlfriend ate light.

"So who exactly are these two in our room again?" Annie had been walking with Harley in the hallway while she'd stopped off in the bathroom.

"I told you, my brother and his girlfriend. Good people, you'd love 'em."

"Hey didn't say I wouldn't."

Annie herself was wearing a blue sun dress with a swirl leading up to her left shoulder, leaving the right should completely bare. Her shoes were open toed sandals, showing off her pink nail polish. She also had a hefty orange bracelet, and in her ears were thin gold hoops, the large kind.

"Anything I should know about these two before we head back in?" Annie said "I'm assuming I didn't follow you into the bathroom to watch you pee."

"Right, yeah." Harley said "Just that, uh, I think tensions might be high. She's wanted him to pop the question for about a year now, and he's a little to, uh, well, spineless is what we keep thinking the problem is."

"Esh."

"Yeah, it's a little bad. Oh, never said their names. They prefer Will and Mimi."

"'Mimi'?!"

"Her real name is Megan but she prefers Mimi."

"Why?"

"Says the woman who goes by 'Annie'."

"Hey, Megan and Annabel are on completely different spectrums of name here."

Harley let out a small snort. "Okay, good point."

Harley and Annie were about to enter their room, but the voices on the other end very much stopped them.

"You know by this point I am getting tired of this." Mimi said

"Look, I'm sorry." Will said "I just. This is just a hard decision and I-"

"OH! This is a hard decision huh! You know it's so FUCKING funny how you don't have any problem deciding if you want me to suck your dick, but making our relationship fucking MATTER is appearing the biggest fucking thing you don't want to talk about."

"It's not I don't want to talk about it, it's that, I, I'm not not ready for it."

"FUCK YOU!"

"Hey I'm trying to be nice about this!"

"Just try to say that again."

"I said I'm being NICE!"

"FUCK you!"

"Fuck YOU!"

Harley turned her eyes over to Annie. "Let's pretend I have to go back to the bathroom."

"I'm okay with that." Annie said, and they both turned back around.

But their destination was not the bathroom, it was straight outside. They walked for a bit behind the building, to the lawn near the parking lot.

"Fucking hell....." Harley said "I've never heard them fight before but I honestly don't think they usually get this bad."

"Didn't sound like it." Annie said "That would be a built-up one. Criticize my lifestyle all you want, I don't stay long enough to get in fights. Especially not the rough ones."

Harley didn't say anything.

Annie rummaged through her purse. "Look I know this'll sound dumb but I need to do this after hearing awful shit like that."

Annie pulled a joint out of her purse and placed it in her mouth.

"I'd offer you one but I don't think this is the best time for your first high." Annie said

"Was thinking the exact same thing." Harley said

Annie lit up. Harley had nothing better to do but watch her, and her technique proved interesting. Without ever doing it herself and only listening to those who did, she was aware of how the process normally went. You would inhale, hold, and exhale. Annie nailed that fine.

The curious bit was her hand. While Harley could not do the motion herself due to never seeing it, she was aware the grip tended to use the thumb and index finger. However, Annie held it like anyone would normally hold a cigarette, between her middle and index finger. If it hadn't been legal in the area, she would have assumed Annie was just trying to pass her joint off as a cigarette.

"Hey professor!" Annie waved over at a professor she recognized, holding her marijuana firmly in the other hand, even taking a puff at one point.

"I thought that shit calmed people down." Harley said

"It does it, oh." Annie said, starting to get slower. "Yeah. It does." She giggled.

Annie and Harley walked back to the room. They had stayed on the lawn for fifteen minutes, Annie had even calmed down from her high, slightly.

To be safe, this time, Harley knocked instead of listening in.

"Yeah." Will said "It's uh, you can come in, it's your room."

Harley entered first, and did not see Mimi anywhere around them.

"She, stepped out for something." Will said

Harley faintly heard Annie whisper "fuck".

"Um, Annabel." Harley turned towards her roommate. "Could you, hang out somewhere for a second?"

Annie looked her dead in the eye. "I, guess I know how to tell you're serious now. Yeah. Annabel will head out for a bit."

Annie left, and the door was silently closed.

"We fought." Will sat up on Harley bed, and his eyes did not leave the view of the floor.

Harley noticed a wet stain on Will's right sleeve. He'd torn a white dress shirt and black dress pants, which only made it more obvious he'd wrecked it by wiping away tears.

"I'm fucking so fucked." Will said

"I don't know what to say to you Will." Harley said "I mean, I. I know what this is about, and, I've given the best input I can beforehand."

"I know. This isn't about you, you don't need to do anything about this. Don't worry about this."

Will continued to stare down the floor. Harley had seen her brother through a lot of pains, this one, this one was very new.

There was a sound from the door knob. Someone had tried to open it not knowing it was locked.

"Here." Harley said "I'll get it."

Harley let Mimi inside.

Mimi was wearing a lovely purple dress, a gold heart necklace, knee-high black socks, and white open-toed shoes. She didn't normally dress like this, and now Harley got it.

Mimi really was hoping this would be the last day they wouldn't be engaged.

Mimi barely noticed Harley, only giving her a simple thank you.

"Hey. Will." Mimi said, and Harley now noticed her mascara had run slightly, and she'd tried to take care of it.

"Hey baby." Will said

Will, however, walked directly to Harley. "Harls." He said "This is something I need to only say to her."

Harley started to form a smile, until Will motioned a hand. His face was, stern.

Harley did turn to leave them. However, she had to know whether or not they even realized her presences that much anymore.

She opened the door to the closet, and hid in there. The sound of a door closing was good enough for them.

"Megan." Will said

"Yes?"

"I. You and I have been together for a long time."

"We have."

"And the fact of the matter is. You want somebody who would have married you by this point, and you really do deserve that."

"Willy."

"Meg, you do deserve it. And that's the thing. If I'm not that guy, then, then you deserve someone better than me."

"…….."

"I'm sorry. If it's taken this long and I still can't see it happening, than it isn't going to happen and I can't just drag you along like this."

"….. fuck you."

Mimi left the room, crying.

Harley stayed completely silent in her closet, nothing. Not a single sound, despite the hundreds of noises she felt like making.

She could hear Will pace around, waiting and hurting.

"Fuck it I'll just text her later about me and Mimi." Will said, apparently deciding it was better than waiting to tell his sister to her face.

Quite honestly, Harley accepted this. This wasn't Will being spineless, this was Will needing to get some air and not having the time to tell Harley something she already knew.

Once she heard the door close again, she spoke aloud. "I'm sorry Will."

Harley had been lying in bed, looking at the ceiling, for almost an hour now. Will had yet to text her about the break-up, but she had texted Annie a few minutes ago letting her know she could come back.

Just before Harley could nod off to sleep, Annie opened the door.

"Alright." Annie said "Shoot. Was this good or-" Annie noticed Harley lying in bed "really really bad?"

Harley mustered up her strength to sit up. "They broke up."

"God." Annie said "I'm so sorry Harley."

Harley stood up out of bed, trying to get her bearings.

"Hey, come on." Annie said "Hug me. We've never hugged but you really need it."

They hugged it out, Harley tried not to cry, but as tears did still happen, she tried to keep them from staining Annie's clothes.

"Are you crying?" Annie said

"Yes. Not much. I'm trying not to." Harley said

"Hey, let it out, it's okay. Do you know why you're crying?"

"I guess, yes I know. I shouldn't be because it wasn't me, but I'm crying. I thought she was going to become my sister."

"Let it all out Harley."

"Harls. You can call me Harls."

"Harls. Okay sweetie. Cry it out Harls."

Harley let a few more tears out after the suggestion.

Erika Ramson

♥ - Chapter 13 - ♥

"UGH!" Harley said.

She was not feeling remotely well. It was her time of the month now, her menstrual cycle had its first step the day before.

Today it had felt worse. It was almost embarrassing to say it made her sick, as that had not happened since she was fourteen. However, for whatever reason, her cramps had hit her very hard this month, she was absolutely sick.

While she had changed out of her pajamas earlier, she only did so to change into another pair. The top was black and had buttons, and the bottom was also black, and smooth across her skin. The color choice was so nothing would be ruined should she fail in replacing her tampon, something that usually never happened. Of course, that was also what she would normally say about becoming ill from the cramps, so precautions were made.

Annie walked through the door, carrying a bag of food.

"Alright, I got ya." Annie said, handing over the bag.

Inside it was a Styrofoam cup filled with soup. Filling, despite very little ingredients, it was only chicken broth.

"Thank you." Harley said

"You have no idea how many dirty looks I got ordering this" Annie said "Everyone thought I wanted chicken noodle, but no, they got so confused over the prospect of chicken broth in a bowl. I heard one of them say 'wouldn't that basically be cream of chicken soup'? I hope he's right, I kind of like that name."

Harley moved her eyes up and down Annie as she slurped her soup. It might not have been the order why they looked at her so.

Annie wore a white frilly skirt, cowgirl boots, a gray scrunchie on her left wrist like a bracelet, and a white t-shirt with a personal logo embroidered on it. The logo claimed "Dude Magnet". To be perfectly honest, it wasn't a lie.

"How ya feelin' girl?" Annie said

"Horrible." Harley said "Embarrassed honestly."

"Don't sweat it, bleeding sucks. Anything else I can do for you? I'll do anything but throw out your applicator."

"You don't have to worry then. Don't use one."

Annie's jaw dropped and her eyes bugged out.

"You're fucking kidding." She said

"Nope. I try to be green, I use the kind without an applicator."

"That's disgusting."

"Really? I thought it was kind of badass. You know, going in alone."

"No it's disgusting. Do you at least have some baby wipes?"

"'Course I do, flushable kind. I'm not leaving clots on my hand."

Annie made a disturbed noise.

"I'm gonna go. I have class." Annie picked up her backpack. "I will," She made another noise "see you when I get back."

Harley finished her "cream of chicken" soup. She wanted to lay back down, but there was enough willpower in her brain to remind her it would be a good idea to work on her class journal.

She struggled to get up, the sick pains changed to her feet as she walked. She wished all of the pain would travel there, but no such luck.

She opened up her laptop to start the journal.

Sick.
Cramping.
Hurt.
Painful.

She stopped for a moment.

Slightly horny.
Kind of understand why.

She was usually more articulate, but today was not the day she could muster more words. She uploaded the entry to the website, and checked her e-mail.

She got one from the very professor she just did homework for.

Hello students,

Now, I have been reading all of your journals privately, as you know.

With everyone's permission, I would like you all to pick several entries you would like me to share with another student.
You will meet these students on our final, it will be scheduled on a date we would have had a real class, so no scheduling conflicts should occur.
I look forward to meeting all of you, and seeing how the quick pairing teaches you about other's outlooks and realities.

Tootles.

"Well." Harley said "I'm not using that last one, but I can think of a few."

Harley opened a drawer to find some over-the-counter medicine. She popped two in her mouth, and walked back to her bed.

She had to take a hard nap.

In her dream, Harley was in a bluish-black void. For whatever reason, she was wearing both a shirt and pants made entirely of shiny gold.

Annie appeared next to her.

"Hey buddy." When Dream Annie spoke, Harley got a good glimpse of her tongue.

It was a flaccid penis.

"Hey how's it going." Dream Harley said, apparently not questioning anything about what was going on.

Suddenly, they were underwater. Nothing was different about the way they behaved.

They chatted until the words they spoke were a made-up dream language with no translation. Dream Harley seemed to understand it anyway.

Out of the crest of the water, Dream Janie made her appearance.

She was a tiger with Janie's head and voice. She spoke English.

"So did you hear about our new neighbors?" Dream Janie said

That was when real Harley woke up.

"Dammit, what did she want to say about the neighbors?"

Harley needed to pop off to the bathroom. It was not easy to relieve herself in this state, but she managed as best as she could. She had diarrhea, or at least it felt like it, but that was in the recent past now.

She walked back to her room, in her pajamas holding her key in her hand. Struggling to walk.

She passed Josh.

"Hey there Harley Millsboone!" Josh said

"Yeah hey." Harley said, not having any excitement or pleasantry to share.

"Pajama day huh? Gotta have fun every once in a while."

"It's not 'cause I'm happy."

"Oh. Well, still. Sure is a nice day to hang around."

"Yep."

"You know you could try to be a little nice right now. Smile more." Josh immediately scowled. "What did I ever do but say hello? I shouldn't have to do anything for you to like me, I'm the RA."

"Yeah and I'm a chick with an inflamed cunt!" Harley said "So shut up for a second and realize I'll probably apologize next time. Cool? COOL!"

Harley marched right out. Although from the look of it, Josh had no interest in changing his mind.

Harley opened and shut her door. She walked straight over to her bed, and crashed back down, trying to get more sleep.

"I better find out what the neighbors are like." She muttered before drifting off to sleep.

Harley woke up to see that Annie had been sitting at her desk for a while.

"Hey." Harley said, feeling better finally.

"Hey sunshine." Annie said "How you doin'?"

"Good. In pain but better. What time is it?"

"Six o'clock."

"P.M.?"

"Yeah. Don't worry it ain't the next day."

"Great. I just remembered, I have to sign up for this class next semester. It's with my old art professor, she recommended it to me."

"Connections can be a good thing."

Harley got up and went back to her computer. It took her little to no time to get to the school's website, log in to her account, and sign up for said class. She'd signed up for her other ones the previous day, but she had to wait for this one to appear on the site.

"Hey." Annie said, moving her chair over to Harley.

"Yeah?" Harley said

"Um. I have to pick a new room tomorrow. And, you haven't done that yet either. I was. I was wondering. Do you want to be roommates again?"

"Yes." Harley said, smiling the best she could today. "Without a doubt."

Annie squealed. "Oh I'm so happy you want to be roommates again! I was afraid I'd have to settle for a random weirdo."

"I didn't even have to think about it." Harley said, and there was no lie in the statement.

"I could kiss you. Can I kiss you?"

"Just not the lips."

"Good. Did not want to do that anyway."

Annie gave her dear roommate a kiss on the cheek.

"I don't kiss girls that much." Annie said "Not just because I'm straight I mean. It's hard getting close lady friends when you spend a lot of time getting to know the guys instead."

"Makes sense to me. "

"Speaking of boys. Just how is that lovely man Max you talk so much about?"

"I haven't even mentioned him in weeks."

"I." Annie blew with her lips. "I guess I'm not good at exaggerating. How is he?"

"Good."

"You uh. Think about fucking him again?"

"By this point it's happened twice, I'm more than aware that might just be part of our friendship, so, yeah, I've kind of thought about it once or twice when I talked with him."

"Maybe you could rush down there now. I hear, but granted, I've never done it. I hear, it is so, so, good, when you're on your period. It apparently fixes the cramps."

"I think I heard that before too."

"Oh you should do it! Text him and see if he's DTF."

"You know what, for you, maybe next time. I am sick and I don't think it's a good idea to do anything that'd make me sweaty and hot."

"Oh come on! It could be exactly what you need."

"Annie. You're fucking crazy. Cool, but crazy."

"Give me his number I'll do it for you."

Harley went back to bed instead of answering. Annie would let it go if she let it go first. So, she nodded off back to sleep.

Harley woke up two hours later. Annie had nodded off to sleep as well. She had a big day tomorrow, she usually didn't nod off until past midnight.

Harley got up to search for a chocolate bar. She was feeling better, and the thought of any sort of food sounded good to her.

She was halfway through the candy when she saw her phone. She stared at it. The thought was there and wouldn't leave.

"I fucking hate you Annabel." She muttered.

Harley picked up her phone, and called Max. really hoping she hadn't just woke him up.

He sounded too rested and chipper for that to be the case. "Hey Harley. Nice to talk to you."

"Yeah, uh. Nice to talk to you too." Harley said "Um. Look can I just come to your room?"

"Sure. Just knock when you get here."

Max gave her directions, and off she went.

Harley knocked on Max's door. When he opened it, she was happy see how alone he was in there. She'd forgotten he roomed by himself.

The room was quite clean as well. Harley liked organizing, but Max was far better at it than she was.

Max himself was clean and organized as well. He wore a gray shirt, covered by a dark gray vest. His pants were dress pants, also gray. He wasn't wearing shoes, only black socks, with dark blue lines.

"Huh." Harley said "Didn't strike me as the guy to not wear shoes at home?"

"So many people say that to me." He said "But honestly, I hate shoes. They look nice but my feet can't breathe after a while."

"Eh. I like shoes. I mean I'm not wearing them right now either but, well, that's the thing."

Harley closed the door.

"I'm sorry if this was something you never wanted a woman to tell you, but I'm on my period right now."

"Uh." Max said, cocking his head "Okay."

"I hear that uh. It's really good when." She coughed. "Do you get me? Really good if you, when I'm, doing this."

Max un-cocked his head, and instead screwed up his eyebrows. "You want to have sex?"

"Annie put the idea in my head and I'm horny enough to go alone with it. Part of the side effects of this stupid time."

"Are you sure?"

"Yes I'm fucking sure!"

She breathed out.

"I'm sorry. I'm horny and testy. I'll just sit down for a bit."

Harley took a seat in an empty chair.

"So how are you aside from," Max said "er, uh, okay I know nothing about what's happening to you right now so I don't have any words to describe what I was going to say."

"I'm good aside from all that." Harley said "My grades are good, some of them are great. Annie's a crazy little peach. Janie's much sweeter than she thinks she is. And, well." She looked at him. "Whatever we have here, I like it."

"Yeah." Max said "I'm getting good grades, I've got some new friends, and you. You're something special."

Max coughed.

"We have something here that's good. Our friendship."

Harley stood up, and walked over to him. "We do."

She sat in his lap. "Hey. I'm not testy anymore. But, I am still horny.

"Funny story." Max said "So am I."

"I call top this time."

Max and Harley moved onto his bed. Max took no time shedding his clothes, and laying down on his back. Harley kneeled over him, taking her clothes off as well.

Everything of her's was now bare. In its current state.

"Huh." Max said

Harley's image was not as strong as Max's, and yet her response was also "Huh."

They stayed in the same position, no connections between their parts, for two minutes. The insanity of the situation had now finally set in for the two of them. No rushes, no grabbing any sort of protection. No real moving of any kind for minutes.

"Okay I can't do this." Max said

"Oh my God I can't either." Harley said

Harley leaped off of him and put her pajamas back on.

"I'm sorry I'm sure this would have been good." Max said, throwing his clothes back on.

"No no, I'm sorry." Harley said "This was stupid, should have known I'd chicken out."

They were both dressed now, and Harley was ready at the door.

"Hey. Before you go." Max said

He walked over to her, and gave her a gentle kiss on her forehead.

"There." Max said "Something for your time."

"Thank you." Harley smiled "We'll have to reschedule."

Harley walked back into her room. She closed the door, and Annie shifted away.

"Huh?" Annie said, before fully waking. "OH!"

"Nothing happened." Harley said "And I'm not saying that to cover my ass. I WANTED something to happen. You try it, it's weirder than you think when it's about to happen."

"Awww." Annie said "Shit. Guess we don't get to find out tonight after all. So absolutely nothing?"

"He kissed my forehead. That was kind of hot."

"Yeaaaaaah, sounds it. Well, goodnight."

Annie immediately went back to deep sleep.

"Fucking weirdo." Harley said, smiling and almost laughing.

Harley climbed back up into bed.

Maybe it they couldn't fully do it, she could dream about it. Or, granted, whatever she felt like dreaming of.

♥ - *Chapter 14* - ♥

Harley found herself whistling happily on the way to the class meet-up. She'd seen the names of her fellow classmates, and recognized none of them. This would be a completely stranger, and she might as well see if she could turn them into a new friend.

She wore a purple miniskirt, a light gray blouse under a thin black open shirt, and light gray low heels. She'd painted her nails red, her lips pink, and her earrings were silver hoops.

The professor had asked them to meet at the baseball diamond. Thankfully there were no games of any kind going on at this time, so they had the entire area just for the class.

The professor was wearing an unbuttoned orange Hawaiian shirt, with a light gray t-shirt underneath. He wore a rainbow hemp bracelet on his left wrist, and torn faded jeans. His shoes were a pair of sandals, and both of his feet were heavily tattooed. On his left middle toe was a silver toe ring, engraved with black roses all around it. Normally Harley found toe rings to be tacky, but considering the professor was already wearing sandals and had feet tattoos, it just sort of seemed to even itself out.

He was also the professor Annie had waved to a few weeks prior.

"Hello. You must be Miss Harley Millsboone." He said

"Yes." Harley said

"Fantast- Hey! I know you from somewhere."

"My roommate waved to you a couple weeks ago."

"Your roommate is Miss Annabel Shaman! Aha! I hope the fumes don't get to your head."

Harley had to admit, that was a good one. She gave it a good laugh.

"Joking aside." He said "Lovely girl. One of the smartest I've ever come across."

"Huh." Harley said. She'd never taken the time to see how good or bad Annie was at schoolwork.

"Now." The professor handed her a sheet of construction paper with the number 2 printed on it. "The boy I've sent your allowed journal entries to will also be carrying a 2. Meet him, chat with him, see if you can bond with him. If you hate him, well, an experience is an experience. Oh, and don't leave the diamond. I refuse to accidently help a serial killer or whatever may happen should two escape without notice."

"Uuuh, I'll keep that in mind." Harley said, and went off in search of the other person with a number 2.

There were plenty of students, and the only hint Harley had was that he was a young man. There were plenty. Some gruff, some tough, some scrawny. One of them was sleeping.

She came across one man, black spiked bracelets on both wrists. A dark gray t-shirt with the logo of an unknown band, and the sleeves had been ripped. He had large headphones around his neck, without a plug, making them only useful for decoration. His pants were black cargo, and in his hand was the number 2.

"Hello." Harley said, holding out her sign. "Harley Millsboone."

"Great." The boy said, holding his up as well. "Damien Timber. Wassup?"

"I'm good. You?"

"Fine."

They stayed silent for a few minutes.

"Hey look I'm sorry." Damien said "I did read the passages it's just it was last night and I don't remember any of them."

"Hey it's alright." Harley said "Really, they're all just how we felt during the day. You sound very laid back though from what I remember."

"Well, what you read is what you get."

Damien leaned back where he was sitting, stretching his legs in a more open position.

"Hell I'm a slob, a procrastinator, everything you were probably thinking the second I opened my mouth."

Harley giggled.

"At least you find it funny. For the record, I said I procrastinate but I never said I don't get the job done."

"That's all that matters I guess."

"What about you?"

"I try to avoid the all-nighters, get the work done when I know I have a good amount of time to do them. Doesn't always work, but it works quite a bit."

"Well I hope you weren't trying to make me jealous, because that did not work."

Harley looked around, searching for something they could maybe talk about.

"I like your headphones." She said

"Funny story." Damien said "You see I do the editing for my friend's band. One night I just fucking broke the headphones I was using, ripped the cord right out of 'em, as you can see. My buddy goes, 'hey, Damien, you hold on to those puppies. One day, when we make it, we'll plate 'em gold for ya'. Don't believe it for a second, but hey, gave me the idea for a quick way to look different in a crowd."

"It works. I noticed them before I figured out your face."

"Good. The only other crazy thing I've done was I just got my nipples pierced. I would take my shirt off but A when just met, and B they are still swollen and no one wants to see that."

"Very risqué of you."

"My girlfriend's idea."

Harley found herself, strangely disappointed, at the news of a girlfriend.

"Loud and crazy little fucker." Damien said "But hey, we work out pretty well."

"How'd she get you to go that far?"

"She's had a tongue stud for a year, told me it's not that bad. Well, I can stand being showed-up, but not that far. She said nips, I said they sounded cool enough."

"Sounds like, uh, you guys know how to work things out." Harley found herself staring at the ground for a little bit. "Sorry, I, lost my train of thought."

"Alright then. We'll just move on to something else."

"Sure. You have anything on your mind?"

"A couple things, and no offense to you, it's mostly what I could be doing with my time instead of being here. I'm so used to not doing anything right now."

"Well what would you do?"

"I don't know. Go fishing?"

"Hm, I guess fishing might be more interesting."

Harley and Damien found some common ground for the next twenty minutes. It was around that time that the professor said they were all free to go back to whatever it was they wanted to do.

"Well. Maybe I'll see you around." Harley found herself saying.

"Alright. Maybe you will." Damien said, trotting off to Harley didn't know where.

Harley herself headed straight back to her room. While Damien proved to be an interesting specimen, she was more than happy to leave the class early. For it was her last for the semester.

She walked up the stairs, down the hall, and straight into her room. Annie was laying back in bed, barely dressed, listening to music.

Annie wore a cleavage-revealing gray blouse, purple pajama bottoms, bunny slippers, and had her "booby headphones" plugged in around her ears.

"Yo!" Annie said, mistakenly loud as she did not remove the headphones. "How you do?!"

"I'm good!" Harley said, trying not to yell too loud. "I'm just packing up and heading out!"

"Ah shit!" Annie said "Didn't realize what day it was! Fuck dude! I guess I'll see you after summer!"

"You too!" Harley turned to pick up a few things, before remembering "Oh hey, the professor was that one you waved to a few weeks ago! With the feet tattoos!"

"Oh shit!" Annie removed her headphones. "Dude you are so lucky to have had him. He's a fucking dreamboat."

"You're kidding."

"No way man. He's younger than he looks, not just younger than the fossils I mean. Only just became a professor. He's so hot."

"You really have a crush on a professor?"

"Hey if he's game it can be more than just a crush. I already passed his class and won't be having him for a while. I don't remember anything in the rules saying there's a problem now."

"Um. I don't know if I completely agree with you on that. I see your point, but, he's still a professor."

"Then leave him to me. He's not married, and I'd like to keep him that way until I get my chance, y'know?"

"Yeah. You do you, I guess. I'm going to get going."

"Right. I'll see you after break." Annie put her headphones back in. "I'll call you!"

Harley had arrived home, and already moved most of her belongings back into her old room. All of her family was home, helping her with her packages.

She wasn't the only arrival that day. Over the last several months, since before Christmas, the family dog had to stay at the vet's after a car hit him. Said dog was now home after all this time, roughly as good as new.

"Hello Clive." Harley said, bending down so Clive the dog could lick her face all over. "I missed you too buddy."

Harley got up to grab a paper towel to wipe her face. She wasn't sure why, but it felt like she took more time than she used to to remove the dog slobber. She figured this was just from forgetting what it felt like.

Her mother and father passed by her, and for whatever reason, her mother seemed to be stifling a laugh.

"Hey mom. You okay?" Harley said

"Nope." Her mother said "I'm right as rain, don't worry. Nothing at all."

"Dear." Her father said

"I said I'm fine." Her mother said "Peachy keen."

Her brother appeared from the other room. "Hey, I just finished with the last of Harley's-" Will caught his sister in his eyesight, and for some reason, broke with his speech pattern and slowed down. "stuff, and. Well it's, uh" he coughed "it's all taken care of."

Harley knew she wouldn't get an answer, so she shrugged it off. She headed back into her room, trying to settle back into the now surprisingly unfamiliar surroundings.

She opened her laptop and surfed through social media and her e-mails. Most of her high school friends and now gotten back from college as well, not to mention the new ones she'd met there.

It seemed Janie had left the day before, but didn't make much of a fuss about it. Annie on the other hand seemed more than eager to share that she would be done tomorrow.

Harley realized, she hadn't connected all that much with her high school friends. She knew that would happen, and yet, it still came across as a bit of a hard hit.

She wasn't the only person who thought so, as she received a call from someone she knew very well in those days.

"Hello?" Harley said, forgetting to check the caller ID.

"Hi, Harley." The voice said "Good to know this is still you phone number."

"Chad!" Harley said, recognized the voice of her former boyfriend. "It is so good to hear from you. How have you been?"

"I'm great. Are you in the area? Because, well, I am, and I feel like seeing someone and you popped into my head as the person I've seen the least recently."

"I am. Where would you like to meet?"

Harley and Chad had agreed to meet outside of the old shopping mall. They'd spent several nice days together at this place, and they used to love sneaking out to the woods around the property.

Harley had not changed, aside from redoing her hair and make-up. The same as before, but touched-up to clear away the smudges and be as fresh as she had looked after her morning shower and breakfast.

She wasn't sure if Chad had freshened up, but he did look quite nice.

He wore a long sleeve white shirt, with the name of his college printed on the front. For a college-made shirt, the quality was fairly nice, and the stitching looked like it would last for at least several years after his education finished. He also wore a dark blue sleeveless vest over it, with no buttons or zippers, purely designed for a opened look.

He wore blue jeans, and a thin white belt. It was a striking color choice Harley did not see very much. His sneakers were brown, and looked a few years old. Taking a second, she recognized them, he'd been wearing those since they were still dating.

On his right pinky was a small gold ring. Incredibly shiny, but subtle, hard to notice at first glance. She hadn't seen it until he used that hand to remove strains of his long brown hair out of his eye. He'd never worn jewelry before, must have been his version of experimenting with new things in college.

"Hey Chad."

"Harley! You look good."

"You look great. I like this look."

"Started taking better care of my clothes a few months ago. My uh,"

Chad stopped to cough. He ran his index finger against his cheek.

He was completely embarrassed.

"My boyfriend helped out a little bit." He said

"You have a boyfriend?"

"Yeah." Chad took a closer look at her face. "Oh! Oh shit did I never tell you? Well, okay there's a reason for that I'm sorry."

"Alright?"

"I'm not gay, both ways, I go both ways. Knew that since I was twelve. Never told you, because, well, we were already dating. Unless it came up I didn't see a point in telling you 'but I totally like guys too'."

"How long have you been together?"

"We started going out about a month after I started college." Chad had gone to college immediately after high school. It was not one of the reasons Harley broke up with him, but she was always glad she didn't have to worry about a long-term relationship.

"He asked me." Chad continued "Kind of like with you."

"Excuse me?"

"Don't give me that bullshit. We both know you asked me out and just pretended to have a cute little question about your homework."

"You figured that out?!"

"Oh from the start. You're a forward girl, I knew better than to say anything."

Chad checked his phone for a second.

"Gotta be kidding me." Chad said "I wanted to show you a picture but I have nothing. Oh wait! Nope, it's too dark in this. Why do I have that one? Gotta delete it."

"I'm sure he's a charmer." Harley said

"Like you wouldn't believe. Actually, I uh, well, both of us, kind of wanted you to meet him."

"Absolutely!"

"Thank you. He is not the jealous type, but he is the type to pester you for questions. I texted him about this and he sent his love, and a request he meet you soon."

"Request accepted." Harley thought about it for a moment. "Hey. We could go fishing."

"Nice! He loves fish."

"You guys are, uh, serious, right? I want to know before I talk while you are both around."

Chad looked around again, finger back on cheek. "How much do you want to know?"

"Anything that'll help."

"He's. The, guy I lost my virginity too."

"Aw." Harley said

"Glad uh, you don't consider that a slap to the face."

"Dude." Harley started beaming. "I'm not a virgin anymore either. It's okay that it never worked out for us."

"Huh." Chad said "I guess that makes me feel better. Actually, no, you know what really makes me feel better about all of that?"

"Shoot."

"It's going to be much easier to be friends now. You know? Not saying you can't bang and still be friends, it's just, I can't imagine that being remotely as easy. Knowing as much of them as you can romantically, and just, trying to pretend you don't."

"Yeah." Harley said, realizing she maybe didn't need to share her whole "first time" story. Granted, she had a feeling Chad would have asked her to stop anyway.

"But it is so nice to chat with you like this." Chad said "And fishing will be great."

"I'll text you back at home with free times." Harley said

"Before we go though, it really is funny how uh, different we both look now, huh?"

Harley didn't answer verbally, only cocked her head.

"Don't tell me you don't like joking like that anymore."

Harley cocked her head further.

"Oh my God no one's told you!"

"Told me what?" Harley said

"You've put on weight."

"No I haven't, look at me."

Harley put her hands under her stomach. She'd never been able to hold the sides up before. She looked down, eyes bugling.

"I have a muffin top!" She said

"It's not bad, really." Chad said "You're not fat or anything."

"I am totally fat!"

"I think you pull it off, if I'm allowed to say that about my ex I mean."

"Why did no one tell me?"

"Your college friends might have not noticed. I hear that happens when you see someone every day."

Harley put her hands on her cheeks. For once, she had trouble containing her face.

"I'm fucking fat." Harley said, closing her eyes.

She let the shock ride out. Once she did, a more calm, reasonable response ensued.

"Let me see myself in your phone." Harley said

Chad turned his phone off, and let Harley see her reflection.

She was fat, by her own terms. Puffy face, chubby hips. However,

"Huh." She said "I. I don't look all that bad."

"I think you're only about twenty pounds over." He said "Maybe. Maybe thirty."

"I'm, okay with this." Harley said "I have been eating more, I should have expecting this. This also means I don't have to worry too much as I already like the look of a fatter me."

"Hey, you do you. It's what they say."
"Yeah. Me do me."

Harley arrived home, every intention of giving Chad a text once she checked her schedule.

More importantly, she had to see her family first. She found them in the living room

"How come none of you told me I'm fat?" Harley said

Her mother bust a gut.

♥ - *Chapter 15* - ♥

Harley woke up that morning, showered, shaved her legs and her pubic area, ready for the day planned. This was the day she'd meet Chad's boyfriend, and hopefully catch a few fish.

She started putting on her class ring. It did not slide on as easy as it used to.

"Huh." Harley said "It, was kind of harder to get on recently." Until she discovered her weight shift, she never thought hard about it.

But the truth was coming to her, her fingers were getting too big. The ring could still fit, but it was getting harder. If she gained more weight, it might get stuck.

Only slightly knowing why, she gave the ring a kiss, and pulled out her box of memories.

It was now sitting at the top. Granted, the box was very little. She had no photos of her younger years, no old sticks she thought looked cool as a kid. She'd only gotten the box just before college.

The only other thing inside the box, was the wrapper to the condom from her first time. Seeing it again made her smile. She carefully closed the box and placed it back where she got it.

Another box caught her eye, a small box she used as a jewelry box, until she would gain enough jewelry to justify buying a real jewelry box. One of the items inside was the metal ring Annie had gifted to her.

She tried it on her right ring finger, but it was still too large. She tried it back on her left thumb, and while not as loose, it still fit. While it was a different finger, the short amount of time in the shower had already caused her hands to feel as if they were naked. It would be good enough, and it would certainly please Annie well enough if she had been there.

That reminded her. She pulled out her phone, and sent a quick text to said roommate.

"Did you know I was getting fat?"

She finished the text, and changed.

She wore a red-and-black plaid button-up shirt. Nothing said "fishing" to her more than that. She decided to be daring, and only her bra, which was a solid pink, was underneath the shirt. It wasn't going to be cold, and the shirt covered her up enough without a second layer.

For comfort and mobility, she wore a black skort. She had very few skorts, and after trying on this one again, she figured she may need more. Mostly, it was due to the fact it had a stretch-band waist. She'd have to do a lot of clothes shopping in general.

Her shoes were typical grey and white sneakers. She hadn't worn them in years, it wouldn't have been a tragedy if they got soaked and she'd have to throw them away. After slight debating, she chose small blue opal earrings, with a gold-platted outline.

Now fully dressed, Harley walked over into the kitchen for a quick breakfast. She figured some cereal and a muffin would do.

Her mother was there as well, cleaning up some of the dishes. There was a snicker at first, then muffled laughter behind her palm.

"The body shaming isn't going to make this easy mom." Harley said

"Oh, honey." Her mother said "Here, sit. I'm not just laughing at my little chubby girl."

The two of them sat down, but not before Harley grabbed the chocolate chip muffin she'd been wanting. She didn't have the time to butter it, so she simply picked off a few bites.

"When I first met your father." Her mother said, her eyes beaming at the memory. "He was a little porker."

Harley almost spit out her muffin bits. "You're kidding?"

"He had the marshmallowy sides." Her mother said "A beer belly. Saggy caves. And manb-." She coughed "His, pecs were more swollen and round."

"He's always been thin from what I remember."

"He didn't lose a pound until I got pregnant. He said he wanted to be able to play with his kids without having to catch his breath. It almost worked, you two were so fast and energetic. Anyway, Harley, that was the shape of the man I continued to go with date after date," She showed her wedding ring "and I have never taken this off since the day he put it on me."

Her mother couldn't stop smiling. She was never a solemn person, and yet, this was the happiest Harley had seen her in a while.

"You alright mom?"

"Memories Harley. You can't remember them without reliving them. Anyway, what I'm trying to say. I'm not laughing because it's funny. I'm laughing because you are starting to look a lot like your father."

A smile formed out of the corner of Harley's mouth. "Thanks mom."

Her mother began to walk out of the room. While no longer a teenager, there was still a small rebellious attitude welling for a short moment.

"Boobies and all?" Harley said, leaning back her head from her chair.

"Um." Her mother began to blush. "His were bigger than yours."

Her mother quickly left the room, and Harley stayed shocked for a good half a minute.

Once she recovered, she headed over to the cereal, and the butter. She began spreading the butter over the chocolate chip pieces when her phone buzzed. Annie had already gotten back to her.

"I didn't notice it but now that you mention it YES! You totally gained a few pounds."

Harley was about to put the phone away, when it went off again.

"Not that that's bad! Some people totally love that! I've dated about a dozen chubby guys, two obese guys. They were all sweet, but you had to be careful when they hugged you."

Instead of replying, Harley texted the same question to Janie. She knew her response would probably take longer, Janie had admitted to her before that summer was when she caught up on sleep, but it was starting to get entertaining watching everyone care about her weight far more than she did.

Which, is to say, she completely forgot about her own fit over the situation.

Harley walked up the dirt path to the small fishing cabin Chad had rented for the three of them. She expected a small wooden hut, a fire pit out front, cement or wood blocks as make-shift seats around said pit, and only a small amount of cleared area, allowing the trees to still flourish.

Aside from the one or two discarded beer cans in the wild, her mental image proved to be true. She also believed she'd stayed in this very cabin before, back in high school her family had taken many trips out into the back woods. Mostly fishing, but they also spent many a time just staying in the cabin to get away from everything else.

Chad and his boyfriend were both waiting near the door inside. Chad himself was a long sleeve white shirt under a brown checked open dress shirt. Closer to that of a hunting jacket than a typical dress shirt, not a bad choice for the scenery. His jeans were brown as well, and he wore brown boots. Chad had been an outdoors type on occasion as well, although he usually only dressed this good when on a date. Apparently, this new love affair got him to dress up more. Enough that he was still wearing the pinky ring, most likely it was an everyday piece of jewelry for him.

As for the boyfriend, he went with a short sleeve light grey t-shirt, with a fishing jacket and hat. There were a few hooks along the side.

Harley herself owned a fishing hat years ago, but lost it in the lake from a bad wind. The idea of a hat still applied, as before she left the home she had placed upon her head a green-and-white trucker hat her bother once gave her for beating him at an arcade basketball game. It also had a fish hook, as she could not think of a better place to store the one she'd brought.

As for the rest of the boyfriend's ensemble, he wore light brown cargo shorts, brown waterproof boots, and a brown bracelet cuff on his left arm.

It did not take Harley long to realize these two were the kind of couple who liked to plan ahead and wear similar outfits. Chad had tried this with her back in high school to no success. It must have been a blast to him to finally get a stupid little thing that he wanted so badly.

"Hey!" Chad waved her down.

"Hey Chad." Harley said, then turned to the boyfriend. "Nice to meet you."

"You too Lydia." The boyfriend said "My name's Dom by the way."

"Yeah….." Harley said "And mine's Harley…."

"You got your pole?" Dom apparently ignored the correction.

"Yep, left it outside the cabin." Harley said

"Great! I say we get going. Fish really don't wait all that long."

Harley and the boys headed back out, grabbed all of their gear, and walked over to the boat Chad had rented out.

"Life jackets are in the back." Chad said "I don't think it's tippy, but hey, let's not be stupid and assume it can't happen."

The boyfriend was the only one who did not need a life jacket, his ensemble had one built in. After they were strapped on, Chad started the motor and the boat headed out with the three on them onboard.

"Chad says you two used to be something special." Dom said "It's nice to meet you, if I didn't say that earlier."

"Thank you." Harley said "And Chad's told me the two of you are something pretty special right now."

Dom looked over at Chad, who did not notice anything but the motor at this point.

"Well, you know what this boy's like." Dom said "Can't image anything with him that isn't special."

"Yeah." Harley said "It's been a few years but I think I remember what you mean."

"He's a looker as much as he is a decent fella. Anyway, Lydia, you want first cast or you okay waiting?"

Harley's eyes formed a minor irritated scowl. "I think I'll cast first."

They'd been on the lake for a little over an hour, and had just moved towards the center. Harley herself had caught an impressive enough perch, and it lay dead in the cooler, every intention to be eaten by her family for dinner that night.

She was hoping for more, but today, there had mostly been sunfish, and those were always thrown back. Chad had caught nothing but the spiky little creatures, while Dom had gotten close to an incredibly nice fish twice. One a mackerel that broke his line, and one an ornery pickerel that bit him.

There were more bandages covered his hand then necessary, but this is what happens when you choose the boyfriend instead of the acquaintance to address your wound. Admittedly, there was still blood, and they all agreed twenty more minutes at sea would be good enough.

Harley decided to quit and just watch, the same action Chad had taken a while before the pickerel. Harley ended up learning one thing about Dom, he was incredibly determined. He was going home with a fish.

Casting was a little harder for him with the bandages, so despite the retiring, both Harley and Chad would occasionally help with his reeling. Mostly, he managed without them.

His current line went taut.

Dom took no time carefully reeling in this fish. Once it got close enough to the boat, they all made out the same image. A green fish with a long mouth and spikes.

"Another fuckin' pickerel." Harley said

"Yeah." Dom said "So no mistakes this time."

Dom reeled the fish in, this time, not touching it, letting it plop into the boat, flopping around with the hook still in its mouth.

Along with a blood stain, and a small bit of brown fabric.

"You're fucking kidding me." Harley said

"No, don't think so Har- Lydia." Dom said, shifting his mouth afterwards.

Harley gave him a side look, which Dom tried to ignore as he handed a hunting knife to Chad.

"Alright babe." Dom said "You know how to end this thing's suffering better than I do. I know it's tempting but don't get revenge on this thing. It's just a fish."

Chad took the knife from his boyfriend, brandishing it over the suffocating fish.

The pickerel lay dead, spiked on a sharp stick over the fire pit. Chad had gone to get extra firewood, the fish had barely begun to char.

"So you know my name, huh?" Harley said

"Of course I do." Dom flashed her a big dumb smile. "I'm just messing with Chaddy."

Harley almost giggled.

"Think about it." Dom said "You were his first love and his first kiss. I'm his first time. Way I see it, the two of us have no choice but to be friends, universe demands it, you know. Jealousy will ruin what I've worked real hard to accomplish, and I wouldn't care about being jealous anyway.

"But you be that nice all the time, and your fella will get tired of it. You have to mess with them a little sometimes. What better way than making him have just a few quick moments of 'Oh God he said it again'?

"As for 'Lydia', okay, I'm a little petty. It's the name of this chick who was in our class and had a huge crush on Chaddy-boy. Jealousy's dumb, but what's the harm in rubbing my victory in her face a little bit? You know how much attention our guy gets."

Harley was never vocal about how Chad was attractive to more high school girls than just her when they were dating. She didn't flaunt it like Dom, but it was hard to ignore. Thinking back, she now realized just how many times it was high school boys who would give him a thoughtful look as well, and that it meant more than she'd figured at the time.

"You gonna cook your fish?" Dom said

"Nah." Harley said

"You're not one of those people that eats them raw, are you?"

"No I just mean I'm saving it for later with my family. Didn't know those people were a kind of thing. I mean, except for sushi."

"Harley there are people that think the Earth is flat, there are people for every mindset."

Chad came back with the firewood, and carefully placed it on the fire. The fish was noticeably cooking faster.

"So how did you two get along while I was gone?" Chad said

"Lydia and I just did a little talking." Dom said "Got to know each other."

Harley saw a weird mix of happiness and disappointment in Chad's face.

"Yeah." Harley said "Damien and I had a few things we found out we had in common." She had to play along now.

She surprised herself though. Originally, she was going to say "Max". Yet, something about it seemed too strong, and she didn't notice it until the other name slipped out.

Until now, she hadn't thought much about Damien in the first place.

Harley arrived home, giving her catch to her father. Her father enjoyed cooking fish, and considering it had been a few years, he was more than happy to start the second it got in his hands.

Harley's phone gave a quick buzz, and she noticed Janie had finally responded to her question from the morning.

"No, why?" It read.

Harley wrote back. "Just curious. No one told me, was wondering if you'd noticed."

Janie's reply to this was instant. "No but I'm kind of surprised you care. No offense."

"I'll get over it. ☺" Was the last text sent in the conversation.

"How'd you like these two?" Will said

"Good guys." Harley said "Cute together, not one of those couples I'd worry about. It's a," She found herself pausing. "a bit of an eye-opener, I guess. Every time you see a happy couple, you just, kinda. I dunno. Think it over."

"That's because you aren't married yet." Her mother said

"That's when it gets so confusing you have to figure it out." Her father set, still focusing on the fish.

"Well, yes." Her mother said "Yes I suppose that fits what I was saying."

♥ - *Chapter 16* - ♥

As much as Harley's family had insisted they would help her move back into her new dorm, she found herself quite content in her decision that she and Annie would simply help each other out.

Annie was wearing a short jean skirt, a loose white blouse with fake paint splatters on the front, and black flats. On her right middle finger, she wore her thin scraggly silver ring, and on her left middle finger she wore a large blue-stone with silver coloring on the ring itself, the entire thing being a gaudy piece of costume jewelry she was still comfortable wearing in public. In her ears were little gold colored anchors. Over the break, she had dyed her hair again. This time, she added red highlights, while keeping the fake blonde coloring.

As for Harley's attire, she went for jeans shorts and her pink frilly blouse. She also wore white boots, brand new, a gift to herself for the start of a new school year. She wore no jewelry today, but put extra effort into applying dark red lipstick.

They were both carrying boxes, in Harley's she had hoodies and sweaters. Annie was carrying numerous textbooks. Whatever Annie was studying this semester, she apparently had to read up.

"So you have any plans for when we're done unpacking?" Annie said

"I kind of want pizza." Harley said "You want pizza?"

"Eh. I was getting hungry but not for anything specific. I can split one with you."

As they walked, they ended up hearing the sound of an electric fan. It was coming from an opened door. Neither usually being nosey, the two ladies glanced inside the room as they passed it. The noise drawing them.

Laying on the floor, facing the ceiling, was the owner of the room and fan. A young lady such as themselves, although something about her said to Harley that she was at least a couple years older.

She had short brownish-blonde hair, and was wearing a white blouse with black sides. Her skirt was red, and had the same black siding as her top. Her shoes were removed, as were her socks, but on the anklet of her right leg, a simple gold chain. On both of her wrists were an assortment of thin gold bracelets.

She seemed to sense the two looking at her, and lifted her head. Instead of saying anything, she simply shot them her index finger. Apparently having no problem saying hello to these complete strangers.

"It's uh," Annie said "nice to meet you."

"Maybe we'll introduce ourselves later." Harley said, then motioned to Annie that they couldn't stay and chat while they were carrying their stuff.

Harley and Annie headed up to their new room, depositing their boxes onto the floor.

"I need to rest a few minutes." Annie said

"Alright. I'll make sure no one steals your stuff."

"Great. Oh, by the way. I have to tell you something."

"Hm?"

"Some of my plans changed a little bit. I ended up getting in this abroad program. I'll be gone for, I think half of the semester."

"Nice. Were to?"

"Europe. Well, okay, sorry, more specific. England, France, a lot of time in Hungary. Barely any time in England actually, France is sort of the middle. I'm supposed to learn language and literature. For France, it's literature, Hungary it's the language. England is sort of like the preparation stage, I guess."

"Sounds like fun."

"Hey I hope so. Going abroad is expensive. You have no idea how many grants I'm already on."

"Remind me to ask you later."

It was getting dark now, the two were eating the pizza that had arrived only ten minutes ago. Between that, and some minor unboxing, they found the time to continue conversation.

"It'll be weird not having you around for a while." Harley said "When exactly do you leave?"

"Two weeks." Annie said "And I need to use that time to fill up on the assigned work of my classes here."

"That's going to be hard, I'd think."

"Yeah, but I'm getting an easier workload than the other students will. Part of the deal."

"You know that reminds me. When I was talking with that professor who knows you-"

"Oooooh, yeah. The dreamboat."

"Again, creepy. He said you were incredibly smart."

"Hey I need to be. I'm studying to be a surgeon."

Harley looked blank at Annie for quite some time. "I'm sorry what?"

"I'm going to be a surgeon. Going to be here forever, unfortunately. The abroad program will help. Plus, my fallback plan if I fail is to be an interpreter. God everything is going to cost my family so much money."

"I can imagine. Still, you got here right after high school."

"Yeah and I had to juggle a lot of application forms while I was in my last year. I'm lucky I figured out what I wanted to be early on, the best loan I'm on only allowed me to take it if I had the full four high school years and was eighteen or over. You believe that? I could have finished high school when I was fourteen if it wasn't for that stupid rule. Granted, helped me learn how to handle a lot of work at once, that's been my saving grace to try and speed through what I can here."

Again, Harley was blank. She had to remind herself that Annie was not good at telling jokes, she would have known by now if she was joking.

"Sorry I never said this shit to you, considering the looks I'm getting." Annie said "Guess I don't act like the type with an IQ of 150."

"Please just stop, I can't take the surprise anymore." Harley said "Wait I thought you almost failed that one class?"

"So did I until I saw the A. Turns out the assignment I thought I forgot about was related to another class, and was an extra credit one. Being smart does not stop you from being a scatterbrain. OH! That just reminded me, I forgot something!"

Harley realized just how right she was, she was a scatterbrain no matter what her IQ test proved.

Annie pulled a large plastic bag out of her backpack, filled with colorful treats.

"I got you some candy from back home!" Annie said

"Great. What are they?"

"There's some 'normal' stuff for your palette. Chocolates, chewy sugar stuff. I also brought you the good stuff. The red ones have chili powder."

"Chili powder?"

"Yeah man. That's the candy flavor of my people."

Harley tilted her head.

"Oh don't give me that 'I don't see color' bullshit. You knew since the day you laid eyes on me that I'm a hot little Mexican number."

"Wasn't aware Mexican candy had chili powder, is what I'm saying."

"We love chili powder as much as America loves peanut butter, Australia loves marmite, and Sweden loves black licorice."

"I'm guessing that you're listing multiple countries candy preferences to rub in how smart you are."

"I'm gunna rub it in your face ever since I saw your reaction. Away, here's yo' candy."

Harley saved most of the bag for a later date, but gave a few pieces a try. The chili powder did not bother her, but that was not to say she liked it too much.

Annie moved her chair closer.

"So," She said "since I'll be gone very soon, this may be the best day for us to just sit and talk. Be good ol' friends and learn things about each other."

"Hey, I'm game."

Harley told Annie about her summer. Her reuniting with her high school love, her mother's story with her father's weight, even a few things she just felt like sharing about herself.

"Oh, sorry I didn't bring you anything." Harley said "That is two gifts you've bought for me, and I've given you nothing."

"Eh don't worry about it." Annie said "I'mma be a doctor. I'll actually be able to pay off my loans and shit, you worry about how much money you have, I can go without a gift or two."

"Okay then, why don't we talk about how you've been? Okay, wait, first things first."

Harley pointed to a cardboard box of Annie's. Written on the side was "condoms".

"Are you hiding something worse in there and didn't want your parents to see? Or are you just that open with everyone about the kind of person you are?"

"In this case neither." Annie said "It is full of condoms and lube and stuff, but I didn't write that on the box until it was out of my parent's sight. They don't really ask or care about my love life. Fam doesn't really care what we get up to aside from being careful. Oh! You know what my mom and dad said when I hit puberty?"

"No, of course I don't."

"Mom said to me, 'Annabel, now that you know about love and sex. I want you to know, it is your life, no one else's. You cannot truly be judged for doing what you think is right.' And dad added 'However, if you are going to be wild, you need to be responsible'."

"Sounds a bit like what my brother told me. Minus the responsible part, since, well, brothers tend to forget that easier than parents."

"Well, I've been taking their advice. Hell, I can share this with you. Day before college, I got an IUD. Those condoms are just for STDs. I ain't getting pregnant. At least not without a lawsuit."

"Tell me more about your family." Harley finished the last of her pizza. "I swear I'll talk more about mine in the near future."

"Well, my mom and dad are awesome, like I said. I have a brother, he's a sweetheart. By the way, no one in my family is dumb but I'm the only one with a high IQ. It's not genetic, which, doesn't really help the bills because if my mom and dad were doctors as well I could fucking shower you in presents, you know?

"Anyway, my brother's a porn star."

Harley came close to choking.

"We're all supportive of him verbally, but it's not like we can support him by watching her stuff. He's family, that's fucking disgusting to watch him get railed. You know he was the good and chaste one for a while, then sort of gave up. Poor guy was bullied in middle school and high school. Got his nose broke once, but to be fair, the chick apologized as it was further than she meant to go. Her folks paid the surgery.

"That new nose ended up getting him some good money down the road. Not enough to help me much. He donates a little to me for my loans, but not exactly anything big, he has to survive too. He's telling me he'll be old enough to have to retire the mainstream stuff soon, but after that he says the internet can hire him for the niche stuff. Apparently porn can be niche.

"But it is because of him I've never watched porn. Always wanted to, too afraid he'll show up and I'd barf everywhere."

Harley spoke "When I was sixteen my boyfriend snuck out an X film from his parents and we watched it at my house. If it was any indication, they're dumb. I've had a better time reading erotic books from the library and the audio stuff I've heard online. Although Chad did have to shift his legs a lot, in hindsight he must have been hiding a boner that whole time.

"Anyway, any other relatives? What about your grandma?"

"Nana's wonderful." Annie said "She's been there for me since my diapers. I try to see her as much as I can now, she needs someone there for her ever since abuela died."

"I'm sorry, who?"

"My other grandmother. It was hard to call them both grandma and grandma, so, yeah. Nanna and abuela. Just about the only Spanish I still say aloud instead of to myself when I'm trying to think."

"*That's* why I can never understand you when you're muttering to yourself!"

"You must have never studied Spanish then. But it's not like I speak it to you anyway. We're not in some shitty direct-to-TV movie where the ethnic characters have to forcedly thrown in non-English slang or somehow forget the English word every other word. Christ, I've never even heard tourists talk like that. I have heard a few American tourists in Mexico ask to go to the 'cuarto del bano', which is completely wrong. If you're planning on Mexico Harls, just say 'bano', adding in cuarto means you want the entire room instead of just the toilet, as in it needs a bathtub. But try saying that to an indie director who couldn't point out Spain or Mexico on a globe."

"Can we get back to the subject of your grandma?"

"Oh, right! Nanna. Well I already told you she's gay so I guess I start with all of that. It's a cute story. So about when she was fifteen, she realized she only crushed on the ladies. Not that she could say anything then. However, around eighteen she met a pretty little lady who felt the same way. They pretended to be close friends so they could live together, and then there's grandpa. Grandpa was a guy who didn't really have any bigotry in him, and was also not all that convinced finding his own love would ever happen.

But he did want a kid or two, keep his family line. They fake-married, and this is my dad's side of the family, so the Shaman name lived on while Nanna still got the lady she loved.

And then, as you know, Supreme Court decided to not be dicks. Grandpa respectfully annulled so Nanna and Abuela could finally be wives.

Then Abuela died a year after they got married. So if I ever seem pissed off at the concept of irony, now you know."

Harley took her turn to speak. "I'm sorry Annie. How's uh, how's your grandpa handling all of it?"

Annie's eyes widened from surprise. "I don't know! I haven't talked to him in a while! Thanks for this conversation, I'm going to go call my grandpa now."

Annie headed over to her cellphone, then pause. She reached into her backpack, and pulled a massive bag filled with marijuana.

"Hey, when I get back." She shook it. "We're setting aside a time."

"Alright. What do I have to lose? It's legal."

"Fucking legal!" Annie dialed in a number. "Hola abuelo."

Harley tuned out so Annie could have privacy, not that she understood a word she was saying anyway. Harley opened to her social media, noticing her picture was a little out of date. Opening the webcam, and remembering her lipstick, she timed the camera to snap a shot of her blowing a kiss.

After uploading it, she wondered if anyone was going to comment.

Maybe Max.

She had to make sure it would not take very long until she saw Max again.

♥ - Chapter 17 - ♥

Harley headed her way to her tracing class. She wore a bright blue frilly blouse, tied off behind her neck, with white bubbles imprinting all of it. Her pants were sand-colored cargo shorts, and she had sandals, and sunglasses on the top of her head. On her left wrist was her pearl bracelet, and her left thumb was metal ring from Annie.

Harley knew this professor already, instead of dressing to make a first impression, she was only trying for a compliment. She remembered how Professor Anghula tended to dress and accessorize, it would be interesting to hear what she would say.

This class was in the same room as her past class with Anghula. Harley couldn't help but look to the side of the building, her muscle memory letting her hope to see Janie sneaking a cigarette. After not seeing her, Harley had to sniff the air. It was odd smelling the area without the side effects of cigarette smoke.

Harley entered the classroom, early enough to gain the same seat she'd always had before. Professor Anghula was facing piles of drawing paper, at the moment she was fiddling with some of her rings, fitting them better on her fingers. The timespan of a year did not change how she dressed her hands, she had likely not even bought new jewelry, from how comfortable she was in choosing them every day. Harley could have felt simpatico until this past summer.

"Ah, Harley Millsboone!" Professor Anghula said, opening her arms and coming over, as if asking for a hug.

"Hey Professor." Harley said

"That is such a lovely top. Your ensemble is gorgeous right now. Sorry if I seem a chattier than usual. I ended up getting tenure."

"Congratulations."

"You're very welcome. It is nice to know that they trust me to do and say whatever I like. By the way, you're a repeat student of mine, you don't need to call me 'Professor'. Just Anghula is fine. And, if you feel friendly, Margorie."

Harley went back to her seat, assuming the conversation was over. Instead, Anghula brought over a small sketchbook.

"In this are several artworks." She said "I've put little dates on each page, that's when your trace of them is due. However, you'll be tracing much more than this."

"Alright." Harley said

"You'll also need several designs not from this book for homework assignments, and for in-class tracing when from-home drawings are required. I've seen you draw, you can use any of your own. However, I'd recommend getting some drawings from people you know. I don't like asking for students to gain access to famous art. In your case, you know a budding tattoo artist, start with her."

Harley agreed with this professor, and took the book from her hands. In the back of her head, she figured she could ask this favor of Max also.

His designs could be fun to trace as long as he felt it was a good idea as well.

Harley opened the door to her and Annie's room. Annie had been changing, and at that point, had only managed to put on her jeans and a pair of red heels.

"Yo what's up?" Annie said, looking around for a bra.

"About to make a phone call, actually." Harley said, before taking a seat "I'm going to see if Max is alright letting me borrow something."

"Well don't leave me hanging here I'd like to know too." Annie found a simple light pink bra and clasped it on.

"Professor Anghula wants me to get extra pictures for tracing." She started looking for his number in her contacts. "Figure he has some scrapped projects he won't mind letting me have."

"Oh! That's smart." Annie slid on a plain grey shirt, slightly too big for her. Most likely a left-over from a former boyfriend. "I figured you'd be asking, uh, I'm sorry what was her name?"

"I'm asking Janie too, but it'd be nice to get as much as I can."

Harley began texting her request to Max. "Hey! I need a favor?!"

It was only a minute or so for the reply. "Okay? What kind?"

"Just come here I'll tell you" She then typed in the location of her new room.

"You'll finally get to meet him." Harley said

"Good thing too, you hear enough about a guy and you picture what he looks like about a hundred times. Be nice to not have to guess anymore. Plus, you know. 'He's cute' isn't as descriptive as you would think."

"Well he is."

"Harley I think all boys are cute! That doesn't help!"

There was a knock at the door. Harley stood up out of her chair and answered it.

"Hey Max." She said, letting him in. "This is my roommate Annie."

"So nice to meet you." Annie extended her hand.

"Same here. Hear about you a lot." Max shook her hand, friendly. Flashing a nice smile Harley appreciated far more than Annie.

Max's attire today was a long sleeve blue sweater, pure cotton from the look of it. His black pants were designer, logos and splatters strewn about, made from silk while the pant material itself polyester. His shoes were very dark gray, with blue laces and outlines. On his right index finger was a gold ring, with a squiggly line design in the middle, in a small ridge of darker gold.

"Do you own a cape?" Annie asked, without as much as a blink.

"Uh." Max said, then began to think it over. "I own, uh, five capes. One of them shrank and got holes in it, but I never threw it out so I technically still own it. Yeah, five."

"I think you'd look good in a cape, looking at you." Annie said

The look on Max's face said that he was too nice to tell her that she wasn't right in her assumption.

"Anyway, I have to go!" Annie said, heading out the door. "I'm having lunch with a friend. I do mean friend by the way, so I should be back in an hour or so."

"Take care." Harley said, as Annie left for her friend.

"Alright." Max said "What's the favor?"

He looked very good in his sweater. Harley often forget sweaters could be a fashion thing, even when it wasn't too cold out.

"Do you have some old designs I could borrow?" Harley said "You remember Professor Anghula? I'm in her tracing class now."

"I think I'd rather let you have finished designs." Max said "In my major you don't just submit them to the professor, you send them out into the fashion world itself. So, you know, I'd rather let you see rejects and things people have already seen instead of the things I decided against."

"Sounds good to me." Harley said

He looked so, good.

"So," Harley said "you uh, you want a favor in return?"

"Oh, now that you mention it." Max snapped his fingers. "If you're comfortable, I have some stuff I wouldn't mind seeing someone model."

"I'd love to!" This was no lie on Harley's part. She knew Max and his tastes well enough that helping him in his career delighted her.

"Great. Um. Some of it may be plus-sized stuff. I think you're a plus-size where I'm concerned."

"Yeah, I think I am too. If I'm basing it right."

"A little hard, right? Plus-size is kind of a joke. Honestly I, well okay I did notice, but it was hard to fully notice you as any different kind of weight after what I do. I've tried training myself to remember there's a difference in what the fashion world thinks is overweight and what reality thinks is overweight. Instead all that happens is I often think anyone who isn't obese isn't overweight. Ended up making my career a lot harder."

Harley laughed. Maybe it was a pity laugh, maybe he was funny. It was hard to tell anymore.

"But you did notice?" She said, playing with her her bangs slightly.

"I saw you naked after the fact, remember. No offense but that made it a lot easier."

"Oh, right. Almost got to try out some love handles." She giggled.

"Again, I. I'm sorry I chickened out. I know you did too, but, I dunno. I figure it would have made you feel better if I'd not acted like I was scared."

"Who cares? It's a funny memory now. Anyway, you send me some drawings sometime, and I'll head to your place and try on some clothes sometime."

"It's a deal. I'll talk to you soon. I should have some things picked out by the end of this week."

Harley and Annie had changed into their pajamas. At the moment, they were both brushing their teeth in one of the sinks in the shared floor bathroom. They happened to be alone.

"It'll be weird when you go away." Harley said, brushing in-between speaking.

"Yeah but it's super helpful." Annie spit "You know you'll have the room to yourself. I say throw some parties of something. Hell, invite Janie over, sure she'll be happy I won't be there."

"I might do that, but I really think you two might end up getting along."

"Nope." Annie rinsed the water in her mouth, and finished up. "See you at the room."

Harley was near the end of her teeth cleaning as well. On the way out of the bathroom, Annie ran into the young woman she and Annie had seen on their first day.

"Hey Izzy." Annie said "Thanks for lunch today. That was fun."

"Thanks. Nice to get to know you." The woman said

As Annie left, the woman walked more into the bathroom. She was also planning on brushing her teeth, if the toothbrush and paste in hand was any indication.

"You know my roommate?" Harley said

"Yeah." She said "Made friends with her just yesterday. Sweet kid, instantly considered me a great friend. Name's Esmerelda Platt, Izzy works just fine if that's too long."

"Izzy it is then. I'm Harley."

"Right, Annie had said that was your name. Spoke a little too much for me to remember everything."

Izzy was wearing pajamas like Harley and Annie had. Her bottoms were dark purple, with white and black sheep patterned on. They looked like men's pajamas, overly large and comfortable. Her top was a thin white tube top. She had no bra, yet the outline of her breasts was minor. She was clearly an A-cup, and this most likely did not bother her considering her attire. In the bridge of her nose was a simple gage, silver. Harley did not remember seeing this when she'd first laid eyes on her, but this was not a new piercing from the look of it. Her feet were covered by simple pink flip-flops

"Love to talk but I'm halfway through a movie. I'll catch up with you sometime." Izzy said

Harley simply acknowledged this, and rinsed out her mouth. Heading back to her room.

Harley found herself appreciating the walk back. While her past floor did separate the men's and women's bathrooms, it was nice that this floor went the extra step by fully separating the sexes by hall. The only boy on her previous floor was Josh, but that had been enough. The realization she could be even less cautious relieved her, she could almost just run through the hallway without any sort of top if she felt like it, it almost made her outright happy to picture it. Especially now, Izzy's outfit reminded her she could no longer even pretend she could go out without a bra.

While she never did before, she was only barely too big for it to be a bad idea. Ever since the weight-gain, it was even less advised. Her previous bras had grown so small that her breasts would pop out of them. She hadn't technically grown a full size, but some of her bras were now a size C. It was her sister-size, and frankly, she barely understood what that meant.

The thought of her own body left her mind once she opened her door, seeing Annie doing a lazy headstand on her bed, up against a wall, pajama bottoms at her ankles.

"What the fuck are you doing?" Harley said calmly, as nothing about this surprised her.

"You took too long and I got bored." Annie said to Harley, although her eyes did not leave her privates. "Wondered what I looked like upside down. Not bad if I'm saying so myself."

"Yeah, well, if you're looking for a further comment you'll have to ask someone else."

"Fair enough. Want to do something?"

"What like tell scary stories?"

"Maybe. More like make some popcorn."

"Alright. Yeah. Popcorn sounds good."

"Cool. Give me a few minutes and I'll get it started."

After five more minutes of staring into her own void, Annie got up, pulled her pajamas up, and made the two of them some popcorn. They ate and talked for the rest of the night.

"Won't be able to do this for a while after I'm gone." Annie said "I'll try to make some stories while I'm away."

"Great. I'll focus on passing my classes." Harley said

"Deal. I'm glad we're still roommates Harley. Can't imagine starting again with some stranger."

"Agree to that."

♥ - *Chapter 18* - ♥

It was an incredibly nice day out. The early cold chills were starting already, but Harley could still wear her comfy light clothes. She wore light blue Capri pants, end low enough just to show off half of shins. Her top was a button-up white shirt, almost light enough to be see-through, over a low-cut light blue blouse without straps. She was also wearing a white beret she'd borrowed from Annie while she was gone. Harley had to promised her to "keep my clothes happy even though I didn't take them all", and hats were about the only clothes of Annie's that fit her. Her shoes were a pair of black Mary Janes.

She was doing some basic drawing, and tracing over once she was done. As she was outside, and had little else to do, she wanted to start from the very beginning with the drawings instead of accidently let the world see Max's old designs or lose them from the wind.

She'd been drawing for around half an hour when a familiar pair of feet entered her view.

"Hey." Janie said, taking a drag from an e-cigarette. "So what was it you wanted to do?"

"Nothing really." Harley said "Just figured having you here with me would make the day less boring." She flashed her a pretty smile.

"Suits me I guess." Janie laid on the grass next to her.

Janie was wearing, surprisingly, a red skirt. Not long, although certainly not a short skirt, it went directly to her knees. For her top, she wore a black leather jacket, over a blue t-shirt with a tiny breast pocket. Her shoes were beige and orange flats.

"That's a lovely skirt." Harley said "I love the color."

"Matt found it at a cheap used store." Janie said "He texted me a picture, asked if I liked it, and now I owe him roughly two dollars."

"Does he go clothes searching for you very often?"

"Not really, but he's got eagle eyes when it comes to other people. You've seen how he dresses, he's a fucking slob, but he's good at picking up what'll fit."

"So basically, who cares how someone thinks it'll look on you as long as it actually fits you?"

"Yep. Don't entirely disagree, but he does seem to try harder if he sees something that would fit me. Eh, to be honest he may do that because of what I think. I'd love to be a slob too, but I care just enough."

Janie continued to suck on her phony electric cigarette. Harley was confused by a completely different smell.

"What is that? Is it flavored?"

"Strawberry. Supposedly the water is better for me. Most likely bullshit, but I'm tired of lighting shit on fire next to my mouth."

"Can I try?"

Janie handed the e-cigarette over, and Harley took a respectable puff before handing it back.

"What do you think?"

"I like it better than the real thing, but, still didn't really like it. You?"

"I think it tastes like shit, but they allow these in more places. Besides, maybe the shit taste will make me quit sooner."

"I have a funny feeling that doesn't work out that way for most people."

"Well, it does for me. Between the two of us I guess we're just immune to the true power of smoking."

Harley giggled. Janie tried to hide a smile from hearing her friend appreciate the joke, but Harley caught it anyway.

Harley had brought Janie up to her room. At the moment, Harley was putting away her school drawings, and Janie was sitting up on Harley's bed.

"That weed yours?" Janie said

"No, Annie's. Sorry if you were hoping we split it, Annie didn't give me permission and she wants my first high to be with her."

"Didn't really care. I grew out of the drug scene. Word of warning though, from what I've heard, you don't always get high the first time with weed."

"Really?"

"Hey, I never did it, just repeating what I heard a few times behind the curtain at the club. Oh, shit, what time is it?"

"It's only 2."

"Okay, good. Was afraid I was losing track of time. I have to DJ tonight."

"Oh! I forgot you DJ."

"You want to come to the club as a VP?"

"Oh fuck yeah!"

"Great. Nice to have a friend with me."

Janie seemed to pause after saying those words.

"I'll, have to change before we go, work clothes." Janie said "Not what you might be expecting, but they did give me a dress code and it's very strict. You have to glow and shit, you'll see."

"You mentioned drugs so tell me, these places have a lot of drugs going around?"

"You sound so dumb saying that. It's a club, we rave. Not everyone's high but it's not hard to find coke and acid and shit. We know some reliable guys who bring their own stuff to share. They're just happy crazy fucks who want to spread the joy, we kick out full-on drug dealers."

"Good to know. Want to get something to eat?"

"Sure."

Harley and Janie had headed back to Janie's apartment. Janie had to go to work within the hour, so Harley planned on waiting in the room while Janie changed.

"Matthew and I carpool, so we have to wait for him." Janie said, changing in the other room.

"I thought you worked at a different place." Harley said

"I was transferred roughly after Matty was promoted to assistant manager."

"Congrats."

"It's the same job."

"I meant Matt. Or Matty or Matthew. What am I supposed to call him?"

"He doesn't care. Any of the three."

Janie came back in her work attire. She wore bright magenta leggings as pants, with a darker magenta used at the crotch. A pair of neon orange panties were visible, as she had pulled the strings up past her hips. Her top was a dark pink short tub top, and over it was a blue denim short jacket. Her shoes were zebra-striped long boots with decently tall heels.

Her hair was made up to be spiky, both of her wrists had spiky leather wristbands, and she was wearing face paint on her cheeks. They were simply red circles. It did not take Harley long to recognize the copywritten character Janie was replicating.

"Laugh if you want." Janie said "I didn't pick out or buy any of these. The club knows exactly what makes those drugged up partyers giddy and grinning."

"I like the face paint." Harley said

"It glows in the dark...." Janie said

"Okay, that's kind of awesome. I've gotten fond of glow-in-the-dark thanks to my roommate."

"Yeah, she seemed like a partyer."

Janie went over to her mirror, taking a closer look at her cheeks. "You know, I am starting to like the idea of designs on my cheeks though."

Harley had barely noticed the new spider on Janie's left wrist. She'd had it since last semester, as she'd told her just before getting it, but Harley had completely forgotten to admire it until now.

"You think a spider-web would be cool?" Janie said, point at her left cheek. "Right here."

"Oh, yeah. That'd be sweet." Harley said

"Good. I'm trying to make my left side my 'spider side'. You know? I'm getting inked everywhere, but I want to try and have something of a rule for some places.

"Um. Hey. Speaking of everywhere."

Janie sat down in a chair, looking mostly at the floor. "Um. So, I'm glad you didn't have a problem waiting in the other room."

"It's no problem at all. I get it, you're a little shy."

"Yeah. Shy. I know you aren't so, I was hoping you'd understand. Um. When we were, at the beach and I stuffed. Er. Did you see anything?"

"I saw the corner of a nip, that's all."

"Yeah, I was, I was afraid you did. When you have silver dollars it's a little hard to hide. When you've got the small-ass chest that I've got."

"I'm sure you look lovely."

"I'm, I dunno. I've just never really liked what God gave me. Whatever you fuckin' call it."

"I'm not trying to tell a joke or anything with this, if you don't like 'em you could just see a plastic surgeon."

"I've thought about that, but I sort of want my boobs tatted at some point as well. I'm afraid if I do it first, they'll warp the ink. And if I do it after, I've. I've looked at a few surgery books and some of them look real, balloony. I'm afraid the gun will pop them or something. That, and, I don't know if I'll ever not be too scared to take them out even slightly so it can be done."

"Hey, I wouldn't know. Annie wants to be a surgeon, maybe she knows someone who's studied implants who you can talk to. Hell, that person could even be herself, never asked what kind of surgeon she wants to be."

Janie moved her gaze up to Harley. "Sure. Thanks."

Janie stood up, moving over to her counter. "Hey you want some free lotion? I get them in my beauty magazines and I didn't really like this sample this time."

"You of all people read maga-"

There was a knock at the door, followed by a slow opening. It was Matthew.

"Hey Janie. Harley." He said "I have to fix this stupid tie so, relax, not leaving just yet."

True to his word, Matt went straight to fixing his tie. That did not mean he was wearing a suit, nor even a suit jacket. He was wearing a gray shirt that was a little too big for him, and dress pants with a small hole in the side.

The question of how he became assistant manager crossed Harley's mind.

"You were saying?" Janie said

"Huh?" Harley said "Oh. You of all people read beauty magazines?"

"I use a lot of face and hand cream." Janie said, awkward grinning. "It's, a little silly, but trust me, every time you've seen me I was lathered with the stuff."

"She even wears perfume." Matthew said, almost finishing with his tie. "Unless she's at school. It's good stuff."

"Shit!" Janie said, heading over to apply perfume. "Thank you Matt! Completely forgot."

"I've never once smelled you with perfume." Harley said

Janie finished with her quick perfuming. "Mostly it's for when I go out. I count going to work as going out, but not so much school."

"What about the beach, you didn't smell like perfume at all on the beach."

"Pfft, no one should wear perfume on the beach. The place stinks of saltwater and fish, nothing you do will fix that. It'll just get washed off when you swim."

"Does the cream work?"

"Oh fuck yeah. Look at me, I actually look me age! My moth-"

Janie stopped for a second. Harley noticed Matt did as well.

"The," Janie continued "women in my family have a history of early crow's feet. I might look like a mummy by the time I'm thirty-five." Janie took a deep breath. "I have to use the bathroom."

Janie headed off to her apartment's bathroom. She stayed there for around half a minute before Matt walked over to Harley, finished tie between his hands.

"Hey, just a head's up." Matt said "Never mention parents around her."

"Okay." Harley said

"No, look at me, say it harder. I'm sure you had great parents, I like mine quite a bit. That doesn't matter. Don't mention anything related to your mom or dad around her. Okay?"

"Okay." Harley looked him dead in the eye.

"Great. Don't expect me to explain why. Not my life to share."

The two of them waited for Janie to leave the bathroom. Harley figured it was good that Janie was not wearing eye makeup, as she probably would have had to reapply it, judging on the way she was carrying herself.

"Alright." Janie said "Fuck this, let's get to work."

"We had this one chick in here one time." Matthew was passing the time by telling Harley stories from the club, as Janie played away for her job. "Crazy fuckin' hair, dark purple and dirty bubblegum pink in the back. Or front, fuck, it was those colors but I don't remember which order. She came up to me, and I was assistant manager by this point already, she asked me if she could snort coke off my dick."

Harley cocked her eyebrows. "Alright, tell me. Did she get the opportunity?"

"I told her I'd think about it. It's not like I'd have the answer to that off the bat, you know. Honestly I still don't have the answer, and I've never seen her since so I might not have to."

"Well if there is a second part to this story I hope I get to hear it."

Harley moved her gaze back over to Janie. She had just changed songs, something quieter, something that sounded like it would last longer than the typical pick.

Janie then spoke into her microphone. "Alright, I've taking a break to vape. You all keep going."

Every though the crowd did hear her, they practically ignored her to continue being the drugged-out airheads the majority of them were.

Harley walked her way over to Janie before she disappeared. "You're doing great!"

"Yeah thanks." Janie said "Look we'll talk after work, I really do need this break." and then headed to the outside smoking area.

Harley figured this may as well be a good time to see if there was anyone else worth talking to. She mostly saw the typical young adults who would attend a rave. A few people a couple of years older, most of whom seemed to know what they were getting into, a few completely confused.

Harley's eyes eventually caught one young lady who was completely topless. In white glow-in-the-dark paint was a drawing of an ejaculating penis, and a phone number, presumably and hopefully her own. The likelihood of her being a prostitute was fifty-fifty.

Then her eyes caught something far more familiar.

"Holy shit!" She said "Damian!"

Damian was barely able to hear her, but her voice was able to cause him to turn his head and see her. Harley invited herself over to him.

"Hey!" Damian said "Harley, right?"

"Yeah!" Harley was now beginning to wish the music had been even quieter than what Janie had picked. "So what are you doing here!?"

"Friend's band plays here sometimes!" Damian said "I got used to coming here after a while! And my girlfriend felt like going!"

Harley had momentarily forgotten about her.

"I guess I'll get to meet her!"

"Yeah, she should be right back! In the bathroom! Why are you here?!"

"I know the DJ!"

"Sweet! Ask her if she can play some jazz! I love the music of my people! Well, okay, all music is the music of my people, but I like jazz a lot more!"

Harley made a mental note to ask. As her mind was opening, a question appeared, on whether Damian dressed himself or his girlfriend.

Like the body paint lady, Damian was at the club with no shirt on. In his situation, it was to show off the barbells in his nipples. They had very much stopped the swelling he'd warned her about last time they met. His bottom was, of all things, a kilt. He when wore high socks and appropriate shoes.

"You like the man-skirt?!" Damian said, noticing her eyes.

"Yeah! Sorry for staring, never seen one in real life!"

"I'm part Scottish! Girlfriend thought it'd be cute for club life, and I really agree! It's nice having as much a breeze as possible with all the heat in here! Also why I'm not wearing a shirt!"

"I figured it was the nipple rings!"

"Those are just an added bonus!" He winked at her after saying that.

Harley found herself oddly lamenting that this was no way a flirt on his part. If he was in an open relationship, or just a cheater, he'd have been far more clear about that from day one. This was just him being funny.

"Ah! Here she is!" Damian said as another woman walked into his view. "Hey baby! This is the girl I got paired with in that class last semester!"

Harley quickly noted Damian's girlfriend, trying hard to note as much as she could before she'd have to focus on shouting a conversation over the music.

She was very attractive, Harley noted, Damian was a lucky man easily. Her coarse long brown hair slightly reminded her of Max's hair, except that hers went down to her breasts while Max kept his short enough. It was also perpetually frizzy, while Max's only frizzed when he was sweaty, a look of his she was more used to seeing than most others.

Her shirt was light green, with a black sleeve jacket sown onto the sides of it, making it a double-shirt. Her pants were faded and torn jeans, cut off at the very bottom into bell-bottoms. Her shoes were purple dance flats.

On both of her hands were silver rings, for the thumb and index fingers. The exact same ring was on both index fingers, a simple design of an eagle on the band. Her left thumb ring was just a thick single band. For her right thumb, another thick band, but with the words "TOTAL BITCH" inscribed. Just as Damian had mentioned, his girlfriend also sported a stud in her tongue.

Harley had a feeling the two of them would get along just fine.

"So what's he told you about me?!" The girlfriend said "He tell you I'm the real deal!? Don't fuck with me?! Come on girl, out with it!"

"Not much!" Harley said "Honestly barely know each other!"

"Too bad bitch!" The girlfriend said "I'm someone to know, and that goes the same for my boyfriend! If he ain't fixing that then I am!"

Damian chuckled a little. "Great ain't she?!"

"I already said I was!" She said "Anyway my name's Sheena! And I am the real deal!"

"I'll keep that in mind!" Harley said "It's great to meet you!"

"One minute in and you admit it!" Sheena said "I'm getting even better! And you just earned a point!"

"Huh?!"

"Bitch I'm great, but I know no one's a God and no one's perfect! I score everyone! Point system! Some people even beat me! Mostly lovers, because let's be fair, they gotta be better than me or there's no point! I don't do pity!"

"I like you already!"

"That don't get you another point, but you are welcome for that!"

Harley noticed Janie come back inside. "Sorry, I gotta go! DJ's back! I'll ask her about the song!"

"You know the DJ?! Alright, fifty points! And whatever her fucking name is, a hundred! Ain't met a DJ I hate!"

Harley walked off smiling. Perhaps she had only been upset by Damian's initial admission of their relationship because she wanted to meet her herself. She was hoping that was a case, it felt, weird, to be attracted to a man with a girlfriend. It wasn't like she could do anything about it, well, of course she could *literally*. But *morally*, she would never do anything, and that was going to be the way it went.

"Hey Janie!" Harley said "Can you play some jazz?!"

"Sure I love jazz!" Janie said "For you anything, give me a minute."

"Thanks buddy!"

"Yeah. Like I said, anything for you."

At that moment, a young man stood up on one of the tables. He gained most everyone's attention.

"I just want to tell you all you're absolutely beautiful and are basically my best friends I've never met! I'm so happy right now there's only one way I can both show it and give back to you, so if any of you don't want to see my penis you should close your eyes now!"

Harley was not one of the people who closed their eyes. Janie was neither.

"Hey. Baby dick. Not bad." Janie said

"I guess so." Harley said

"Meet me in the bathroom!" Said the topless body paint woman.

Harley and Janie had headed back to her place. Harley planned on driving back to school in the early hours of the morning. She had class, but she'd done her homework way ahead of time, so she was in no rush.

"I need to crash." Janie said "Sorry if you wanted me to bring you back."

"No problem Janie, I'm going to stay here if that's okay."

"Eh, alright. Door's always open I guess."

Janie immediately laid down on the couch without changing. "If I sleep until midnight, tell me to get up and brush my teeth. This is supposed to be a powernap."

Harley looked over at the time, 11:00 P.M. "Sounds good to me."

"Help yourself to anything you want." Janie nodded off.

Harley headed over to the pantry. Only now did she realize she was hungry. She figured she could make a peanut butter sandwich, after seeing the very ingredients she would need to make one.

In the middle of crafting her dinner, she came across a pile of the beauty magazines Janie had subscribed to. With her free hand, she opened up the newest one, reading as she began to ate.

She found Janie was right, and the magazine proved a good read, despite skimming the much longer sections. At the very end, she found a personal quiz. She thought about doing it herself, but saw Janie had already filled it out.

The questions were about self-esteem. Her answer read as followed:

It seems to us that you lack a lot of self-love and appreciation. We can't see why! You do you! You're great as you are! If you don't like something about yourself, maybe you're just overthinking it more than you think! It's our opinion that loving and excepting yourself for whatever you are and whatever you like is the true step to happiness and real beauty, whether or not you want cosmetics to feel better!

Harley gave the magazine a sad smile. It was just as right as it though. And as right as, most likely, Janie didn't think it was.

♥ - *Chapter 19* - ♥

There had been a few things on Harley's mind about what she could do now that the room was hers until Annie's trip was over. For all of the ideas that popped in, there was only one she truly cared about doing. It had been months since the last time, and without having to worry about Annie barging in, Harley was going to give herself the best time she could.

To start with, she was going to shower with her lavender shampoo. She rarely used it, and today was the right occasion. She felt the warm water rush down her body, hair to toe. The sweet lavender smell already intoxicating her. She was not fully ready yet, but she could feel herself already getting close to it.

She was content with her cleanliness, and turned the water off, reaching for her towel to wrap around herself. The walk back to her room made her feel a slight cool breeze that both helped her dry off faster, and helped contrast the remaining heat from the water droplets.

She opened her door, and immediately shut it. Dropping her towel into her laundry hamper, she picked out her clothes for the day.

She choose a frilly light sea-green button-up blouse. A black bowtie was attached to the neck, and she made sure to tie it up correctly. Her pants were blue capris, ending just above her calves, showing off the majority of the bottom of her legs. Her shoes were black strappy low heels. In her ears were silver studs.

She started on her way to breakfast.

"I'll take scrambled eggs, some bacon, and French toast." Harley told her server.

During the morning, the school cafeteria was very complacent in the idea of cooking breakfast for whoever asked. It never took them all that long, and many times the food tasted as such. However, Harley was ordering a bigger breakfast than normal, and she was going to be happy either way.

Her eggs were cheesy, her bacon was crispy enough, and the toast melted in her mouth. She ate that specific item as slow as she could.

Before she could have her planned activity, she needed to finish the in-class work Anghula had given her. At that same moment, Anghula was also going through all of the homework her students had given her.

Anghula was wearing a short red dress, the collar of which had a slight fishnet design, which was mirrored on the end of the sleeves as well. Anghula was also wearing brown sandals, showing off her painted red toe nails. Her fingernails were painted the same, which Harley found a little pointless. With all the rings Anghula was wearing, there seemed little point in doing anything else to make her fingers stand out, but to each their own.

Suddenly, Harley was called over. Harley asked for just a moment, as she was almost done anyway.

"I just wanted to say how much I like these drawings." Anghula said "Tell me. Is this Ms. Olber's work?"

"Yes." Harley said

"Ah. I figured as much. You too truly got along in my classes. I miss seeing her work, I always get attached to the artwork of students who are pouring their heart's desires whether they know it or not. Pay her a compliment for me when you can."

"I guess so, if I remember."

"Wonderful. Now, give me what you have, and you can start with the next one."

Harley quickly handed over her work. Admittedly, it was sloppier than usual. She was trying to finish as soon as she could, without horribly messing up. She was getting tired of waiting.

Harley was now naked in front of her computer. She had just downloaded an audiobook, and her headphones were in.

"The grass had been kept hot by the sun. She was still but yet a girl, as far as she could care, while in the presence of this lovely powerful man."

The main character of the book, either on purpose or due to bad writing, had been given absolutely no definable character traits other than the fact she was looking for true love. In this exception, Harley was completely okay with this, as she allowed herself to fill in the cracks by asserting herself into the role.

As for the one trait this fictional woman had, Harley was not looking for love, but pretending to share this trait helped with her real goal of quick and on-the-spot lust.

" 'I've finished patching your roof Madam.' He said, buffily, all of his gleaming glow shining in her living room.

'Oh, thank you.' She tried to hide the meekness of her voice. 'Why don't you, come, and sit next to me so we can talk.

'Why madam, I can tell you would like much more than to talk.'" He told her, and her eyes and mouth watered for him."

Harley turned on her vibrator.

Harley laid back in her chair. Spent. Satisfied.

And then, regretful. Ashamed. Every single time. She knew she could do better than this. She knew she didn't need to do this.

She didn't need to think about that, after doing a simple act she knew everyone did. All she did was masturbate, and her brain was now berating herself for it.

She looked at her phone. A rash thought came to her. She considered finding Max's number in her contacts, quickly texting him "Come over here and fuck me!"

It took less than a second for her to know that was an awful and impulsive idea. Max was wonderful as a sexual partner, no question about it. He also meant more to her than just a friend-with-benefits.

She put her clothes back on, and spent the rest of the day on her homework. Drifting between the elation of the act, and the self-humiliation of the act.

♥ - *Chapter 20* - ♥

Harley was heading out to meet with Janie. Annie would be back in only two days, so they planned to spend the rest of the day together. Harley's plans, which she had yet to share with Janie, involved shopping, lunch, and whatever they felt like doing afterwards at either her dorm or Janie's apartment.

Harley wore a red warm short sleeved sweater, wooly at the touch and looked it. Over that, she had a grey overcoat that cut off at her waist, and looked similar in design to a trench coat. Her skirt was white, went to her knees, and had vertical frills. On her head was a grey skullcap, in her ears small silver hoops, and on her feet were black flats.

Harley had told Janie to meet her in the parking lot on campus, and was not surprised to see Janie had already arrived, vaping up against her car.

Janie also wore a sweater, however hers was black and long sleeved. She also wore dark blue jeans, and short black heeled boots.

"So," Janie said, placing her e-cigarette back in her purse. "Where are we headed?"

"The mall." Harley said

"Oh fuck off. We're clothes shopping, aren't we?"

"Yep."

Janie sighed. "Alright. Guess it's something."

Harley had dragged Janie into a dress boutique. Little did Janie know, Harley had done some searching online, and she had found something she believed Janie would like.

"Alright. Just give me a second. Ah! There we go. Come over here Janie."

"Why?"

"I want you to look at this."

It was a simple black fabric dress. In the middle was a buckle to tie around the waist, leaving the bottom short enough to come just above the knees.

"Do you like it?" Harley said "I thought you'd like it."

"Huh." Janie decided to touch said dress. "Okay. Maybe this wouldn't be bad."

"I'll buy it for you."

Janie turned around to look at her. "Why?"

"Because you're my best friend, and I think it'd look really cute on you."

Janie's mouth, for whatever reason, seemed to wobble a little after Harley spoke. After a few seconds, Janie turned her head back to her dress, and noticeably also titled it down.

"You don't have to buy this." She said "But you're right, this will look cute on me. I'm going to try it on."

Janie took the outfit with her into the changing room. In the meantime, Harley looked around the store. A lot of moms shopping for their daughters. A lot of men trying to impress their girlfriends. A few women all on their lonesome, perhaps assuming good looking dresses were the exact thing they needed. Superficially or otherwise.

She couldn't judge them if that was the case. She remembered just how many times a certain someone's smile made her nothing short of happy inside.

Janie came out of the changing room. She had left her jeans on, but the dress still did it's work or looking gorgeous on her.

"How does this look?" Janie said "There, was a mirror in there, and. Well. I like it do you still like it?"

"You look beautiful."

"I. Sure, okay. I'm buying this."

"Any reason you left your pants on? I don't think that comes up high enough to worry about not wearing a bottom."

"It's fucking cold out Harley. I'll wear it by itself in the summer."

There was less venom in how she said that than usual. Harley had gotten so used to Janie's temper that this completely shocked her. So she simply said nothing as Janie walked over to the cashier.

"You'll have to scan this tag on the side." Janie said "I'm not taking this off."

"Um. Okay." The saleswoman said.

The saleswoman seemed the pinnacle of "housewife trying too hard". Her blonde hair had been curled, her eyelashes were big and fake, her blush was heavy, and none of it went with the green smock, white t-shirt, and blue slacks the job forced her to wear.

Why they didn't force her to wear a dress in a dress boutique, Harley would never know.

As Janie was buzzed, she flinched at the price, and paid anyway.

"Come on." Harley said "We've been here long enough. Let's get Chinese."

"Oh God yes!" Janie said "It's been fucking ages since I had Chinese."

Even though they had gone to the restaurant to order it, they both agreed it was better to head back to Janie's apartment with the food instead of eating it there. There was something nostalgic about it, of all things, to both of them. Eating Chinese food out of boxes in their bedroom.

Harley hadn't even been allowed in Janie's bedroom before. The walls were painted a quiet mix of cream and beige, most likely from an earlier tenant. Janie's bed was as lumpy as she'd described it before, and her sheets were pinstriped, light gray. She had three pillows, one of them completely squished under the other two.

"You know this sweet and sour shrimp is a little better made than I was expecting." Janie said "Never been to this place. How'd you hear of it?"

"My brother used to eat there a lot." Harley said "There are times where he ingests almost nothing but salt and msg."

Janie actually laughed. "Matt says the same thing about himself with curry powder and sriracha. I swear he could eat fucking molten lead."

"How did you and Matt meet, anyway?"

"It's uh," Janie paused for a moment, and then, closed her mouth. Breathing in. "Fuck it. You can know. I was kicked out of the house at seventeen."

"What?!"

"Yeah. Still had some school, parents figured I was good enough on my own. Matt's about, three years older than me. Hold on." She began speaking mostly to herself for a moment. "He's twenty-two, yeah, three years." She went back to talking to Harley. "I think he felt sorry for me. So, he told me a few things I could do to pass my classes quickly while trying to figure out how to live.

When I graduated, he was ready to finally move and get a better job. He didn't mind telling me a few places he'd passed up in the area in case I was interested. Told me where the local college was while I was trying to smooth things out with my old high school and still technically graduate. He kept in touch with me in case I needed more favors. I didn't but think much about it, but, I don't know, I guess I appreciated it because I decided he was worth trusting after the random help."

"Fuck."

"Not surprised he never told you. Don't tell him this, but he is a lot shyer than he lets on." She let out a tiny smile. "You know. It's not like he saved my life or anything, but, there's quite a bit I'd due to repay him."

"Oh?"

"Sure. Like I said, I like him, that's the rules."

"Hey. You think maybe he helped you because he thought you were cute?"

"God no. Matt's not that shallow. Besides, look, Harley. I know you're just being nice. Alright. You can be honest."

Harley scooted closer to her friend. "I am being honest. I get it now why you don't think so, at least part of it, I hope all of it. You're sweeter than you think."

"Shut up....."

"Janie."

"Yeah?"

"You're my best friend."

Janie's eyes went wide.

"I love you." Harley said

Janie's eyes were wide, and now, they had grown wet. She took no time at all wrapping her arms around Harley, dropping her food box onto the floor.

"I can't believe you've been so nice to me." Janie said

"It's okay." Harley patted her back. "Cry it out. I'm here for you."

"Yeah. Yeah, I get it. Okay. It's just, I didn't actually expect this. Not just you, I. Fucking. No one's ever loved me before.

"I thought. You know, I thought that. When you first said hi to me last year. When you were all nice to me. I just thought you were flirting with me, trying to get some action from a bad girl sneaking cigarettes before class. And then you kept talking to me after it was clear you weren't interested in me like that.

"I love you too!"

Harley let Janie cry on her for roughly two more minutes. When Janie was done, she let go, and wiped away her tears and snot with her wrist.

"I'm sorry." Janie said "I've never really cried like that."

"It's okay." Harley said "You ruined my clothes, but it's okay."

That made her laugh. Not hard, but considering the circumstance, it was the best she could laugh.

"Hey, if it makes you feel better," Harley said "before I forget, Professor Anghula mentioned you recently."

"Fuckin' really? Does she not have the spare time to think about her current classes?"

"She complimented the art of yours I'm tracing over."

"Oh. Okay, yeah. I get it. Maybe that makes me feel better. I dunno. Fucking hated Anghula, you know that."

"Did you know her first name is Marjorie?"

Janie snickered. "I should have, but I didn't. Fucking Marjorie! Hah! Holy shit that's the most embarrassing name I've ever heard."

Janie finished wiping away the wet off her face. Taken both of her hands, she tried rubbing her cheeks and then the rest of her face. She gave one last rub of her eyes with the back of her wrist, and tucked back her hair behind her ears.

"Anyway, you wanna watch a movie?" Janie said

"Sure. I wasn't planning on heading back until tomorrow anyway."

"Cool. And, thanks. I don't know how this'll work now, but, it's nice having a best friend."

♥ - *Chapter 21* - ♥

It was now Thanksgiving, and Harley was happy to be back with her family. Thanksgiving was always a lazier time for the Millsboone family, and as such, Harley was only wearing a white t-shirt and a light blue skirt. Her shoes were a pair of white flats.

At the moment, she and her brother were setting the plates at the table. They had been given this assignment since Harley was eight. It never took long between the two of them, Harley would tend to set her and her brother's plates while her brother set the ones for their mom and dad.

"So tell me." Harley said "What are you looking forward to the most? Turkey or potatoes?"

"Honest." Will said "I'm just waiting for the main course to be over so we can get to the pie."

"Hm, alright. I'll accept that answer."

"And you?"

"Uh. Huh. I guess potatoes. It's easy to like the thing that just gets stuck to everything anyway. No matter what, you can find a way to be eating it."

Will and Harley continued chatting while they waited for Thanksgiving dinner to be served. Once the table was finally ready, the whole family sat down to eat.

"Now who's first?" Her mother said "Hm? Who wants to say something first?"

"Well." Her father said "I'm just happy having all of you here. Both of my kids are healthy, smart, taking good care of themselves. I'm a proud dad, that's what I'm thankful for."

"And I am as well." Her mother said "Nothing makes me happier than seeing my babies grow up so good. Harley, how about you?"

"Me?" Harley said "Well. School's going really well. I'm made some really good friends. I feel good. Yeah. I guess I'm thankful that I like school and that I've made enough friends to feel good about it."

"I uh." Will said "I, guess I'm okay."

They all just looked at him. It took a while before anything said anything.

"Hey, Will." Harley said "You'll be fine."

"Yeah, I know." Will said "I did the right thing. I'm, almost over it. I mean it."

"It'd be okay baby." Their mother said "I know I didn't exactly pretend to like her, but, that doesn't mean I don't understand. I'm sorry."

"Thanks mom." Will said "Hey. Let's eat. I think that'll make me happy."

They proceeded to do so.

Harley and her brother were in the living room. Harley was sitting lazily on the couch, watching whatever she happened to end up on while surfing channels. The family dog was resting his head on her lap, and she returned the favor by placing her hand between his ears.

Will was standing up against a wall, eating a slice of pumpkin pie without a plate or silverware.

"You could just turn the thing on." He said, teeth plastered orange.

"I don't want to stream." Harley said "I stream all the time back at school, I've missed cable."

"Hey. Can I talk with you about something?"

"I'd be a shit sister if I said no."

"So. I've been thinking a lot about what Mimi and I had."

Harley turned to look at him now. "Okay. Good or bad?"

"Mostly good. I don't really regret dating her, only dating her for so long. Stringing her along. I should have figured it out. It uh, it's been making me think. If I missed one obvious thing, I may have missed another."

"Okay? I see the logic."

"There," For a moment, she saw her brother blush. "there was this other girl I used to know. Thinking back on it. I think she really liked me. I. I've been wondering if it would hurt to find out."

"It's your call."

"Alright. Yeah. Guess you can't tell me to just go for it or not too. I'll think it over." He shoved the rest of the pie into his mouth. "Thanks." She was only barely able to make that out.

The channel she had changed to was playing a cartoon. One that instead of being full of original ideas, instead copied an already popular one. Harley figured this out as the theme song was playing.

"OY Kids are you ready for an adventure?!"

The prerecorded sound of a bunch of children agreeing played.

AAAAAAARGH!

This is the show WITH the yellow round thing!
He's yellow and round and he's yellow and round!
Oh what adventures await when you do anything!

Does whatever he wants to, adventure abound!
He'll be singing and swimming and eating pound by pound!

He's a yellow thing that's round!
He's a yellow thing that's round
HE'S A YELLOW THING THAT'S ROUND!

YELLOW THIIIIIIIIIIIING!

THAT'S ROOOOOOOOOOUND!

AR HAR HAR HAR HAR HAR!

"Alright fuck that noise." Harley said, turning off the TV.

♥ - *Chapter 22* - ♥

"Anyway!" Annie had spent the last forty-nine minutes telling Harley everything she had gotten up to during her time abroad. "I learned a lot of things and boy do the boys still know how to have fun over there."

"Glad you had a great time." Harley said "It's nice to finally catch back up with you.

Annie's trip had ended just a short while ago, but she'd been so busy keeping up with her missed class work that she hadn't had the time to talk until now.

"Yeah well you'll have to wait even longer for me." Annie said "Today I have to meet with every single fucking one of my professors." She sighed. "I've done all the work they assigned to me for the abroad program, and now, now I have to meet with them all in private for separate lectures and special assignments. I'm glad I went because I'm never travelling while in school ever again."

"Wouldn't have known 'til you tried."

"Exactly. Anyway, don't want to be late. Peace out." Annie picked up her backpack and headed out the door.

Harley went to her computer, finishing up a few pieces of homework she needed to get done. It was due on Monday, and it would be nice to have the full weekend to herself.

After a few minutes of homework time, her phone rang. According to the ID, it was Max.

"Hey!" She said, her happiness as genuine as it was sudden.

"Is this a good time?" Max said. There was a slight bit of anxiety in his voice. "To uh, to do the modeling thing?"

"Oh fuck I forgot about that! Sure Max, I have time."

"Oh, great. Thank goodness, this is the first time I've been free in a month! Just come over as soon as you can. I have a lot of pictures I need to take, so, yeah anytime is great. See you soon."

Max had hung up. Harley placed her phone back on her desk, taking a little bit to think something over. Max had not said if she should do anything to look her best. Realistically, she was now going to be a temporary amateur model. She was sure Max found her attractive after nearly three sexual encounters, but these were pictures for the world to see. She should do something else.

Having little make-up of her own, Annie had let her know long ago that she could borrow any cosmetics she wanted. She walked to Annie's side of the room, and grabbed Annie's rather impressive make-up set.

She started with black eyeliner. Normally, when Harley wore eyeliner she would try to wear enough that it could be noticed easily. She cared little for subtly tricks. Today, she only needed it for a quick reason to trick someone into paying brief attention to her eyes, so she went lighter than she ever had before. She did the same with a red lipliner.

Her eyes, however, were not done just yet. She looked around Annie's near collection of colored eyeshadow for something, unique. Being close to an upcoming fashion designer meant Harley had seen several examples of modern fashion magazines, and the models on the cover. This generation's fascination with new ideas shown through, be it whacky eye-catching jewelry or eyelids that could be painted something either than blue or green.

She found gray. It intrigued her enough to open it up, and apply it on. Hopefully the professor who received these picture would like it. She wasn't too worried on whether or not Max would like it, she already knew he would.

To finish, her nails. She glossed them, letting their natural color stay intact, while still being shiny and clean.

After her beautifying, she fluffed up her hair, checked her teeth, adjusted her breasts, and was ready to head out. She realized it was funny how when she first woke up today, she'd only chosen a quick pair of faded jeans, a white t-shirt, and sneakers; a lazy day ensemble. And now she was about to go and wear, most likely, some of the nicest clothes she'd ever wear in her entire life.

As soon as she took care of one more thing.

Harley knocked on the door to Max's room. It was not long at all before he opened the door for her.

Max looked as stunning as always. He wore a pair of white slacks, a blue buttoned-up vest over a light purple long sleeve shirt, and designer white-

and-gray socks. On his left thumb was a spiraled silver ring in the shape of what could be best described as a spiky crown, and around his neck was an HD digital camera.

"Oh thank goodness you're here already." He said "I have everything set up when you're ready."

Harley walked into Max's room. It was bigger than her's, and bigger than the one he'd been in the previous school room. Up against the back wall was a large sheet of white cloth, this was what she would be stood up against for contrast, she assumed. In a different corner of the room was a makeshift changing station.

Max took a breath out before he spoke, and it served to calm his nerves as much as he had hoped. "Alright Harls, I have a good bit of stuff for you to try on. There's a changing station over there for your privacy."

"Does it matter?" Harley said "You've seen everything I've got."

"I know, just, I figured you might still want the privacy. I mean, I would."

"I'm comfortable changing in front of you. Incredibly comfortable, really."

"Well, hey, I certainly don't mind making this go slightly faster. I'm, sorry if I seem nervous. I am. This is due in a little over a week and I've had no time until now."

"I'm sure a lot of your classmates are waiting until the night before."

"Well, they aren't me. And I'd like to get these pictures shot tonight and edited and filtered tomorrow. Oh."

Max came over to her, taking a closer look at her face.

"You dolled up." He said "Thank you, I was afraid to ask. Don't get me wrong, you're very pretty, but it's basically the rules that models have to go beyond how they look normally."

Despite not being surprised by the statement, having Max refer to her as pretty made her happier inside than she expected.

"It's no problem." Harley said "I figured that was the case."

"I had some make-up on standby just in case, glad I don't have to bother. Now, you will need from jewelry in a few shots. It looks super expensive, but, they're all adjustable costume jewelry. Little secret of mine I figured might be useful. It's like when fast food uses plastic burgers on their menu."

"Then make me beautiful."

Harley took little time removing her clothes. She was now down to her underwear, a light blue bra and panties with pink silk highlights.

Max handed her the first items to wear.

"Now, I've eyeballed your size." He said "But if anything doesn't fit, let me know. If you need help zipping anything up in the back, also let me know."

Harley slipped on the light green floral sundress Max had handed her. I went as far down as her knees, and the barely visible zipper in the back was able to get as far as a few inches below the top before she needed Max's help. It wasn't small, she was just unable to twist her arms backwards and up high enough.

"This fits great." She said as Max finished her zipping. "You've got a great eye."

"Yeah, well, they taught me that." Max said "A theater class, apparently a lot of backstage people need to learn how to guess accurately, so I took a class in costume design. Good fun, I have at least one more theatre class I'm taking next semester, and then I'll see after that. They count as part of my major."

"Sounds more fun than what counts as part of mine."

With her dress securely on, Max handed her the accessories and shoes. The shoes were a pair of platform-heeled straw-colored sandals, with numerous straps covering her feet. She was also given a large sun hat, straw-colored like the sandals. Finally, she was given a fake gold ring with a massive fake ruby, the size preferred by baronesses.

"You know, gonna admit it." Harley said "I feel incredibly pretty."

"You look it." He flashed her a smile. His worries were already melting away. "Okay, I'll just find something for you to sit on. This is supposed to be market as outdoor loungewear, so you need to look like your easing back in the sun on a nice summer day. It'll all be edited in later."

"I do get to see these photos, right?"

"Of course you do. Hang them on your wall if you like. You'll get a shitload of compliments from them."

Max found a fake rock, and carefully moved it over to the white area. He motioned for Harley to sit down. The way she was told to sit was to lean her back against nothing, turned to her right side so the camera could capture it. Her left leg was on the rock, bent at the knee so her foot was firmly planted on it. Her right leg lazily hung down, barely in frame at all.

Max snapped a few quick pictures, Harley counted three of them.

"Dammit, hold on." Max removed the ring on his thumb. "Sorry, sometimes fashionable doesn't mean practical. Okay, now, take off the hat and hold it in your left hand, and dangle it over your left leg, hat facing the camera."

Harley complied. It took her a few seconds to understand, but Max guided her when she was about to do it wrong. Max snapped two more pictures.

"Lovely." He said "Okay, we can move on to the next one now. You're looking great."

Harley moved off of the rock and removed her clothes again. She took the time to ask why Max was using a digital camera instead of his phone.

"Class requirement." He said "This camera is a little easier to filter and edit with than a smartphone, apparently. Hey, it was supplied for me, so I'm not going to complain."

Max grabbed a fluffy light gray turtleneck sweater. "How do you feel about the hipster look?"

"Oh boy." She said "This should be interesting."

"We've got this top, a miniskirt, a beanie, and a lot more accessories. We're going for the 'hottie going to the coffee shop' look."

Max handed the outfit over to her. Harley put on the turtleneck, black miniskirt, and red knit beanie. Next in Max's hands was a pair of black rim glasses.

"The lenses are real but they aren't any kind of prescription." He said "They shouldn't fuck with your eyesight but if they do I'll be as quick as possible."

"Why lenses in the first places?" Harley said, placing the phony glasses on her face.

"It's easier to spot a pair of glasses without lenses than you'd think. It looks fucking stupid. How are your eyes?"

"Pretty good. Not seeing anything different than usual."

Max selected a few finger rings from his box. A thin gold band with three pearls, a long silver domed ring with several trees inscribed on it, and what looked like a small gold chain.

"This one wraps around your finger." He said "Here, I'll help. Little complicated."

Harley was easily able to slip the pearl band onto her right ring finger, and the long silver piece onto her left index finger. She held both hands afterwards for Max. After a quick thought, Max chose her left hand, middle finger. The trick turned out that the middle of the chain touched the center of the finger, and the rest wrapped around it.

There was a weird feeling, she found, in depths of her gut. It shouldn't have affected her, but the gentle touch of his hands on hers. His touch was as soft as his kisses, and careful on her skin. She almost gulped, but for whatever reason, she held it back.

"Alright." She said "Tell me how to pose."

Max instructed her to lean up against the wall, on foot pressed up, and her arms folded behind her.

"Okay, now, come over here a bit." He said "Take your left hand and move the glasses down a bit."

"You mean, like, super sexy, or?"

"Yeah, yeah, the sexy eye thing."

She complied, and found herself enjoying the pose, when directly at him.

"Okay, you can have some fun now." Max said "Do what you want, spontaneity. Give my professor your natural beauty."

This made her smile, hearing him say that. He smiled back at her. She never forgot how good that made him look, and she sure was happy to see it again.

"Oh! I got it." She said

Harley took both of her hands, and cupped the inside of her breasts with her palms.

"Yeah I can guarantee you they won't allow that." Max said

"Okay then, how about just one pic for myself?"

"Sure. You want the added backdrop?"

"No, I think the natural backdrop is good enough for me." She wanted the background to remind her of this time in his room.

She smiled as Max took her personal picture. Once he was done, he told her she could remove and prepare for the next look.

"I'm not entirely sure which to do next." He said "Sorry, I just need a second."

"Take your time." Harley said "This has been fun."

"I'm glad you think so. It hasn't been bad for me either."

After short deliberation, Max picked out her next pieces. A long poodle skirt, a short jacket, and sneakers.

"Okay." He said "Rebel 60's look. Sort of. I'll be honest, this is one of my least favorites, but shit like this still works so we might as well do it."

Harley began putting the jacket on. "Did you make any of these?"

"No." Max said "All borrowed from the department, but they are my styles. I haven't been able to work with any of my own stuff yet, I haven't been chosen. Apparently very common, usually only juniors and seniors get their designs made."

"Makes sense to me, but I've seen your stuff, I think they should consider."

"You and me both Harls. Okay, turn your cheek."

Max snapped several pictures of Harley in her "rebel" outfit. There was a lot of sitting, fake anger for the camera, whatever seemed to give her attitude.

"Okay." Max said "I think we need a break."

"Fuck yeah." Harley said "Can I have some water?"

"Oh, yeah. Sorry, I should have offered."

Max turned to his fridge as Harley removed her outfit. She carefully placed it with the others, and then grabbed the water from Max.

"If it's all the same to you." Harley said, taking a quick drink. "I think I'm going to stay in my undies for right now."

"You sure?" Max said

"Yeah." Harley said "I'm already sick of putting clothes back on. I'll just hang out almost naked until we start up again.

"Alright then. Hey, um. Can I say something real quick?"

"Sure. I'm guessing it's a compliment?"

"Well, yeah. I like that uh. I like your taste in panties. I. Look, when you work with models you see fucking black bras and panties almost every day. It's so nice to see something different. Give me the name of the designer if you can, I really like the work they do."

"Will do."

Harley sat up on Max's bed, her water already drank. She kicked her legs around as she waited. Max looked through his fridge for something for himself. He settled on a lemon-lime soda.

"Would you like a cupcake?" Max said "They gave us some after a runway show and I don't know if I want all of the ones I got."

"Fuck yeah!" Harley said "What kind?"

"Triple chocolate." Max said "Um. I can look for a bag or something for you?"

"Worried about me getting it on my clothes?"

"Not so much right now, but you'll stain your teeth and that's a nightmare for picture taking."

"I'll just grab it before I leave."

Max sat on the bed next to her. He turned to her, giving her one of his amazing smiles, which as always, she returned.

She also decided to take this time to do something she hadn't done enough, look directly into his eyes. It had been his eyes that made her want to know him last year, and she was practically relearning their charms all over again.

She decided to use her own. Flittering them around for his sake. To give him something to look at, and, to say something without words.

"Aright." Max said "I getcha."

He leaned in to gently kiss her. Their lips pressed together, wet with a quick passion.

"You lipliner tastes really good." He said, just inches from her mouth after they had finished. "As does your mouth."

"I think yours tastes better." Harley said "If I'm being honest."

Harley ran her finger down Max's sides.

"Do you want me to even the playing field?" She said, biting her bottom lip ever so slightly.

"That would be perfectly fine with me." He said

Harley slowly unbuttoned Max's vest and pants. She did not work as slow when it came to removing them, leaving him in his green boxers. She continued to run her fingers over his sides, then moved them onto his chest.

"Sorry I don't have any muscles for you." He said, smiling. "But I hope what I do have feels good."

"You've got more than enough." Harley said

It was true, he lacked defined pecks or abs. However, he was a healthy thin, fit all the same. Any small amount of fat still in him proved to be fun to play with.

She pressed her breasts up against his chest.

"Sorry I don't have any muscles either." Harley said "But I think that may work out for you, here."

"I have no complaints."

"Tell me. When we first had sex, you told me you weren't sure what I'd let you say about my boobs. You have my permission to tell me what you were really thinking."

"Well, it's a little, different, now. In case you can't tell, they're bigger."

"Trust me, I know. Have a feeling you're happier about it than I am, and I'm not exactly upset about them."

"Let me think. Oh, yeah. I remember. Going to show how old I was last year, but all I was thinking was how much I wanted to touch 'em."

"Well then."

Harley took both of her hands, and let her bra gently fly down onto the bed.

"Go for it." She said

Max took a bit to figure the exact way to approach. In the end, he simply took his left hand, and gently grabbed her right breast.

"Whoa." Harley said. A slight surge she was not expected eased through her body.

Max scooched over, and placed his other hand over, cupped both of her breasts. Gently moving them around, sometimes taking his thumb and rubbing her nipples.

"Holy shit." Harley said "This is really good."

She was unaware she was sensitive. Not only was Max the only man to play with her chest, she had never done so either, he was in the fact only person to make her fully aware of how good her breasts could make her feel.

"Can, I put my face on them?" He said

"Yeah." Harley said, moving his face onto them herself.

After a moment, she could feel his tongue emerge, licking her cleavage and eventually moving to her right nipple. She came close to making a noise.

"Fucking hell." She said "Don't stop this is so good."

He continued for another minute or so, before looking up to catch her eyes in his.

"Too bad I didn't come prepared." He said "This is fun, but it's all we'll get to do."

She flashed him a cheeky grin, and she moved to her discarded purse. She unzipped it, and pulling a condom out between her left index and middle fingers.

"I know us too well." She said, placing the wrapped condom up against her lips. "And don't worry, I brought more."

He leaned up to kiss her, the condom barely in the way of their mouths. He continued to fondle her as she unwrapped the condom, and removed his boxers.

Before running the condom down his shaft, she took it by the hand, and gave it an upwards lick, from ball to head. She felt him quiver against her tongue. Once she had slid the condom down, she pinned him against the bed.

"Remember last time?" She said "I still want to be on top."

"You're more than welcome." He said, moving his hands back onto her breasts. "Just let me grab on so you don't fall."

She had to give him one more hard kiss, before they fully moved into position.

Max and Harley, still absolutely naked, were sitting on the edge of Max's bed.

"Wow." Was all Harley could say.

During the act, a new surge had gone through Harley's body she had not felt before. A sort of pitting in her stomach that moved her entire body. A rumble, something she had always felt the build-up to, and had now finally felt the full force of.

Max had given her an orgasm. Her body was still in the aftermath.

"Are you okay?" Max said, taking a careful and empathetic look at her, not knowing she was far from troubled.

"I'm great." She said, barely able to contain herself.

"You look like you're crying. Are you sure you're okay?"

"I'm amazing. I came."

"And, you're crying?"

"A little, I think. That was really fucking good."

"You were great too. It was hard holding in near the end there. Hell, it was hard holding in at the beginning. If this had been the first time I think I would have jizzed before I'd made contact."

Max looked over at the clock. "Ah fuck!" He said, as they had made love for thirty-five minutes. "We're going to be here all night."

"Well." Harley said, batting him an eye. "*I* thought it was worth it."

He chuckled, and gave her a tiny smile from the side of his mouth. "Alright, fair point. Time well spent."

"Besides, I don't might staying here all night anyway." She found herself, pausing, before the next thing she wanted to say. "If it's alright with you, I could spend the night here."

"Really?" Max said

The last time this was offered, Max ended up turning it down. Harley waited to see if it would be different this time, and she was hoping it would be

"Yeah, yeah that would make this easier. Won't have to worry about when you need to get back."

They looked at each other, deciding there was no need for more words. After that, Harley found her eyes going down. She had been sitting in a wet spot, and it only occurred to her now to look at it. This cold stain did not bother her, she simply wanted to see for herself what it was.

Next to it was her hand, and next to her hand, was Max's. Max pieced this together as well, and they quietly motioned their hands together. They held their hands for a short while, looking only at their shared grasp.

Harley wasn't entirely sure what she was feeling. It was, nice, more than likely more than that. She didn't let go until Max needed to get up. He slid his clothes back on to start on the next part of his homework.

Harley looked over to check her phone. She had gotten a text she wasn't aware of, from Annie.

"Yo where are you?" It said, sent over forty minutes ago.

"Sorry." She replied. "I'm a little busy with someone. I'm gone for the night."

After only seconds, she got another text from Annie in response. "You sly dog! See you tomorrow. :3"

Harley got up to put her underwear back on. By the time she was finished, Max had picked out the next outfit.

For whatever reason, she gave him a quick kiss on the cheek before getting ready for the next shoot.

♥ - Chapter 23 - ♥

Harley woke up next to Max that morning. It was now Saturday, her need to wake up was minimal at best. As she had awoken first, she got to watch his eyes open after her slight movements managed to wake him.

It did not take them long to realize how close they were to already naked.

Max was now fully dressed. He wore a long sleeve white shirt under a white buttoned vest, and a light gray tie. His slacks were light purple, and his designer shoes were a combination of all three colors. He had showered and brushed his teeth while Harley had simply stayed in his room, still naked and bidding her time.

"So, what are you going to do now?" She said

"I have to bring the camera to the lab and take care of the pictures." Max said "Wish I could stay and chat, but I really should take care of these as soon as possible."

"No problem." She said "How long will that take?"

"Most likely, all day."

"Oh."

When she had first gone to sleep the night before, she had begun to believe they might be able to spend a good portion of the day together. Be it sex, talking, anything they would normally do when they hung out.

"You uh." Max said "You, think you might want to do something when I'm done, you mean?"

"Well. I did." Harley said "But it sounds like you might not have time now."

"Yeah. Yeah, I was thinking that. I mean, at least we did a lot yesterday. I really made you cum?"

"Hard!" She said, spirits restored from the memory. "I think I was still kind of feeling it afterwards."

"Oh. You sayin' I should have fingered you afterwards or something?"

"No, I don't think that would have done anything. Thank you very much for the after-the-fact offer though."

They stood there, now suddenly, awkward.

"I. Guess I should put my clothes on and head back." She said

"Yeah." Max said "Um, like I said. That was amazing. Oh, and, thank for so much for helping me out with this project. I'll get you the first copies as soon as I can."

"Looking forward to it."

Harley slid on her clothes, and headed out of Max's door. She began the walk back to her room, and found she was walking very, very, slow.

Harley opened her front door, not all that surprised to see Annie sitting in a chair up against the end wall. Once the door was closed, Annie spoke.

"So how'd it go?"

"That was the best I've ever had."

"Way to go Harley!"

Annie jumped up, almost about to hug her, then refusing at the last moment.

"I think I'll wait until you've had the chance to shower." She said

"That would be the right call."

"Man he did a number on your hair. I'm surprised you can see with how messed up it is. All of that from last night."

"Hm? Oh no, he brushed my hair back in place afterwards so we could keep going with the photoshoot. Totally forgot, this is from this morning."

"You had sex with him this morning as well? Twice in a row!?"

"Yeah. We just woke up, looked at each other, next thing we knew we had a quickie. Sure you know what I'm talking about."

"Actually. No. I've never just woken up and decided the person next to me was going to have a quickie with me. I always just, get all hot and we cuddle for a while, normal stuff."

"Huh. It was, pretty natural here. We just, really liked being in each other's arms and, sex just happened. Felt like the way to start the morning between us."

Annie seemed to think over what Harley was saying. Her flamboyancy and general bounciness, was, lowered, when she spoke again.

"Huh. Okay then, I, guess that's just how it worked for you. Anyway, you should work on that shower."

Harley looked over in the mirror, wanting to see how bad a shape she was in. Her make-up was smeared, she hadn't removed it as well as she thought, and she hair truly was all over the place like Annie said.

"I need a haircut." She said

Harley was sitting in the barber's chair, she planned on only getting a trim. She'd been getting her hair slightly long since the fifth grade, after she stopped liking the pixie cut. It still needed to cover her ears, but she did not want it past her neck like it had been.

Under the smock she was required to wear, she was wearing a red blouse with short sleeves, blue capris, and white sneakers.

The barber was a man, older than her by at least eight years. He wore a black button-up shirt, grayish blue jeans, and brown sneakers. His hair had two colored streaks on the left side just above his ear, the bottom on blue, the upper one gray. The rest of his hair was simply black.

"Alright." He said, barely seeming to care. "Long short?"

"Just past my ears." Harley said "I don't want anything radically different, just a little shorter."

"Suit yourself. I guess this will only take ten minutes."

The barber was fairly quick in his snipping. Harley felt no hurry in what he was doing, he was just naturally good at cutting hair fast.

"Alright, tell me." He said, monotonous as earlier. "What are you studying? That kind of thing. If you want to talk that's the best I can care about."

Harley told the barber her major, her plans for the future. He barely commented.

Harley considering telling him about last night, that maybe it would convince him to at least say something interesting. However, it caused another thought to enter her mind. Maybe he'd say something useful, something to help explain the weird feeling in her head since she had left Max's room.

It didn't matter, because after a few more minutes, he was done.

"Nice." Harley said, seeing herself in the mirror.

It was as short and as long as she'd requested, and there was a small layering job to ensure her hair would not tangle as much once it started growing out again. This suited her very well.

"Great, fantastic." The barber said "Now we'll go to the counter, and we go back to our lives."

Harley and Annie were playing poker in the middle of their room. It was Annie's idea, and unfortunately for her, it was also the day she was learning the rules.

Even more unfortunately for Harley, Annie was a fast learner and skilled player.

"Fuck you." Harley said, losing the sixth pot in a row.

Annie laughed. "We need to play this all the time."

"No we fucking don't."

"Uh huh, and the second I lose you'll be saying the exact opposite."

They played halfway through the next hand before someone knocked on their door. Harley placed her cards face down, and answered the door.

Max.

"Hey." He said "You uh, you forgot your cupcake."

Max handed her a large chocolate cupcake, covered in thick chocolate frosting, with noticeable hard crunches of sugar. Harley did her best to not drool.

"Thanks!" She said, taking it from him.

And then, another silence.

"It's uh." He said "No problem. Like I said, wanted to get rid of them. I mean, too many for me."

Why was she struggling to think of something to say?

"Yeah." She said "I can tell. I. It looks big, I bet you had too many of them."

Max scratched the back of his head with his hand. "You know, we should uh,"

That was as far as he got, before he just plain stopped talking. Annie had been watching the whole thing, Harley took a look back and saw her. For her, she looked, slightly sad.

All Harley could think of was two words.

Say something.

"I, guess I should go." He said "I haven't finished the editing yet. Again, you'll get your copies first."

"Yeah. Yeah, great." She said "I'll see you soon, okay?"

"Yeah. Real soon." He said, and gave her a friendly wave goodbye.

Harley slowly closed the door after watching him leave down the hall. She went back to her seat on the floor, and looked at the cupcake.

She love cupcakes. She was heavily fond of the young man who gave this cupcake to her.

So why, did this feel exactly the same as when she was sad? She couldn't be sad, but it felt exactly like it.

She took another look at the cupcake, and then buried her face into it to eat it.

Annie only looked at her.

"Don't judge me!" Harley said, nearly spitting globs of chocolate frosting all over the room.

♥ - *Chapter 24* - ♥

It was after Christmas now. Harley was wearing a light purple sweater with a snowman and snow sewn in, a gift from her father. She was also wearing a pair of red slacks, something she had bought herself. On her feet was a simply pair of gray sneakers. She was headed to the mail.

Inside were two more presents, both addressed to her.

"Ooh!" She said, immediately taking them.

She was not surprised she got the presents themselves, only how fast she had gotten them. They were from Annie and Janie, whom she had added to her Christmas list this year. They returned the favor.

She took them inside, figuring which she should open first. Janie's was a smaller box, wrapped carefully in red paper with elves and trees. She must have tried extra hard, Harley had admitted to her how much she loved the holiday around a month ago. Annie's box was larger, and the wrapping was nearly a disaster. However, this suited her personality just fine, and in all honesty, if she had wrapped it perfectly, Harley would have been terrified by the unexpected twist.

She started with Janie's gift. A small bronze band ring with swirly and curled designs, and an onyx stone in the center. She slid it on her right middle finger like a glove. She admired it for a short bit before opening the next box.

Annie's gift was a collection of children's fantasy books. A series Harley had read as a kid, and had once mentioned to Annie that she'd wanted to go back and reread them for years, only to remember the copies she read belonged to the school and she didn't actually have her own copies.

She carefully placed the books on her bed, deciding she could start the first one later, after school started up again. As for what she'd do today, originally, she was stumped on what to do, but her trip to the mailbox inspired her.

She opened her dresser drawer, and grabbed her pair of gray jogging pants. Removing her slacks and replacing them with the jogging pants, she decided it was just cool enough outside to enjoy a nice jog.

She went to the kitchen, only to see her brother and the dog.

"Hey Will." She said

"Hey Harls." He said "You're going for a jog?"

"Yeah. Want to come?"

"Was just about to ask. Clive needs to go for a walk, this will be more interesting."

Harley waited for her brother to grab the dog's leash, and they all left the door together.

The three of them had been walking for about an hour. Harley noticed Will check his phone.

"Expecting a call?" Harley said

"Maybe." He said "From Sarah."

"Whoa whoa, wait." She said "Sarah who?"

"You remember her, she went to school with us."

"You mean the Sarah with the pitch black hair, blacker eyeliner?"

"Yeah. And sweetest deposition if you remember."

"Hey I didn't say I forgot that. Everyone liked Sarah, the goth girl who pumped iron and let people cheat off her homework."

"Well, she's not really goth anymore. I uh, I've been talking to her. She's the, remember what we talked about at Thanksgiving?"

"You think you have a shot with her?"

"I did, so far it's looking like I was right, really hoping I'm still right."

"Wasn't this also the Sarah with huge boobs?"

"She was. Reduction. I mean, between you and me I kind of miss them but I'll get over it."

"Really? She wasn't even that big, remind me to tell you about my art professor."

Will's phone began to ring.

"Oh fuck oh fuck oh fuck." He said, over and over again.

"I'll hold the dog." Harley said, taking the leash from him.

"You're the best little sister in the world." Will said, before all of his words were directed into his phone.

Harley decided it best not to listen in, only because it involved her brother.

"Alright Clive. You have to shit?" She said

Clive responded with no words at all, being a dog.

"Well, I'm not going to risk it." She walked him over to some bushes.

It was now getting dark. Harley had tried taking a nap on the couch, but had only managed to sleep an hour or so instead of the attempted two or three.

Will came in to sit in the chair next to her, once he saw she was awake.

"Hey. Tell me." He said

"Tell you what?" She said

"Are you okay?"

"I think so, just really tired. Do I have resting bitch face?"

"No, not that. Just. You've kind of, fallen off the radar while you've been here. It's like something is bothering you."

"Well. Kind of. I feel like I'm trying to make a decision, but, I can't fucking figure out what the decision is. Sometimes it's really clear, but it jumps away before I can think of it."

"Maybe you're lonely. I was a little lonely my first few years at college. I know you're around loads of people, but, it's a big jump. A lot of the obvious shit becomes impossible. You think doing something you should do would jeopardize everything. Like, breaking up with the woman you don't even love anymore. …. That kind of thing."

"Hm. I haven't even been dating. I mean, okay, I have been sleeping with this guy but we're not dating."

"Do you like him? Aside from the sex thing?"

"He's great."

"Okay then. I told you before, you do what you want, just be careful. If he's a great guy, sounds like you're doing the smart thing, or, I don't know, something I don't need to give a shit about. I guess that's your answer."

Harley tried to figure out what he meant. That it was okay to value a friendship while being intimate? Perhaps. She remembered what Chad had said last summer had bothered her, maybe she needed someone else to tell her the opposite, as superficial as that seemed.

"Care to give me any big brother advice?" She said

"Well, I guess one thing." He said "If this guy means a lot to you, make sure you always feel that. Treat this like it needs to be treated, and I'm not you, so I can't tell you what that means. Any help?"

"Yeah. Yeah, I think so. Thanks Will. Love you."

"Eh love you too shithead. Have a nice nap."

♥ - *Chapter 25* - ♥

It had been two days already since Harley had returned to school. She was sitting at her desk, she had just finished up her homework and was listening to music. Harley was wearing a button-up purple blouse with dark lines running down the side, and a white frilly skirt. On her head was a gray skullcap, and her shoes were Mary Janes of the same color.

Currently, she was alone. Annie's classes were not going to start until tomorrow, so in her own words, she was taking the time now to "get other shit done" before heading back, as all of her belongings were still in the room from last semester.

After three rather long songs, Harley took out her headphones and stood up to stretch. Now that she was up, there was something she remembered she wanted to take care of.

She headed over to a box of hers, and opened it. Out of it, she took the finished picture from the photo shoot. Seeing it for herself, Max was a talented photographer. He may have been a better artist and fashion designer, but his photography skills were nothing short of impressive to her. He made her look beautiful, even doing something as stupid as cupping herself in a sweater while wearing fake glasses.

Damn the rules, she was hanging this on her wall. From what she heard, there wasn't a single RA who actually enforced the rule anyway. She had gotten it framed, it deserved to be in a spot where everyone could see it.

Just after she had finished, the door opened. Annie walked in wearing a short light green dress, and black high heels. On her right index and middle fingers were blue rings, simple bands, most likely plastic or hard rubber. On her left wrist was, of all things, a watch. Nothing expensive, just a brown band and a blue face, but the time was at least accurate.

On her head was some kind of wrapped towel. She'd had her hair dyed again.

"What's up?" Harley said

"So much!" Annie said "Check this out!"

When Annie removed her towel, she made some sounds that phonetically would have looked like "ah ba ba!"

It was short, almost pixie-cut, and two colors. The front was bright blue, the back a bright pink. Small spots of the opposite color were found on both halves.

"What do you think?" Annie said "Am I wild or what?"

"You look like this cotton candy flavored yogurt I used to eat as a kid." Harley said, without any trace of insult.

"You know, I can see that." Annie said "Anyway, you have any classes later?"

"Nope."

"A'ight! Here's the plan. I'm taking you to a movie."

"Sure, sounds fun."

Annie spotted the framed picture on the wall. "Oh my God, you look gorgeous in that!" She then walked over to it for a closer look.

"I know, right?" Harley said "I'm getting a whole list of things I know Max is great at."

"Yeah." Annie said "Hey, you think he's busy?"

"Don't know. Max has classes like you and me but they're more sporadic, he has to spend a lot of his time as mock fashion shows and shit like that."

"Call him, see if he'll go with us. Three people is fun."

"Hm, alright. Hope he doesn't mind."

Harley dialed the number into her phone, it rang a short bit before he answered. "Hey Harls. How are you?"

"I'm good, was just admiring your work actually. Hey, do you want to go see a movie?"

There was a mix of surprise, and, stutter, in his voice. "Uh. I, yeah, um. Are you, is this uh. How many people are going I mean?"

"Annie's idea."

His response now, will not fully sounding like disappointment, seemed to have a slight air of it. "Oh, okay. Yeah. Sure, sounds like fun. Did you mean now?"

"Yep. Is it a bad time?"

"No, no not at all. Um, meet you in the parking lot?"

"Sure, we'll go in my car. See you in a few minutes."

"Yeah, you too. I'm, happy to do something."

Harley ended the phone call. Looking over at Annie, she seemed to be almost beaming. Not odd for her, all things considering, even if a little out-of-place considering they hadn't even left yet.

The three of them were now standing in front of the movie theater. Annie was staring down the movie list, deciding almost randomly what the three of them should see.

Max was wearing light blue, a color Harley had once told him he looked great in. It was another designer sweater, different patterns than the last. This one was closer to a shirt, while still having the fluff of a sweater, almost like a short-sleeved sweatshirt without a hoodie. There were white diagonal lines on the ends of the short sleeves.

His pants were designer jeans, comfy and more practical than most of his other clothes, yet still dazzling on him as far as Harley was concerned. They made his butt pop out more, and she was now realizing this needed to happen more often. His shoes were simply white, with hints of green and red to stand out.

Harley also noticed, his hair seemed more brushed and combed than normal. Considering how good it normally looked, only someone who'd seen his hair as often as Harley would notice it. She appreciated the effort, even if in the back of her mind she wasn't sure why, or why he bothered in the first place.

"Hey!" Annie called over to them. "I got one, starts in ten minutes. Let's get inside."

Annie practically walked Harley and Max into the theater with her. As the movie was her idea, she asked and paid for the tickets. The group then immediately headed to the concessions. Annie picked out a chocolate bar.

"So how much popcorn should we get?" Harley said

"Um, huh." Max said "It depends I guess. I want popcorn so I guess I'll buy one."

"I want popcorn too, so maybe we can just put our money together and get one of those big tubs." Harley said

"You know." Annie said "I don't actually want any popcorn. The two of you can split one."

"Alright." Harley said "Fair point. You know what, Max I invited you here, I'll cover you."

"Really?" Max said "Thanks that's, nice. You sure?"

"Hey don't let a nicety go questioned, you know?" Annie said "Just eat the free popcorn."

Harley bought herself and Max a large popcorn, while Annie paid for her little chocolate bar. The three then found their way over to the theater number printed on their tickets.

"WOW!" Annie said after entering, there was not a soul in sight besides the three of them. "I've never seen it empty like this!"

"How long until it starts?" Harley said

As if he was thinking the same thing, Max was already looking at the time on his phone. "It's, oh, three minutes, wow. I don't think anyone else is going to come."

"Well if they are." Annie said " I say we pick our seats now."

They had been sitting in the second row, watching the movie for twenty minutes now. Back when it had only been five minutes, Harley had figured out the movie was completely garbage. She felt a few gentle tugs on her right sleeve, Annie was trying to get her attention. Once she had, Annie made Harley slouch herself over incredibly close to her.

"I need to change my tampon." Annie hushed "I'll be right back when I can."

"Alright." Harley said "I'll be here."

Annie stood up and left the theater, much less quietly than she whispered her bathroom reason.

"Where is she going?" Max said, also whispering.

Before answering, Harley looked around. She spoke at a normal volume. "She's going to the bathroom. Don't bother whispering, there's still fucking no one here."

"Alright by me I guess." Max said

Harley went for some more of the popcorn. Max had already placed his hand in the bag as well, this had happened several times. They'd quickly adjusted to moving their hands around so they could share the bag, absolutely nothing awkward or inconvenient about the situation.

"I'm glad you came with us." Harley said, followed by a mouthful of popcorn. "Would have been a lot more boring with just the two of us."

"Glad I could help." Max gave her one of his smiles.

It was all Harley needed to realize a conversation with him would be far more riveting than this terrible movie. Frankly, it would be more riveting than several okay or even good movies.

She thought of a few topics. After a while, there was on major thing she knew she needed to ask.

"Hey, Max."

"Yes?"

"Tell me about yourself."

"Hm?"

"Like, I know a lot about who you are, what you're like. I know your major, the way you laugh, all great stuff. What's your story? Why a fashion designer? What makes you tick? I feel kind of, dumb, for not knowing any of this by this point."

Max continued to smile. "It's not your fault, not even a problem. Hell, you want to know, alright.

"So, I grew up kind of average, I guess. Income wise I mean, I'm from a small middle class family, just my mother, father, and me. My aunt from my father's side used to live with us, but I'll get to that. Do you want to know the fashion thing first or can I keep going?"

Harley said "Keep going, sounds like you're leading up to something."

"Yeah, but it might not be all that interesting." Max said "I grew up next to a farm. I don't like farm work, as I found out when we would do them a favor, but they were nice folk. My aunt had an affair with the man of the house, didn't know that until just before college. It explained why we always got free milk.

"Anyway, it's a shame he had to leave after the divorce, but I did kind of like this wife more than him. She used to cut my hair. God, I should show you some pictures, my hair used to be so frizzy. Like, I don't think I ever had an afro, but I came close, I had to have. It still curls in the humidity, but you've seen that."

"I like your hair now." Harley said "But the curls are very cute. As is your outfit. I know you like the nicer stuff, but this simple stuff is very cute."

"Yeah, I, figured you might think that." He seemed, embarrassed maybe, when he said this. "It's nice to be understated sometimes anyway, and, you've mentioned to me a few times that this works. I thought, I dunno, it sounded right."

"Did you date much in high school?" Harley had no clue where the question came from, but she asked it anyway.

"Yes and no." Max said, and this time he was without a doubt embarrassed. "I uh, I've not always been as great with being forward as I would like, or, sometimes even just talking when it comes to some situations, but, mostly, you know what I mean. But, that wasn't always a problem since I did get asked to a lot of girl's choice dances and shit like that. Like I told you before, I have a lot of experience with kissing."

"And it shows. I didn't peg you as the awkward type."

"Well, I'm, not entirely sure that's the right word. Also, I, around you I'm a little easier flowing. Something about your blunt and forwardness, didn't feel like I could screw up by talking to you."

"Not ever?" Harley raised one eyebrow.

He looked her in the eyes, and seemed almost sure of himself. "Yeah. Ever."

They continued looking at each other for the next few seconds.

"I." Max said "I, I just uh. I, I'm sorry this movie fucking sucks."

"You can say that again. At least until Annie comes back, we can break that news to her later."

Their eyes shifted back to the film, begrudgingly, considering it only proved to get worse and worse.

Annie came back after three more minutes. There was a bit of toilet paper stuck to the bottom of her shoe. In her hands, was a bag of popcorn. She went back to her seat.

"I thought you didn't want popcorn?" Harley said

"I changed my mind." Annie said, still whispering "What did I miss?"

"Max was just about to tell me why he became a fashion designer." Harley said

Now on the spot once again, Max turned to both of them. "Oh, right. My family won a lottery."

"Huh?" Harley said

"Four hundred thousand dollars." He said "The three of us got one hundred each, and the final one got put into emergencies and part of my college fund. With the extra money, I did what I'd wanted to do since I was about eight, and I finally bought designer clothes. A few years of that, and, well, I realized I actually wanted that to be a part of my life. Here's hoping it pays off soon, the career is a lot of money and it'd be nice to help pay my parents back a little for the funds. And buy shit for my friends, you know, something I kind of forgot about after the lottery."

"You know that's very determined." Annie said "And quite noble too, wouldn't you say Harley."

"Yeah, I guess so." Harley said "A bit fancy to put it that way, but, yeah. Dead on the money."

Max smiled a little.

Someone in the movie promptly died, and Annie was the only one of them to give a crap about the loss of fictional life.

Harley was opening the door to her and Annie's room. As nice as it was to spend time with her and Max, Harley was happy to no longer be at the movie, and immediately went to her bed to lay down and continue reading the first of the books Annie had bought her for Christmas.

"So what'd you think of the movie?" Annie said

"Fucking terrible." Harley said

"I meant the outing, sorry, not the movie movie. What'd you think of that."

"It was nice hanging out with the two of you."

"Well, I wasn't exactly there the whole time. I did end up giving you and Max some alone time you know. Was that fun?"

"Of course it was, Max is a great guy."

"You guys talk about anything?"

"Yeah." Harley closed the book now that they were clearly having a conversation. "Yeah, just, chatted aimlessly until I asked him about his life. It was, really nice. I don't know, I guess Max is the kind of guy to make his past sound really cool."

"Mm-hm." Annie said, almost passively. "Well, yeah. Sounds like a good trait."

"It is. He's, something else. It was really nice to just, talk with him. Spend some time with him for no real reason."

"Great! Next time I won't even show up, promise me."

"Alright?"

Harley laid back down to continue reading the book. It almost sounded like Annie sighed, but Harley could not tell what kind of sigh it sounded like. She simply ignored it, there was enough confusion that surged through her mind lately.

♥ - Chapter 25 - ♥

Harley had a special class today, one she was looking forward to. Fate had decided to smile on her this semester the same way it had her first. She and Janie were in the same class together. Harley was in fact waiting for Janie to arrive so they could head out together.

Harley was wearing a white t-shirt, with a pathetically small pocket in the left breast. She had no clue what could possibly put inside the pocket, but she liked the feel of the shirt regardless. Her pants were olive green capris, and her shoes were light blue flats with small holes to see the slightest hint of her toes. On her right middle finger was the onyx and bronze ring she'd gotten for Christmas. She figured Janie would be glad to see her wear it, although she also assumed Janie wouldn't actually say so.

There was a knock on her door, and not a doubt in her mind who it could be.

"I'll get it." She said, as Annie was at her desk and was not yet aware Janie was coming.

Harley opened the door, and saw Janie clearly had a similar thought when she dressed herself this morning. She was wearing the cute little dress Harley had bought for her, along with a pair of ridiculously dark purple jeans. Harley didn't know what shade of purple it was, and that Janie probably didn't care enough to know either. If it crossed her mind, maybe Max or Annie would know.

In the belt of the dress, securely in place, was Janie's e-cigarette. There was also a patch of gauze taped to her left cheek. Thanks to a picture message, Harley already knew this tattoo was a spider web.

"Alright, let's get going." Janie said

"See you later Annie." Harley said before leaving, closing the door behind her.

They two of them walked down the hall, and out of the building. After a while, they reached a small area with grass and a couple of trees. It was meant as a relaxing area for students between classes, like a cheap version of stress relief.

"Hey." Janie said "Let's stop here for five minutes."

"Why?" Harley said

"Class doesn't start for ten minutes." She said "It doesn't even take one minute to get there. I don't want to be early."

"Alright, fair enough. Just don't lose track of time. I try not to be tardy."

"Neither do I, I just also don't want to be there before most of the class. It's creepy and I get kind of bored."

Harley looked around the small yet pleasant area. She and Janie did not talk while they waited here, they only stood there, quiet and as serene as they could be.

Harley noticed someone else close to them, someone familiar enough to her.

"Hey Izzy." Harley gave her a friendly wave, inviting her over it she so wished.

Izzy complied. "Hey here. Oh, hi, don't think we've met."

"Jane Olber." Janie said

"Izzy Platt."

Izzy was wearing a thin pink shirt that ended above her bellybutton, revealing its multiple piercings. There were also two rings in her left eyebrow. Her jeans were simply dark blue.

"So, what's up with you?" Izzy said

"We're just waiting to head to class in a few minutes." Harley said "History of industrial technology."

"Oh, shit." Izzy said "Same here. I just transferred into it."

Harley noticed Janie move her eyes down to Izzy's breast, and then sport a small yet satisfied smile. She clearly enjoyed no longer having the smallest chest in the room. Room of course being relative when outside.

"You know that guy?" Izzy said, pointed her Harley's shoulder with a look.

Harley turned around to see her old RA, who for some reason had the compulsion to walk over to her. Unlike before, he didn't hide it under a façade, he has mad from the start.

"Have any of you seen my girlfriend?" He said, just barely non-hostile.

"No, sorry." Harley said. She remember said girlfriend from the year before and onward. Mostly around Josh, as she had no classes with her.

"I don't even know what she looks like." Janie said

"Hey, shut up." Josh said "Look Harley, you fucking sure you haven't seen her?"

"Yeah no, positive." She said

"You better be fucking honest with me Millsboone." Josh said "I was your fucking RA. If you think it's okay to lie to me, I may not be your RA anymore but you still have to respect me."

Janie was apparently more sick of him than anyone else Harley had known. She punched him right in the face.

Josh wasn't hurt all that badly, his ego was bruised harder than anything else. But he still wobbled off, holding the side of his face and trying to not let anyone see that he was crying.

"Fucking creep." Janie said

"Should you have done that?" Izzy said

"I'm going with yes." Janie said "Anyway, come on, asshole's almost made us late for class."

Harley and Janie were walking back to Harley's room. She needed to prepare for her other class today.

"It's nice having another class with you." Harley said "It's been a while."

"Yeah." Janie said "I guess so. I honestly prefer seeing you without a professor involved."

"Then I'll head to the club with you again sometime."

"Door's always open as long as I'm working."

"Still, I do hope we have even more classes together before this is all over."

Janie stopped walking. It took Harley a few seconds to notice.

"Oh." Janie said "I forgot to tell you."

"What?"

"I'm on a two-year plan."

"Oh. Well, are you at least on track with it?"

"Yeah, yeah. Thanks for worrying, but, don't worry. I'm not an A student but I don't fail classes. I will graduate in a few months."

"Congratulations."

"Thanks. I mean it, thank you."

The two continued walking to Harley's room. Once they were at the door, Janie began to say her goodbyes.

"Yeah I'm not going to get in bubbly's way. I'll see you around."

"You too. Hey, I turn 21 this year, maybe we can do something at a bar. Or I can buy us some beer and we chill at your place."

"Fine by me. Love ya Harls, see you later."

Janie turned and walked away. Harley let herself breathe a little bit before entering her room.

"'Bubbly' huh?" Annie said "I think she wanted me to hear that, too."

"Maybe." Harley started preparing her supplies.

"All shit aside, how was your class?" Annie said

"Good. I met up with your friend Izzy, we're all in that class."

"Cool, at least someone there is nice."

"Oh, and Janie punched Josh in the face."

Annie was clearly trying very hard not to smile. "Doesn't mean I like her now."

♥ - Chapter 26 - ♥

Harley and Annie were sitting outside, behind a tree that was behind the soccer field. Harley was wearing a new blouse from her mother. The middle was pink, from collar to bottom, and the sides were white. To separate the color changes, there were vertical white frills. It felt comfy and breezy on her, a perfect new thing to wear. Her bottom was a pair of blue jeans, with a flower stitched into the left leg. It was a replacement for an older pair that no longer fit, bought from the same store.

In the collar of her shirt were her pink-rimmed sunglasses, just in case she needed them later. Her shoes were a simple pair of gray sneakers. On her left thumb was the black heart metal ring Annie had bought for her, and on her right middle finger was the bronze and onyx ring Janie had bought her.

Annie was wearing a yellow blouse with purposefully made tears. The left strap was in place, but there was no right strap, and her light green bra was visible from an angle. Her skirt was a mix of blue and pink, like her hair, and also torn apart at the bottom. According to her, this was Annie's "trapped on a deserted island" look. Despite the rough look of her clothes, her shoes were fancy white flats, with butterflies carved into the toes. Her new watch was still on her left arm.

"It feels weird that we're hiding." Harley said "Weren't not breaking a law."

"One, force of habit." Annie said "Two, this is a great place when there's more than one person. See the view?"

Harley turned her head to see the overlook. It was admittedly very pretty, but she saw little point in that. Roughly any overlook would probably look the same.

"Try staring out into it when we're done here." Annie said, grabbing the weed from her backpack.

"I've heard it doesn't always work on your first try." Harley said

"Pfft." Annie said "Whatever Harls. I know it kicked me when I first did it, so it should work for you too. This is the good stuff."

"I just can't believe you're not busy today."

"Hey, the second you told me this was your birthday, I called off everything I had. I've barely been seeing him anyway, and if he has a problem with me hanging out with you instead than it's guaranteed that I'm ending it."

Annie handed a marijuana joint to Harley, directly into her mouth. She lit it for her, and instructed Harley on the correct way to puff. Instead of sharing, Annie made a separate one for herself. She wanted it to feel like an actual birthday gift, instead of just something she had to split.

Harley had taken a deep breath, and held exactly as Annie had told her. And then, nothing.

"Um." Harley said "What am I supposed to feel?"

Erika Ramson

"Just keep going dude." Annie was laying on her back now, many small clouds had already circled around her. "You'll know."

Harley continued smoking pot. She could swear nothing about her felt different. She took a look at the overlook again, deciding she may as well look at something. Somehow, the sky and the grass combining together seemed, far more pleasant than it did before. A peaceful scene, the air gently brushing against her face. She was doing nothing, and yet, the feeling of content flushed around her.

It was okay that the weed wasn't apparently doing anything to her, as far as she could tell.

"So," Annie said "when does your friend get here to pick us up?"

"In, fuck." Harley said, someone losing track of mind. "Um. Twenty minutes."

"Great, plenty of time to blaze it up."

Annie offered more drugs to Harley now that she was finished.

"What about you?" Harley said after a long drag.

"Nah." Annie said "I just wanted to clear my head a bit before *she* shows up."

"I thought you promised not to complain." Harley said

"She's not here, that means I'm not complaining. Besides, that's the point. If I'm a little at ease, I think I can handle drinking with you two. It's your birthday, I'm willing to look past her being kind of, well, okay that would be complaining if I finished that sentence."

Harley decided to just ignore Annie and go back to gazing at the sky. The sky never looked so peaceful. She should have been bored, but, the activity was alright with her. At least it did something, she was still wondering exactly what marijuana was supposed to do to her.

Janie had driven them all over to the bar. The intention was for Harley to get drunk, and since Annie did not even own a car, Janie had it covered.

The three of them were sitting at a table, at roughly equal distance to each other. Janie was wearing a lot of black. She had a slightly low-cut black t-shirt, not low enough to reveal a neckline, and over that was a thin black jacket with short torn sleeves. Her jeans were black as well, although a shade lighter than her shirt and sneakers.

A waitress came over to take their order. She was dressed the part, a nice green t-shirt cut lower than Janie's, and grayish-blue jeans. A nametag was supposed to say her name, but it was smudged and faded. On her left hand were two black rings, for her middle and ring fingers. Both simple but shiny bands.

"Uuuuuh." Harley said, craning her neck back instead of turning around.

"We should get bread." Janie said

"Why?" Annie said

"Because Harley's 21, and she'll need a sponge."

"Oh, right, yeah." Annie gave a big fake smile, trying to prove she hadn't completely forgotten how alcohol worked.

"Um." Harley said "Yeah, bread. Breadsticks, um." She trailed off. "I don't know."

The waitress noted her eyes. "Alright, breadsticks. Will there be anything else?"

"Get her a shot of that buttery stuff." Annie said "You'll love it Harley."

"I need to see your IDs." The waitress said, and the three girls confirmed.

"Okay." The waitress said "Brunette, you're good. Technically I can't give you the drink unless you actually ask for it though, sorry blue-pink."

"Okay…." Harley started rubbing her eyes. "Whatever the buttery stuff is. What did you say exactly?"

"Close enough, I'll be right back ladies." The waitress walked away to get their orders.

"You okay?" Janie said

"Hey, of course I am." Harley said, now no longer touching her puffy red eyes. "Just uh, I dunno. Tired?"

Annie had a little giggle, and after that , Janie seemed to figure out the problem.

"What's so funny?" Harley said, and then giggled herself. "Now you got me laughing."

"Just how much did you give her?" Janie said

"Hey I gave her enough." Annie said "It's the good stuff, she'll calm down after some drinking."

"Don't expect that to take long." Janie said "We've drank together, she does not have enough experience to be a heavy drinker."

"Uh-huh." Harley said "And what are you taking about? I'm not even high."

"Whatever." Annie said smirking "I think the waitress is coming back to us now anyway."

Sure enough, their waitress appeared with breadsticks and a shot of buttery-flavored liquor.

Harley took a breadstick and took not too long to eat it. Neither Annie nor Janie even started on them.

"Alright girl!" Annie said "Slam it!"

Harley shrugged her shoulders, took the shot, and drank it. "Hey that's not too bad."

"Alright, my turn." Janie said "Order a rum-cola. I think you'll like it. Just get a single."

"Alright." The step in Harley's shoe was now coming back. "I'll take a rum-cola. Single."

"Coming right up darling." The waitress said

Annie and Janie took a breadstick, followed by Harley.

"To save some time." Harley said "What would you two recommend after this?"

"Whiskey sour might be up your alley." Janie said "I mean, granted, it's up mine."

"Take a vodka shot!" Annie said "Oh! See if they have any flavored kinds!"

"Maybe she should have some more bread first."

"Hey, look, Harley can handle herself, it's her 21st. Let her run loose!"

"Yeah well I'm not a fan of cleaning up vomit."

"She's not going to throw up!"

"The way you're pumping her full means she will!"

"Why don't you fucking shut-"

"Hey." Harley said

The other two looked straight at her.

"Calm down, alright?" Harley said "It's my birthday. You can hate each other all you want some other day."

Instead of playing nice, the two just stayed silent from that point onward. Harley was happy, it was close enough.

The waitress came back with the rum-cola.

"Thank you!" Harley said "Now I'll also take a shot of vodka and a whiskey sour."

Harley let out a loud belch. There were no more breadsticks, and two of her glasses had been accidently knocked over. They were already empty by that point, being emptied in fact being a factor to Harley accidently knocking them over.

"I love you guys." Harley said, belching again.

"Mm-hm." Annie said "And we love you too."

The waitress came back, bending over to pick up all the empty glasses. Harley ended up catching the fact that she wasn't wearing a bra.

"Nice nips. Sorry…" Harley said, slapping her cheek out of embarrassment.

"Uh huh." The waitress said "For being drunk I'll give you a warning, say it ever again and my wife will kick your shit out. 'Kay?"

Harley nodded.

"Alright, time to pay the bill." Annie said

She and Janie begrudgingly worked together to make up the money. Annie was handed every dollar Janie had to pay, and she tried giving the sum directly to the waitress.

"Look, again." The waitress said "Probably can't legally do that, has to count as her paying me."

Janie and Annie both sighed.

"Fine!" Annie handed the money over to Harley.

Harley had to stare at it a little bit before handing it over to the waitress.

"Drive safely." The waitress said, taking the money and heading to her next patrons.

Harley belched again. "Who was driving me home again, I forget."

Janie and Annie walked Harley back to her room.

"That was fun you guys." Harley slurred. "We need to, do that again."

"Maybe." Janie said "Not much time left."

"It's only Feburarly." Harley said

"The semesters are going by faster now." Annie said "You get used to it and it just speeds by."

"Well," Harley said "I'd like it if this one didn't go by so fast. Okay, who wants a kiss?"

Harley walked closer to her friends. Janie effortlessly pushed her back, hand directly on face.

"If we're going to kiss I'd wait until you're both not drunk, and at the club." Janie said "Would probably get a raise if I made out with you in front of everyone."

"Yeah and I'm good." Annie said "Thank you for the offer."

Annie unlocked the door, and Janie bade Harley goodbye. Harley walked messily over to her bed, leaning up against it once she got there. She spotted a pile of papers on Annie's desk.

"What's that?" Harley pointed to the pile.

"My V-Day letters." Annie said "I get a lot from old boyfriends. Most just saying hi, some of them do ask to take them back. I got one from my new guy though, looking forward to it."

Annie began sifting through her pile of love letters. She stopped after seeing a specific one.

"Hey!" She said "This one's yours!"

Annie handed over the envelope to Harley. Harley's name was written on it clear as day, not a smudge or mistake in sight. She opened it up to find a birthday card. A nice yellow card, a few balloons drawn on it from the card company.

She opened it.

Happy Birthday

-Max

"Aw!" Harley said "Max wished himself a happy birthday. Wait, that doesn't make sense."

"That's nice of him." Annie grew a little smile "He thought of you."

"He did." Harley said "I'm gunna go thank him!" She then left the room.

"Hold on!"

Harley was now banging on Max's door. Annie was trying to tug at her arm.

"You're wasted, not the best time dude." Annie said

"Whatever, he gave me a card, I should thank him." Harley said

Max opened the door, clearly not expecting anyone. "Oh, hey Harls."

Max was wearing a short-sleeve black collared shirt under a purple vest. Around his neck was a white tie, the same color as his slacks. His socks were a clean white.

"I got your card." Harley said "That was a nice thing."

"Oh, thanks." Max said, almost blushing from the look of it.

"Can we come in?" Harley said

"Uh, sure." Max said

Annie stifled a hard sigh.

Harley and Annie walked themselves into Max's room. There was someone else there, a young man around Max's age. He wore all black, a well-fitting t-shirt and slacks. Around his waist was something similar to a thin black see-through skirt, and around his neck was a dark blue boa. He had dark blue eyeliner under his eyes, pointing outwards. Nothing on the upper side of his eyes.

"Who are you?" Harley said, although she burped out the last word.

"Clyde Feathers." He said "Art-fashion major. Max and I were supposed to work on a few projects together. The idea was two single guys wouldn't be doing anything today but if I'm wrong I'm wrong." He immediately pulled out his phone and started playing a game.

"Oh." Annie said "We shouldn't stay then, you sound busy."

"I, would kind of appreciate that." Max said "The both of us get a little busy."

"I just wanted to say thank you anyway." Harley said "You and Clyde can do whatever. But thank you for my birthday card."

Harley tried walking backwards during this, and that caused her to lose her footing. Annie tried to grab her, but Max ended up getting to her first. Simply grabbing her hand and pulling her forward.

"Wow!" Harley said, smiling like a goof. "You're real strong."

"Not really." Max said, having a hard time looking her in the eye after the compliment.

"Nah! I'm a hefty girl, you didn't even had to try."

"Again, not really."

Harley buried her head in Max's chest, almost giggling. She closed her eyes. Happy and content.

Then her eyes bolted open, she pulled back, and put her hand over her mouth. She swallowed what had happened, and that was enough to almost entirely sober her up.

"I should go, nice to meet you Clyde."

Harley and Annie were back in their room. Harley was starting to breathe a little heavier.

"Okay!"

Annie rushed to her with the trashcan. She removed Harley's rings and placed them both safely on the desk, while Harley leaned over the can. Annie held her hair as the vomiting commenced.

♥ - Chapter 27 - ♥

Harley was laying upright in bed today. It was a nice March Saturday, the perfect time to finally finish up the book she'd started reading at the start of the semester.

To accommodate her relaxing, she wore a simple white t-shirt. Her bottom was a short, thin, and flowing blue skirt. She wore no shoes or socks, but her aqua-marine sandals were by the door for when the bathroom trips would happen.

Despite the laid-back and relaxed nature of her outfit, there were a few things she did above that. Her nails were painted, a cute and bright yellow. It radiated a sunny calmness, perfect for her attitude of the day. In her ear were small purple gemstone studs. They were a gift from her brother during Christmas. He'd been so embarrassed from the gift he'd given it to her in private instead of in front of their parents.

They were subtle additions, that added a lot despite having no reason as she wasn't going anywhere. She'd spent enough time with Max that dressing nicer felt fun. Although she could never style half as good as he could.

She was just at the start of the final chapter when she heard the door open up. Despite the fact it was the weekend, Annie did still have classes. She walked in the room completely overworked and tired, and it clearly took a lot for her to refuse the idea of just crashing onto her bed.

Annie wore a beautiful lavender and bright green dress. While not a vintage dress, it was close to the rough shape of one. Two straps, no cleavage, all the way to her feet. The green was the majority, while the lavender was the colorful spiral circulating around the entire ensemble. Her shoes were shiny black high heels. There was a small red hairclip getting her bangs out of the way, and she was currently double-checking her watch.

"Hey Annie." Harley said, putting the book down. "How's the class going?"

"Not bad, but they sure are long." Annie said "I only have about twenty minutes to talk, I'm getting a sandwich before I head to my next one."

"I've been meaning to ask, what's with the watch? It's super cute."

"Thank you! My dad bought it for me. It's not a secret I kind of act like an airhead, so my dad figured I might as well have something that hints at my intelligence. It's also a lot more useful than I thought. Who fucking knew? I seriously thought phones were better, but this watch kicks ass."

"Hey, whatever works."

"How's the book?"

"Great! It's a lot like I remember. How did you find the collection anyway?"

"Okay, so here's the thing. This series, not popular. Like, didn't see much hate for it, but not popular. I found that thing at a used book store for ten bucks."

"No joke?"

"Uh-huh. They listed it on their site, ordered it, picked it right up the next day. Said they were holding the complete collection copy for a while now. Two years or so. Glad you enjoy it."

Annie turned to grab her purse. A nice blue little thing, many pockets on the outside. She hadn't brought it to her first class, as everything was provided for all the students, but now she was going to need her money.

"Cute nails." Annie said "If you want I could paint little daisies on them for you."

"No, but that does sound cute." Harley said "You just worry about getting lunch."

"Yeah. Oh, so spoil it for me, what's the book about?"

"It's this underwater story with a bunch of mermaids and shit. The main mermaid befriends this frog who can magically live deep in the water, and they solve a bunch of mysteries and have huge adventures. Oh fuck! I just remembered the third book. It had this pollution subplot, it's super nineties. Fuck, I think a seagull raps to them or something."

"Yeah, now I see why it never caught on."

"Hey, it made it to five books. I'd say that's good enough. I kind of like the friendship between the mermaid and the frog, though. Something about them seems nice, like real friends. Like you and me."

"Do they become anything more?"

"No, not that kind of story."

"Hm, well. Maybe that's why. People like stories where the friends fall in love. Granted, there are times that is what should happen."

"Yeah, I guess so. Makes sense."

Annie flashed a little smile. "Take care sweetie. When I get back we'll order pizza and talk about boys."

"I'm game."

Annie said another goodbye, and quietly headed out so Harley could keep reading.

Sadly, her neighbors did not decide to be quiet in their new activity.

"Oh fuck me! Fuck me! Fuck me! Fuck me!"

She could hear them even louder than the bedsprings.

Harley banged on the wall and shouted "Why would you ask him to fuck you when he's clearly already fucking you!?"

❤ - *Chapter 28* - ❤

Despite their best efforts, it had been well over a month since Harley and Janie had actually been able to hang out. Today, however, Harley was welcomed back to the club during Janie's shift. Either they were going to spend a good deal of time together while partying up, or they would get as much time together as they could while partying up.

Harley decided to dress for the occasion. Her shirt was a white spaghetti strap, and over it was a faux leather black jacket, lacking zippers. Her bottom was a pair of black jean shorts, and her shoes were black heeled boots with gold chains across the front and pink fuzz on the top.

Her nails were black, and Annie had painted two electric blue zigzag stripes, with one white stripe in-between them. She offered to paint some of the strips green, but Harley did not prefer the idea of some nails being different, no matter how popular that look had become. Her earrings were large silver hoops.

Janie was also dressed in black, a button-up blouse with thin straps that revealed a sizable portion of her neckline. Knowing her, this was an outfit the company had picked out for her, but she still seemed happy enough to wear it for once. Her jeans however were faded blue, with many purposeful tears and stains. She was allowed to wear sneakers today, as her feet were not visible behind the booth.

"It's a good night tonight!" Janie said "We're packed!"

"I could tell!" Harley said, tapping her feet to the music.

"I have a break in a little bit!" Janie pointed over to the dance floor. "Why don't you have some fun for now?! I can wait!"

"You sure!?"

"Yeah! We have all night!"

Harley shrugged her shoulders, and headed out to dance.

Harley had always found dancing to be a fun time, but never exactly took the time to learn how to do it very well. This made the club more exciting, there was an appeal to being an idiot trying to dance alongside a bunch of other idiots trying to dance. She shifted her legs around, threw her arms around, bobbed her head to the music.

Most everyone else was doing the same. Some of them were waving around glow sticks, and a few more did the same with their drinks. Alcoholic or otherwise, they were often glowing florescent in color. Harley figured it was the glasses that did this, but she wouldn't have been surprised if it was the drinks themselves.

The song changed, a more upbeat track than the last. Harley decided to dance faster, as did everyone else around her. By this point, she wasn't entirely sure exactly what she was doing, she was moving around too fast to figure it out. She was making herself dizzy, but in the best possible way, she decided.

It was only a two-minute song, so she cleared her head by standing in place and breathing. A few others kept dancing, but most everyone else had the same idea. She noticed many of them took this time to make-out with their dancing partner. Harley would have to remember this should be ever bring someone special.

"Yo girl!" Harley heard from the crowd, and did not even know it was addressed to her.

"Harley!" The voice said again, and Harley turned to see her.

"Sheena!" Harley said, surprised to see her there without Damian. She was sure it was their thing to go together.

Sheena was stunning in her dance wear, blue platform heels that did not look as garish as usual. Her top was a blue and black tub top, fitting to her shape perfectly. Her bottom was a lovely slightly long skirt, same color pattern as the top, that flowed elegantly as she moved. On her right hand, every finger, was a silver band ring. No special engravings, barring the one she always wore on the thumb, the same as Harley had last seen her.

"What'sup !?" Sheena said

"Janie's graduating so we're clubbing together!" Harley said "Once she's on a break!"

"Nice! I know she had to be here, but you picked a good place to hang out!"

"Yeah! Didn't know clubbing was my thing until Janie showed me!"

"Used to say that to Damian a lot! But I guesses that's passed!"

"Huh!?"

"Shit girl, guess you didn't know! Damian broke up with me!"

"Oh!" Harley was fully genuine in her words. "I'm sorry Sheena! You two seemed good together!"

"Yeah, well he had problems and I kind of see some in him now that it's over!" Sheena said "Between you and me he's a lazy slob! Still lovable, but it can get bad!"

"Guess that's good to know!" Harley said

"I'm glad he said we can be friends still! I'm not going to dive into it, but, Damian and I went to high school together he saw a, me, that I didn't feel right about back then! Never got in his way, I'll always kind of love him for that!"

"I hear ya! I'm still friends with my high school ex!"

"Stick with that! Exs can be assholes when they aren't your friend! You know, if we're talking about these kind of things, I might as well ask! You the kind of girl who would dance my way!?"

"Sorry! Super straight!"

"Well, that's definitely unfortunate for you, and probably unfortunate for me! I know I'm good, got a feeling you are too! Looks like your friend's not bad either!"

Sheena pointed with her left hand, and Harley turned to see what it was.

Janie was up against a wall, making out with some stranger.

A smile crooked from the side of Harley's mouth. "Way to go!"

Janie guided the club stranger's hand up her shirt. She was giving him free reign of her breasts, while still also being in control of exactly where his hands were going.

"DJ's got spunk!" Sheena said "I liked her before, but since I still haven't actually met her, I guess I like her already!"

"She's a peach!" Harley said "I mean, also kind of a bitch! You can tell her I said that if you want, she doesn't give a fuck! She loves me and isn't trying to impress anybody anyway!"

"Only thing I notice right now is you clearly won't be hanging out with her right now! I've seen what she's doing, that takes a while!"

"Yeah, well I'll have to find something to do! I'm not just going to stare at her until she's done!"

Sheena and Harley continued talking for a short while. About boys, clubs, even a little about Damian and what Sheena missed about him. Music, candy, anything that crossed their minds. They ended up swapping numbers midway through the conversation.

The next song was Sheena's favorite, so she had to go and enjoy it. Not long after she did, Harley turned to see Matty trying to survey the floor.

As usual for his job, his lazily put together suit jacket and tie were on. It was funny to see such a fun place still needed its higher-ups to dress like boring professionals.

"Hey Matt!" Harley said, walking up to him.

"Oh, hey!" Matty said "You enjoying the club tonight?!"

"Of course I am! This is a great place! Janie's enjoying herself too, and someone else!"

Matty turned to see Janie and the stranger. A smile broke out on his face.

"Heh!" Matty said "Yeah, that's Janie! It's been a while since she's done that! Good to see her happy! I guess I should thank you for that, she told me about the talks you have!"

"I'm not surprised! We're both her best friends by this point!"

"Yeah! Wish she had more! I mean, I know she's trying not to, but!" Matt's gaze went over to her again. "She is great! You know, I have to admit I'm a little jealous of how she can do that! Just, jump down someone's throat! I know she said she'll go back to regular dating after school, but, yeah I'm jealous of what she can do now!"

Matt's smile was becoming more, content. He cocked his head a little, folded his arms. He was not just happy to look at her, he was happy to know her, to see what she could do.

Happy she existed.

"You uh," Harley said "ever say any of this to her!?"

"Eh...." Matty said "Maybe! I mean, no I haven't but! Maybe I will! Fuck I just remembered I'm working!"

A young woman was walking in front of them. With pink and purple hair.

"Oh my God it's you!" She said, a little high-pitched but not as annoying as that could be.

"Oh hey!" Matty said "Long time!"

"Yeah! You have an answer for me yet?! You interested?"!

"Um! You know, the thing is! I never really asked the full details! Like, you want me to get hard so you can snort off of me!? Like, is anything supposed to happen after that?!"

"No, and you don't have to get hard! If you want more, sorry, I just think snorting coke off a dick sounds cool!"

"Yeah! Actually, yeah, it kind of does! Fuck it! Harley let me know if someone does anything bad! This shouldn't take long!"

Harley agreed to keep an eye out, and Matt took the young lady into one of the executive rooms.

Harley figured the best way to keep an eye on everyone would be to head back to the DJ's station. Janie would possibly be done with her other business by that point anyway. Harley passed by many more brightly colored glow sticks and costumes. Eventually, she came across a very strange sight for her.

"Hey!" Harley said to the man. "Why are you handing out baby pacifiers?!"

"You don't know?" He said. He was carrying them all around on a tray, and had several of his own wrapped around his arms. The only other thing he was wearing was a pair of black swim shorts, not the strangest outfit she'd seen there to be frank.

"They're laced!" He said "Acid! LSD!"

"Oh!" Harley said "Okay!"

"You want one, they're free! Just trying to make people happy!"

"I think I'll pass, you'll know if I change my mind!"

Harley continued over to the station. To her delight, Janie was now done. She was readjusting her blouse.

"Caught an eye of what you were doing!" Harley said "How was he?!"

"Knew what he was doing!" Janie said smirking "Asked if I wanted his number but I didn't want it! Nice guy though, hope someone else gets him tonight!"

"Matty told me you were going to date after school! Maybe you should have taken it!"

"Nah! He was nice, but I don't think he would have been want I'm looking for! When it comes to the settling down stuff I'm kind of picky!"

Harley was going to ask more, but she didn't want to forget the other question on her lips "Hey! Is that selling handing out binkies legit?"

"Who!?" Janie went to look "Oh him! Yeah, he's here every once in a while, I fucking forget his name but he only spikes with the shit he promises he did!"

"Okay!"

"Why, are you saying you want an acid pacifier?"

"Honestly, I don't know! I've never done hard drugs, but I'm not all that scared of what I've heard of acid!"

"Well, it's your life! Speaking of that, do you remember your birthday?!"

"Um…" Harley started hiding her face "only up until a few drinks from the bar!"

"Ha!" Janie grew a big smile "Too bad, I was looking forward to the raise!"

Harley raised her eyebrow, and as Janie walked back to end her break, she blew Harley a mock kiss. The reference going completely over her head.

Harley looked back at the drug handler. "Ah fuck it!"

She walked back up to him. "Changed my mind!"

The man whose name Janie forgot handed Harley a pacifier. She placed it in her mouth, and began to suck it exactly like a baby.

It started out pretty okay.

The lights and bright colors mixed perfectly with her vision. Everything seemed even more colorful, and yet, nothing was hurting her eyes in the slightest. It was just as wild and bizarre as everything had been before, but now, she also felt a strong calming.

She noticed Matty and the young lady step out from the executive room.

"Thanks dude! That was awesome!"

"Thank you! You sure I uh, wasn't a little disappointing for what you were expecting?!"

"You kidding?! I've wanted to cut down anyway! I'd thank you more but I'm saving the really good stuff for marriage!"

Harley watched the pink and purple girl walk back into the crowd, sniffling her nose a few times. She was a gorgeous dancer, now that Harley was watching her.

She could have sworn her hair was shifting a lot more than normal.

Harley continued sucking her pacifier, and decided to get back into dancing. Letting the music envelop her into the crowd, another face like everyone else.

They were starting to melt together. Harley could feel herself getting dizzy. She looked down at her nails for something to focus on. The blue and white squiggles were a great distraction.

Until they resembled little mouths. Fangs spread out, clawing up to her face. Ready to rip her flesh to drink her blood. She held back any sort of scream.

But now the floor was swirling together. Swallowing many people's feet. Harley closed her eyes, and when she opened them, everyone was safely dancing again. She braved looking at her nails again, but the tiny mouths had already started their eating with the back of her hand.

She backed up over to the wall, almost crashing into Sheena on the way.

"Hey baby you okay?!" Sheena said

And Harley could not find the words to answer her. Only the shivering and shaking.

"Oh fuck!" Sheena said "Come on, we're going to DJ!"

Sheena hurried Harley over to Janie by the arm. The speed of the journey did not help calm her down, but the fast way was the best thing Sheena could muster for her.

"Hey, DJ!" Sheena said

"Only special people get to make requests!" Janie said, animosity as strong as ever.

"You're friend's tripping bad." Sheena showed her Harley.

"Ah fuck." Janie said, then turned to the crowd. "I have to bug out everybody. Back in a few." She gave her shift to Matty to take care of, and the ladies headed into one of the VIP rooms.

Harley was sat down on the couch. Her eyes were bugging wildly, and she was keeping her hands as far away from her body as she could. Janie removed the pacifier, something Harley was not in the right mind to think of.

"Thanks." Janie said, trying to be nicer.

"Can you handle this?" Sheena said

"Yeah, I think so. I OD'd on heroin when I was 16, this should technically be easier to handle."

"Alright, I'll head back out. You need me, shout. I'm Sheena."

"Great, whatever. I mean, yeah, I'm Jane."

Sheena bowed out of the room, letting Janie and Harley alone to try and deal with the bad trip.

"What do you see?" Janie said

"My nails are trying to eat me." Harley looked up "And you're melting. Now you're on fire! Janie you're on fire!"

"No, no I'm okay. Breathe out Harls. I don't think this will last too much longer."

Harley did as instructed. While the visuals on her hands stayed, Janie no longer melted before her eyes.

"Okay." Harley said, sounding calmer. "What do we do now?"

"I guess we should talk about something. Anything to get your mind off of it."

Harley searched her head for a question. The only one, was a recent one.

"What do you think about Matt?" Harley said

"Matt's great. I told you this." Janie said "He's, one in a million."

"So, like. Do you think he's special?"

"Very."

"You'd date him?"

"Eheh." Janie was scratching the back of her head. "Well, yeah. Yeah, I would. It'd be, weird though, I've. Never had anything that serious, and I can't imagine having something with Matty that wouldn't be serious."

"That's good. Do you think he likes you?"

"I kind of doubt it, but, well it wouldn't be that much of a surprise and I'd be happy about it."

Harley looked over at her hands. She did not have as many imaginary gashes as before, but the mouths were still chomping down on her.

"It really hurts." She said "I can feel it."

"Hey, hey, look at me." Janie said, and Harley obliged. "It's just a bad trip. You're perfectly safe. Do you want to go home?"

Harley nodded her head. "I drove here. Will you keep my car safe?"

"Security is tight here." Janie said "Don't worry. I'll drive you home in my car."

Janie carefully helped Harley up off of the couch. Once she had, Matty entered the room.

Harley tried not to scream at the fact Matty looked like his skin was peeling off in bloody chunks. She decided to close her eyes hard.

"So, what's exactly happening?" Matty said

"Harley's on a bad trip." Janie said "I'm driving her home."

"Uh, hey. Wait just four minutes, I'll sign out and give power over. You can keep her happy in the back while I drive you back."

"Really?"

"Yeah. Yeah, that looks like a bad one. You should focus on her, I'll focus on the paperwork."

"You're a sweetheart."

Janie's eyes shifted downward. Even in her current state, Harley could tell Janie had never called anyone "sweetheart" before. Matty's expression mirrored hers almost perfectly.

"No, I'm uh." He said "Just a decent guy. Eheh. Again, four minutes, promise."

Matt and Janie were carefully moving Harley towards her room. The trip was not over just yet, and Harley was not sure if the worst was yet to come. Every step introduced fear, that something might pop its way out of the floor, walls, or ceiling.

Her hands and nails had returned to normal, but she could still vividly remember the imagery. The possibility of it coming back was all too real for her.

She had trouble unlocking her door, all of her fingers fidgeting to no end. Janie took gentle control of her hand, and took the key from her. With the door now open, Harley was gently pushed into the room.

Annie was in her pajamas, a white t-shirt and purple fluffy pajama bottoms.

"Uh," Annie said "what are you doing here?"

"Harls is on a bad trip." Janie said

"Oh. Oh, okay. Here, I'll help her into bed."

"Yeah, sure. Just don't get in the way."

The other three set Harley down on her bed, sitting. Matt took the time after to loosen and remove his tie. Harley watched him, and to her, it was looking like it was moving on its own.

"Ugh." Harley said "Do you think I can sleep it off?"

"Maybe." Janie said "I had to sign in, so, I can sleep in here with you."

"Okay." Harley said "But, I don't want to hit you if I see something."

"And you're not sleeping with me." Annie said

"Cool, cold ass floor it is then." Janie said

"If you need me, I'll be in the car." Matty said

"You sure?" Janie said "You can head back home if you want."

"No, no I'm fine." Matty said "Just let me know when things subside."

"Okay. Just, be careful." Janie almost found herself blushing, from what Harley could see.

Harley leaned back, not wanting to see anything else. She heard the door gently close from Matt's departure. She heard Annie crawl into bed, and Janie squeak the floorboards from laying on them.

Harley's eyes closed.

Her dreams were vivid.

She found herself on a giant plate of spaghetti. Nothing harmful to her, she figured maybe she was just hungry. Even in the dream, she realized it had been several hours since she last ate. The spaghetti began a little dance, one that was interrupted when they all lunged for her.

Harley jumped out of the plate, never crashing into a floor. Spaghetti following her, until, they no longer existed.

Bright white blared at her from the bottom of the endless chasm. She could feel herself resist the urge to cry, to scream.

The bottom of the pit now revealed itself. Red.

Red fires, red spikes, blood. Monsters formed themselves from the blood. Savage clawed, frilled giant monsters. Most of them, lizards. Alien in their design. Something Harley could eventually no longer process as familiar.

They all crawled to her once she finally landed. In this dream state, her legs had shattered from impact, the blood and gore from which forming one last monster.

A red-eyed, upright beast. Crab-like claws for its two hands, two legs like a cow or a goat, in front of six more legs like ones of a giant scorpion.

It's tongue sharp as a blade, radiating heat. It's face, Harley had no comparison. Hideous, odious. It's movements, unreal. It stayed still for several seconds, then jutted rapidly, as if the in-between movements did not exist.

It lashed its great tongue again, stabbing her through the heart.

She woke up.

Nothing.

No visions, no head pain, no flushing of the eyes. She rubbed them for good measure, and looked hard at her nails afterwards. It was over. She breathed the hardest sigh of her life.

Harley looked over at Annie's bed. Annie was facing the wall, sound asleep. To Harley's amazement, Janie was in bed with her. Hugging her side, most likely without even knowing. Janie was just as sound asleep.

According to her clock, it was just now eleven o'clock. Harley decided she would spend the witching hour letting Matt know she was now okay.

All of her clothes, shoes including, were still on, so she simply headed out the door. She traveled down the hall, a skip in her step now that the horror was over. Although she eventually toned it down, in case she accidently woke anyone up.

Once outside, she needed her phone's flashlight setting. Thankfully, Matt was parked and sleeping in his car near a street light. Harley gently tapped on the door, and Matt woke up without much jumping.

"Hey." He said, opening the door after. "You're awake. You better?"

"Yeah." Harley said "How long was I out?"

"Pfft, fuck. Um. Three hours."

"Not too bad I guess. I think I know what the devil looks like now, but I'm fine."

Harley scooted into the car.

"Just wanted to let you know." Harley said "And see how you're doing. This isn't a bad school or neighborhood, but I don't think car sleeping is the best move."

"I have a gun in the glove compartment." Matty said "And I'm not jumpy when I wake up, so, no chance of shooting someone without meaning to."

"Don't think that's allowed on campus."

"It's not, if it leaves the car. Loophole, thankfully one that actually works in favor of people who aren't crazy."

"So what are you going to do now?"

"Well, I'm going to head out. I need to say goodbye to Janie first, I'm sure she's waiting for it, even if she's sound asleep."

"Anything else you want to tell her?"

"Hmph. You're persistent today. Okay, tell me. What makes you think that would be such a good idea right now?"

"I dunno. I just want Janie to be happy."

"Between you and me, I don't entirely know if I could. Or if she would want me too."

"You'll do fine."

"I might piss her off."

"Janie may have a short temper, but if she likes you half as much as she likes me, she'll let it slide. Besides, she'll probably be too tired to be pissed off."

"Yeah. I guess so. I, do think she deserves someone nice. It'd be cool if that was me."

"One way to find out."

"Yeah. But I don't think I can do that right now."

"Alright, fair enough. Let's just get back to my room."

Matty and Harley stepped out of the car, Matty locking it behind them. Harley had to take the lead, Matt did not remember the way from earlier. They were lucky in that they passed by no one. While Harley had no problem letting people assume things about her and Max, it would be different with Matty. For one, they'd be wrong. For two, it would feel like crushing Janie's heart, even if she didn't end up caring.

Harley gently unlocked the door, finding the two girls still sleeping.

"Hey." She whispered.

This was enough to wake up Janie, who after moving her hand, caused Annie to wake up. They seemed to quickly agree to not mention or think about the sleep-hug.

"You better?" Janie said

"Much." Harley said

"Which means I have to go back home." Matt said "Are you staying or do you want a ride?"

"Honestly, I should stay in case there's a relapse." Janie said

Harley could see the unpleased look on Annie's face. She immediately fixed her bedsheets.

"I'll walk you out." Janie said

"Thanks." Matty said

The two left, but it wasn't long before Harley quickly joined them.

"Hey, Janie." Harley handed her the room key. "Just let yourself in. Don't need to knock."

"Alright." Janie said

Harley flashed Matty a smile. He started to smile as well, and then, a different expression seemed to grow. She heard him mutter "fuck it."

Harley started to walk away, and heard Matty ask Janie to hold up a moment before they left. This caused another smile on Harley's one, one far more satisfying.

Harley entered her room, and pretended to fully close the door.

"What are you do-" Annie started to say, she was stopped by Harley placing her index finger to her own lips.

"I'm a dirty eavesdropper." Harley whispered.

True to her words, Harley leaned into the crack of the door to listen in. Annie simply wandered back near the bed.

"Um. Hey." Matt said "Janie, um. I know you said this kind of thing would be after you finished school, and. Maybe it's close enough but. Would you, like to see a movie or have dinner or. Do, something that counts as a date?"

Harley could imagine the smile on Janie's face. "I'd love to." Janie said

"You mean it?" Matty said "This isn't sarcasm or being nice or something?"

"I'm sorry if it sounds like sarcasm, I really would love to."

"Wow, I wasn't sure if you would. I'll do my best to be worth your time."

"I look forward to it."

Harley could hear their footsteps, and after enough of them, she closed the door for real.

"I hope whatever you heard was worth it." Annie said

"Very." Harley said "So you caved and let her sleep with you?"

"Yeah…." Annie said "No one needs to sleep on the floor. And no, you've been through enough tonight. Unless she wants you, she can keep sleeping with me."

Harley waited sitting on her bed for Janie to come back. It wasn't all that long before the door opened. Janie shut the door, and carefully set the key on Harley's desk.

"Good night Harley." Janie said

"Good night Janie." Harley said "Love you."

Janie smiled at her in response.

Harley laid back in bed, waiting for tiredness to drift her back to sleep. Janie walked over to Annie's bed. Harley decided to turn and watch the two of them, hoping they might finally start to get along.

"So." Janie said "I still sleep here?"

"Yeah." Annie said, arms folded. "Anything you need different?"

"Well." Janie took a small vial out of her front jean pocket. There was clear embarrassment on her face, Harley could tell even from the back of her head. "I, wear a facemask."

"Put it on then." Annie said "Try not to mess up the pillow. ... Too badly, I mean."

"You carry your facemask in your pocket?" Harley said

"Well normally I sleep naked so I do this to remember it." Janie said "Not that I'll be doing so tonight."

Annie cocked her eyebrow. "If that's how you sleep, I don't care."

"Too bad, I do." Janie said "Just be happy I'm not putting lotion on, it'd be all over your bedsheets."

"Ick. Alright, get the mask painted on and climb in. Oh, as for hugging me, belly or boobs are okay, but touch my pussy and I'm punching you in the face."

"Deal."

Everyone settled into bed. Harley noticed Janie almost immediately grab Annie's side once they fell asleep.

It was fruitless to hope this meant they liked each other now. However, if it meant they could put it aside because of her, that was more than okay.

Harley drifted off to a gentle nightmare-free sleep.

♥ - *Chapter 29* - ♥

Harley planned on going out to eat today. There was a small restaurant she'd heard great things about. Max in particular had recommended both the cheddar broccoli soup and the potato skins. She wasn't sure if those foods would go together, but today seemed like a good day to find out.

Her outfit today consisted of a lot of white. Her blouse, tied at the back of her neck, was white and frilly. Enough to cover her, but not spacious, and a snug fit. Her bottom was a frilly white skirt, with pink as the bottom layer. Her shoes were a pair of black heels, she felt a perfect contrast.

With no pockets of any kind, she slung a purse around her shoulder. A tan one, many zippers and pockets for everything she needed. She truthfully only needed her wallet, but there was also lipstick, elastic bands, nail polish, and some coin rolls from the last time she went to the bank.

"I'm heading out, want to come?" Harley said

Annie was currently eating from a plate of rice. "No way. There's not a single restaurant in the world that can convince me to stop eating my mom's Mexican rice."

Annie was dressed in a quiet green blouse, tied above each shoulder. Her skirt was also green, with little bubbles sewn into it. Her shoes were just white flipflops.

"Hey, fair enough." Harley said "I'll be back in a few hours, probably. Don't worry if I take a while."

Harley pushed open the door, and started the way to her lunch.

"What can I get for you today miss?" The waiter was dressed nicely. His black shirt was pressed, and his red velvet vest seemed as comfy as it was stylish.

"I'll take the cheddar and broccoli soup," Harley said "the potato skins, and a cola."

"Diet or regular?"

"Oh, regular. Sorry."

"Not a problem, madam. I'll bring your order when it's ready."

The waiter left her to her own devices. Which at the table, was not much of anything at all. Eventually, she was brought her drink and some silverware.

Harley took a small sip of the cola. It tasted as she expected, but she wished there was less ice. Most restaurants put ice in their drinks, and the middle ground was not always found. Admittedly, this place did not try to stiff her with nothing but ice, like some places she had been to, but it would have been nice to just have a cold drink without ice being needed.

Her glance was brought up to the other side of the table. The empty seat.

Harley did not suffer from loneliness. She was well-adjusted with the number of people she spent time with. But now, today, she had a weird pit in her stomach realizing she was eating at a restaurant all by herself. In the back of her mind, there was this, puzzling idea. She didn't necessarily need to be eating alone. There was some other way this could have played out today, at this specific place.

The waiter brought her food over. Maybe she could think it over more on a fuller stomach.

Harley was walking back from the parking lot. It was a nice day out. Maybe she'd sit up against a tree and get some air. Her body was admittedly getting a little tired, as she had walked to the restaurant instead of taking her car.

She tried looking up at the sun, but it was brighter than she expected. Now, rubbing her eyes real quick, she caught a glimpse of something far more interesting and attractive than the sun.

"Max!" She said

She, completely subconsciously, fluffed out her hair and perked up her breasts before walking over to him.

"Hey." He said, flashing her a gorgeous smile.

Max was dressed as sharp as always. A fancy and expensive pair or gray slacks. Black-and-white sneakers, new from the look of them. A long-sleeve purple dress shirt under a lovely gray vest.

"What brings you here?" He said

"Just getting back from lunch." Harley said "I tried out that place you told me about. You were right."

"Oh, great. What did you have?"

"Potato skins and the soup."

"Huh. Funny, kind of didn't expect you to actually order what I said was good. I feel like that doesn't happen all that much."

"Hey. You have good taste, they sounded delicious. Price was alright, so, I'll experiment next time."

They chatted with each other as they walked. A new subject always found its way in. They more or less refused to run out of things to talk about.

Eventually, they reached Max's room.

"Oh, um." Max said "Did you have somewhere to be, or, do you want to keep talking?"

"I have nowhere to be Max." Harley said "I'd rather just keep talking with you."

Max opened the door, letting them both in.

"It's been a while since I've been in here." Harley said

"Yeah." Max said "Funny how I get used to it, and then I have to move out. You got your room situation handled?"

"I let Annie take care of it. We're going to room again, and well, Annie knows how to get paperwork done a lot faster than I do."

"No joke, exactly why Clyde's doing mine."

"Who's Clyde?"

"……..You don't remember…?"

"Remember what?"

"You uh, you kind of barged into my room on V-day."

Harley, for once in her life, flushed scarlet with embarrassment. "What did I do?! Did I do anything stupid?! Did I say anything stupid?! Did I do anything to you?!"

"You knocked on my door," Max said "almost broke it down in all honesty. You had Annie with you, so, no. Nothing embarrassing really happened. I kind of, didn't care all that much. Until you fell down and almost threw up on me."

"Um, yeah. Annie did mention throwing up, but, nothing about any of that."

"You met Clyde then. Clyde's a friend of mine from the fashion department. You'll meet him again in about half an hour, he's coming here so we can. Ahem, this sounds funny out loud. We're fabric shopping."

"You mean like, dress fabrics?"

"Yes! Right on the money, actually. Clyde and I met about two semesters ago, and we ended up liking each other's stuff. We're going to try and be business partners when school is over. He's a genius at make-up."

"Sounds like a good fit for you then, you're a genius at clothing style."

"Hey, and design too. Eheh. But seriously, next year all the fashion majors have to focus on mock and real runway shows. Me and Clyde pairing up meant we could think about this early. We all also have to move into his special dorm building, and you need roommates, so again, Clyde and I pairing up early is great. He understands personal space as much as I do. And is almost as clean as I am."

"Hope that works out. I've heard you don't always know until it happens."

"Clyde's good people, we should be fine. Next year will be good for our work as well, he doesn't have to focus on the art part of his major, he did almost all of it already."

"Art? He's a combined major then, that's cool."

"Very. Oh! Oh, my God. Um. Okay. I'm not entirely sure I should show you this, but. Okay, no, I need to show you this."

Max moved over to his laptop, opened it, and started moving to a specific site.

"Okay, um." Max said "Before I show you this, um. Eheh. Okay, with you I guess there's not need to hide that I uh. Sometimes have to go online to look at. Um."

"Porn?" Harley said

"Okay, yeah. Here's the thing though, I'm not the one who found this, a friend of Clyde's found this and showed it to him. It's not my kind of thing anyway, and it's not actually, even, and, okay I'm sorry I'm over explaining but it's really something that should be explained before you look at it."

"Okay. Go on then."

"Um, you know cam girls? Like, the idea."

"Yeah. Show your boobs to a webcam for money."

"Okay, good. I'm not calling you dumb it's just, I actually didn't learn about them until a few months ago. I tried watching and, it's kind of dumb and almost creepy. And, well, this one didn't help matters. Just sit down."

Harley did as asked, sitting down in front of the computer. Max pushed the play button.

"PROFESSOR ANGHULA!" Harley said

"Yep….." Max said, already looking away.

"Hey friends." Said Anghula.

"Why would she call us her friends?" Harley said

"Art has evolved since the days of original man, our concepts and our own evolution has created many styles and methods."

"Oh. She's, doing teaching on the side? On a, porn site?"

"And the canvas can sometimes be our own bodies, to the best degree."

Then Anghula's top was removed.

"Okay I'm done!" Harley simply slammed the laptop shut.

"I think you lasted longer than I did." Max said "Like, you know from experience I like nice tits and all. But, fuck. First day I met Anghula I decided there was a threshold."

"Any idea why she's in the cam girl thing?"

"Normally I would say salary when it comes to a professor doing another job, but. Okay, Anghula's weird, she might just do that for fun now that she can't get fired, so she's doing the risqué stuff online that would get a few eyebrows if she did it in class."

"I wouldn't be surprised. I also wouldn't be surprised if this makes her popular."

"Or if she'll let students watch it in her class as some weird art project. Clyde says she'll sometimes show these art movies her and her boyfriend make. They weren't porn, and I'm hoping it stays that way personally. I don't want to see those two bone."

"I think tenure can be broken in extreme circumstances. The cam girl thing might not count but if doing legit porn doesn't than I suddenly hate tenure."

Max sat down on the edge of his bed. He breathed out, already trying to get the image out of his head.

Harley couldn't help but noticed his handsome qualities already. She too was trying to get rid of the image, and replacing it with Max was a good idea.

"So." Harley said "How long until Clyde gets here anyway?"

"Uh." Max said, looking at his phone. "Twenty-five minutes. He's punctual, so, I'm not expecting him to be late. Still plenty of time if you want to make out." He hid his face. "Hang out, sorry. Fuckin'. Honestly did not mean to say that."

"Making out sounds fine too." Harley smiled at him. "It's not like I wasn't also thinking it."

She sat next to him on the bed. They looked into each other's eyes. Max's, beautiful as they were, seemed more awkward than usual. The eyes of a man who thought he just said the wrong thing. Harley could only imagine her eyes were trying to tell him it was perfectly alright.

"So, uh." Max said "What do you actually want to do?"

There was his smile again. Harley thought back on all the things Max had done for her. Between simple smiling, oral sex on her birthday, letting her be on top and making it the best time of her life. She knew, whether on top or on bottom, she had always been the one really in charge of the sexual encounters. Maybe it was time to let him have the chance, and all she had to do was do unto him what he once did unto her.

"Would you like a blowjob?" Harley said

"Uh." Max said "Eheh. The thing is, yeah. Just, um. I've kind of never expected to get one, I mean. Blowjobs sounded like a thing the more dominant guys got, and, between the two of us I think you're the dominant one."

"I am. So why don't we let you know what it's like?"

Harley got onto her knees, unzipping Max's pants. Out of her purse, she grabbed an elastic to tie back her hair. Why risk it getting in the way?

"Um, I should just undress." Max said "I'm not going fabric shopping with cum on anything."

Stark naked on the bed, although his penis was only at half-mast. Harley removed her blouse, and the problem was already fixing itself.

"Thanks." He said "I uh, still couldn't entirely get her out of my head."

Harley looked closely at the erection. Now that it was in front of her, she realized she had no clue how to give a blowjob. She had licked it last semester, and that was as close to the experience she'd ever got.

She looked up at this beautiful face. He was worth finding out.

Harley was coughing over a trashcan. While she had not thrown up, the white contents of her mouth had been forcefully spat out. Max was rubbing her back, doing what he could to help her feel better.

It was more than appreciated.

"I'm so sorry." Harley said

"Hey. It's no big deal." Max said "The idea was you blow me, and you did. What's there to be upset about from my end. You just focus on getting your breath back."

Harley looked up to see Max's eyes. He was happy, and also worried only about her. She had tried everything she'd heard about. Breathing through her nose, working your hand as much as your mouth, and still she was one of the many women who had to spit and almost throw up.

Max was now holding both of her cheeks, gently.

"Um." He said "Maybe this is gross, but. Can I, kiss you?"

Harley gave a smile, and allowed the kiss to happen. She swore it felt better than she could have expected.

"Hm." Max said "So that's what I tasted like. Well, at least you taste good."

"Yeah." Harley said "Well, you taste good too, don't worry about that."

Max began to dress himself, and Harley looked at the clock. From the time they had started, it had only been seven minutes. Max had told her he would try to speed things up, after how many times she stopped for air. She appreciated the effort, as fruitless as it proved, and she was now simply watching him dress. Max also opened his fridge to drink a quick soda. He offered one to Harley as well.

"This might help with the taste and the smell." He said

Harley took a quick sip. "Thanks. Wow, yeah, that helped a lot."

"Hope it does for me too. If Clyde smells my cum I won't mind all that much, but if he smells it in my mouth because I kissed you, well. He thinks I'm alone in here so I know what he would think I did."

She couldn't think of a thing to say to him now, deciding awkwardness might prevail if she did. So, the two of them waited until Clyde knocked on Max's door.

Max told her she could stay there if she wanted, and walked out to talk to Clyde.

"Hey Clyde, ready to head out?" Max said

"Yep." Clyde said, and Harley heard him making sniffing noises. "Couldn't help yourself, could you?"

Harley decided this was the perfect time to open Max's door. "Nope! He couldn't."

Max jumped back, and Clyde decided that was worth a smile.

Clyde today was wearing all white, clean t-shirt and slacks. The see-through black skirt-thing he wore the first time he and Harley meet was still around his waist, not that she recognized it. Harley noticed that his face had foundation, cleverly applied, you could only see it if up close, and it completely covered his pores and facial impurities.

"Hey Harley." Clyde said

"Uh, yeah. Hi." Harley said "Look Max explained but I totally don't remember meeting you, super drunk."

"You looked like it. Oh! Hey, I just remembered where I saw your face before. You were his model last semester. The only one to actually make that fucking awful 50's stuff look good."

"Thanks."

"There's good money in being a temp model for the fake runway shows. I'd say you should consider it."

"If my schedule is open enough, sure."

Max now took interest in the conversation. "Really?! That would be, well, great. You'll look great, I got a lot of compliments about you from the class. I meant to tell you, just, it was hard to find the best way to say it."

"Wow. Alright then." Harley said "I'll see what I can do next semester."

Clyde was in the middle of giving her a friendly wave hello, when his hand instead turned to a point, towards her left cheek.

"You may want to clean that up."

Harley touched her cheek, and did not need to be told what had splashed onto it. She licked her finger and wiped it again.

"I'll see you around Harls." Max said "I-ahem, sorry I lost my train of thought."

Max and Clyde left to go shop, while Harley headed back towards her room.

Harley opened the door, and noticed in the mirror she still had her hair in a ponytail.

"Oh, that's cute." Annie said "You going to keep it like that?"

"Um." Harley said "You know what, yeah. Just until next semester, but yeah. I think that would be best."

Annie was laying back in bed. No interest in sleeping, just enjoying her free time. Maybe this was a good time to ask what Harley knew she had an answer to.

"Hey, Annie." Harley said "How do you give a guy a blowjob?"

"Well-" Annie's explanation took fifty-seven minutes.

❤ - Chapter 30 - ❤

Harley was ready for her second-to-last history of industrial technology class. This would be one of the last times where school forced her and Janie to see each other, and she planned on making it count. Today, they sat next to each other. Like school girls, including passing notes to each other. The honest truth was that they were watching an incredibly boring movie, it was the professor's idea of rewarding them for everyone's good grades.

Harley's outfit today was a nice quiet white blouse. Nothing frilly, just soft and pretty. Her jeans were green, and her shoes were black flats. In her ears were little pink hearts.

Janie was wearing a gray t-shirt, black cargo pants, and black-and-white sneakers. Harley noticed she kept her hair cleaner and tidier than Harley had ever seen it before. Janie's nails were free of dirt and chips, and she seemed, happier.

The movie ended, and the professor let them out early. Harley immediately invited Janie back to her room, and the two walked out of the classroom, across the campus, right up the stairs without barely a word.

At the top of the stairs though, there was a bit of panting.

"Okay." Harley said "Forgot, still need to take more walks." She wiped her forehead, happy to see she at least wasn't sweating.

Janie began coughing, loudly. "Fuck it!"

Janie took her e-cigarette from her pocket, and walked over to the window at the end of the hall. She cracked the window open, and tossed the e-cigarette away, to land wherever it landed.

"You okay?" Harley said, regaining her composure.

"Yeah." Janie said, throat rough from coughing "That was a good one too, black cherry and orange."

After taking a breath, they headed over to Harley's room. Annie was dressing herself.

"Hello." Annie said, sliding her cute yellow blouse with pink flowers down her head. "Oh, hey to you too."

Janie and Harley finished walking in, while Annie put on a matching short skirt. Harley invited Janie to sit on the bed with her so they could talk.

"You know," Harley said "I think we should try to do something. After the semester."

"Alright." Janie said "Fine, I think I'll have time. What do you want to do?"

Harley thought it over for a short bit. One idea came to mind, maybe a bit much, but if Janie liked it then they could spend a great deal of time together.

"Want to go camping?" Harley said

"Camping?" Janie said "Huh. Never been camping."

"There are these lodges you can rent for up to a week or so. I mean, you can rent them for longer but I don't have that kind of money."

"You're saying we go camping for a week?"

"Um. How about five days?"

"Sure. Five days in the woods sounds cool."

Harley noticed Annie casually sitting at her desk. She had yet to put her headphones in, so she had heard the conversation, more than likely.

"Hey." Harley said

"Yes?" Janie said

"Um. Can Annie come with us?"

Annie stopped putting her headphones on.

"Eh." Janie said 'Whatever. If she wants to. Yo, Anne. Did you catch that?"

Annie turned around. There was a weird mix of emotion on her face. Both happily surprised, and, a bit perturbed.

"What do these lodges have?" Annie said

"They're decently sized cabins." Harley said "These aren't the fishing lodges, if you've been to those. There's electricity, wi-fi, these really big showers that I think four or five people can fit into. Well, okay, the shitters are outhouses. Every year they say they'll upgrade but they never do."

Annie was clearly actually thinking it over. "You know what, sure. Can uh, I invite someone?"

"If we all know them." Harley said

"Izzy." Annie said

"You mean Esmerelda Platt?" Janie said "She said she knew you, hope she likes camping."

"I'll check now." Annie took out her phone and started the call.

"Well, if she says no." Harley said "It's still the three of us. We'll need to think of a time."

"Hey Izzy, how you do?" Annie said to her phone. "Hey, me, Jane Olber, and Harley Millsboone are going camping at these kind of nice sounding cabins. You want to come?"

Annie paused for the response, and then cuffed the phone to say the answer to the girls. "She says if it's the first week after school, she can make the time easy."

"Alright then." Harley jumped off the bed. "We can worry about what everyone should pay later. I'm making the reservations now."

♥ - *Chapter 31* - ♥

There were two pairs of cars for the girls' camping trip. Janie and Harley in Harley's car, and Izzy and Annie in Izzy's car. They had all packed accordingly, enough for leisure and comfort. They all had four pairs of clothes, with two extras, and all of the needed bedding and personal health items. Harley brought a fishing pole, Annie a laptop, and Janie brought art supplies. In lieu of something more fun, Izzy took the practical decision of being in charge of all the food supplies. There was a general store less than half a mile away, and a diner, and Izzy's plan to pay for all of that helped the others cover the renting fee.

They were now unpacking their supplies, keeping the chatter to minimal until they were almost done.

Harley choose her red-and-black flannel shirt, still comfy against her body without another shirt underneath. Just as the last time she wore it, it was paired with her black skort. Her shoes were brown sneakers, perfect for if she wanted to take a nature walk.

Annie wore a cute blue blouse, frills at the bottom. Her skirt matched, and her shoes were pink flats. In her hair was a large red bow, she was getting tired of how her hair looked so she was trying accessories, as she had told Harley just the day before. Janie was wearing a black top with thin straps, not thin enough to be spaghetti straps. Just an average black shirt without sleeves, to show off her many tattoos. Her jeans were very dark grey, almost black until you got close enough to see. She wore hiking boots, brown ones. They looked new, but Janie claimed to have bought them from a second-hand store two months ago.

Izzy wore a light and thin pink shirt, barely showing the bottom of her stomach. It was not thin enough to be see-through, but enough to reveal both the lack of a bra and the existence of nipple rings. Unlike the usual matching set Harley assumed people with nipple rings would have, Izzy chose a barbell for her left and a hoop for her right. They were not the only piercings in play, she'd also covered both of her ears in silver pieces, too many to identify each other, and enough to hide all of the flesh of her outer ear. Her jeans were a very light blue, with both tears and sewn butterflies all over them. Her shoes were red and strappy, with a low heel, comfortable enough as long as she didn't plan on hiking anywhere.

Most of the unpacking was now done. Harley took a quick second to sit down and catch her breath, Janie leaning up against the wall near her.

"I think one of us should go turn on the generator now." Harley said "We won't get any power until we do that."

Harley got up, cracked her back, and all of the lights came on.

"The fuck?" Janie said

Annie walked into the room, generator instructions in hand. "We have power for three days, then I have to reset it."

"Oh." Harley said "I was just about to do it. Thanks. Didn't know you could work a generator."

"I took a quick class in emergency protocol. This generator's a lot weaker than the one I worked on, but they all run basically the same. I'll set up the wi-fi now, I'm hoping it doesn't take more than ten minutes."

Annie headed into another room, to find the internet hook-up.

"Tell me." Janie said "She's not one of those 'cute and crazy but also incredibly book smart' girls, is she?"

"Yep." Harley said "Genius level."

"Of fucking course she is." Janie said "Whatever, maybe she'll be useful until the trip is over."

"I'd say so. Hey, you've got hiking boots, want to go for a hike when the unpacking is done?"

"Eh. I guess so. Smart girl's probably going to want the internet since she's the one who fixed it."

"Annie's a lot less selfish than you think."

"I don't care."

Harley did some stretches as Janie got the last of her belongings. Janie decided she didn't have to warm-up, as they weren't actually working out. Harley reminded her it might be a long hike, but Janie's attitude remained the same.

Harley was glad she decided to keep the ponytail an extra month or so longer than she original planned. Sweat had started to appear on her brow, and wet bangs were not among her favorite things. Janie, now a former smoker, did not sweat but did noticeably have to breathe quite a bit.

At first, they'd only been walking on dirt roads, but after Harley had seen this mountain, she decided it wouldn't stand in her way. Janie was neutral enough to go along with the idea.

"So while we're up here." Harley said, reaching the very top. "Have any girl talk? I figured you didn't want to say anything of the sort to the others."

"Oh." Janie's face was becoming pink. "Yeah. Um. Matty and I are, kind of, fantastic."

"You're starting to look like some silly school girl with a crush from how red your face is getting."

"Yeah. Well." Janie's normal roughness and gruffness was melting, Harley assumed she really want to make sure she got the point across on how well this was going. "I've uh. I've, never had an actually serious relationship. I mean, you know I've had one-night stands and I did go on a few dates in high school. But, nothing I ever thought was more than just that. Matt is, Matt's a serious boyfriend."

"That's good. You're clearly happy with him, it's going the right way."

"We um. We knew we wouldn't see each other for a while so. Last night we had sex."

"That's great!"

Now Janie's face looked, embarrassed. "It was, for what it was. I. Look I've always, I'm kind of scared what something might think of me. I wanted to tell you that, and, well you might have figured that out after the whole beach thing."

"Janie, I guarantee you Matty liked what he saw."

"He, didn't see anything. I. Most of the time, when I fuck, I just unzip my crotch and tell them to go from there. Only about, two guys were charming enough that I slipped down out of my pants, but no one's ever gotten my shirt off. Not even guys I've let play with them. Matt's so, different, and. Look, you know that bullshit about fireworks?"

A fond memory appeared in the back of Harley's mind. "Yeah."

"It's not bullshit." Janie said "So, enough though he was restricted, I felt fireworks a little bit. You know, he, he wanted to make it fair game and only unzipped his pants too, but." Janie took a quick pause. "He's small and it got in the way. Which sucks because I'm small there too so he fits really good. I've got a guy who respects me be being scared more than I thought possible, has a perfect dick for me, and I didn't let him see anything."

"It's okay. I've heard that good relationships make people change over time. This sounds like something he can help you overcome."

"I hope so. I think, I mean, I did already tell him, and it's not like I've said it before. That I love him."

"Wow. That's big. You know, I have to know, what's that feel like? Love."

"It's hard to explain. My chest feels funny, and I feel like, it's all okay. That, whatever the point was, it was all good. I dunno, I kind of think that sounds stupid but I can't think of a better version."

"Hm. I'm sure it's hard. When I dated Chad, I always felt, fine. As nice as he was, I could tell I never exactly got to the point where I loved him. Actually, be it random crushes or my only relationship, I've never been in love. I really don't have a clue what it must feel like, I really hope I do know it when I feel it.

"You know, I hope you do to. You deserve it, after all you've done for me. You know, there's something I think I can show you now. Just give me a moment to get a good hold of my shirt."

"You want to get naked in front of me?"

"Well, no. I don't see a point in getting naked on a mountain. But, um. Here, I have to show you something."

Janie lifted the left side of her shirt, just barely.

Thanks Harley

"That's adorable." Harley said, admiring the design of the tattoo.

"Good." Janie said, putting her shirt back down. "I was afraid you'd say you'd wished I'd asked you first."

"Nah. Hell, get me tatted all over you if you want."

"Just the one. I had to pretend you were the name of my boyfriend though, it was a quicker explanation."

"Hey, no problem pretending I was your man."

"Well, I mean. Matt was there in the room so he had to respond to your name."

Harley started laughing. After a bit, so did Janie.

Harley and Janie returned back to the cabin. On arrival, they found out Annie had gotten their internet connection perfectly, and Izzy had made them all grilled cheese sandwiches. Harley and Janie both took one, enjoying the hard work someone else did for them.

Although in the back of her mind, Harley was also happy Izzy didn't decide to also make them tomato soup. She was willing to not think grilled cheese meant 'kid's food', but only to a certain limit.

Harley asked for the laptop Annie was about to put away.

"Sure I guess so, why?" Annie said

"I want to check my e-mail." Harley said

"Let me just sign out first. By the way, this is a spare. It's not school related, this is the one I bought to personal stuff, please don't add bookmarks or anything."

"Can I still go wherever I want?"

"Oh, yeah. I have good anti-virus."

With those words as Annie left, a terrible idea sparked in Harley's head. After checking her e-mails, she turned her gaze towards Janie.

"Hey." Harley said "I'm sorry, but I think I should show you something."

"This isn't an internet reviewer is it?" Janie said "Too many of them are shit, and trust me, I've tried looking very hard."

"No, no." Harley said "But this is something worse."

"Alright you got me, now I have to see it."

The second Janie saw the face and chest of Professor Marjorie Anghula on the cam girl site, Janie's face made her look like she was little else but dead.

Annie walked back into the room a few seconds later. "Hey guys what are you watchi- JESUS CHRIST!"

"I hate her I hate her I hate her." Janie said, still looking like a corpse.

"This is our art professor." Harley said

"You had Anghula!" Annie said 'This is Anghula! My last boyfriend warned me she was doing this shit!"

"Oh, so the school does know." Harley said, nonchalantly. "Had a feeling."

"I heard she can get it counted as an art experiment." Annie said "To which the school said she can't be paid for it, or they will break tenure law."

"And she'll be even more popular." Janie said, color draining from her face even more. "Big boobied cam girl who doesn't charge."

Izzy walked into the room now. "Hellooooooo, what's this?"

Annie started hugging her chest. "Girls I love you! Don't let her think she's better!"

"Please turn this off." Janie said "I don't want to know if she does the other cam girl stuff."

"I'll take it off your hands." Izzy said "I need to see how this ends."

There were no objections to Izzy taking the laptop off their hands.

The four young ladies were settled up near a campfire. For the most part, as it was the middle of the night, they were changed into pajamas.

Annie wore a gray t-shirt, and big fluffy men's blue pajama bottoms. By this point, Harley no longer believed she only owned them from old boyfriends. Most likely, it only started that way before she decided to buy them outright.

Harley herself was wearing a nice light blue button-up pajama shirt, and a matching pair of bottoms with no buttons or ties.

Janie was still wearing her clothes from earlier, but had put on her facemask, and was currently rubbing lotion on her arms and legs. Her belly and back as well, but only when she was sure no one was looking.

Izzy wore a pink pajama shirt with polka-dots, and after asking if it was already with the rest of them, stuck with just her white and pink panties. They were granny panties, so her request seemed ridiculous after the fact.

"Well." Annie said "I guess we play a game, tell spooky stories, or do girl chat. What would you like Harley, this was your trip?"

"Fuck it, let's play a game." Harley said

"Never have I ever." Izzy said

"Fuck, really?" Janie said "Last time I checked I wasn't nine."

"To be honest." Izzy said, no regret in sight. "I ran out of other ideas."

"Alright." Harley said "I've actually never played this game, so, yeah I'm in."

"Fuck." Annie said "You're the bluntest person I know Harley, you're going to kick ass at this game. But, hey, I'm in. It beats the Sudoku and cross-words that I brought."

"Why did you bring them if you don't like them?" Janie said

"Well," Annie said, letting animosity get the best of her tone. "I thought a brain tester would be a great way to pass the time. Doesn't work when you beat them too fast."

Izzy and Harley lifted up their open-fingered hands. This was nicer than just yelling "shut the fuck up you two."

Janie and Annie followed suit.

"Never have I ever." Izzy said "And sorry if this seems mean, bad at ideas. Slept with someone I wasn't dating."

Harley and Janie put their right thumbs down.

"Never have I ever." Janie said "Snuck liquor when I was little."

Annie put her left thumb down. "And yes, I did get caught."

"So quick question." Harley said "What are the rules for my question?"

"Has to be something you yourself have never done." Izzy said

"Oh, okay." Harley said "Never have I ever, um, pierced my genitals."

Izzy put her right thumb down, and everybody stared blankly at her.

"Just got it done a week ago." Izzy said, proudly. "We wanted to start offering them, and I love being the guinea pig. My snatch took it like a pro too!" Izzy tapped her vagina, and immediately winced. "Ow."

"Hold on." Harley said "Um, were do you work exactly?"

"Oh!" Annie said "I never told you! Remember that place in the mall I got my ears pierced?"

"Yeah, of course I do." Harley said

"That's part of a local chain! Izzy's family owns it. The lady who pierced me was Izzy's older sister."

"Annie decided we needed to be friends when she found that out." Izzy said "I hope you liked Sharon. She's a sweetheart, very good with the customers. I don't pierce, like I said, I'm the test subject. I've got so many holes, I change it up every day just because I might as well. I like what Sharon does though by just keeping them all in all the time, but I like what I do better. Anyway, Annie, your turn."

"Right." Annie said "Um. Never have I ever, cheated on a test?"

No one put their fingers down.

"Wow." Annie said "We're super boring."

"Just that I'm too smart to cheat." Janie said, smug little grin appearing.

"Oh ha ha ha." Annie said "Alright Izzy, back to you."

"Alright, sorry if this sounds familiar to earlier." Izzy said "Never have I ever, been a cam girl."

Harley put her right index finger down.

The other three all stared at her in disbelief.

"Nah I'm just fucking with you!" Harley said, and put her finger back up.

"Funny as that was." Janie said "I feel like someone lying is supposed to mean the game is over."

"Eh, I guess you have a point." Izzy said, and the both of them put their hands back down.

"Fine then." Annie said "Then I say we girl talk. Any of us seeing somebody?"

"Nope." Izzy said "Mostly of my own accord, really. I'm in school now just in case we ever lose the family business. I try to only be distracted if it's very much worth it. Which I tell myself they are every single time."

"Well, I also have no one." Annie said "I broke up with my last boyfriend a little while ago. Good guy though, I could just tell it had run its course. You know how it is. Sure wish it hadn't."

"No one special in my life." Harley said "Well, I mean I don't have a boyfriend." She wasn't entirely sure why she needed to state the correction.

"I have a boyfriend." Janie said, starting to look away, blushing.

"That's nice." Izzy said "Hope he's a good guy."

"Trust me," Janie said "you don't need to hope."

"Maybe it's because I'm a little older." Izzy said "But, hey, maybe it good to think about this early on. What do you expect? Later on. Any of you getting married? Kids?"

"I'd." Janie said, actually trying to look at the others now. "I'd like to have some kids. And, well, getting married to the father, yeah. I messed around a little, but, I've always wanted to settle down and get married, have a family of my own. Teach them right from wrong. Love them."

"I don't know if I call what I do 'mess around'." Harley said "But I'd like to get married too. Two kids, just like my parents. Boy and a girl. I learned a lot by having a brother and he learned a lot by having a sister."

"Marrying sounds fine by me, I guess." Izzy said "Not too sure how much I care. I mostly just think I'm not opposed to it. Now, meet the right girl, who knows, heart might melt apart. And then adoption if she can convince me."

"I for sure messed around." Annie said "But I've been waiting for the right guy since I was ten. Sue me, I want the fairytale ending, no matter the slutty way I'm going about it."

Harley had to look twice to confirm she did in fact see Janie grow a little friendly smile from that response.

"You're getting funny Annie." Harley said

"Yep." Annie said "I'm the biggest riot that, um."

Dead silence.

"Fuck….." Annie said "Look, honestly it wasn't a joke. I want a husband when this school shit is over, or hell, at least after his school shit is over. Fuck I'll be here forever until I get my medical license. Oh, and kids! Lots of kids! I only got one brother and a kind of boring little sister I love anyway. My kids need at least one more sibling than that."

"I think that subject's spent." Harley said "Now what? We talked love, do we talk about sex?"

"If you have any good stories." Izzy said

"Okay then." Harley said, and she decided to not hold back.

She said everything she had Max and gone through. Janie and Annie had heard many of the details before, but she wanted to be vivid now. Max, to her, was wonderful, someone other women needed to hear about in full. Not out of jealousy, or bragging rights, but because it was a disservice to other women to not know just exactly how wonderful a lover he could be.

"He made you orgasm?" Izzy said "Nice. That is someone I've only had once."

"What are you talking about?" Annie said "We don't have orgasms."

"You're kidding!" Harley said "No, Annie, women orgasm."

"Honey my number is way higher than yours and it ain't happened yet." Annie said "Learned pretty quick it's a myth."

"Trust me, it's not." Harley said, almost getting offended.

"Hate to tell you then." Izzy said "I think I know why you don't stay with any of these guys. That, or you're just the unlucky kind who never gets to experience it. What about you Jane? You've been silent. It's okay if you're shy about it."

"Um." Janie was looking at the fire, her eyesight closer to the girls than before. "I squirt." She almost smiled after the words.

"Hey." Izzy said "I only knew one other girl who did that. I regretted not asking her, but trust me I had a lot more on my mind at the time. What's it like?"

Janie looked up more. "It's, pretty good sometimes. The last time it was really good, actually. Like a big release of pressure. Other times, it's kind of, awkward. Sometimes it almost, hurts. It doesn't actually hurt, I don't think, but it feels like it wants to."

"Isn't it just pee?" Annie said

"I don't think so, but it kind of feels like it on the worst days." Janie said "And, on the better days too, actually. But it doesn't smell like it, and I don't think it is. I think it's like that stuff that leaks out a little when I start getting wet."

"Hm, okay." Harley said "I can picture that now. Sounds like it makes things interesting."

"Yeah, well, yeah. It does." Janie was smiling now, but she was a few inches away from fully looking at everyone.

Then she did, and her face went back to embarrassment. "How about scary stories now?" She said

"Oh yeah!" Harley said "I forgot, I love scary stories."

"Eh, I can take them or leave 'em." Annie said "I'm a bit easily scared. And, well, sometimes that does make it better but. Okay let's be real, it's not like I'll be going to any of you for comfort if I get too scared."

"Who's telling the first story?" Harley said, looking around. "Janie?"

"Look," Janie said "let's not pretend I hang out with the girls much. I like me some scary stories but I don't have any."

"Hey don't look at me." Annie said "Scaredy-cats try to forget scary stories."

"I think I have one." Harley said "But, it's kind of dumb."

"Okay then." Izzy said "I only have one as well. It's not dumb. I'll go."

Erika Ramson

There was a simple town, smack dab in the middle of the United States. 1998. It was rural, wooded areas all over the place. These places always had one shared legend: Bigfoot. The giant, hairy, humanoid ape stalking the land. Maybe to eat, God knew what.

In this town, an opportunist realized what he could do. How could the police investigate if anyone seeing him would just claim he was Bigfoot? His name, who knows? His profession? Passion? He dressed as the monster, and was a bigger one inside. Anyone lost in the woods, he made sure they were gone.

Calling him a hunter wasn't fair, he neither hunted out of necessity or even for the sport of the hunt. It wasn't the tracking he loved, he simply just wasn't sociable enough to fake a good enough personality to trap anyone. He saw this as nothing, the only personality he needed as the faces he would make when cutting this victims apart.

Always starting at the thigh. He wanted to look them in the eye on the first cut.

A young couple and they're friends were spending a long weekend in the woods. They didn't believe in Bigfoot. It probably wouldn't have made a different.

"Whoa-ho!" Shouted Tabitha. She was the fun one of the small group. Hair extensions, drawing the eyeliner on the bottom, stretching it in a line past her cheekbones. Believe it or not, she was the one in a stable relationship.

Her boyfriend, whom many people liked to call Bones, had driven all of them. Bones was the kind of guy to were dark purple shirts, skulls or daggers imprinted on the front.

"Alright babe, calm down." He said "You can use that excitement to get the beers out of the back."

The gang, five of them in total, started unpacking their party supplies. It was just going to be a campfire near the swamp. No idea how easy it was to be watched.

Mandy, Jack, and Lyndie were the other three. Jack was the one trying to be ahead of the curb, a carrier of the then new cell phone. He gave the others all business cards with the number on it, in case of any sort of emergency. They were all there for reckless fun, but this was not an idea they thought sounded stupid.

Mandy was Jack's sister, she went wherever he went. She did not detest friends, she just figured it was easier to steal from other people's success in obtaining them.

Lyndie was a doormat, except when she was drunk. Most people becoming annoying, or irritable, or confusing when they drank, but Lyndia simply became sociable.

"Well." Lyndie said "I guess we're here. I'll uh, I'll go get the fireworks. I guess?"

"Nah." Jack said, whom always had a huge crush on Lyndie. "I can get it."

"Oh." Said Lyndie, who did not return Jack's crush but was decidedly okay with it. "I'll just sit here then."

Jack set off, crunching through the leaves.

XXXXX

It was not long before Jack had found Bigfoot. Now, laying against the wall of the hidden cabin, Jack was bleeding heavily down to the souls of his feet. The man dressed as Bigfoot simply watched him. He was waiting in anticipation for him to die.

Jack's phone rang.

Bigfoot stared at it hard. He was smart enough to realize it had to be Jack's friends calling him. No answer could be very bad. His luck with the police could not last forever, but he was not ready for the slaughter to stop.

He was, however, not smart enough to know how to use this new piece of technology.

Bigfoot picked up the large phone, handing it to Jack. With his other hand, an arrow, the head of which pointed at Jack's irises. Bigfoot's pitch black eyes showing all the evil intended if Jack answered.

Jack did nothing. He was not going to lie to his friends, and he knew that no serial killer would just let him tell his friends where he was. Let them worry, and go for the police. Save themselves and just let him pay their price.

The phone stopped ringing. Bigfoot decided to do what he would have done regardless of Jack's decision. The arrow slowly cut across Jack's bare eye. Ocular gush and blood leaked from the pool, the process was several minutes made to feel like hours.

Jack was left with neither eye, both plucked out after being torn. His nose and tongue were left, he was forced to either bleed to death, or swallow enough of it to drown.

XXXXX

Mandy was told by the others to just call Jack again. That resulted in the same. As did the third.

"Okay." Mandy said "Fuck this, I'm getting the cops."

"You sure you need to leave?" Bones said "Let's wait five more minutes."

"It's been half an hour." Lyndie said, who'd been drinking by this point. "She has a good point."

"Yeah, okay. Fair enough." Bones said "We don't anything to worry about anyway. Lyndie's of age, so I guess the rest of us can wait until after the cops are done."

"I'll be back as soon as I can." Mandy said, who then turned to privately talk with Lyndie.

"H-hey." Lyndie said "If he's hurt, tell him that, well, I do still like him for what he is. Don't let him think I don't appreciate him."

"I'll try to make that sound right."

Mandy drove away.

"Alright." Bones said "Let's move the beer into the cooler. The local cops are cool enough to believe it's just Lyndie's as long as we stay out of 'em."

"Going to be honest, don't like this." Tabitha said "I think to be safe, I'm going to look for a kitchen knife or something better. Could have been attacked by a rabid animal for all we know."

Tabitha and Bones, unable to leave his girlfriend alone after she sensed danger, walked into the kitchen. That left Lyndie alone to put away the beers, and look out the back door. It was glass, sliding. She cracked it open for the breeze, but decided actually going outside wasn't worth it. Another beer, and the fear was through out of her.

And Bigfoot was on the edge of the woods. Waiting for his chance. Lyndie rubbed her eyes, seeing for herself a hairy man-sized ape. She started to laugh, thinking she had to be truly drunk to start seeing Bigfoot. She laughed hard enough for him to walk out of sight unnoticed.

Tabitha and Bones returned with several kitchen knives.

"Alright. Let's close that door," Tabitha said "it's getting drafty. Mandy will be back soon with the cops."

"How soon?" Said Bigfoot

XXXXX

The gory piles that used to be their remains, were found.

♥ - *Chapter 32* - ♥

Harley woke up that morning enjoying the crisp country air. They had all enjoyed a nice sleep after telling stories, each one cheesier than the next. Harley wiped the crust from her eyes, and moved to her yellow and pink fluffy towel.

The walk to the shower was not far, but it was long enough to enjoy the crinkle of grass and leaves under her aquamarine flipflops.

"Oh!" Annie said, in a green towel and large brown strapped sandals. "You need it too huh?"

"Yep." Harley said

"Which one of us goes first?"

"Annie, I told you, these things are massive. They make them that way in case field trips or sports teams rent these out. If you want, we can just head in together."

"Eh, alright."

Annie and Harley headed in, choosing shower heads far enough away from each other to have their own space. They were separated by small glass panels, but they were still open, no doors, they were not stalls. This also meant they could hear each other through the water.

"You liking this trip?" Harley said

"Yeah!" Annie said "Camping's pretty alright. But, I can't say I like the fact there's snakes around here."

"Don't like snakes?"

"Not the kind that rattle."

"Ah, yeah, they can be a bitch. Just walk away if you hear one."

Harley and Annie went through the cycle of washing and soaping. It was a while before they talked again, they didn't want to waste the entire time just chatting when they did in fact need to wash away the sweat and stink from sleep.

"Hey, honest opinion." Harley said "Is my butt flat to you?"

"Now that you mention it." Annie said, taking the effort to look. "Yeah."

"Doesn't that take the piss?" Harley said "I don't mind being a little heavy, but with a flat butt I don't know what I am, I'm not curvy."

"Hm. I don't know what to say about that really. I've kind of always weighed what I weigh."

"Max says I'm plus-sized, which I buy. I'm not curvy, I guess puffy or hefty. I'm not chunky, but my muffin top makes me feel like I might be a little bit lumpy."

"Be glad you don't have stretchmarks. My little sister has those because she was a fat kid. They're going away, but they get straight-up purple sometimes."

"Eesh."

The door opened. The two girls turned to see the next occupant. Janie, in a black towel with basic black sandals.

"Um." Janie said "I can wait outside, if you want."

"Nah, join the party." Harley said "Plenty of shower heads left for you."

Janie looked over at not the shower heads, but the dividing glass. In truth, they were very short. They could not cover much. Janie moved to the

Erika Ramson

chair at the end of the showers instead, sitting down, waiting for privacy.

It was Annie, her sworn enemy, who spoke.

"Do you need us to leave?"

"Uh." Janie said "Well. I think I can do it with Harley, but, I need you to leave."

"Okay then." Annie turned her water off.

"You don't have to go dude if you're not done." Harley said

"Yeah, I can wait." Janie said, apparently realizing she didn't need to answer as rough as she did.

Annie walked up close to her, drying her hair off with her towel, trying to keep her voice low. "Look, it's not exactly the same thing, but I was a late bloomer. I kind of understand being afraid, even if I'm not anymore."

Without another word, Annie left the shower stalls.

Janie walked over to an empty shower head, one close to Harley. Janie was shaking her hand on the top of her towel. After a good while, he released it to the floor, picking it up and throwing it aside once she realized it would get wet.

"You okay?" Harley said, making sure she did not actually look at Janie's body.

"I just." Janie said, turning on the water. "I don't get it."

"Get what?"

"I mean. I'm sure it's not uncommon, but. I can't go to the beach or a pool without stuffing my suit like I'm fifteen. I've seen some women just drop their towels in the changing room and chat like

377

nothing is going on, and I can't even chat when the towel is on. I don't get it. And, I don't know why anyone would be fine with just seeing what I have anyway." Janie placed her head against the tiles of the however. "I've got nothing good enough to show. I'm smaller than you, and that's fine. I'm smaller than Annie, and, I don't know, I'm trying to be okay with that. I'm bigger than Izzy, but, she just uses that as a reason to not bother with a bra because it would just get in the way. I'm big enough for a bra, and too small to be anything interesting."

"Want me to look at you?" Harley said "You know me, I'm blunt. I'll tell you exactly what you look like."

"......Okay. But, do everything. It'll be better if you tell me what's good or bad about everything."

Harley gave Janie a few good once overs. As she already knew, Janie's breasts were barely a B-cup, her nipples were large, and she had been right in calling her vagina small.

"You look, dainty." Harley said "Yeah, kind of dainty. I guess it is a little weird your nipples are almost as big as your boobs, but that doesn't make them bad. Your skin is still gorgeous, you take amazing care of it."

Even though Janie's forehead was still smushed against the wall, a smile was visible on her face.

"Thanks. From you that means something." Janie said

"Okay, how about I shampoo your hair for you, huh? Take your mind off things."

Janie started to laugh. "You've asked to kiss me before and this is still the gayest thing you've ever said to me."

Harley's face went white. "I'm sorry could you please say that again?"

Harley was just finishing changing. She wore green rubber pants, tall brown boots, a blue plaid shirt, and a fishing hat. She burst into the room with her pole in hand.

"Who wants to go fishing?" Harley said

"Nope." Annie said, placing a ring on her index finger.

It was a silver bunny, hugging its legs to make the design round. Its eyes were pink gemstones. Annie's top was a simple dark purple t-shirt, with her own name written in fake sparkly gemstones. Her pants were simple blue jeans, and her shoes were green flats.

Harley turned to Janie and Izzy. Izzy was making eggs for everyone, while Janie was simply sitting in the big comfortable armchair.

Janie was wearing a black t-shirt, and a pair of tan cargo shorts. Her shoes were brown and black sneakers. Her answer was "No offense but fishing's dumb."

Izzy was wearing a white and light red frilly short dress, with a red bow in the middle, and white heels. Her piercings were two in the left eyebrow, her tongue, and magnetic studs on her right cheek. "Fishing isn't my thing." Izzy said

Harley felt her heart drop down into her stomach. "Oh. I figured fishing was something fun we could all do together."

Admittedly, she was hoping this might convince them to change their minds. Also admittedly, they didn't fall for it.

Annie started randomly searching online maps of the area. "Oh shit! There's a hair salon, with great reviews! Harley, could you drive me to this hair salon? I'll pay you."

"NO I'M GOING FISHING!" Harley said "Sorry...."

"I'll take you." Janie said

Harley and Annie down looked hard at her. Even after the personal growth, this was new.

"Why?" Annie said

"You name something else I can do right now." Janie sat at the table, as Izzy started handing out plates with the sunny-side up eggs on them.

Janie simply grabbed hers by the hand and shoved it all into her mouth. Annie started cutting hers before she talked.

"Fine." Annie said "Just don't be a bitch about it on the way there or anything."

"You either." Janie said

"Just get along." Izzy said "It's going to feel like forever if you two act like bitches to each other."

"Hey she's been a fucking cunt to me almost every time I see her." Annie said

"And you've been a fucking cunt right back." Janie said

"Oh come on!" Annie said "What you're saying that once you rail into me, I'm supposed to be all fucking smiling and sunny!"

"I don't know." Janie said

"Lighten up! If you want me to be nice to you, you be nice to me first! Your bitch act may not piss *everyone* off but if it pisses me off you have no right to assume I'll hide the fact from you."

"And I have no reason to treat you like an actual friend when we're only friends because we both know Harley."

"I'm your friend?!"

"Close enough."

"Oh bullshit!"

"Look, whatever. Do you still want the ride?"

"Hrm. Look, considering you at least calmed down. Fine, but if I ask you to bring me back, that's what you do."

"Cool by me."

Janie wiped the egg yolk from her mouth. "Thanks for the food, Esmerelda."

"Like I said, Izzy is fine." Izzy said

"Yeah, well. Eh, fuck it. Fine, Izzy. But try to stick to calling me Jane."

"Whatever."

"Pfft. Fine, okay. Call me Janie if you want."

Harley was not an avid watcher of anime, but she decided that the look on Annie's face when she puffed up her cheeks after what Janie just said was only comparable to something she would see in an anime.

"Well, that's settled." Harley said "And dinners on me tonight because I'm getting all the Goddamn fish in the lake!"

Harley's only catch was a tiny minnow. She carried it with the rough opposite of pride.

"Fucking stupid tiny fucking fish." Harley said, hanging her head. "Now they're really going to be happy they didn't go with me. How can you not like fishing?"

Harley returned to the campground to see Annie walking around to show off her new haircut. She had dyed it black, a deeper black than her first semester when they first met. The left side had been shaved, and the entire remaining amount of hair was combed directly to her right, making it drip to her shoulder.

"Check it!" Annie said "I decided to go back to my punk rock phase from high school!"

Annie started proving her skills at head banging, while also singing "du nuh nuh nuh du du nuh nuh du nuh" for a good short while.

Janie walked over to them from the direction of the outhouse, placing her phone in her pocket. "Hey, Harley, can I talk to you real quick? It's, important."

Harley looked back at Annie, who simply rolled her eyes and said "Just go."

Harley and Janie moved to the side of the cabin. "So," Janie said "I just got off the phone with Matty."

"Aw." Harley said "That's sweet."

"Well, actually, it's more than that." Janie said. Her face was unreadable, except, she was clearly happy. "So, after school. I'm supposed to get an internship at a real tattoo parlor until I can start on my own."

"Right, yeah. You told me that."

"Um, yeah. Apparently, the school really did put my contact information out there in the open like they said. I figured they were joking. And, I didn't hear them in the shower so they called Matt. I, got an offer."

"That's great!"

"In Idaho."

"….. Oh."

"Yeah. You know, this state is a lot of things, but, it's not Idaho."

"Yeah."

"Matt told me he's coming with me if I go. And I told him, I am going. I know you can't keep that same promise, and you have no reason to."

"I'll miss you."

"I'll miss you a lot more, I mean it. I'm glad you can just skip to that, you know I need to go."

The two of them just looked at each other. Neither ready to cry, but both feeling like they had.

"Anyway," Janie said "Matt's actually coming here really soon."

"Aw, you couldn't actually stay away from each other?" Harley said

A far less happy expression appeared on Janie's face. "No there's a fucking huge rattlesnake in the outhouse and he's the only person I know with a gun."

Dinner that night, was rattlesnake. Harley's minnow was barely an appetizer.

♥ - *Chapter 33* - ♥

It was the first day of Harley's junior year. She and Annie had just finished unpacking, the room that Annie had secured for them was bigger and comfier than the last two. It cost more money, but Annie had secured more loans and grants due gaining the third best GPA in the entire school.

Harley's outfit was a quiet white dress, with small pink petals stitched all over. The back was technically open, guarded by two diagonal straps, yellow with a thin outer edge of black. Her shoes were white open toed flats.

Annie outfit was also a dress, shorter than Harley's. It was dark red, with streaks of brown at the neck and bottom. Her shoes were flats of the same color pattern.

Today was also the day that Harley was going to say goodbye to Janie. They were going to meet once the unpacking was done, so Harley now had to send out the text telling her that it was.

"Okay." Janie's reply text said "I'll see you outside the building."

It had gotten almost dusk by this point. While Harley and Annie had been unpacking, Janie had been packing up all of her belongings with Matt's help. Harley brushed off her dress, double-checking that she looked decent.

"Hey," Harley said "did you want to come?"

"Pfft." Annie said "She won't want to see me, but I guess so.

Harley and Annie walked out of their new dorm, and straight down the hall about out the door.

Janie and Matt were waiting by Janie's car. They had packed it well and heavy. They now only had the one, Matt sold his once they decided they really were moving into Janie's new place together.

Janie was wearing a black blouse that revealed nothing and had short sleeves, and a pair of blue capris. Her shoes were white sneakers with brown accents.

"So." Harley said "You guys are, all ready."

"Yeah." Janie said "I'm going to start my life as a tattoo artist. That's the whole point, isn't it? To leave school and jump into what you want?"

"We don't all get to be lucky like you Jane." Annie said, crossing her arms. "You should think about that if you think this was all easy." Annie let her hands down, uncrossing her arms. "And, if you starting thinking it's too hard. It's not like you're the only one. You'll be fine."

"Thank you." Janie said, somewhat looking at Annie. She turned her gaze fully to Harley. "I, guess we still have social media."

"I'll call you and can chat with you as much as I can." Harley said "I'm not letting state lines interfere as much as they could."

"Me neither." Janie said

Then Janie hugged her.

"I'm going to miss you." Janie said, and Harley could feel a few tears drip down onto her shoulder.

"I'm going to miss you so much too." Harley said, now doing her share of the hug.

They held each other for a short while, but both were ready to move on despite how much it was finally starting to fully hurt. Once they ended, Janie walked over to Annie.

"Um." Janie extended her hand. "I don't know how you feel, but, we should shake hands?"

Annie started to lift up her hand. Something inside her was stopping from fully growing through with it, and her face showed nothing but, confusion.

Janie balled her hand up. "This?"

Annie smirked, and nodded. They fist bumped.

"I'm sorry." Janie said

"Fuck." Annie said "Thank you. Well, if you're man enough, then I'm sorry too."

Janie run up to Annie to give her a much quicker hug than she had with Harley. Annie's response was to blink, and she wasn't given enough time to even think about hugging back before Janie walked back away.

"I do need to go." Janie said "Maybe we'll even see each other again."

"Who knows?" Harley said "I sure hope so."

Janie waved the both of them goodbye, and entered the car. Matt drove the two of them on their way to Idaho.

Annie breathed out. "Shit." She rubbed her eyes, and turned back. "She's actually convinced me to miss her."

Harley smiled in Annie's direction, and then simply just smiled up at the sky. It helped, no matter how bad she was feeling inside.

It was now dark, Harley was trying not to fall asleep at her computer. Suddenly her cell phone rang. She looked at the caller ID.

"Oh shit I forgot I told Max to call me when he gets here!" Harley said, immediately answering after she did. "Hello."

"Hey." Max said "Um, it's late but I figured not too late to let you know Clyde and I finally finished moving in. There was a shit load of paperwork, I don't know why they made this so hard when we filed for it last semester."

"Eck." Harley said "Anyway, where are you? We can just talk on the phone if you'd like but if you could, I'd like to see you in person."

Harley caught a broad smile on Annie's face, which did not seem out-of-place and yet still through her for a little bit of a loop.

"Um, well I'm in the new dorm now." Max said "It's connected to the fashion studio, thing. I don't know what to call it since it's not technically a real one. Um, right, sorry, I can meet you there in front of the doors. I'm sorry but I don't want to go further than that, it's getting kind of dark."

"No, I understand." Harley said "That's good enough for me. Hell, you can wait inside if you want and just wait for me."

"It's no big deal, I can wait for you outside. I, really want to see you."

"Me too. I'm leaving right now."

Harley and Max hung up after quick goodbyes.

"So whatcha gonna dooooooo?" Annie said

"I just want to say hi to him in person." Harley said "I don't start every semester saying hi to him, but, it does kind of feel right. It's, kind of special I guess."

Annie started happily burying her face into the edge of her bed. "And?"

"Don't know." Harley said "Not planning on anything. Well, okay, a hug."

"Really?" Annie said "Go on."

"Just. No offense to you, love you too and everything, you and Janie still didn't get along. It's, a little hard for me to get some consoling from you on this. You're good every other time, but not now."

Annie raised her head back up. "Oh. Okay, yeah, no. That sounds good. Hey, he is a good guy you know. I think you picked the right person to console you."

"Thanks." Harley said, walking her way out of the room.

Harley could see Max under one of the street lights the campus used during the night time. He waved at her, trying to flag her down. She waved back at him.

Max was wearing a long-sleeved yellow shirt, under an orange vest. His slacks were a beige-cream color, the same as his designer shoes.

"Wow!" Harley said "Don't often see you in bright colors. This makes you look gorgeous."

Max was slightly taken aback. "Thanks. It's uh, I figured I should try brighter colors, and, I guess it was a good idea. I, didn't know how quickly I could be gorgeous."

"Hey, come on, it's not like you're a bad looking guy." Harley gave him a smile. "To be honest, you always look very good."

"That, I uh." Max said "I, already had a feeling. Thank you a lot though. You try something new, even just new colors, and it can be a little worrying until you hear from someone impartial."

Something in the back of Harley's mind prevented her some admitting she was probably not impartial.

"You look great too." Max said "I'm, not just returning a compliment. I've always, liked your style. You wear dresses as well as you wear pants."

"Yeah, I mixing things up." Harley said "Hey, uh, you remember Janie Olber?"

"Of course I do." Max said "You me and her had art class together. She's an amazing artist, and I hear her temperament is starting to get a lot better."

"Yeah, well." Harley could feel a sniffle coming on. "She's gotten a job in Idaho and just moved out a few hours ago. We said goodbye."

"Oh. Oh, baby I'm sorry."

The same little something in the back of her head made her refuse to question why he had just called her "baby". Although his stutter afterwards seemed to imply he sure did.

"What I, ahem. I know you and her were really good friends." Max said

"I was hoping you could console me a little." Harley said "My roommate fucking hated her, and, all I need now is a hug and being told she'll be alright."

"There's no problem with that."

Harley and Max embraced in a hug. They lasted longer than the one Janie had given her, and Max went an extra mile but gently rubbing her back. This little extra thing, did a lot to help. This, melted her, in terms of the pain she'd been feeling earlier. She could have kissed him for it. On a better day, she most likely would have, but she knew that once this was over she needed to head back and prepare for school.

"Thank you so much." Harley said

"It's no problem." Max left his arms on her shoulders. "Hey, Harls. If you ever need anything, you know I'm here for you. Okay? No matter what you need, or how you feel. I'm here for you."

Harley could swear she'd heard someone tell her this before, but neither a name or face appeared in her memory. Instead, this was just something that sounded familiar, but far sweeter and real than it ever could have the first time.

"I know." Harley said, and there was nothing but truth in her words, even more than usual. "And I will, and you can do the same for me. You mean a lot to me."

Max seemingly blushed. "That's, great to know. I'll see you soon enough."

"You too."

Max walked back into his dorm building. Harley turned around, ready to make the trip back to her own building. It was funny. On the way there, it was hard for her to walk without remembering the sadness from earlier. But now? She was practically walking with a spring in her step.

♥ - *Chapter 34* - ♥

Harley hadn't been to a Halloween party since she was seven. She'd been invited by a friend of her brother's, and she could remember a pleasant enough time. Today, the person who invited her was Sheena, and her expectations were much higher.

Annie's costume was a simple footie-pajamas ensemble with a hood, horns on top.

"So what's your costume?" Harley said

"I am the devil!" Annie said, trying to be in character.

"Since when is the devil pink?"

"I'm the devil who put her costume in with the whites and the color ran! Argh!"

"Argh is a pirate thing."

"Argh I don't fucking care anymore!"

Harley costume consisted of the following: a black-and-white miniskirt with many tears across the sides and the seams. A dark blue blouse, lowcut with no sleeves, and revealing tears on the sides. Under it was a grubby white t-shirt that still exposed a noticeable amount of cleavage. On her right wrist was a wide, obviously fake gold bracelet that looked rather heavy. In her ears were large gold hoops, and on her feet were cheap red high heels. She put temporary dark brown streaks in her hair, excessive eyeliner was drawn on every corner of her eyes, and she was chewing bubblegum.

"What what's yours?" Annie said

"I'm a hooker." Harley said

"You're kidding?!"

"Nope. I figure since most everyone just does the slutty costume thing now, I'd just go as far as I wanted. I'm dressed as a hooker."

"You are the coolest girl I've ever met!"

Annie and Harley's first stop before the party was to Max's room. Sheena allowed her guests to invite people as long as they'd vouched for them, and Harley had invited both Annie and Max. Max had already agreed, but with a caveat that he may end up being too busy.

They arrived at his room, and knocked. Max answered the door, in little more than an incredibly clean gray t-shirt and blue jeans.

"Is that your costume?" Harley said, followed by blowing and popping a bubble.

"No," Max said, embarrassed. "this is what I wear when I need something breathable because I'm working too hard."

"Oh." Harley said, continuing chewing. "I guess this means you can't go?"

"Probably not." Max said

"Can we come in? Might as well chat for a minute or so since we came all the way down here."

"Sure, just try to only be a minute or so. I'm so sorry, I'll explain."

Max welcomed the girls into his room. Harley noticed his roommate Clyde sitting upside down at their TV playing some kind of video game. His shirt and slacks were solid pink, his regular skirt-thing was absent, and his lips were just as pink as the rest of him.

"Hey." Clyde said "How's it going?"

"We're good." Harley said "Anyway Max, what exactly are you working on? You're usually good at getting your homework done."

"It's not technically homework." Max said, gripping a large rolled up wad of drawing paper. "They're designs. See, one of my classes, the kids who've been around long enough get to hand in some stuff that will be shown in the real fashion world. If all goes well, I could be one of three students to get picked. They'd put my stuff in the mock fashion shows, and then, they'd move on to the real ones."

Annie whistled.

"Yeah." Harley said "That's hot shit. I'll root for you."

"Thank you." Max said "I mean it, the competition will be fierce, there's thirty-eight people in total, mostly juniors like me but a handful of seniors. And one kid who's expected to be top knot, just a freshman. Fuck, those one's always tend to get it. Fucking prodigies."

"You help in any way for this?" Harley said to Clyde, blowing another bubble afterwards.

"All of them are allowed a make-up modeler to help add accents to the faces." Clyde said, still playing. "Which I did. I think only the prodigy and two others didn't do that, but I will get credit if Max passes, even if they don't notice my work." Clyde's in-game character was then killed by someone he was playing online with, and he barely made a sigh in response.

"I can hand it in anytime." Max said "Which for me, is going to be tomorrow. I don't want to rush it or prolong it. About ten of them have handed theirs in already, so I'm betting my timing is as accurate in my head as I think it is."

"I guess we should leave then." Harley said "This is too important to make you wait for us."

"Yeah." Annie said "But tell us, what was your costume going to be?"

"Uh, eh ha." Max said "I didn't trick-or-treat much as a kid, I kind of forgot Halloween parties need costumes until a few days ago. That's the other reason I'm not going, I can't justify suddenly putting a costume together. That's not something I can personally feel comfortable half-assing."

"Makes a lot of sense." Annie said

"Except for the trick-or-treating part." Harley said "Don't you like candy?"

"Not entirely." Max said "I mean, I'll eat it, but I have only a small tolerance for sweets. I think I told you this, but, fuck I'm a little frazzled right now."

"Well, I can bring you back something." Harley said "It's the least I can do, it'll help get your energy levels up, pick your clichéd saying."

"I guess a candy bar." Max said "But just one, I mean it, my sweet tooth is a total joke."

"Define then." Harley said "Nougat, peanuts, just chocolate? Caramel?"

"Huh. Well, not just chocolate, those are too boring. Just got something with shit it in, I do like those. I'm not allergic so, run free."

"What about you Clyde?" Harley said "Do you want anyway slash do you have any allergies that affect what I'm getting."

"No," Clyde and "and no. Not hungry, and I'm grabbing some tai food for us later, so I'm not worried about chocolate."

"Alright then, I guess we're headed out." Harley said "I'll stop by after we leave to bring your candy to you."

"I'll be here." Max flashed her a smile.

Harley was surprised that a girl her age could suddenly become weak in the knee, but went out the door regardless.

"Tell me." Harley said "Is it me, or does he have such a great smile."

"It's okay." Annie said "He has remarkably clean teeth. It's not a whitener either, trust me, I tried that once. It's not bad or anything, but you can tell the difference after you've done it. Too bad he can't go with you to the party."

"Yeah, but hey, I wouldn't want him to miss such a great opportunity. You don't have to come back to his room with me later if you don't want to, by the way."

"I wasn't planning on it. You two are perfectly okay with having alone time together in my book."

"Thanks. That's, pretty nice. It feels right, I guess."

"Maybe it should. Anyway, come on, this Sheena's sounded pretty awesome from how you've described her, I'm dying to check out this party."

Sheena's costume was a Roman toga, a golden laurel on her head, and simple sandals. Despite being in costume, she still wore her "TOTAL BITCH" thumb ring. Harley could never think of a time she didn't wear it, so this did not surprise her.

"Alright." Sheena said "All ya'll are here, so this is how we're doin' things. Now, we're going to be loud, so loud I am expecting the cops to ask us to calm down, I don't got a problem with that. Now, as for what we're doing for fun, I have it covered in a way you better not complain about. We've got food, lots of junk as this is Halloween. I have no plans to make this one of those dumb college parties where everyone just gets drunk and they pretend that's a good time."

Annie's face began to sink.

"I'm not sayin' there's no drinking." Sheena said

Annie's face lit back up.

"You just have to be of age." Sheena said

Annie's face feel back down.

"If what you smoke is legal, I've got ashtrays and a campfire area just for you." Sheena said "On the TV is nothing but shitty cheesy monster movies, and you are encouraged to make rip into them as much as you want. I'll be pumping the music, and you need something else, you better ask instead of just thinking I've got nothing good. This is a party babies, just because we're not being stupid, doesn't mean we're not partying."

Most of the guests were close friends of Sheena, the speech was mostly for the extras who'd been invited. As such, most of the guests, including Harley, cheered once she was done.

"At least we can get high." Annie said

"Well, you can." Harley said "I'm uh, gonna continue to pass if you don't mind."

"Fine, I hear ya. This better end up being good, I can't believe there's rules in a Halloween party."

A familiar guest walked over to the both of them. "Sheena's mother is a judge and her father is a warden." He said

"Uh?" Annie said

"Oh, hey Damien." Harley said "Nice to see you here."

"Nice to be here." Damien said "Sheena's too bombastic to throw a bad party. But like I said, considering her parents of course she's going to try and be legit as she can in her own house."

It was a nice little place. Not too away from the road, a driveway big enough for all the cars to park. Close to the campus, driving distance. Harley decided she'd have to ask how Sheena afforded to live there by herself.

"So, what's your costume?" Harley said, although she was certain she'd already pieced it together for herself.

Damien's costume was a red and white striped shirt, and matching bandana on his red, and blue jeans torn as the bottom. His shoes were small black boots.

"Can't tell?" Damien said "I'm a pirate. What about you two? I think you're a pink bunny, but the horns are throwing me."

"I'm the devil but pink." Annie said "Incident with the washing machine. I'm going to get so sick of saying that….."

"And Harley, I have no idea." Damian said

Harley popped a fresh piece of bubblegum into her mouth. "I'm a prostitute. Not the fancy call girl kind, the pick 'em up on the street kind."

"Original." Damian said "You should share that with Sheena, she'll love it. See you around."

Damian walked away to continue the party.

"So you know him?" Annie said

"Yes." Harley said "Damian, something. Timber I think. We were in that psychology class a while back, and he's Sheena's ex."

"Ah. Okay. You know uh, you honestly don't know him that well."

"Well, no. I guess not. Don't know what your point is."

"Just an observation. Anyway, I'm hangry."

Harley and Annie headed over to the concessions. Despite her claims, Annie only needed a chocolate bar. Harley decided to load up on nachos and the paired cheese sauce.

"I'm going to go mingle." Annie said "Either I get a date, or I kick everyone's ass at a trivia game."

"Good luck to both." Harley said "I'm going to catch up with Sheena."

Annie walked over to the other guests, while Harley made her way into the kitchen. It was the place she'd seen Sheena heading, and was hoping she was still there.

"Hey Harls." Sheena said "Gotta say, nice costume."

"Thanks." Harley said "I love yours too. Roman or Greek?"

"I think I'm an ancient Roman, but in all honestly, I just wanted to wear something comfortable."

"Fair enough."

"You want a soda? You 21?"

"Sure, and yes."

"Maybe a beer instead."

"Eh, I'll just take a soda right now."

Sheena handed Harley an orange soda. Harley cracked it open before reading the label, simply enjoying the drink no matter the company who made it.

"Shit, not bad." Harley said

"You've gotta pick the best if you want people to stay at the party." Sheena said

Harley leaned up against the wall to finish her drink, while Sheena moved around some other refreshments planning to bring them in. They chatted a short while.

"So, you havin' a good time?" Sheena said

"Pretty good." Harley said "Nice to take a break from everything. I haven't celebrated Halloween in years."

"Trust me, this was the right way to finally do it. This ain't a dumb college party, this is full on Halloween. Those movies I picked out, those bad ones are just for the start. I've got the real ones for later, the ones that are going to scare half of them so bad they'll be afraid of the dark all night."

"Nice. Oh, hey, I promised a friend of mine I'd bring him back some candy."

"You can take a bag from under the sink if you want. I stow the paper bags from the store under there in case I ever need them, so there's plenty. Now, better subject, mind helping me carry these in? Wouldn't ask but I think I can trust ya."

"Sure, no problem." Harley downed her soda, and grabbed a cooler full of drinks.

The two of them placed the new items on the table. The guests, however, were currently preoccupied with something else. Something not surprising to Harley, but clearly surprising to everyone else. Annie was playing checkers with a boy wearing a white wedding gown with fake blood smeared through the stomach section. All of Annie's pieces had been kinged. Her opponent was down to only two left, neither of them kinged.

"Hey I've got all night if you can't think of a new move bro." Annie said "I'm patient."

The opponent moved. Annie immediately jumped both of his remaining pieces. He groaned loudly, and everyone else half-heartedly clapped. They all saw it coming.

"Alright, what's next?" Annie said "And who's next?"

"You're not beating me like this." The checkers opponent said "You think you're smart? Chess is a real smart man's game."

"Ooh! I've never played chess before."

"Heh, you are going down then."

Harley rolled her eyes. She was expecting the rest of them should have figured out by now

Erika Ramson

Annie was a fast learner. The rules were explained
to her, and she asked no questions. To be fair to the
other player, he hid no information from her. He
was planning on beating her fairly.

A few moves in, and the look on his face
proved he already started kissing that prediction
goodbye.

"HOW!?" He said

"Hey I'm just following the rules." Annie
said "Based on that, I figured what you would
probably be trying, and countered it."

"Speed chess! We're starting again with
speed chess!" He threw the pieces off the board, and
grabbed the chess timer. "We've got a combined
total of fifteen minutes to beat the other!"

In two minutes, he'd been forced into
checkmate.

"Okay fuck you!" He said, then calmed back
down. "You're really smart."

"And don't you forget it." Annie said, smile
brimming. "Alright ya'll, I've got to use the
bathroom now. If you still want to challenge me,
hey, feel free the second I'm back."

Annie walked over to Harley, and started to
whisper. "Please walk me to the bathroom, I have
no fucking idea where it is."

Harley walked Annie over to the bathroom,
chatting about her victories along the way. Once
they arrived, Annie simply stepped inside, and
Harley decided to walk around the corner and
simply watch the party for a while. It wasn't long
before she had company.

"Hey." Damian said

"Hey to you too." Harley said "So what's up?"

"Just Halloween. Your friend was something to witness just now. It was kind of hot."

"I'm sure it was."

Harley started thinking. Maybe someone like Damian and someone like Annie wouldn't be such a horrible idea. Of course, she was probably still trying to forget how attractive she'd first found him, even though he'd been dating Sheena at the time.

"You know," Damian said "you're not bad yourself, really."

"Oh." Harley said, trying to stand a little taller now. "Thanks. That's very nice of you to notice."

"I hope you don't mind being straightforward, but I'm single now so. I don't know. If you wanted to do something, I'm free."

Harley let this sift through her head. She was single. She liked Damian's personality, and found him attractive.

So how come something in her, quested the idea of actually dating him? Some, other reason, some obstacle that made it sound like, she was already good with what was going like. It was funny, because the last time she thought about men like that, was when she had a boyfriend and this one other boy didn't know and asked her out. She didn't have one, but this circumstance seemed to feel similar, and she couldn't find the reason why.

"You know." Harley said "I actually don't know."

Damian scratched the back of his head. "If that's a no that's the weirdest nice way I've ever heard it."

"It's not a no." Harley said "Just a, maybe. I kind of have to think things over, and I'll tell you when I know."

"You want my number then?"

"Yeah, yeah. That makes sense."

Damian gave her his number. He didn't ask for hers in return, claiming he'd rather know once he heard her voice on the other end. It seemed sweet in its sense of surprise.

Damian walked back to the party, allowed her to think it over without outside influence. Sheena appeared not long after, with a brown paper bag.

"Here ya go baby." Sheena said "I had a second so I thought I'd grab one for ya."

"Thanks." Harley said, taking the bag. "I think I'll fill it up now before I forget."

"Take as much as you want, there's a shitload for everyone. So, I see Damian just left."

"Yeah."

"You know, if anything was to go between you two, fine by me."

"Oh. Cool. He did ask, but, I don't know."

"Hm, well it's also okay by me if you don't think he's your type. I like the both of you a lot Harley, Damian more of course. I'm just happy to see my friends like each other."

Sheena walked back out to tend her party. Harley walked over to the candy and sodas.

"Eh." Harley said "Better to just get an assortment and hope he likes one of them."

Annie walked back to her now, done with her priorities involving the bathroom.

"This ain't bad." Annie said "Glad you brought me along."

"Yeah." Harley said "I think it's good we came here tonight."

"I'm going to stop at Max's room." Harley said "You can go ahead if you like."

"Yeah." Annie said "I'm pooped. See you when you get back yo."

Annie left towards the direction of their dorm building. Harley started off towards Max's. She was about to text Max to open the door, but someone else was just about to. Clyde.

"Oh, hey." Clyde said, leaving the door open for her.

Harley ran up so Clyde did not have to hold the door for long. "Thanks Clyde. Just bringing the candy over."

"I see." He said "I'm getting the tai food. Guess that's good timing. He'll be happy to see you."

Clyde walked out to get dinner as Harley continued down the hall. Remembering she still had some, she popped a new piece of bubblegum into her mouth. She blew a bubble, louder than she expected, but decided it wasn't a problem unless someone asked her to shut up.

Erika Ramson

While it wasn't a long walk, Harley decided to call for the elevator. There was a young man inside, around Harley's age, and he politely moved over for her. He wore round glasses, had dyed his hair blue, wore a black dress shirt and gray jeans, and designer shoes. She pressed her button, the doors closed, and they started the ascend.

They'd been quiet only a short bit, until the young man got out what he was trying to say.

"So, uh." He said "Is fifty bucks enough, or, that's all I have."

"Just a costume." Harley said, popping a bubble. "Sorry."

"Oh. Oh okay." He said "It's just I, I totally thought you were. And I don't, I don't date much and I'm not good at. I'm sorry the thought just-"

The doors opened.

"My floor." He said "Again sorry I, I'm bad at this." He walked out.

Harley shrugged her shoulders as the doors closed, and the elevator brought her to Max's floor. She exited, spat her gum into a trashcan, and walked to Max's room. She knocked gently, and she could hear Max jump from the other side. She probably should have texted him like she'd first planned.

He opened the door, the stress and sudden shock quickly starting to drain. Happiness replacing it.

"Oh, hey." Max said "Kind of forgot you were coming."

"I guess I'm a pleasant surprise." Harley said

She walked herself in, Max closing the door behind her. They sat at the edge of Max's bed, and Harley handed over the paper bag to him.

"I just took a few handfuls of shit." Harley said "Take whatever you want."

"I'll be fine with this." Max pulled a king-sized candy bar from the bag, and tore it open.

He took a small bite after handing the bag back to Harley. She let him swallow, waiting for what she was planning on telling him.

"So how was the party?" Max said "Did I miss much?"

"It was a really good time." Harley said "You would have liked it. Fun costumes, bad movies, free sodas, board games. Yeah. It was an, eventful night."

Max took another bite of his candy.

"This guy I know, asked me out." Harley said

Max tried not to cough, and the effort did not go unnoticed.

"You want some water or milk?" Harley said, staying on alert in case he moved onto choking.

"I'm fi-, not choking." Max said "Anyway, you were talking."

"I told him I don't know. And I'm not sure why." Harley said "I like this guy. He's cute, he's laidback, I've talked with him a few times before and would very much like to know him better. It's just, I don't know. Some funny little part of me feels like there's something stopping me."

Max breathed out. Harley assumed he was regaining his composure from the coughing fit.

"Well." Max said "I, can't really tell you what to do. There's nothing right about me telling you what to do, especially not in this situation."

"Huh. Thank you, that makes a lot of sense, and was, nice to hear." Harley said

Harley kicked her feet a little bit, she figured maybe it was the best way to think quickly.

"Fuck it." She said "I should at least give him a chance."

"Cool." Max said "Hey, I. Can't eat all of this, I expected too much of my stomach. You want it."

Harley more or less ate the candy right out of his hand.

"Careful!" Max said "Jesus Christ, you're a fucking shark."

"Rargh." Harley said "And I don't even look it. Oh! That reminds me, some dude thought this wasn't a costume."

"Guess you made it look real enough." Max said, smiling, yet for some reason it seemed, forced.

"He offered me fifty bucks." Harley was already just laughing about the sad exchange.

"Fifty bucks!?" Max said "How can anyone look at you and think fifty bucks is enough!?"

Max swallowed. Maybe there was some residual chocolate in the back of his throat.

"Do you want any more of this candy?" Harley said

"I don't think so. I mean, definitely not right now." Max said

Harley carefully took some of the candy from the bag, and dropped it into Max's hand. "Just eat it another day. I doubt it will go bad for a year or so. I'll see you around. Hopefully I won't be too busy with this guy to stop hanging out with you and my other friends, huh?"

"Yeah." Max said, quietly moving the candy over to his desk. "I'll see you when I see you."

Harley walked out of Max's room, and pulled out her phone to give Damian her answer in a quick text.

"Yes, when? Harley"

She then started the walk all the way back to her and Annie's dorm.

Harley walked through the door, seeing Annie almost asleep in her chair. Annie started to rub her eyes to slightly wake herself up.

"Hello again." Annie said

"Hey Annie." Harley said, then took a seat. "So hey, I guess I'm back on the dating scene."

Annie raised both of her arms straight up in the air. "About time! I've been waiting for this news."

"I guess it has been a while." Harley said "And Damian's a pretty good guy."

Annie's arms went back down. "Damian?"

"Yeah, Damian."

"Oh. Yeah, he's a nice guy. You uh, sure you want to go out with him?"

410

"He asked me, and, I thought it over and, it made enough sense."

"Okay then. If you're super sure. You're super sure?"

"Well." Harley said, now looking slightly at the floor. "I guess so."

Annie sighed. "Cool. Good luck with him."

Annie turned back to her homework. Knowing her, it would only take at most an hour for her to get everything done for the coming week. Harley simply sat at her desk, ready to reply now that Damian had texted her back with the time and place he had in mind.

While she was replying, both Annie's and now even Max's reaction was burning into the back of her head. For some reason, she was getting the same feeling she got when she knew she'd made a mistake.

♥ - Chapter 35 - ♥

Damian had picked a breakfast diner. It was a complete change of pace from what Harley knew first dates normally were. Not a movie, not dinner somewhere fancy, just breakfast at a decent place. It was a cozy little transition, and was already helping her decide if there would be another date to follow.

Harley wore a quiet white blouse, the collar was see-through with diagonal crosses stitched in. This design was mimicked on the bottom. Her pants were a simple faded pair of blue jeans, and her sneakers were black-and-white. On her right middle finger was the bronze and onyx ring, and on her left wrist was her pearl bracelet. She also chosen to wear noticeable pink blush and black eyeliner.

Damian wore a dark blue t-shirt, clean and pressed. For his pants, a pair of faded grey jeans. On his head was a gray bowler hat. As Harley expected, he continued to dress on a date the same way he normally did. For some men, this would make them look lazy or stupid. For Damian, he was simply pulling off what he normally pulled off. There was a slight bit of effort though, in the fact that he'd removed the headphones he usually always wore. She was starting to miss them.

"These are for you." He said, handing her a wrapped bouquet of flowers.

Pink roses.

"These are lovely." Harley said, giving them a sniff.

"They had red ones and yellow ones." Damian said "But I had a feeling pink was more up your alley."

"They are." Harley said "Thank you."

Harley set her flowers in the seat beside her. The two of them started to chat while waiting for their food, getting to know little details about each other. Damian's interests did not surprise Harley, after all, it was what she both knew and assumed about him that made her decide to agree to the date.

Their food was brought to them; Damian had ordered pancakes and scrambled eggs. He seemed to not be too careful when it came to pouring his syrup. It didn't really matter to him that the eggs were now covered in it as well.

Harley had ordered waffles and sausage links. She was not too careful either, but this was because the waffles held the syrup in place. She managed to not cover the sausages, but she had every intention of using the sausages to wipe the extra syrup up.

After trying a bite of her waffle, it was clear Damian had chosen a good spot.

Harley was politely being walked back to her dorm by Damian, as she carefully carried her flowers.

"Maybe I can find something to put these in." Harley said

"Yeah." Damian said "I didn't think about that. Well, hey, still better than getting you plastic ones, right? I dated a girl in high school once who said some guy did that on their first date and she broke up with him right there."

"If it was a first date, you can't really call that breaking up."

"You know what, yeah, that makes sense. Speaking of. Did you like ours?"

"Yes. This was a great first date."

"Does that mean they'll be a second?"

"Yes. I think you've earned a second date."

The two of them were now at the head of the building. They'd said quick goodbyes, and Damian started heading out, but quickly changed his mind.

"Can I do one thing first?" Damian said

Harley figured what this one thing was, and chose the appropriate response. "Lay it on me."

Damian gave her a kiss on the cheek.

"Maybe I can do something better later on." He said "I think that's good for now."

"Yeah." Harley said, holding her kissed cheek with one hand. "I'll see you soon."

The two now went on their opposite directions. Harley decided she had done enough walking for the day, and went into the elevator. She took the short time inside to admire the tingling feeling from the kiss, and again smell her beautiful flowers.

With how great this one date had gone, she must've been wrong about that odd feeling she'd felt about the decision not that long ago.

She must've, she told herself.

♥ - Chapter 36 - ♥

While not a holiday the Millsboone family usually celebrated, it was still technically a holiday. Black Friday. Normally, there would be no plans for anyone, they would just sit around the house and do whatever they felt like. However, Will had made some quick but special plans.

Sarah was going to come visit him.

He was sitting at a chair, noticeably happy while waiting.

"You seem excited." Harley sad

"She's great!" Will said, gaining a broad smile. "You know, she hasn't met you guys yet, so, I'm just happy to introduce her. Plus, well, remember how nervous and twitchy I would get when I was dating Mimi?"

"Of course I do."

"I have none of that with Sarah. I, don't want to be mean to Mimi, but I think there were a lot more warning signs now that it's all over and I can look back on it. This is going really good. You'll like her."

"I'm sure I will. I barely remember her, so, hey, she's still kind of new to me."

Harley was wearing a yellow t-shirt, fitting and comfy. Her skirt was frilly and white, just slightly below her knees. Her shoes were white flats.

Will was wearing a black t-shirt, and blue jeans. His sneakers were black-and-white, and he was remarkably clean. Not that he was ever actually filthy, but Harley could see the extra effort.

There was a knock at the door, and Harley decided to get it. "Hello."

Sarah was wearing a black athletic top. For her pants, they were grey sweatpants, which looked warm and comfy against the outside cold. Her sneakers were black-and-white, just like Will's. Harley also noticed a Celtic cross tattooed on her right upper arm. Sarah was incredibly fit, in fantastic shape. Thin because of exercise instead of being born skinny. What used to be DD breasts were now D, and Harley decided it was now okay to judge Will a little bit for "missing" the old cup when she'd barely went down at all.

"Hey." Sarah said, her eyes nervously trying to lock onto Harley's. "I'm Sarah. You're Harley, right?"

"Yep." Harley said "Great to meet you."

"You too." Sarah said "Um, yeah. Sorry, really, it's great to meet you."

Sarah walked over to Will. They were immediately happy to see each other.

"So, guess what we're doing?" Will said, absolutely giddy.

"What?" Sarah said, and Harley noticed it was much easier for her to look him in the eyes.

"I figured," Will said "you would like to help me rearrange my dollies."

"Oh!" Sarah said "Yeah! That sounds fun. I like organizing."

"I know." Will said

Will and Harley's mother came into the room. In a quiet white robe and slippers. She immediately eyed Will's new girlfriend.

"You're Sarah?" Harley's mom said

"Oh," Sarah said, once again trying as hard as she could to look someone other than Will in the eye. "yeah, yeah. Sorry I'm, yes I'm Sarah."

Harley's mother pointed at Sarah's arm. "Celtic cross?"

"Oh, yeah." Sarah turned to arm to make it more visible. "I got it a few years ago. I'm not super religious but, I like crosses."

"Mm-hm." Harley's mother said, now moving to get coffee. Admittedly, still paying attention to the young woman talking to her.

"I also have these." Sarah lifted up her pant legs. Her right leg was a colored-in forest of trees, and her left was a colored-in beach side with calm waves and seashells. "They really hurt, but I like the beach and the woods. They go up to my thighs."

"How interesting." Harley's mother said

"Okay." Sarah said, rolled her pants back down, seemingly dejected at the reaction.

"Now let's take care of the dollies." Will said "Harley, want to come with us?"

"You mind?" Harley said, aiming the question mostly at Sarah.

"Oh no!" Sarah said "Please, yeah, you can hang out with us."

The three of them moved into Will's room. Will had gotten his childhood dolls onto his bed, Harley had forgotten just how many of them he owned. She very much remembered how they used to play with them together when they were little, but without seeing them for several years, there seemed to be millions when there were really just more than a dozen.

"Oh, I remember this one!" Harley said, referring to a little cloth doll in a cute sun dress.

"There's the stitch where you tried to bite her head off." Will said, with no malice, only humor in the old story of theirs.

"Hey I was three." Harley said "I had no intention of actually ripping her head off, it just sort of almost happened."

"I know. Good thing mom didn't mind fixing it." Will gently took the doll from Harley, giving it to Sarah so she could look it over too.

Harley decided to take up a chair, it was best to let them go about their own thing and just sort of be there if needed. Sarah and Will openly flirted while arranging the dolls, and eventually Harley just grabbed a magazine and started reading it in quiet.

"Hey, I have to use the bathroom." Will said "I'll be right back, okay?"

"Okay." Sarah said

He gave her a quick kiss on the cheek before leaving. He'd been gone for a few seconds before Sarah started talking.

"Am I doing good?"

"Huh?" Harley said, leaning her head back to talk.

"I've, never had a real boyfriend before." Sarah said, grabbing her arm in nervousness. "I've been on dates before, these things get guy's attention but I, I guess they find me annoying or they don't like how much I exercise or, I kind of stopped trying to figure it out. And, I was scared

Will would be like that, but, he just kisses me or tells me I'm great and that he's happy, and then he actually asked me if he could be my boyfriend.

"And, Will was special to me anyway. I've had a crush on him since I was nine. I was willing to accept even he would leave me, now I'm just, really worried and confused about how this is going good."

Harley got up, and gave her a smile. "Will likes you. He was freaking out in the best way when he thought you might be a thing. Don't worry about it."

Sarah smiled back, it was all she needed to say.

Harley went back to her seat, and Will eventually came back. Even though she was mostly reading, Harley still took the time to look up and watch just how cute they were together.

Sarah said her quick goodbyes and then left for home. Will wished her luck in case of any traffic, but thanks to her area, she promised there would not be much of a problem.

Harley's phone beeped with a text. Damian needed to cancel a date they had planned. Harley sighed, and replied. This was something Sheena had already warned her about, so she was not as upset as she could have been. Damien was not always great at remember how many things he needed to do, dates were not the only thing he would flake on.

Will came back to the table with Harley, sitting down roughly after she was done texting.

"That went so well." Will said "You see how happy she was?"

"I did." Harley said "That was clever, letting her just do something she finds fun."

"You have to get creative." Will said

Their mother returned to the room. The microwave beeped, and Harley grabbed the mug of hot chocolate she'd been preparing.

"So, you're getting serious with her?" Their mother said

"Yep." Will said "Sarah went to school with us, so, we're kind of getting serious fast."

Harley lifted the mug up near her mouth.

"Good," Their mother said "I like her."

The mug dropped straight to the room, shattering in an uncountable amount of pieces.

"Harley clean that up, I raised you better than that." Their mother said

Harley went straight to cleaning it up, while still talking. "I'm just surprised. I mean, you hated Mimi."

Their mother gave a harsh deep sigh. "Megan was pretending to be so nice and so thoughtful. Sarah's regular nice. Did you see how that girl was still looking me in the eye even though it hurt her to do it? She respects me and never met me, that's a good-hearted girl. Sure, the tattoos are out there, but it's so much better than that dumb little lip ring Megan was so happy to pretend was permanent. At least Sarah's body modifications are actually permanent."

"I'm glad you like her." Will said "I have a very good feeling about her."

"You should." Their mother said "This one, this one's not an idiot." She then left the room.

Harley threw the pieces of mug into the trash, had wiped up the drink, and she started to prepare the second cup, hopefully to drink it this time.

"You like her?" Will said

"Very much." Harley said "You know, we were talking when you were gone. She said she's had a crush on you since she was nine."

"Nine!?" Will said "Christ, here's hoping I don't end up disappointing her."

"I think you're doing fine." Harley said "You want hot chocolate?"

"Eh, fuck it, sure. Nice way to end the day."

♥ - *Chapter 37* - ♥

It was now December, crisp and fresh despite it now being as cold as the state would get. Harley was walking back to her dorm, it being her first day back from vacation. Technically, it wasn't the first official school day back, she had skipped the day before to spend more time with her family. Her grades were good enough to justify the decision in her head.

Her outfit today was a nice white puffy coat, blues jeans, and brown boots with fake fur on the top. Under her coat was a white blouse, no frills, slightly thick to combat the cold.

She opened the door to find Annie laying on her bed, over the sheets. Fully dressed in a flowing red t-shirt and a light blue jean skirt. She was blasting music through her headphones, eyes closed to fully enjoy the rhythm.

She moved her left index and middle fingers over the crotch of her jeans. She pressed down, with a noticeable amount of force.

"Hey!" Harley said

Annie immediately jumped and fell out of her bed. She rushed back into standing position, ripping out her headphones. With her back turned to Harley, she reached into her skirt, and pulled something out. Wet drips splashed onto the floor.

"Oh hey I didn't think you'd be back for another hour or so!" Annie said, roughly as fast as humanly possible.

Annie ran over to her closet, trying to squeeze past Harley, to hide the exact device she'd just pulled out of herself back where it belonged.

"So how was your trip I bet you had a lot of fun with your family!" Annie said, exactly as fast as before.

"Good." Harley said, not as surprised as Annie most likely expected her to be.

"Well. Good." Annie said, now turning to Harley and trying to calm down.

There was silence for five full minutes.

"Um." Annie said. "Oh, check this out."

Annie lifted up her shirt.

"I got this done over the break. Izzy gave me a friend discount." She said

The belly-button piercing was shiny and silver. As she had an innie, she'd been able to not only have a small hoop in the top, but the bellybutton itself was filled with sparkling silver and gemstones.

"It's the best jewelry I have now." Annie said "I'm thinking this'll look so good when I can go back to short shirts in the spring."

"You won't have long to wait." Harley said "We get noticeable warmer as soon as January as far as I'm concerned. It is lovely too, Izzy's family know their stuff."

"That's why I'm wearing it every day." Annie said

There was a fast knocking at the door.

"Oh, shit." Harley said "Someone's here."

Annie noticeably became embarrassed again. "Eh heh, hooray. You know what I think I'm going to get something to eat."

Annie opened to door to leave, letting Max into the room. Max tried saying hello, but Annie was already speeding off. She likely didn't even see who it was with how fast she was running.

"She okay?" Max said

"Oh, just a girl thing." Harley said "No real problem, just forget about it."

Max was wearing a long sleeve black dress shirt, and over it a light gray vest. His pants were pinstriped gray dress pants, the strips being white. His shoes were blindingly white, brand new, and around his neck a white bowtie. He looked like something out of a 30's cartoon, a look Harley assumed only Max could make incredibly gorgeous.

"So!" Max's eyes lit right up. Harley had forgotten how they could glitter. "I won!"

"NO!" Harley said, her eyes lighting up almost as bright. "That's wonderful!"

"I came in second." Max said "The prodigy came in third. I beat the fucking prodigy!"

"I'm so proud of you." Harley suddenly took one step back. It was, weird, to use that specific word, and she could not place why.

Perhaps Max felt it as well, and he was suddenly taking a dry swallow.

"Hey." He said, starting to gain energy back. "Look, second place also gets me a free dinner to this place, and I can give it away, so. How about you and Damian take it?"

"You don't mind?" Harley said, cocking her head at this level of kindness.

"No." Max said, now gaining a smile. "Not at all. I don't care much for the coupon, and you've got a boyfriend so you need it more than I do anyway."

His tone turned different, more excitable. "Oh! There's one thing I'd like you to do for me if that's okay!"

"Shoot." Harley said

"Well, actually I guess it's situational. Is Annie seeing anybody right now?"

"I have a feeling she isn't. Why?"

"I have a friend within the major. He's a little loud, energetic, gaudy but he pulls it off, gets around. See where I'm going with this?"

"OH!" Harley said "I get it! They sound like a perfect match."

"Please set them up!" Max clasped his hands together. "I've wanted to set two people up since I was in high school. It's so adorable."

"You've got it."

♥ - *Chapter 38* - ♥

Max's borrowed coupon and Harley's schedule lead to the double-date landing on another important time of the year. Christmas eve. The four of them would simply eat, and then go back home to their families to prepare for the following day. The shops were crowded with the forgetful and lazy people attempting to finally get something nice for their loved ones. As such, it was too busy of a shopping day for many people to be at a restaurant. It was a nice, slightly empty, holiday atmosphere.

"So where do we sit?" Annie said

They had arrived at almost exactly the same time, so they decided to pick out the table while they waited for the boys.

"You and me will be over here." Harley said "These seats."

"We're sitting together?" Annie said

"Well yeah. Do you want to look your date in the eyes by just looking up, or do you want to do it by craning your fucking neck the whole time?"

"Fair point."

Annie was wearing a beautiful white frilly and flowing skirt, with blue accents. It was split in the middle, and almost reached her ankles. Her shoes were strappy and gold in color, high heels, a style Harley could not remember seeing Annie wear all that often. On her right wrist was a black long bracelet, and on her right index and middle fingers were simple blue rings. Her shirt was an expensive looking low-cut red blouse with short sleeves, and bundled on the left breast made to resemble a flower. On her left middle ring was a large plastic silver ring with a fake plastic gray butterfly on it, almost big enough to cover the two near fingers. She'd left her watch at home, "to look prettier".

She was also sporting the new haircut for the upcoming semester, a pixie cut dyed a gray-pink. It was surprisingly adorable, not that it surprised Harley too much that Annie managed to pull it off.

Harley herself was wearing black flats, white jeans rolled at the very bottom. Her top was a pink t-shirt, purple sparkles firmly stitched in, none of them were going to fall out and leave a mess, like so many other shirts that resembled it. She was understated, which compared to Annie was nothing unusual, but today is was because he'd already met and impressed her date enough that she didn't feel the need to bother.

Versus Annie, who was already re-applying her red lip-gloss.

"You know anything about this guy?" Annie said

"Nope." Harley said "I'm completely in the dark. He's not my date, didn't feel the need to ask other than the quick things Max told me."

"Well, I guess I'm in for a big ol' surprise."

Damian had now arrived, and found their table after directions from the head waiter. Damian was wearing his broken headphones around his neck, he had listened when Harley mentioned she missed seeing them. His shirt was red on the right side, and black on the left side, a regular button-up. His jeans were dark blue, and his shoes were brown, mostly likely a little old. Harley spotted a small tear on the rubber sole, and realized just how much time she'd been spending with fashion designers.

"Hey babe." Damian said, sitting down. "Hey Ann."

"Hi." Harley said

"Now we're three." Annie said, starting to get a little over-excited. "Now to wait for my blind date!"

"You're very excited for a blind date." Damian said

"This is one of Max's friends." Annie said "Max may be closer with Harley, but I trust him by this point. He's a good guy. If he thinks we'll like each other, than I have a very good feeling about him."

Harley and Damian chatted, while Annie decided to scan the room for whoever the mystery man could be.

Visually, she ended up not being disappointed.

"Hey." He said "I'm Malcolm."

The first thing he did was remove his winter jacket. The rest of them had felt it wasn't very cold today, so they dressed normally. Upon the removal, they realized why he'd bothered with the jacket. Underneath it, he was only wearing an open vest. Harley could see Annie's urge to drool.

Malcolm was fit, no doubt about it. Not jacked, but muscles quite happily existed on his arms and chest. He had a slight tan, not an artificial one, he'd apparently done the hard work of getting a tan when the sun did not come out as often. His pants were simple green jeans, and his shoes were a shiny black. There was a large ring on his right middle finger, something rivaling even Annie's fashion choices, the band being gold, and the center being a large black stone. There seemed to be an image ingrained in it.

"What's that?" Annie said, verbally asking the question Harley was thinking.

"Family photo." Malcolm said, passing over his hand for Annie to see. "Me, my brother, and my mother. We've all been very close, I already had an extra of this picture so it wasn't hard at all choosing it for the ring. You like it?"

"That is perfect!" Annie said, and suddenly, she was carrying her cheek with her shoulder. "My family and I get along very well too, you know. It's all important, especially my grandma really."

"That's cute. It's good to be close with the people you have to know, huh? Make a great situation out of something you technically didn't need to."

"Yeah. You have cute hands by the way."

"I work part-time as a hand model, aside from the regular modeling stuff. My hands are a little dainty and long, so I have his androgynous look to them that ad people eat right up. I can wear men's or women's rings as the public doesn't question it."

"Mmm."

Harley looked over at Damian, giving him a little smile. This was going to work out.

The double-date ended smoothly, Harley was now walking back to her car. She and Damian had shared a kiss, quick but satisfying. She caught Annie on the way out, and noticed she and her date were ending with a kiss as well.

Except theirs's was taking a few minutes. When they were done, Harley walked over to her dear roommate, and saw her lipstick revealing its inexpensive nature by being smeared all over her mouth.

"Tell Max this is the best first date I've had since, fuck Oh my God maybe ever!" Annie said

"He'll be glad to know." Harley said, already picturing his adorable little face light up.

"So yeah, I just asked him to share a hotel room with me."

"WOW!"

"Hey, I've never first-date fucked but this guy's a good one. He said yes, so I'm satisfied. We'll both still be heading back to our families after so if you want to call me or whatever don't worry."

"Tomorrow, then I can wish you a happy Christmas."

"I'll wish you one too Harley. Hell, Merry Christmas Eve. Take care."

Harley arrived back at home, it was now almost nine. She walked through the door, not too surprised to see her brother playing with the dog.

"How'd it go little sis?" Will said

"Great." Harley said "Annie and Malcolm got along better than I've ever seen her with a guy, and I've sat through a lot of times where she'd be talking with a new boyfriend."

"Maybe he's her one."

"You know, that'd be cool if he was. Personally, he's a little flashy but I can see why they connect."

Their father walked into the room. "You have a moment you two?"

"Sure dad." Will said

"What's wrong?" Harley said

"Ha." Their father said "Harley if anything was wrong I would have lead with that. Look, to put things as honest as I can, your mother just went to bed and I've decided to make a decision that will piss her off but for the right reasons. Will, you can invite Sarah to Christmas tomorrow."

"Oh my God thank you so much!" Will left the room within a second to call his girlfriend.

"Wow she is going to be really mad." Harley said

"Eh, she'll just throw up her arms and get over it." Harley's dad said "A little advice for when you get married sweetie, sometimes you figure out what pisses them off and what only slightly pisses them off, and you have to decide which times the latter is worth it. She does really like this one, she'll be mad at me, forget about it, and then secretly coo over the two of them."

"Yeah." Harley said "You know, I can see that too. Sarah's on mom's good side."

"Alright, so since I'm already doing this, what about you? You have a boy, he can't stay over but if you want him to pop in for a minute I can let that slide."

"Huh." Harley was not entirely sure why, but she knew this was the right response. "No, I think I'll be okay without Damian popping in. Thanks anyway dad."

♥ - Chapter 39 - ♥

Today was the mock fashion show. Harley was excited to get the chance to meet so many of Max's colleagues in the fashion department. She'd brought Damian with her, it seemed liked a cute little idea, letting her boyfriend watch her prance around and look great while doing it.

She was changing at the moment, an open back white dress with many yellow streaks. Horizontal on the arms, vertical on the skirt. It was slightly puffy on the bottom, letter her knees and legs feel open and comfortable, while the top gently hugged her, tight while not restrictive. Her heels were shiny and black, Max believe they would give a lovely contrast, and she was already agreeing with him.

She stepped out of the changing room, and gave a quick spin for Max to double-check her dress-up work.

"Great!" Max said "Everything looks like it fits."

Max was wearing a long-sleeve gray shirt, under a dark black vest, and a bright blue tie. His pants were dark gray cargo, to carry all of his extra supplies. His shoes were dressy and black. He'd done his hair cleaner and nicer than usual, which must have been loads of effort, Harley figured, considering how nice it usually was already.

"Before I head out." Harley said "Mind pointing out a few of your friends here?"

"Of course not." Max said, and pointed towards a woman of at least thirty. "That's Luna."

Luna was wearing a quiet black dress, small frills on the bottom and a fake flower on the side of her waist. Her shoes were beautiful, shiny black heels. On her right hand were two enormous jeweled rings. Her middle finger was sparkling with light blue diamond, and her index finger a cool and clear white. Her left hand was also adorned, a yellow diamond on her middle finger and what seemed to be a wedding band on her ring finger.

"She's an expert jeweler." Max said "She wanted to try and get a degree so she could fill her life back up after her husband died."

"Oh God that's terrible." Harley said

"Yeah, she says they really loved each other. She might be ready to move on after school, but now she's just going to be an older student who wants to be a jewelry maker. Turns out, she'd also amazing at men's clothes. She's the one who beat me."

"Wow."

"I don't blame them for picking her first. And even though he's great at men's stuff, I think she's right at sticking with jewelry. She's taught me a few things, a bunch of us really. Quick stuff about what designs can look good, not even a fraction of what she knows. Oh shit, there's her model."

A young adult of Max's age walked into the scene, striking up conversation with Luna. He was wearing lovely blue jeans; a perfectly faded color Harley rarely saw outside of expensive clothing stores. His top was a designer white shirt, and he had a long green scarf that accented his eyes. There were silver bands on both of his middle fingers, and his right ring finger had a large round stone, a mix of purple and black.

"Old friend of mine." Max said "Went to the same high school. Victor is a funny story wrapped up into a great friend."

"Do tell." Harley said

"You know how some guys get caught bringing porn into the school bathroom?"

Harley started to blush. "I mean I once thought about bringing in this erotic audiobook I had. I got too embarrassed by the idea though."

"Well Vic actually did it, and multiple times."

Harley whistled.

"And he's not a perv. The guy's into S&M, and not the way most people are. He loves the leatherwork, a lot. He's here to learn how to make and sell the stuff. It was so weird, and so cool, when I told him about my college choice. His eyes lit up because he didn't realize you could major in fashion, and he immediately sent them a form. When he graduates he's going to reopen that shop that was closed up a few years ago. Unlike Luna I can't say firsthand how great his stuff is, but, he's very open about asking and people have yet to be afraid to tell him it's good shit."

And a young, fresh face was the next person Max pointed at.

"And that's the prodigy." Max said, clearly wanting to sigh. "Fucking prodigy."

"What's his name?" Harley said

"Alex." Max said "And I guess he's not a bad guy, but fuck is he arrogant and loud-mouthed.

435

Surprisingly not in the bad sense, I'm trying not to dislike him but I'm a bit too jealous. Granted, I beat him, so that helps a lot. He is a genius, and he's only half a fashion major, he's in the business major too. He wants to open a dress shop. Hey, good for him. I mean it."

Alex was shorter than the other fashion students, and had wavy blonde hair. His shirt was buttoned up, his slacks were clean and pressed, his bolo tie perfected done up in a way to prevent it from looking stupid. His black shoes also seemed clean pressed. He looked exactly like the business major he partially was.

Max and Harley continued to chat friendly about all of Max's friends from his major. It was nice to see him smile so much, he was clearly getting along well with everyone. Just then, Damian came back from the bathroom. He, as usual, had underdressed for the occasion. A plain black t-shirt, his headphones, ripped gray jeans, and gray sneakers. Harley was just happy he didn't own one of those black t-shirts with a phony tuxedo painted on the front. She never once understood why people would own that, let alone wear it anywhere.

"Hey babe." Damian said

"Hey you." Harley said

They kissed. Harley noticed that Max did the polite thing and looked away.

"So, how's this thing go buddy?" Damian said, turning to Max now. "I don't know anything about this, so, does Harley just walk out there or what?"

"Er, well, yeah sort of." Max said "She's on a schedule like the other models. Um, shit, I know she goes on in ten minutes but I can't remember the rest of her timeslots. I'll go get the clipboard real quick while I have time."

Max headed over to his station. Harley decided to watch him, it might have been interesting to see how he carried himself. She was wrong, he walked like a normal person usually does.

"Hey." Damian said, scratching the back of his head.

"What?" Harley said, cocking her head in his direction.

"You know, he seems cool. I like him. Don't take this as anything but curiosity. Did uh, did the two of you have something going on at some point? It kind of feels like it."

"Oh." Harley took a second to figure out how to phrase. "Yeah, sort of. We sort of slept together a couple times since we met. You know? Nothing more than that, last time was quite a while before you first asked me out."

"Like I said, I'm not concerned other than the fact I'm curious."

"Well, cool. Because. Yeah. That was all we did. …. You know."

Harley had no clue why every part of her body wanted to trail off right now. She looked back over at Max, who currently was chatting with Luna.

A tiny, cute smile appeared. For once, not from Max, but from Harley.

Damian looked over at her. "Um. Hey, look."

Harley looked back at him.

"Hey. I'd completely understand it if you decide that you'd rather-"

Harley was called onto the stage.

"Fuck!" Damian said "Break a leg, good luck, shit what do I say here?"

Harley giggled, and headed out to show herself off on the catwalk.

Harley had gone out to the catwalk seven times now. It had been a great two hours for her, each outfit beautiful and fun to wear in its own regard. Right now, she was wearing a simple white top, no sleeves, just short enough to barely show the bottom of her belly and sides. Her bottom was a pair of shorts of the same color, and her flats were dark gray. They were the clothes she'd originally brought, easy to change out of in a heartbeat.

Her time was now over though, she was not needed for anything else. Her plan was to stay though, as long as she could. This was a big day for Max, having his model stay around for moral support was a good thing. There were still things he had to attend to, despite finishing with Harley,

She sat down in a chair, breathing out a bit. She was more tired from the experience than she thought she would be. She was happy they provided free water for her.

Damian took a seat next to her. He gave her a cute smile, brushing some loose hair out of her eye.

"Thanks." Harley said "So exhausted I didn't even notice it."

"Hey, no problem babe." Damian said "So what do we do now?"

"Don't know. Just hang around here for a while."

"Oh. Cool."

Harley noticed Clyde come from around the corner. She gave him a wave, and after a second, he noticed and returned it.

Clyde was wearing all back; designer pants, shirt, unbuttoned over shirt, and dress shoes. Around his waist was a blueish-black skirt-type piece, as usual for him. He ended up walking towards a mirror, and started applying a light pink lip gloss.

"I'm going to stretch." Damian said "If that's alright."

"Sure, take your time." Harley said "I'll be right here when you get back."

Damian gave her a lovely kiss on the cheek, and headed out.

"So how are you Clyde?" Harley said

"Alright." Clyde said "I don't have much to do for these, so I'm just kind of hanging out back here."

"Hey, I hear ya. That's all I'm doing now."

"Huh. Think you might mind helping me with my homework then? I'm in a Diversity in Make-up class, and we get graded better depending on how many races we cover. You're white, right?"

"Yep. Well, there's a bit of middle-east on my mother's side, but it doesn't show up on her at all and even less so on me."

"Great. I basically need Asian, black, and white before I think my grade will be good."

"Max won't help you? I mean, I know he doesn't really like the stuff."

"I'd rather work on someone who enjoys having make-up on though, he'd pretty much be a very last-ditch effort. He said he'd do it if I couldn't find someone else who's black, but I hated even asking him, and I'm sure he did too."

"Well, I doubt Damian would want to get make-up on him either, but I have a friend named Sheena who might be able to help you out."

"Great. Anyway, just sit there for a second."

Clyde reached into his seemingly skirt, and pulled out several vials of make-up.

"That's what that is!" Harley said "I just thought you were a cross-dresser."

Surprisingly, the usually stoic Clyde gave a gentle laugh. "No. My parents weren't lucky enough for me to be that much of an effeminate gay."

Clyde quickly walked over to her with his supplies. He was not quick in the applying, very diligent and careful with every brush.

"Can we talk at all?" Harley said

"Sure, I guess so." Clyde said "About what?"

"I don't know. Just figured it was better than being silent."

"Alright. I'll try to be topical. That was your boyfriend, right?"

"Yep." Harley let out a smile that she originally expected to be bigger.

"He seems very nice. Not bad looking either. Headphones are a little silly."

"There's a story behind them, and I kinda like 'em."

"I guess that makes public outings a lot easier to swallow."

"What about you? You have someone special."

"No joke, I'm the only gay guy in the fashion department."

"Ouch."

"And the guys in the art department can fuck themselves as far as I'm concerned. There's so much pretense in everything they say. They're all beat poets basically."

"Okay than, now that I'm wondering, what exactly do you look for?"

"Whenever a guy hits on me, I always ask him 'Can you throw a football?'. If I hear 'no', the conversation's over. My last boyfriend was the high school star quarterback, he was gentle with me but only when I wanted him to be. Get me?"

"Shit yeah."

"I ended up making him ball his eyes out when I broke up with him. Poor little darling, but it needed to be over. Would have hurt him more if I'd started to pretend I still loved him. I haven't been able to find a guy since then."

"You're not as rare as you might think. Everyone thinks the rest of the world is dating so much more than they are. Plenty of people barely do any dating at all."

"Yeah, that sounds about right. Still, I'm not entirely on baited breathe anyway. Alright, how's this look?"

Harley looked at herself in the mirror. Her eyes had gorgeous attention paid to them from eyeliner, and fuller lashes than she'd usually had before. Her cheeks were a lovely red, deep but also subtle. Her lips were now full, and to her surprise, looked stunning in orange. Both the lipstick and the slightly darker lipliner.

"I look amazing!" Harley said "Thank you so much."

"Hold still for one second, need to take a picture."

Harley turned back for the picture. A simple closed mouth smile, face and head perfectly in place. Only two pictures were taken, apparently Clyde only believed in one safety.

Damian found his way back. Harley flagged him down.

"Huh." Damian said "Looks like a lot happened while I was gone."

"Just got made pretty." Harley said

"You do this?" Damian said to Clyde

"Yep." Clyde said "Had homework for a make-up class. And now I just remembered I have to do something for my Haircuts and Dye class."

"Great, yeah. Sounds great." Damian said

Damian sat back down, and let out a loud sigh. His face showed he didn't mean to do it that loudly.

"You okay?" Harley said, whispering to keep everything just between the two of them.

"I mean." Damian said "No. I find all of this shit really boring. I'm happy to support you, so I didn't mind the runway stuff or anything. Just, I don't know, I'm going to be bored until you think we should leave."

The debate began in Harley's head. Max needed the moral support, she'd seen how easily pressure could freak him out. And then, there was her boyfriend clearly not wanting to be there, and technically having no real reason to be there. He wouldn't leave unless she did.

Harley got up and looked around. She was hoping to see Max somewhere, anywhere in eyeshot. She even tried listening for him, and, nothing. She found herself hard swallowing.

"Hey." Harley said "We'll get out of here. Just give me a second."

She walked over back to Clyde, getting his attention.

"Hey, when you see Max. Let him know I headed out."

"…. Okay. I'm a little surprised you don't want to tell him.

"I know, but. I should get Damian out of here and I don't know if I should wait for him. See you later Clyde, please tell Max I had so much fun."

Damian walked Harley back to her room, his hand gently around her waist. With his hand around her, and being so close to him, she got to notice and appreciate just how nice he smelled tonight.

"Well, here we go." Damian said "Your room babe."

"Thanks Damian." Harley said, giving him a quick kiss.

"Hey. Thanks again for letting me bale. I know that wasn't easy."

"Yeah." Harley said "Yeah. Yeah, it wasn't."

Damian kissed her neck, only a little bit of passion due to the fact they were in public. However, it was still plenty enough.

"I'll call you tomorrow." He said "I'll see you as soon as I can."

"Great." She said, a dumb stupid grin plastered over her face. "Look forward to it."

Damian walked away, and Harley's arm shook as she tried to open the door, still overtaken by sudden emotion.

The emotion quickly changed once she saw what Annie was wearing. Her normal lab work clothes; a white lab suit, globes, sneakers, acceptable jeans.

All of it covered in blood.

"………. Didn't go great?" Harley said

"No!" Annie said "The fucking text dummy died!"

"Oh. I'm sorry. That sucks. Things just happen sometimes."

"No! Bullshit, this is medicine, you don't get to think like that. I made a mistake and it killed the pretend person. I was able to find out what I'd done wrong, so I still got an A, but it's not exactly an A I'm proud of."

"You'll save 'em next time."

"I better! I can't afford to lose any more patients! My GPA depends on it!"

❤ - *Chapter 40* - ❤

As countless couples were celebrating their love today, Harley was now adding another year to her age. Damian promised a special surprise for the day, and Harley already had to remind herself several times that it was in fact because of the holiday. She was positive it was too early in the relationship to tell him about her birthday, let him only focus on one thing instead of having to juggle two.

Harley dressed for the occasion, new pink jeans down to her knees, dark pink at the bottom. Her top was a light pink blouse, and over it was a dark yellow button-up shirt. Her shoes were black flats, with pink lines on the side.

Underneath her clothes was a swimsuit. The plan was that she, Damian, and only four others were going to enjoy the campus's pool. Annie and her boyfriend were two of the others.

Annie was wearing a pair of blue jeans, and a brown sweatshirt. Her shoes were white flats.

"I'm surprised you're not dressed up for the holiday." Harley said

"Eh." Annie said "I kind of don't like doing much on V-day. You know? Just sort of sit back and try to have a pleasant time. Which, is probably exactly what swimming will be like."

"Maybe I can use to time to get to know Malcolm a little better." Harley said "Honestly, I feel like I don't know anything crucial about him other than the fact he's your boyfriend."

As Annie was about to open her mouth, there was a knock on the door. Harley was not surprised to see Damian on the other side. What did catch her off guard, was that he'd brought her a gift.

"Oh!" Harley said "What's in the box?"

"Here." Damian said, opening it up.

They were half a dozen doughnuts. Two with a red glaze, two with a pink, and two with a sort of magenta.

"The first two are cherry." Damian said "Then strawberry, and raspberry. I custom ordered them, and they made them, I want to say an hour ago."

"They look amazing!" Harley said, grabbing a strawberry.

"Oh, wait." Damian said "They kind of fancied it up a bit without telling me beforehand. I mentioned they were a Valentine's gift and they just did it, I don't think they charged me more but I wish they'd told me yesterday. Okay, so, the cherry ones also have cherry filling, so I hope you really like cherry."

"I do." Harley said, through what was left of the strawberry-frosted doughnut.

"The strawberry ones either have something or they left them alone, I can't remember. I wrote it down I can check in a second. And the raspberry ones have peanut butter in them. You're not allergic, right?"

"Nope." Harley immediately reached for a raspberry one.

"Great."

"Oh, and the strawberry one had no filling."

"I think I just remembered it now. I think one had nothing and the other was Bismarck or Boston or some kind of plain cream. I heard one lady there say the strawberry ones are popular so they don't feel the need to do anything special to them to get people interested."

"Can I have one?" Annie said, noticing just how many there were.

The response she got from Harley was a glare.

"I mean okay, I guess they're all yours." She said

"You have your suit on too?" Harley said, once again debilitated by talking with doughnut in her mouth.

"I've got it in a bag." Damian showed the bag he was holding under the doughnut box.

Damian was wearing shorts, dark blue with white diagonal lines. His shirt was a simple red t-shirt, not even a pocket or a button.

Harley swallowed her food. "Then we just have to wait for my brother and his girlfriend." She carefully put the box on her bed, and closed it. "Then we can head over to the pool."

The three couples were having a fun time splashing and swimming around. Harley was currently only ankle-deep, sitting on the edge. She wanted to watch everybody now. Specifically, she couldn't help but watch how her brother and Sarah were interacting.

Currently, Sarah was sneaking up on him as he, like Harley, was simply sitting on the edge. Sarah suddenly jumped out of the water, quietly shouting what sounded like "RARGH!" as she pulled him back into the water. In an instant, he was back above water, and they took no time in splashing water in each other's directions. Suddenly, Sarah squeezed together her breasts, sending a small personal puddle of pool water directly into Will's face. She couldn't stop laughing, although Will seemed a little less than thrilled.

Harley could swear she lip-read something along the lines of "Payback!" from Sarah. This ended up putting a smile back on Will's face.

Sarah ended up getting up, walking towards Harley.

"Hey Sarah." Harley said

Sarah was caught off-guard. "Oh! Wasn't going to, I. I was going to the bathroom."

"I'll head in with you. I wanted to talk with you."

"Uh. I'm going to poop."

"I'll plug my nose."

"Alright...."

Harley got up to join Sarah on her bathroom adventure. On the way up, Harley got a closer view of Sarah's stomach, and the absolutely impressive work she'd put in to her abdominals was finally noted.

"You're ripped you know." Harley said, now walking alongside Sarah.

"Oh, thanks." She said "It's uh, I've been working out since I was 14."

"How often?"

"Two hours, six days a week. Sometimes it's just cardio, but I stomach crunch, and, stuff like that."

"So tell me, what do you do on the other day?"

A blush crossed Sarah's face. "Here's the stall."

Sarah found her way quickly onto the toilet, almost slamming the door. Harley appreciated that she was polite enough to not actually slam it.

"There's no reason to be embarrassed." Harley said, meaning every word.

"It was, kind of nothing." Sarah said "I, sat at home and. Wanted to do something."

"Oh. Sorry."

"It's okay. I wasn't lonely or anything. I mean, well, Will came along and he tries to make every one of those days a date night. It means I'm not too tired so it's really helpful."

The first of what would surely be many farts came from Sarah's stall.

"I'm sure he's good to you." Harley said "I'd hate to think my brother was a pinhead."

"He's beautiful and amazing." Sarah said, a fart following. "I didn't know a guy could even be so good for me." Fart. "And he's so gentle." Fart. "Which is not entirely what I can say about me."

"Care to clarify?"

"He's wearing that shirt because he's embarrassed by all the scratch marks I put in his back."

"AH! That's why! I thought it was weird he was wearing a t-shirt to the pool."

The sound of urine now came from Sarah's stall.

"Wow you really had to go." Harley said

"Sorry, suddenly needed it." Sarah said

"You love him?"

"So much! I mean. Yeah. Okay, yeah. I really love him."

And then came the question Harley was, slightly dreading the response to. "You think you, want to marry him?"

"Um. I know it's soon to say but, I, I have liked him for a long time now. Yeah. Yeah if I asked I think I would."

"Okay." Not the worst response.

"But, I mean. I really can't say anything. Even if it wasn't too soon. He gets a little, funky, with some things. Tongue-tied. I don't think we could be the kind of couple to talk about that kind of thing."

This made Harley breathe out. "You know, he tell you about Mimi?"

"Mimi? Yeah, a little bit. They were together for a while, but, he talks about breaking up like he ended up realizing it needed to happen."

"Very much so. She pestered him to propose, none of us thought it was pestering until she was gone. Plus, well, you know how you two played at the pool just now?"

"Of course!" Sarah now walked out of the stall. "We love doing stuff like that. It's like we're kids again expect, well, it means more since we're together."

"Mimi hated that. She'd put up with it only a few times."

"Ugh. She doesn't sound like fun."

"No, maybe in her way, but not Will's. And not yours."

Sarah went to wash her hands, a smile was on her face. A happy, satisfied one. "I guess it's good he loves me. No matter what happens later, at least I got to be the girl he wants right now."

"He's told you he loves you?"

"All the time. Since a month ago. He calls me sometimes just to tell me, and because I really like hearing it."

"Alright, enough about my brother." Her wide smile showed how happy enough she was with what she'd already heard. "Something's been bugging me for a bit. Why did you start working out?"

"Oh!" Sarah pointed at her chest. "These things. When I first got them, I thought I needed to get strong so I could hold them up. I guess I bloomed too big too early so my kid brain tried to make sense of them."

"You got a reduction thought right? Were they too much too handle anyway?"

"They got in the way when I bench pressed. Blessing and a curse!" She smiled "Still, couldn't forget that they got me fit in the first place, so I only went down a size. Or is going from DD to D just half a size?"

"I don't know. I'll ask my phone when I get my clothes back from the locker."

Sarah and Harley walked back to the pool. They split-up quickly to reunite with their partners.

Harley walked down the pool steps, wading over to the area where Damian was. Leaning up against the side, he was steeling himself to swim laps with her once she felt like it.

Anni and Malcolm were rubbing noses in the deep end. They looked adorable together, and not half as steamy as Harley figured they might get. Neither of them were calming with age, even when it came to the simple acts they did in public. Seeing the two of them do something simpler and quieter was, romantic, Harley figured. She was truly rooting for them by this point.

Sarah jumped straight into the pool, cannonballing. She was rewarded for her bravery with a kiss from Will, and she was clearly taking it as full-on as she could.

Her hand-play slightly lifted his shirt, and Will was apparently no longer embarrassed by the scratches.

"Whoa." Harley had to say to herself. "She wasn't fuckin' kidding."

The swimming was done for the day. Will and Sarah headed out for a jog, while Annie and

Malcolm had a last-minute decision to have dinner at the closest restaurant that seemed pleasant.

As for Harley and Damian, they were heading back to her dorm.

The love surrounding the holiday meant the hallway was clear. Everyone else was spending time outside or in bed. Harley unlocked her door, and Damian asked if he could open it for her.

"Hey, why not?" She said, appreciating the offer.

Harley walked back into her room, walking directly back to the doughnuts. She opened the box, eating a cherry one.

"Would you like one?" Harley said "It's super nice of you but I don't actually know if I can eat all of these. I was kind of joking when I glared Annie down."

"No, I got them for you, I'm happy seeing you eat them. Give them away if you have to, but not to me. Okay?"

"Makes sense to me."

Harley finished her doughnut, and the two just. Stood there.

"Okay." Damian said "So. Are we going to do anything else?"

Once again, they simply stood there.

"Um." Harley said "You know I. I do like you a lot. I'd like to do something with you soon, or, well. Actually, I'd like to do something today but. Look, I don't know why but I don't want to have sex."

It had been bugging her since she'd woke up. Just the night before, she was looking forward to everything she figured they would be doing together. Once the thought of sex entered her mind, it froze it all up. She was never a prude, she'd proved that several times already. And yet.

She could not convince herself to do the same with this boyfriend.

"Hey, it's alright." Damian said, giving a smile that showed his words were completely true. "If I'm pent up later I can just nut at home."

Harley giggled. "Yeah. And I mean it, there are things I think we could do together. Well, I don't want to just say think. I know there's something. Do you, have anything in mind?"

"We could feel each other up. Clothes on, get a feel for each other."

"I'm, a little sensitive in my boobs. I mean, that's not a no! I was just, letting you know. In case anything seemed weird. Yeah. Yeah I can do that. Without a doubt."

"You sure?"

"Oh! Sorry, I still sound a little less confident, don't I?" She gave her face a tiny little slap. "There we go, needed to wake up a little."

"If that's the case, you go first. I just want to make sure."

Harley walked over to Damian, placed her hand on his shoulder. Despite her earlier worries, she was confident in this action. She traced her hand down his chest.

"Okay." Damian said. "You're convincing me."

He placed his hands on her back, rubbing her gently. Firm, gentle, every good feeling from the hand of a man. She could feel his hand trace over her bra, and the respect in not trying to undo it.

She herself, was moving towards his crotch. From what she could guess, there was a little bit of length to him, and the tip was, odd.

"I'm not circumcised." He said

"Oh." Harley said

"Just a guess you were going to ask. Everyone who's touched or looked at it asks. You uh, be careful if you can, my zipper's pushing up against me."

"Don't worry. And my zipper can rub up against me if you'd like to try it."

He did. The gentle movement of his palm and fingers caressed the crotch of her pants directly against her panties. The pressure was increasing, all to her delight.

His other hand finally managed to grab her left breast.

Harley let out a sound. Almost the beginning of a moan, but Damian was going to have to work just a little harder before he got to hear just how she really moaned.

"Well." Damian said "You weren't kidding."

They kissed, and continued the feeling for a bit.

And, the feeling only went that far. As much as Harley was liking what Damian was doing, there was no build to it. It, stayed that way. After five minutes, she called for a break.

Damian shrugged. "Maybe we should just stop then. You know? If we break we'll just be tired later and won't want to keep going."

"Yeah." Harley said "Won't want to, keep going."

Harley was now laying in bed, looking up at her ceiling. Today was, good. Today was, interesting.

She heard the door open, not at all surprised to see Annie. Or the state of her make-up.

"Yo." Annie said "How you make out?"

"Good." Harley said, and yet it somehow sounded like a sigh. "You want a doughnut now?"

"Sure buddy!" Annie said

Annie went to the box, seeing only one left. A raspberry.

"Wow, saved me the best sounding one." Annie said, then took a bite. "Shit, this had to have been the best one. Are you sure you didn't want to rest of it?"

"Yeah, I'm good for the day." Harley said "Damian is a real nice guy, you know. I uh, actually, I don't know what I was going to say. I don't have anything to go after that."

"Yeah." Annie said "Well, that's just something you have to figure out."

"Come again?"

"I don't know, just saying something that might or might not make sense."

"Yeah. Thanks Annabel. I'm going to sleep, see you in the morning."

♥ - *Chapter 41* - ♥

Harley and Annie now had to start thinking about classes for the next semester. They were in the last third of the current semester, and planning this early was important. It would be the first semester in Harley's last year, and Annie wanted to make sure they could still spend time together with a good schedule.

"You know." Harley said "I've done a lot of the art and math classes I need already. I have one last advanced class for both of those, but one can wait until my last semester. I still have a few electives I need to get out of the way."

"Are there any electives you need from a specific department?" Annie said "They've pulled that trick on me a few times already."

"Huh. Now that you bring it up, I need something exercise related."

"OH! Dancing counts as exercise here!"

"They offer dancing classes?"

"Yes they do! I need a few exercise classes too, I was thinking about doing a dance class once I found out, so honestly this would help me out a lot."

Harley did a quick search for a dance class her major would allow as her elective. Annie had her laptop at the ready so she could do that same, double-check it would work for both of their majors.

"Hey." Harley said "Alternative Dance with Janet Hoffman. Apparently, we try out different dance styles over the semester. Shit, five of them. We have to come as close to mastering two of them, but it's apparently just a course to let loose and have fun."

"I have always wanted to learn how to flamenco dance!" Annie said "And I took ballet for two years, wait, no, I still did it when I was ten. Three years. I definitely haven't 'mastered' it so maybe I can use that experience and have it count."

"I'm gonna be honest. At some point I will probably give up and dab."

"And I'm gonna be honest. Even though that sounds like something I would say, I very much kind of hate that you just said that and it's not out of hypocrisy."

Annie did her double-checking, and the course also counted towards her major. The two signed up for the same timeslots, and Annie started to prepare for the other activity of the day. She brushed out her hair, placing a black clip on the left side to keep it in place now that her bangs were starting to grow back.

She changed into a white frilly skirt, purple sneakers, and a sporty white top. The top had a pink and red heart symbol, and a thin outline of yellow glitter to off-set the rest of it. On her right middle finger was a large plastic blue ring, and on her left index finger a thin gold band.

The plan was to go have brunch to Izzy, as the two had not seen each other in a while. Harley was invited, but she had her own plans now that the room would be hers for the next few hours.

Extra sleep, with the promise that Annie could not possibly interrupt her by accident.

It was that exact reason why she was still in her pajamas. A thin but fuzzy purple bottom, with pink and blue bubble-shaped dots, and a plain white t-shirt on top. The shirt was a size too big for her, making it completely comfy for not getting out of bed.

"Hope you have a nice nap." Annie said "Anything you'd like me to get you?"

"If you could get my fat ass some fries that'd be nice." Harley said "If they don't serve them this early, then I'm fine."

"You know you're not really fat, just fairly pudgy."

"Hey I'm well aware of my pounds Annie, I'm just having some fun. Try to deprive me of that again and I'll hip check you to the next county."

There was a knock at the door.

"Ah, there's mah friend." Anni said, who then headed to the door.

Izzy entered the room, giving a quick hello to both Annie and Harley.

Izzy wore a green button-up vest, mostly hiding a thin white blouse underneath. The very bottom peaked out, as well as just the jest of the short sleeves. Her jeans were a faded blue, and looked almost bell-bottom, just shy of being wide enough. Her flats were shiny and black, looking new. There was a stud in her bottom right lip, a ring in her left nostril, and a gage through the top of her nose.

"Sweet shoes." Harley said

"Gift from my new girlfriend." Izzy said "She's the rebellious daughter of a banker. I always tend to get the rebel type, don't always get the ones with cash though. I'm usually the one who pays for things."

"Well, don't worry about that today." Annie said "Well, I mean, for anything you don't order. My bank account's pretty stable right now."

"Glad to hear it." Izzy said "Let's get going."

"Hey, hold on." Harley said "I'll walk you out. Might as well do something today besides sleep."

The three left the room, gently closing the door behind them. Like normal, the walk down the hall was not long. Not tedious. However, the door at the end opened before they reached it first.

"Out of the way." Josh said. His hair was slightly a mess, a stink of sweat around his collar.

"Okay." Annie said, moving to the side.

"I said move." Josh said, apparently not caring he'd already been answered.

Josh took a few steps forward, looking around the hall.

"Goddammit." Josh said "Goddammit. I'm checking the whole campus for you, you need to show up at some point."

Josh pulled out his phone and started angrily texting. Despite the rushed and hard movements of his fingers, the rest of his body stayed perfectly in place. He breathed heavily, not in the fashion to calm himself down. He was clearly fine with acting the way he already was.

"You." Josh turned to the others, pointing specifically at Harley. "Seen my girlfriend?"

"Nope." Harley told the truth, but had a good feeling this would have been her answer even if she had seen her.

"'Nope'?" Josh started walking forward. His footsteps were normal in volume, but the way we carried himself felt as if they were loud and pounding.

"Are you being sassy?" He said "It sounds like it. What I wanted was a straight answer. Okay?"

Despite the obvious angry, Josh did not raise his voice by a single octave. It was, calm, controlled anger. He'd been like this several times before and knew how to throw it around.

"You." Josh moved to Annie. "What about you?"

Annie ended up backing up against the wall. "I. I uh."

"I didn't realize I had all day." Josh said

"No, I didn't." Annie said

Josh turned to Izzy. "You?"

Izzy refused to look him in the eye. "Haven't either."

"You all really like wasting people's time." Josh said

"Lay off." Harley said "It's the middle of the morning, we've barely been out of our rooms."

"You don't talk to me like that." Josh said "You're little fucking friend isn't here to beat me up this time. Okay? You don't get to coward out and send some dog after me."

"You know I could call her." Harley said, and took no time in digging out her phone.

There was a moment of fear on Josh's face, which he quickly tried to hide before leaving. "Fucking I'll find her on my own. Lot of help all of you were."

Annie breathed out once it was clear Josh was completely gone. "Shit."

Harley reached out her hand, at first to place on Annie's shoulder. A part of her decided that, this probably wasn't the right time, and moved it back down instead.

"You all right Annabel?" Harley said

"Hey, I'm fine." Annie said "Just. Creeps, you know. There's nothing else to it."

"Yeah." Harley stood there for a second. She knew Annie was going to wait another minute or so before leaving, not wanting to see him again on her wait out.

"Wh- When I was seventeen." Annie started "Never mind I'll tell you later." She turned to walk out, Izzy not far behind.

"Fourteen." Izzy said to Annie as they left.

Harley could at least take a small comfort in knowing Izzy could be the person Annie could talk to. She could guess what Annie was most likely going to say, and what Izzy was most likely now saying. It was, however, an area Harley had fortunately no experience with, and she was not going to pry Annie for anything unless Annie really was ready to talk.

Harley turned back around, down the hall, opened the door, and slid into bed. This really was a good day to just sleep instead of anything else.

♥ - *Chapter 42* - ♥

Harley was packing up her things from the last class of the day. The end of the semester was right around the corner, and the college was already accepting book returns. She had every intention of dropping them off for what little money she would receive in return.

Her outfit today was a lovely dark blue shirt, unbuttoned and gently blowing in the breeze. Under it was a frilly green blouse, buttoned to the very top. Her jeans were a dark grey, and her sneakers gray and white. On her left thumb was the ring Annie had bought her only a few years ago. There was something about it that complemented her outfit today, and she could not resist.

The bookstore clerk rushed her through the process, giving her a full eighty dollars for the four books returned. She planned on using it for her own personal interests, instead of next year's book. She only needed one, and she was thanking both God and her lucky stars.

Suddenly, her phone buzzed in her pocket. A text from Damien. He wanted to spend an hour or so with her. She replied that she didn't have a problem with that, and headed back to her dorm, where they planned to meet.

"So, what do you plan to do?" Annie said

"I dunno." Harley said "He only texted me about fifteen minutes ago. We'll only have an hour."

"Is that enough time?"

"Between you and me, no. I'd rather we go on a date or hang out, and I can't think of anything we can do in just an hour. Except, I don't know, grocery shopping?"

Annie was wearing a puffy pink shirt, gold sunglasses hanging in the collar. Her jeans were ripped, faded, white, and only went as low as a pair of capris. On her head was a backwards black hat. This ensemble was left-over pieces from a fashion show Malcolm had been part of, an attempt to cash-in on urban influence and rap music in the media. Annie was the only person Malcolm, or Harley for that matter, knew who would unashamedly wear left-over costume clothes.

"Well, I'm sure you'll have fun." Annie said

'Oh yeah. Damien's a great guy." Harley said "Hell, being around him reminds me of-" Harley paused for a moment. Her gaze simply, there. Not at anything in particular.

"Oh." Was her first word out of the pause.

"What?" Annie said

"I was going to say that Damien reminds me a lot of what it was like to be with Chad."

"Makes sense."

"Yeah…. Yeah."

"I'm going to get a sandwich, you okay here?"

"Of course. Have a nice lunch."

Annie peaced out, giving the actual sign, and headed out for her food.

"And I just remembered what happened between me and Chad." Were the words Harley had struggled to say. Only saying them now, after Annie could not hear them.

Harley did the painful wait for Damien to knock on the door. What was only two minutes felt longer than hours.

"Come in." She said

Damien was wearing a blue t-shirt, and tan shorts. While it was certainly no longer cold, Damien was one of the few people on campus who felt the need for shorts. His shoes were brown sneakers, a tear on the left one.

"Hey babe." He said

"Hey." Harley said, giving herself some air. "Look, I. I need to say something."

"Okay, shoot. Is this, bad? You're not making it sound like it's any good."

"It's just that. There's a lot I've been thinking about, and, I kind of didn't even realize what I had actually been thinking about. And, what it is, is that. Shit, look, Damien you're a really great guy and I like being your girlfriend."

"….Okay."

"But, I mean. No, I *did* like being your girlfriend. I did, I think you're really cool but. This isn't. I'm not, into, what's been going on. Something doesn't, feel right. About how fast we're going in some ways and not fast at all in the others. I don't think we're right for each other. I'm sorry.

We're cool, I'd like to stay cool. Just. I want to break up."

There was silence, and not for as long as Harley was afraid there'd be.

"……Okay." Damien said "Yeah, yeah yeah, okay. I wasn't really expecting this, but. Don't worry, we'll still be tight. I'm not going to throw everything we've gone through away. But, well. I guess we're, over. I don't think I can say anything in favor of changing your mind, can I?"

"Damien it's sudden to me too." Harley said "But only because I just, didn't notice how much I didn't like what I didn't like. I've never been, all that smart at this kind of thing I guess, but I do know where this is going and I didn't want to spend a few years with you only to be just as disappointed as I am already."

"I, kind of wish you hadn't kept explaining."

"I'm sorry."

"It's alright. Really. I'll, see you some other time then. Just, without it meaning much of anything."

Damien turned to walk away. He had already opened the door, when he stopped again to say one more thing.

"If it's because of him, like I said, I understand."

Harley wasn't quite sure what Damien meant, but he was gone before she could ask. Maybe for the better, she figured. Still, her curiosity was peeked in one regard. She walked over to the peephole, wanting to check if Damien was going to handle himself as well as she had hoped.

Through the hole, he just stood there. Suddenly, he kicked over the trash can. It was barely a few seconds before he calmed himself, and cleaned up his mess. No harm, no foul, a little burst of anger.

Harley moved away from the peephole, and sat down in her chair. She was the dumper, theoretically, it wasn't worth crying or feeling too sad over.

That didn't remotely make it easier. Her head still went into her hands, even if her eyes stayed dry.

Annie opened the door around an hour after the break-up. She had stopped at the convenience store on-campus, based on her grocery bag.

"You alright?" Annie said

"I dumped him." Harley said, finding no easier way to say it.

"Here you go." Annie pulled a carton of ice cream from her bag. Neapolitan.

"Did you buy this now?" Harley said

"I've dumped and been dumped enough to see it coming. It's why I left the room."

"Oh. Thanks. You're a lot better at figuring all of this out than I am."

"Hey, don't beat yourself up. He seemed like a really nice guy. You could have been stuck with much worse."

"I don't think that matter at this point. You have a spoon?"

"Coming right up."

Harley began eating. She didn't entirely get the idea of eating her sorrows away, but at the end of the day, it was good ice cream, and maybe that could help her feel at least a little better.

♥ - Chapter 43 - ♥

Tomorrow would be her final day of the semester, and Harley had finished all of her packing. She would leave the second the professor ended her last class. Until then, no plans had been made.

And then her phone went off. It had not been long since she'd gotten a phone call, but it had been the first time in a long while that the caller ID caused her to screw up her eyebrows and almost cock her head right off her shoulders.

"Mimi!?"

Harley almost cautiously put the phone to her ear. "Uh, hi."

"This is Harley right?" Mimi said

"Yeah. It's Harley."

"Good, was afraid for a second you changed numbers. Look I'm sorry this is out of nowhere, but you know my apartment right?"

"Uh, it's been a while. Why?"

"I'm getting rid of some things, and I think you could use this box I have. Can you get here today?"

"Well, yeah, actually. I'm free."

"Great. See you in a little."

Mimi ended the phone call, and it did not end Harley's confusion.

Harley walked into the apartment building. She was wearing a cute orange blouse, a few spots of white, too erratic and random to be called polka-dots. Her shoes were white flats, they matched her capris. On her head was a pair of orange tinted sunglasses.

She took a solid few knocks on the door that, and it opened after a short bit.

"Oh hey," Mimi said "earlier than I thought. Guess that works. Come in."

Mimi kept her apartment nice and clean, in most areas. Harley noticed several corners where clothes, papers, anything that could be made into a pile had been made into a pile. Will made mentioned a few times that she could be a slob sometimes, but the odd precision of what could and couldn't be dirty was unexpected by a long shot. Propped up on a dressed, was a framed photo. The one she took of Harley and Will at Christmas roughly three years ago.

As for Mimi herself, she was a little hard to recognize. Her top was beige, held together by one button. It exposed both of her shoulders, her midriff, and the straps of her bra, which were a light purple color. Her bottom was beige as well, a short skirt with purple accents on the top and bottom. Her accessorizing was a far cry from what she used to do. Her lip ring was now gone, and it seemed to be a recent decision, as Harley could still see the hole. On her left middle finger was a large gold and shiny ring, the letter M, big enough to hide her index and ring fingers under it as well.

Most jarring of it, she'd gotten ink. On the left side of her chest, in big, black, cursive letters, was the words "TATS". Harley appreciated the wordplay.

"Nice ink." Harley said

"Thanks, got it a few months ago." Mimi said "Okay, sorry, not true. I got it the day after Will dumped me. I figured, fuck it, I wanted a tattoo since I was twelve and I could get the shitty idea one done since I didn't care anymore. Don't regret it, came out better than I thought it would. You want a beer?"

"Thanks but no thanks, I don't drink all that much."

"Me neither as far as I care to discuss."

Mimi headed to her refrigerator. She grabbed a beer, and immediately cracked it open. She sipped on it, never going for the full gulp. Apparently, she actually savored the stuff.

"So how's life?" Mimi said

"Uh, fine." Harley said "Semester's almost over, about to become a senior."

"Good for you. I didn't pay too much attention to how school was going for you. I kind of left the picture when you hadn't been very long in though, right?"

"Uh, yeah."

"I heard you have a boyfriend now."

"Well, I did. How'd you know that?"

"What, you think Will and I don't talk at all? Okay, okay yeah, I try not to talk to him that much, but it does happen. Apparently, he's dating Sarah now."

"Yeah."

"Eh, good for her. I never did that cutesy stuff well enough. Don't need to tell him, but as pissed off as I am, one of us needed to end it. She better do a better job than I did is all I can say."

"They're very happy. Anyway Mimi, what did you want me to come here for?"

"Megan."

"Huh?"

"Call me Megan. I went by Mimi because I thought Will would find it cute. Never giving myself a nickname for a guy ever again. Anyway, over here."

As Megan directed herself over to a box of items, a thought ran through Harley's head.

"Oh my God mom was absolutely right about her!"

Megan lifted the box, brushing off some dust as she did. She brought it over to Harley, who took interest with what she saw inside.

"Dirty love books!" Harley said

"Yeah, both my mom and I used to collect romantic novels." Megan said "Before you ask, no, I'm not disillusioned or anything like that, I just have a lot of these and I don't like all of them. I kept about five or six of them, but these ones are a little too boring. Old ladies, vampires, melodramas. Each subgenre you could ask for, you want them?"

"Hey, I'll take 'em." Harley said "I needed something new to read. These should work for a little while."

"Not too long, they're all really short. Anyway, take care."

Harley was now laying down, halfway through the first of Megan's novels. Despite Megan's lost interest, Harley found herself immersed in what the story was telling her. When she was little, she'd eat them all like candy, and now as an adult, she discovered she still had her joy to gain out of them. After her latest break-up, Harley had admitted to herself more than ever that maybe she really didn't understand how love was supposed to work and feel. At least that could be one thing these dirty books could possibly help her solve.

Annie opened the door, and stayed in the doorway long enough to catch eyes with Harley. And to notice only one hand was being used to prop up the book. The other one, under the sheets.

"……. I guess we're even?" Harley said

"…… Yep." Annie said

"…….. Mind closing the door and going somewhere else?"

♥ - *Chapter 44* - ♥

The semester had ended, a little rougher than Harley expected. While now a few weeks in the past, her final class had been completely brutal. She'd been personally e-mailed by the professor that she'd barely passed the class, even if they tried to be nice about it.

She had the house to herself right now. Will was doing some grocery shopping while their parents were off to the national park. It was their wedding anniversary, and they deserved the day completely to themselves. They would not be back until the next morning.

Harley found herself scrolling through her phone, wondering if it would be okay to call and talk to somebody. Annie, Janie, Sheena, many people in her contacts sounded good enough to call, but for whatever reason, she turned all of those ideas down.

Her eyes passed across Max's number. There was a strange, feeling in her stomach. Pain? No, she figured, maybe regret. She had never said she was sorry for running away after the fashion show without really saying good-bye. It was one of those small things that ate at her whenever she thought of it. It also wasn't something she could just say over the phone. If she was going to apologize, she was going to do it in person.

She scrolled back up the the top, seeing if maybe there was a name she skipped. There was, a name she had forgotten was there in the first place. Clyde.

"Alright, sure." Harley said "Better find something to talk about though."

She sat up in bed, her hair flopping onto her eyes. The subject was chosen.

"Hey." Said Clyde, was bored as he usually talked.

"It's Harley." She said "Sorry to bother you, but you can dye hair right?"

"Sure I can." Clyde said "Pretty good at it too."

"Could you dye my hair for me sometime? I'll pay you."

"I guess so. You've kind of called me at the only free time I'll have for a little while. I'm doing summer classes on campus."

"Oh." Harley sat up more, now finally moving the hair out of her face. "Well, hey, how about I just drive down there? You still in the room you had last semester?"

"Me and Max's room, yeah. Okay, sure that will work. I have some hair dye here. I don't have orange or pink or silver."

"Eh, I'll just see what you have and pick whatever I like for myself. See you in an hour."

Clyde hung up first, simply muttering an "okay", and Harley sent a quick text message to Will about where she would be.

Harley looked in the mirror, double-checking if her outfit was suitable. A black skirt, flowing at the bottom, and long enough that she could spin around or run without her panties being on display for the world. Her top was a light blue blouse with frilly short sleeves. Low-cut, her cleavage covered by a light white undershirt. Her shoes were shiny black flats, which she decided to change into high heels of the same color. She hadn't worn heels in a while, and for whatever reason, she felt like prettying up.

On that note, she decided to apply some light make-up. Foundation to cover the slight acne she'd gotten from a dessert binge a few days ago. Slight green eyeliner, light in color, just enough to make her eyes pop. She debated lipstick, and eventually choose a light pink.

With her make-up now on, she went to her jewelry box, placing on her steel black heart ring and her onyx and bronze ring, on the left thumb and right middle finger like she always respectively chose for them.

She was not overdressed for a lot of occasions, but she was overdressed for a hair dying appointment. There was something about that fact that made her happy.

Harley was sitting on a comfortable enough stool. A warm towel wrapped around the top of her head. There were only a few minutes remaining until it could be removed.

Behind her, checking his work, was Clyde. Clyde was wearing an all-black ensemble, with his thin make-up bag still flowing around his waist.

"Tell me if you're not happy." Clyde said "This'll be the only day I can try and fix it, and I can't do too much while it's new."

"I'm sure it's great." Harley said "Thanks again. How much do you want for this?"

"Considering how many colors." Clyde said "Pfft. Let me think. I'll need to ask for at least thirty bucks."

"Sounds like I should have gone to an ATM first."

Clyde looked-over the bottles of dye. Having never done this before, Harley was not aware it could be slightly expensive. Still, Annie had made it clear how fun the idea of changing your hairstyle could be, and it would have felt weird if Harley had actually gone through college without trying something adventurous.

She kicked back a little in her seat, waving her legs back and forth. She did this until she heard a key start to open the door. She screwed up her head, there was only one person she could be expecting, but she hadn't heard of him being there today.

The door opened, and there was Max.

In a pair of green boxer shorts, and a black t-shirt with the words "Fuck me hard" in gold foil.

Their eyes met, and Max's face turned redder than she'd ever seen. He ran into the closet and slammed the door behind him.

"Don't look at me like this!" Max said as he escaped.

"He uh, he looked surprised." Harley said "You did tell him I would be here, right?

"Of course I-" Clyde said "Wait, no." He had an incredibly small giggle. "I totally forgot. Whoops."

Having nothing better to do, Harley waited for Max to finish getting dressed. In only a minute, the door opened. His jeans were a light purple, with dark purple on the sides for contrast. There was a green shirt of obvious good quality underneath a dark blue over shirt with long sleeves. His shoes were white with black accents, and clean as a whistle. On his right hand were two thin silver rings, next to each other on the middle and index fingers.

He cleaned up fast, and he cleaned up well.

"So!" Max said, clearly trying to stop being flustered. "When did you get he- Why is there a towel on your head?"

"Well." Harley said "To answer what I think your first question was, I've been here about forty-five minutes. And the towel is because Clyde dyed my hair."

"Oh." Max said "Forty-five minutes, huh?"

"Yeah. How the hell did you not see me on the way here?"

"Um. Aha. I feel asleep on the can….."

Clyde entered the conversation. "Oh, I just figured you went for some food."

"In my underwear!?" Max said "Me of all people?! You really thought I would go outside in my underwear? I was terrified just going into the hall."

"You have designer underwear, you look better in that than some people look fully clothed." Harley said

"Thanks for the compliment but I can't pretend I believe it." Max said "Maybe with a better shirt. I do like that shirt but it's not one I can wear when there are people around."

"We're people." Clyde said

"You're my roommate and Harley, uh, Harley's somebody who's already seen everything…."

"So I'm guessing it was the shirt you didn't want me to see." Harley said

"I don't even know." Max said "Maybe I was just surprised you were here, maybe I'm more self-conscious than I thought, whatever, at least I'm dressed now. Probably needed it, certainly needed that nap."

"Your hair should be done now." Clyde said

"Sweet!" Harley said, removing the towel the second after.

She'd dyed it jet black, and had done extra work on the ends. On her left side, she had dark blue hair where it touched her shoulders. On the right side, a dark red.

"What do you think?" Harley said

"Your hair looks like a magnet." Max said, as an honest reaction. No jokes, no kidding, just a simple point.

Harley smiled. "How does that work?"

"Huh?" Max said

"Never mind. You like it?"

"I like it. It looks good on you."

Harley looked at the time on her phone. "Can we talk more later? I don't have enough money so I need to drive to an ATM. I think the closest one is in the mall, right?"

"Yep." Clyde said "We'll be here."

"Cool." Harley turned to Max, there was something she really wanted to ask. "Could you walk me to my car?"

"Sure, why?" Max said

"I dunno. It's been a while, I guess I want to really talk to you."

"Well, okay. That sounds good enough to me."

Opening the door for her first, Max and Harley walked out of the dorm to head to her car. They chatted briefly about Max's day. He'd slept little last night due to e-mailing a professor back-and-forth for his online class. He had already handed everything in, and was now guaranteed to pass, but it took a huge toll on him today. The bags were noticeable, but Harley had to admit he still looked good.

Harley got in her car, giving a quick good-bye and a rough estimate of when she would be back. She started her car, and it began its trip on the way out.

Then it stopped.

"Oh no!" Harley said "Oh no no no no no no! Don't tell me the fucking thing's broken! Goddammit! I can't afford to fix this! Dammit! Dammit! Fuck!"

"Uh." Max said

Harley craned her head back, trying to calm down for his benefit. "What?"

"You're out of gas." Max said

Harley turned her eyes to the gas gauge.

"Oh." She said "Hey look at that, I'm out of gas." She gave herself a moment, and then started to laugh. "I told myself to get gas back when I saw Mimi. Ha! Of course I forgot. Ah, this is a day. This is very much, a day."

"I'm sorry this sucks." Max said "Are you going to call a tow truck?"

"That's money I probably don't have." Harley said "All I needed was an ATM. I hate to ask, but did you have plans?"

"Nope."

"Could you please drive me to the mall? I'll pay for your gas."

"Huh. I, guess I could think of a few things I needed to get anyway. It doesn't seem entirely worth it for one stop, you know?"

"I understand, no worries."

"Okay, let me call up Clyde. I just remembered something I needed to do, so this works out for me."

Max called Clyde on his phone. Clyde figured as long as he still got his payment, he was fine with however they got it. Harley turned off her car, left it in neutral, and the two pushed it back into a spot. She would have to buy a gas can and fill it, but that would be a worry for later.

Right now, she just had to focus on a nice car ride with Max Turtle.

Harley was currently waiting in the mall food court. She's picked out a table while Max got done what he needed to get done. It turned out, Luna from the fashion department had taken up a summer internship with the jewelry store in the mall. The two had been working together last semester, and Max wanted to gather back some of the supplies they had worked on.

Harley had already ordered for herself. Currently, she had fries with ketchup lathered all over them, and a large cola. There were a few places she had in mind to eat from. A pizza place, an ice cream shop, and maybe a small Italian sandwich.

What she didn't want to do was get her lunch before Max came back. It felt, right, having lunch with him. Even if she did need to tide herself over a little first. So, she patiently waited. Her stomach was happy to see him approach.

"Is this all you felt like?" Max said, sitting down across from her.

"No." She said "Just waiting for you to get here."

"Oh. Okay. Do you know what you want?"

"Not entirely. Let me know when you know. Anyway, like we were saying earlier."

In the car ride, the two had talked a lot about Max's past semester. Harley had talked about hers as well, but she was very interested in what Max had gotten up to. To Harley, it barely felt like she did more than have a break-up.

"Anyway," Max said "I'm actually starting to get some recognition. When I just went to see Luna, the manager of the store knew my name. Never seen him before, he saw my face online through the school's newspaper."

"That's great!"

"I know. I think I can actually start my career once I get out of school. I can't believe it. I got so much exposure after the fash-"

Max stopped his words. Harley could practically hear the lump in his throat. It had to have matched her own.

"After the, fashion show." Max said

"......I'll bet." Harley said

Not only could they not say anything, at that specific moment, they were unable to look at each other. Harley had faced awkwardness before. This was, different. Harder.

She had to say something. Anything to break the tension. Surely, anything could work.

"It's a little funny in hindsight after I ended up dumping his ass anyway." Harley said, completely forcing a smile.

Max looked at her now, after a complete jolt through his body. "You broke up with him?"

"Oh. I guess, you didn't know about that?"

"No. You didn't tell me until now, no one did."

"Well, I told Annie and my family, and, they get the word around."

"Yeah and I still didn't hear about it, I guess."

"I, should have told you."

"It's fine, you didn't have to tell me. It's just, I figured at least you were happy."

"What do you mean?"

"I mean I figured it would be okay that you completely abandoned me because I thought you would be happy, but considering you were barely even with the guy you basically just left me alone on an important night of my life for a guy who didn't even matter."

Another silence. This one, not as long.

"I'm sorry, just." Max said "That was such an important day, and. I wanted someone to support me, and you promised it."

"I mean," Harley didn't fully mean what she was about to say, but her basic instincts wanted to defend herself. "it's not like I didn't show up. I left after I was done."

"Yeah and you had someone else tell me like a coward." Max was not, mad, in the traditional sense. Pissed off, sure, but not furious. He wasn't calm, but he wasn't shouting. "You mean so much to me and I thought that was at least a little bit mutual, and you decided it wasn't without you even telling me."

Harley wasn't sure why she felt the way she did now. She was regretting her most current words, and her actions, but there was something, more to this. Was she, hurt? Her stomach seemed to turn, so maybe. Maybe she was hurt like she didn't expect.

"I'm sorry." Max said, rubbing his face. "I mean, I mean what I said just. I would have been fine if you had tracked me down and said something first. You just, left. You never even tried to explain it to me."

Harley sighed. "Yeah. Okay, yeah. I don't know why I did it. Damien was bored and, I don't know, I didn't want to keep him waiting. I don't know why I fucked up that bad."

"It's fine." Max said "Just. Never mind it. I think I went on about it too much. Right now, I just want some pizza."

"I'll get it. What do you want?"

"Um. Cheese? I think they're pre-made so, that'd be simple."

Harley stepped up out of her seat, heading straight for the pizza place. There was a fully made whole cheese pizza, the right size to split.

"Hey, can I get that one?" Harley said

"Sure sister." The clerk said "Twelve bucks."

Harley reached for her debit card, about to pay in full before also ordering another large cola.

"Your boyfriend's gonna be real happy with ya." The clerk said

"I broke up with my boyfriend." Harley said, trying not to show confusion before the clerk tried to start a conversation with her.

Harley walked back with their pizza, placing the box onto the table, and handed Max his large soda.

"Oh, thanks." Max said "How much was this?"

"Who cares?" Harley said, giving him a smile. "This is on me, 'kay?"

Harley sat down. She took a slice of pizza for herself, shoved it into her mouth, and was able to look up fast enough to see one of Max's gorgeous smiles.

"Alright." He said "Fine by me."

Harley's phone started to ring.

"Oh, sorry." Harley said "Just when the atmosphere was getting really good, you know?"

"A-atmosphere?" Max said

"Hello?" Harley said, talking to the person who called her.

"Hey little sis." Will said "Um, so when do you think you'll be back?"

"Well I'm at the mall now. I need to stop at a gas station, then head back to my car. A friend of mine is driving me, I ran out of gas."

"Ouch. Well, um. I really want to tell you something and I don't have too much time to do it. Could you please stop by home first?"

"Hang on one second." Harley cupped the phone to talk to Max. "This is sudden but could you drive me home first? Will has something to talk to me about and apparently it can't wait."

"I'll text Clyde to know I'll be late. As long as you fork over the gas money I have no complaints."

Harley spoke back into the phone. "Alright Will, I'll be over. Can I at least get gas first?"

"Well, sure, but hurry."

"With bells on, I guess. See you bro."

Harley ended the call, and couldn't help but give a quick shrug at the situation. Max decided to get up and try to close the pizza box. As he did, the clerk from earlier passed by him and tapped him on the shoulder on her way out.

"Hey better luck next time buddy." She said, leaving before anything else could be said.

Max looked over at Harley.

"What the hell she mean by that?" Harley said

"I uh, have no idea." Max said

Will was pacing back and forth in the kitchen. He was dressed nicely, his shoes were new and shiny black. His top was a white t-shirt and a black unbuttoned vest, and his bottoms were a pair of black slacks. Looking him over again, Harley was sure all of his wardrobe was brand new.

"I'm gonna do it." Will said, with no elaboration in the slightest.

"Uh." Harley said "Please give me the context if you could."

"Sarah's coming here in about five minutes." Will said "I don't have much time to explain it, and I think if I try to just say it I'll throw up from nervousness."

"Oh!" Max said "I get it."

Will and Max seemed to have gotten along the second they met.

"Oh thank God you understand!" Will said "I'd say tell Harley but, fuck, maybe it'll jinx it if she does figure it out now. I don't know, just. Harley how do you not understand what I'm trying to say?!"

"I still don't really get it." Harley said "But, good luck I guess."

Sarah politely knocked on the front door, and Will was the one who opened it.

She was wearing a lovely white frilly dress, the kind of outfit Harley had never seen Sarah wear before.

"That's looking pretty relevant, isn't it?" Max whispered.

"Yeah." Harley said "Don't tell Will but I know what he meant. Just kind of wanted to mess with him a little bit."

"I don't have siblings so I assume that's a sibling thing."

"Yep."

"Sarah, you look so beautiful." Will said "And I, I have a lot of special things planned tonight."

"Are we going to have sex at the abandoned playground again?" Sarah said

"Well we are now! Hadn't thought of that. That's the perfect place!" Will then turned to his sister. "I'll be back when I'm back!"

The couple left the house, immediately for the special once-in-a-lifetime date that Will had planned.

"You nervous?" Max said

"No." Harley said "I was so nervous from the last time I thought he'd do it. Now I'm just happy he's found the one for him."

"….. Maybe, you'll find that person too."

"Yeah. Yeah, I think it has to happen at some point."

The family dog had now realized Max's existence, and started licking the bottom of his pant leg.

"Your dog is adding some new flare to my look." Max said "Mind if I pet him?"

"Go ahead, he clearly likes you." Harley said

Max squatted down to Clive's level and scratched his head. "Good puppy. You're a friendly type."

"Clive's about as much of a puppy as I am." Harley said

"His name's Clive?"

"Yeah. Because he's a barker."

"Ah, clever."

"I made you drive here for all of five seconds. Wanna hang out?"

"With you? Of course."

"Well. It's either the living room or my room. If you want to watch a movie, I have some in my room anyway so, I guess we start there anyway."

"No complaints."

Harley led Max into her bedroom. She let him take in the room, look at the walls and everything she had. She couldn't help but want to see if he was impressed by how tidy she was.

"Whaddya think?" Harley said

"It's cute." Max said "Pretty much what I'd expect given your dorm room. Hey, you still have that picture I took of you."

"Of course, I do." Harley said "I remember more from the night other than the fact we banged."

"Hm. You know, it's funny. You're so, open about all of this. I'm a little more scared of starting rumors than you are. I only barely told Clyde about it, and that was just because we wanted to be open about ourselves so it'd be easier to live together."

"Yeah." Harley said "I told Annie, Janie, Izzy, Sheena, Damien, Will-"

"You told your ex-boyfriend? That's, really brave of you."

"Not really, he didn't give a shit. I mean, he seemed, not at all surprised by it. I remember he wanted to say something about it but he got distracted. And I think that he thought he did tell me, never really pressed him about it. He clearly wasn't mad about you and me being friends so it was a non-issue."

"What would you have done if he was pissed off?"

"I'd have dumped him on the spot. You're too important to me to let myself date a guy who hates you."

Harley sat down on her bed. There was another silence, like before, except this time, it did not feel as awkward. It was as if, she'd said everything she thought she could say, and thinking of anything else seemed, boring. Mundane. Minute. Just not worth mentioning.

Or, maybe, there was only something to do.

Max sat down next to her. "Hey. Since you're paying for gas, is there any place else you needed to go today? I can take you anywhere."

"Anywhere?" Harley said

"Yeah. Anywhere."

"Can you take me to pound town?"

"Alright" Max said, getting his keys from his pocket. "Where's pound town?"

".....It's, a euphemism."

"Oh. OH!" Max said "Wow, twice in once day I don't get what you mean."

"What are the odds?"

"Apparently just as high as the two of us having sex."

Harley held Max's amazing face with her hand, and they took no time in starting to kiss.

"So, what are we doing?" Max said "Up for anything here."

"I wanna be on top," Harley said "and there's no way you're not cupping me."

"Fair enough."

Mas slide his hands to Harley's breasts. He hadn't lost his touch.

"Hey, remember that time I ate you out?" Max said

"That's not something a girl forgets." Harley said

"I've wanted to do that again for a real long time. So, can I make a suggestion?"

"Suggestion granted." Harley removed her skirt. "But you have to pull the panties off yourself."

Max removed his shirt, pants were quick to follow. "We have a condom?"

"Shit. Let me think. Oh!"

"You remembered."

"No, you just felt me up real good and I had to express it."

"I do what I can."

"Now I remember. I kept some condoms Annie gave me in that dresser drawer over there.

They were from a while ago, but they should still be good."

Max found one of the condoms, and Harley had no problem placing it on him.

"May have been a little early Harls." Max said "Remember, my tongue's going first."

"Hey, before you get there." Harley now removed her shirt and bra. "Let's shoot for over an hour this time. Think you can do that, stud?"

"I'll do what I can."

"Oh, and call me baby. I like it when you do that."

"Then baby, you're about to have the best fuck of your life."

Max and Harley were now laying peacefully in her bed, naked under the sheets. While they didn't last the over-an-hour hope Harley had, she had no problem with the total fifty-seven minutes.

She turned to look at the man who always pleased her. He seemed more tired than he usually was after sex, his eyes has almost shut several times already. He'd lasted long enough for her to orgasm, so she had no complaints if he needed to fall asleep, he'd earned it.

"Anything you want to talk about?" Max said, fighting off a yawn.

"Well. I'm not sure." Harley said "I think I told you most things I wanted to. Um. Did you know I almost failed a class for the first time?"

Max pushed himself up with his elbows to try and not fall asleep. "No. That sucks, I've had that fear a few times but I always ended up being completely fine. You alright?"

"Yeah. Yeah I guess so." Harley said "I mean. I sort of got my hair dyed today because it was still stressing out even thought it was a while ago."

"Sometimes things eat at you." Max said "You do what you have to do to feel better."

"I know. Still, good to have someone tell me."

Max and Harley laid there for a while, chatting about anything else that came to mind. They'd never done that until now, normally Max would have to head back, or there was something they needed to do. There were no more plans, and Max was staying as long as he felt like. They talked, Harley was sure this was what pillow talk was supposed to be, although she always figured it would involve her partner asking how good he was.

She was, content. Happy just to be there talking with him. Despite doing nothing at all, being there talking with him was all she needed at that point time.

"So uh," Max said "was that the best you've had?"

Harley smiled, glad her prediction was right after all. "Well let's see. That was the best you've ever been, and you're the only guy I've had sex with. So yeah, that was the absolute best I've ever had."

Max gave her one of this amazing smiles. "Good. It was the best you've ever been too."

"You know. Your smile is one of your best features."

"Really?"

"Yeah. You smile like I've never seen anyone else smile before. It's, cute. Adorable, I don't know the right word, but I really like it. It makes you look good."

"Glad I could make you so happy."

Eventually, the sad truth of the sheets being wet and cold got to them.

"Hey, I wanna watch a movie." Harley said "How about you?"

"I'm super tired, but I guess so." Max said "I'll try to stay awake."

"Cool." Harley got up, changed back into her clothes, and grabbed a few random DVDs without really looking at them.

"I'd like a shower first." Max said

"Alright." Harley said, slipping her clothes back off. "I might as well help you out with that."

Harley had finished her shower first, and she'd given Max enough information on where the towels were, what the specific settings were, and had a hand in helping him soap up. Now, she was clean again, aside from recycling her early clothes by wearing them again, and had popped in a romantic movie. After the books she was reading from Mimi, she was in the mood for romance on film.

Max returned from the shower, also in his earlier clothes, but without any of the ruffles or creases that Harley left her clothes in. She didn't know how he did it, but the secret behind it was intriguing enough that she wanted to leave it a secret.

"So, what are we watching?" Max said, sitting down beside her.

"Some crappy romantic movie." Harley said "Do you mind?"

"Nope." Max shifted his eyes to her. "No. I'm, okay with watching this kind of thing with you. Uh, anyway, what's this one about?"

"Some impossibly buff guy with long blonde hair gets his heart softened up by some uppity business woman who learns to cool her jets a little bit."

"Er, that sounds kind of dumb."

"Oh it is. I love this movie, it's terrible. You know, I've read a fair share of slightly erotic romance books, and watched a lot of these dumb movies. There's a lot to like, but, there's some things I don't get. Why don't they spend more time together before they decide they are meant for each other? What's their personalities, why is she so flat a person just so you can pretend you are her? But, hey. I like how some of them drag it out. I like the intimate stuff, I like the villains who realistically lack any good traits and yet are never as relevant to the story as you think they will be. I like the big scenes you remember the whole story for. Even the bad ones have almost all of those things."

"I guess so. I never really cared enough to get into them."

"One thing. I wish they really said how you are supposed to feel. I haven't had many boyfriends or anything, but. I, feel like it would be nice if something could spell out for me what love is supposed to feel like. I'm twenty-two years old and I still don't know for sure what it feels like."

"I think, you're just supposed to figure it out. It, maybe I guess, feels similar for everyone but you can't pin it to anything exact."

"Have you ever been in love?"

Max turned his whole face over to her. He took a second, and then gave a little grin. "Deeply."

"I hope you made her happy."

"I hope so too."

Thunder crashed outside of the house.

"Fuck!" Harley said "I guess there's a storm out there, huh?"

"Whoa." Max looked out the window, the rain started immediately. "I'm not driving back in this. Can I stay here? I'll call Clyde if it's okay."

"It's fine by me. I'll call my family, see how they're doing."

Harley tried calling Will, but got no response. Immediately after she received a text message from him saying not to bother him right now, and that he'd be back when the weather cleared up. She tried her parents, and this time she got an answer.

"Hey honey." Her mother said "Is the rain bad there too?"

"Yeah." Harley said "I just wanted you to know that I had a friend over, and he's going to be staying here now that the rain happened."

"Thank you for the heads up." Her mother sounded happier than usual. Not that she shouldn't or couldn't be happy, but she was clearly enjoying whatever she was doing for her anniversary. "Grab him a sleeping bag from the closet."

"I was going to, do just that, thanks mom." Harley hung up. She may have been okay in discussing her sex life among friends, but trying to explain Max being in her bed to her own mother sounded like a headache she didn't need.

"Yeah, I can't come back until tomorrow probably." Max said into the phone. "What? ... Yes, we boned, look I'll tell you tomorrow." He hung up.

"Needed to tell your roommate about your conquests?" Harley said

"Eh, you know how it is." Max said

"Hey, my mom wants me to get out a sleeping bag for you. Honestly it'd be drier than my bed so maybe it's a good idea."

"Cool, lead the way when you're ready."

After watching the movie, their fatigue from the day finally set in, and the two were ready to sleep for the night. Harley asked Max to wait in her room while she grabbed an old sleeping bag from the closet.

"Do you guys have guests often?" Max said

"Oh no." Harley said "We just go camping a fair bit. This is one of my old ones, but it's still full size."

Harley laid the sleeping bag down onto the floor. After doing so, it looked a lot more familiar to her.

"Oh!" Harley said

"What?" Max said

"Well." Harley figured she and Max had been through enough, encounters, that there was no harm in telling him the story. "This is the sleeping bag I used when I was thirteen."

"It's a pretty nice size for a teen's sleeping bag."

"We just bought adult sizes so we could always reuse them. The thing is, that's not the embarrassing part."

"Oh?"

"I sort of, explored myself for the first time in this thing."

"At thirteen?!"

"Yeah. Lots of us figured that out early on."

"Not me! I didn't jack-off until sophomore year of college."

"So, you lost your virginity before ever masturbating, while I was cutting after-school activities and not joining clubs because I didn't want it to cut into my jill-off time."

"What?!"

"Yeah. One of the only things that's ever embarrassed me was that in my teen years I masturbated as much as my friends told me guys do. Eheh."

"You don't mean-"

"Every day."

"Wow."

"Yeah. Ended up getting caught by my brother twice. He learned to knock the first time, and then learned to not really bother me for much of anything the second time."

"Well, I guess that's one thing I can be glad about when it comes to not having siblings. Anyway, um, I've never used these things, how does it work?"

Harley easily unzipped the sleeping bag for Max. He gave her a smile, and tucked himself in.

"Good night." Max said "See you in the morning."

Max was already turning over to sleep. Harley pulled back her sheets, happy they seemed suitable enough despite the utter work they had been through. She sat down, and looked back over at Max. It was going to be nice to wake up and have him be there, she realized. Not just for the normal friendship or the casual sex. She was going to be able to wake up and, talk to him. About nothing. Just like earlier.

"Hey Max."

"Yeah?"

"Do you think there's room in there for me?"

"I can manage it."

Harley wormed her way into the sleeping bag with him. As Max didn't have pajamas with him, they two simply wore their underwear, and they were now brushing bare shoulders. It was not intimate, and that was fine, because it was still warm and pleasant.

"Good night." Harley said

"Good night Harls. See you in the morning."

❤ - *Chapter 45* - ❤

Harley awoke that morning bursting with energy. She and Max had discussed their plans for the rest of the day, how well they'd slept, and were now both ready to take on the day. Max had to change back into all of his clothes from yesterday, which by now must have been bugging him, Harley figured. She couldn't imagine a fashion designer being comfortable in yesterday's clothes.

As for her, after her hot shower she changed into a pink blouse, and a jean vest. Her pants were a very light green capris, and her shoes were white flats that exposed her toes.

"You look great." Max said

"I know." Harley said "Not as good as you."

Harley couldn't help but look at her hands in the mirror.

"Man." She said "You spend a few years with a ring on your finger and you suddenly feel like a bit of you is missing when you look for it."

"You mean your class ring?" Max said "You could get a college ring if it's really bothering you that much."

"Oo!" Harley said "That sounds like a nice little investment. You know jewelers, think you could get me in touch with someone who won't break my bank account?"

"Of course I do. Start texting me some ideas and I can probably get the whole thing done for you."

Harley hugged Max's neck. "You're too sweet. I'll get started on that soon."

"Just do me a favor and wear it on the same finger you used to wear your last one on." Max said

"Sure, why is that?"

"Just a huge pet peeve I have. Okay, actually it sort of pisses me off more than it needs to. The right ring finger is for important memory rings, like high school, college, armed forces, or anniversaries. Just like how the left ring finger is for engagement and wedding rings."

"I knew about the left one, but the right hand one makes sense too."

"Good! You have no fucking idea how many people just throw a random ring on those fingers. I mean, I can almost understand the one on the right hand, but I've seen fuckers do it for their left ring finger too. I've heard so many people go 'what, I'm not married, why do you ask?' and they never figure out why. For fuck's sake," Max moved the rings on his middle and index fingers for emphasis. "you have two great spots for finger rings right here, both hands."

"What about thumb and pinky?" Harley said

"Thumb rings are fairly cool." Max said "Hell, I owe a lot."

"I know, I've seen them. They're very nice. A little jealous of the jewelry you wear."

"Does my ego good to hear that. As for pinky rings, never liked them myself. The fad seems to be dying and replaced with thumb rings, so I'm fine."

"Anyway, I think I can get my ideas sorted out soon. My last semesters won't be that hectic, I'll have plenty of time before November, well, maybe by December."

"Huh, I'd think those would be the most hectic."

"Only if you didn't pick out your needed class, and I made sure to get those out of the way soon. I barely have any classes left I need. Hell, I can just pick a class to fill up the time I need and skip it when I want to by this point."

"I picked needed classes too, but they expect a lot out of my last year. Less classes, more homework. I think I'll like it though."

Harley heard cars drive into the driveway. She looked out the window, seeing the rest of her family returning.

"Hey, everyone's here." Harley said "Convenient. Guess I'm introducing you to my parents."

"I uh." Max suddenly grew obviously nervous. "Yeah sounds great. I'm ready."

Max and Harley walked to the front door, where Harley's mother had already walked in. Will, Sarah, and Harley's father were still just outside.

"Hi mom." Harley said "This is Max Turtle."

"M-Max. Maxwell Turtle." Max said "Hey, hi Mrs. Millsboone. Harley and I are, old good friends now."

"Hello Maxwell." Harley's mother said. She was beaming, it was been a while since Harley had seen her this happy.

The others came through the door. Will took no time in running to Harley, she could almost feel the wind shift from how fast she'd gone.

"She said yes!" Will said

"What are you talking-" Harley said, until she remembered what he was trying to say yesterday. "OH MY GOD!"

"Congratulations man." Max said

Without much warning, Will shook Max's hand. "Thanks man! I have the greatest girl in the world."

Max looked over at Harley. "Make her happy."

"Every day." Will said

Sarah now came over to them.

"So, anything I can look at?" Harley said, shifting her yes to Sarah's fingers.

"Nope, sorry." Sarah said "We didn't have time to get anywhere after the rain. Will proposed to me in the abandoned playground while we were getting poured down on."

"So, you are getting one then, or just skipping to the wedding?" Harley said

"Oh I'm getting a ring!" Sarah said "Biggest one I can! Only ring I ever wore before was an orange flower I got from a cupcake, but this one. This one's gonna be so big it'll be like I'm working out my whole hand at all time."

"Great…" Will said

"Relax, my daddy will pay for it." Sarah said "Daddy always said that when I found the one for me that he'd finally take out that money he kept in the back of his bank account so I could walk down the aisle with whatever I wanted."

"Oh thank God." Will said "I can use my money getting us an apartment."

Sarah gasped. "That's right! We'll need to live together! I can't wait."

A kiss was shared by the two of them. Harley noticed, it wasn't an unusual kiss for Will and Sarah, even if it was to celebrate something better than they'd celebrated before. It wasn't, however, the kind of kisses she had shared with her own boyfriends. The passion levels, the raw connection so obviously there.

It kind of remembered her of, kissing, Max.

"Sweetie, where's your car?" Her father said

"That's right." Her mother said "I wasn't too concerned about the strange car after your call, but I was surprised I didn't see yours."

"Don't worry, I just ran out of gas." Harley said "Max was kind enough to bring me to the station, but one thing lead to another and, I mean, we just ended up here for a few reasons instead."

"We should probably go get it." Max said "I'm sorry to suggest leaving before I get to know anybody, but, uh. It's important."

"Fine by me." Her mother said "But it was a pleasure meeting you. Bring my daughter back to her car safely."

"I will." Max said, awkwardly saluting her. It ended up getting a laugh from her father.

"I'm going to go get something." Harley said "Be right back."

"I'll, be here." Max said

Harley turned to go into her room. A hand tapped her on the shoulder. She turned again, seeing her mother.

"How long have you known this young man?" Her mother said

"Oh, we meet my first day of college." Harley said "He's," she looked back at him, and couldn't help but smile from his presence. "a great guy."

"I see." Her mother said, and gave a quick whisper. "I approve. Oh, and" Her mother touched her hair, giving it a little flick. "I don't know why you felt like changing what you had, but I guess I'll have to live with it until you dye it back."

"Wait, if you don't like my hair what did you mean by-" Harley said, and her mother simply walked back to continuing cooing over Will and Sarah's engagement.

Max was carefully driving Harley back to her car.

"Since I was there for the announcement." Max said "Would you mind texting me a picture of Sarah's ring when she gets it?"

"No problem." Harley said "I just hope it's not bigger than my phone."

Max laughed "We'll have to see. Oh, I just remembered to ask. Did you know about the New Year's Eve party for the fashion department?"

"I do now."

"It's for everyone in the department, anyone we invite, and anyone who has been a big help to us recently. They asked me for your name after the photo shoot and the fashion show, so you'll be getting it in your school e-mail soon."

"Nice! Hey, speaking of the fashion show. Are you still, it's okay if you are, are you still kinda, mad at me?"

"I won't lie, learning you and he hadn't even slept together really does a number on the whole 'you weren't even serious with him' thing, and that makes me a little upset about it. But, the thing is. I don't have a single part of me that can be that mad at you. I, really care about you. And no matter how mad I wanted to get, I do still know you care about me a lot too. It was either a big thing or it wasn't, but I'm just going to look at it as a minor little thing I don't need to stay mad about. Sound good?" Max ended his words with a delicious little smile.

"Very good." Harley said, giving him a smile in return.

Max continued driving to the campus. They were only a short ways off, when Harley remembered why she had to stop off at her room first. She reached into her purse, grabbing a wrapped piece of rubber the two were becoming more and more familiar with.

"Wanna have car sex?" She said

"I'll just pull over into theses woods here."

♥ - *Chapter 46* - ♥

Harley was in the middle of her dance class with Annie. Like every semester, Annie had changed up her hairstyle, even if this time, it paled to the work Harley had done. It was a simple brown, braided to her left side to make a tail long enough to reach past her shoulder.

The two of them were in their dancing clothes. Annie wore a long red dress with black frills, and currently had roses pinned near the top of her head. Her shoes were stunning black heels.

Harley wore gray leggings, a black tank top, and a blue open jogging vest. Her shoes were simple gray sneakers.

Annie had been doing well in learning flamenco, while Harley simply did whatever she felt like doing. They both ended up working up a sweat by the time classes would be over. They were currently halfway through today's class, and the professor wanted everyone paired up to try dancing together. Without needing much thought behind it, Harley and Annie paired up.

"Let's slow dance, face to face." Annie said

"Could be fun," Harley said "why are you suggesting this?"

"We can smush our boobs together!" Annie said "It'll make the guys super jealous."

"Eh, maybe." Harley said "Maybe we should do what we've been practicing. Plus, I'm kind of in the mood for some beatboxing."

"Alright, you have a point. But sometime in the future let's get super close and see if anyone starts blushing."

"You try way too hard sometimes. Still, I guess there's no harm."

A student Harley did not recognize came in through the doors, directly to the professor.

"Can I have a word with you?" The student said

"If you're trying to join, it's a little too late." The professor said "I suppose it's possible to get a note from the administration but I very much doubt it by this point."

"It's not about that." She said "It's about Muriel. She won't be coming by anymore. I'm telling all of her professors."

"Oh?"

"Yeah. She'll be away for as long as she needs to. And I'm not about to say exactly where or why. You catch my drift?"

"Don't worry, I do. A few of her other professors and I noticed a few too many things between her and the man who calls himself her boyfriend. We've been looking into it to bring it up, I'm glad she's done something too."

The student left. The professor turned back to watch the class, nothing needed to be said to them. Harley and Annie seemed to be the only ones who noticed.

"Wasn't Muriel, Josh's girlfriend?" Annie said

"Yeah." Harley said

"Then I think the both of us know what they were talking about."

"Yeah."

"Well, it looks like we can't do much of anything for her now. If she comes back, different story."

"I know. Anyway, let's get our minds off of this and start dancing."

"You lead partner."

Harley was chugging down the water bottle she'd brought with her on her and Annie's trip out from class. After stopping off in their dorm to change, they were going to head to go dress shopping.

"Any idea what you'll look for?" Annie said

"Nope." Harley said "But, I'm going to drop some serious money. Feels right, after leaving Max's last invite early, I'm going to dress up and stay until they don't want me anymore."

"This is a date night for me." Annie said "Can you believe Malcolm and I are still together? Be honest with me."

"I guess with your track record it's a little surprising." Harley said "But, well, I'm just happy for the both of you."

"Not as happy as I am. I have to thank Max for all of this. I haven't been this happy with a guy for such a long time, and I've had plenty of good times. This is, kind of different. Great different."

"Sounds like Malcolm should be the one you say all of that too."

"Trust me, I have."

"How long until New Year's anyway?"

"About a month, roughly."

"God. I've been really losing track of time. I'm so, bored of this year. I've been paying zero attention."

"You sure that's the reason?"

"Huh?"

Annie sighed. "Nothing. Race ya!"

Annie ran up ahead of Harley. Harley didn't give chase after her. She'd been holding back a nasty fart for the past few minutes, and Annie just gave her the chance to blow it right out.

Granted, the looks she got from the people across the street were a little much.

♥ - *Chapter 47* - ♥

Her semester flew by, and before she could barely blink, Harley was at the promised New Year's Eve party. She'd spent a lot of money on her outfit, and now that she was there, she was feeling more justified in doing so.

It was a blue and purple dress, puffy and frilly on the bottom. The blue was full on the top, with sparkles to add effect. The bottom skirt was vertically striped in the two colors, completely equal with each other. Her shoes were purple heels, and just for the hell of it, she'd bought long purple gloves. They were a snug fit, and had sparkles just like her top. In her ears were sparkling crystal earrings, dangling down enough to almost reach her shoulders.

She applied more make-up than usual as well, she could almost pat herself on the back for all the extra effort. Light pink blush, applied heavily enough to be seen. Black eyeliner, purple eyeshadow. As for her lipstick, a musky peach color.

She was not overdressed or underdressed, the fashion students pulled all of the stops out as well. Thankfully, either from thinking it was too much, or because they could not afford it, they did not go as far as Harley expected. It was mostly a red carpet, but not the million-dollar sort of red carpet she was afraid of. Now she did not stand out too much when in a large crowd, while still looking gorgeous enough to stand out when the crowds were small or if she was by herself.

Which, she figured, could possibly happen at some point. Just as she figured, there was dancing. Many of them couples, friends, more than likely at least a few of them had never even met until now but felt a connection anyway. Good for them, she believed, it was always nice to have a good time. Even if, likely enough, she would not be dancing with anybody. Dancing sure sounded fun, but, she wasn't sure. It was probably just nice enough to be there and eat the free food and enjoy the free music. Probably.

An entire building on campus was reserved for the event. The fashion department had enough funds and power to rent it out, even during winter break. Harley was sure her major couldn't ever dream of that kind of hold. Granted, she doubted any of the professors in her major would have cared, so it likely worked itself out.

There were streamers on every pillar, all over the ceiling and walls. Colorful banners and posters, somehow nothing felt tacky. Months of effort were evident, and Harley's respect had been earned by every single decorator.

But, as nice as everything looked, what deserved her attention right now was the food. Little hors d'oeuvres, from fancy fish and cheeses, to the simple stuff. To Harley, the pigs in blankets looked good. She still enjoyed hot dogs as a food for special occasions, ever since that night four years ago.

It started playing itself back in her head. How straight-forward she couldn't help being. How much of an adorable dork Max had been. The absolutely lovely moon. The passion; brief, sloppy, and awkward as it had been. They'd gotten so much better, but it was the way she wanted to remember that night. Warts and all, as they say.

She had to snap herself out of the thought, not sure if she would just space out if she thought about it too hard. She took a seat, taking her platter of food with her. Taking the time to people watch as she did.

There was Annie, dancing with her boyfriend Malcolm. Annie was wearing a powder blue dress, big and puffy and past her ankles onto the floor. If she hadn't been in the room when they'd dressed, Harley wouldn't have known Annie was wearing blue high heels at all. They were completely hidden. Annie had also painted her nails the same blue, and her hair. It was short once again, pixie. This wasn't her new semester haircut, it was only for tonight. She was inspired by a movie she loved, according to her.

Malcolm was wearing a black suit, black shoes and tie. He did not wear the flashy stuff Harley had seen him wear tonight. He blended with the crowd, and not in a bad way. He was still clean, and it was very clear how happy he and Annie were together. Harley had a feeling they both dressed fairly normally for a party today so none of their normal clothes could be a distraction. They could only focus on each other, no costume jewelry or wild colors to get in the way. Even Annie's blue hair seemed very normal, and they were locked in eyesight.

Harley moved her gaze, hoping to see anyone else she recognized, or at least something interesting. She saw a few couples dancing, a few people getting food or standing in the corner to take a break. The music was now starting to die down, everyone could relax until the next song played.

"Maybe I'll dance next." Harley said, and got up to stretch.

She took her platter back to the table, there was staff who would take care of it for her. She bumped into a familiar face.

"Sheena!" Harley said "How's it going?!"

"Hey girl!" Sheena said "I got invited by this guy Clyde, did a make-up assignment for him. Wait, you're the one how told him about me, right?"

"Yep." Harley said "Clyde is a friend of a friend. Thought you might like to help out."

"Any chance to look good in front of a camera is a'ight by me." Sheena said "Guy new what he was doing too. I can't even get my face to look as good as what he did for me. No way I was going to turn down a party invite after that."

Sheena was wearing a lovely pink dress, down just past her knees. Like Harley's dress, it was two tones, stripes on the side of the skirt were darker pink, while the rest of the body was light pink. Her shoes were red heels, and silver crescent moons dangled in her ears.

"Tell me," Sheena said "find yourself a dance partner yet?"

"Nope." Harley said "Be nice if I got one though. Have a little fun I guess."

"Well, find one before midnight. You'll be happy you did. I'm going to try my luck, I'll catch up with you some other time."

"Alright." Harley said "Sure you don't want to catch up now? I don't mind."

"Sadly Harls, I do mind. Tonight's not a night for just friends. You understand."

"Yeah. I do."

Harley simply stayed put as Sheena went back out to try her luck with the others. Poor Harley was dying for someone to talk to by this point, but her options were thin. It was rude to try and talk to Annie when she clearly had her hands full, as well as 100% unlikely.

Everyone else seemed to have their hands full as well, not just the people she knew. As for that small number though, Luna and Victor were talking together, and from the look of it seemed very happy being in their own world. A few rumors were circulating they were more than just friends after all the times Luna had gotten help from it, and just in case they were true, Harley left them be.

After them, she managed to scout out Clyde. It was easy to do, he still wore his blue waist skit, make-up bag, whatever he called it. The rest of his outfit was black tie, and with strong but subtle make-up.

Another walked up to Clyde, carrying his hips as he walked. "Hey there!"

"Oh. Hey." Clyde said back

"I know you. Art major like me, you've sounded like a real smart guy from what I've heard."

"Cool."

"Hey, you wanna spend a little time with little ol' me on the dancefloor?"

"Can you throw a football?"

"Pfft, no!"

"Then I'd be wasting my time." Clyde just walked away after that.

It was rude to laugh, so Harley stifled it with her mouth the best she could.

Clyde walked past her after that. She went to open her mouth, but Clyde just gave her a friendly nod and kept walking. It ended up reminding her how Clyde really wasn't the chatty type unless you were the only person around or his attention had to be on you.

She gave up and went back to get some more food. There wasn't anybody she would be able to talk to before midnight. A shame, especially when she did know of one man she really would have liked the chance to talk to.

There was something about the smell of the little fish that piqued her interest, so a small fistful of them seemed like a good idea. If she didn't eat them all, maybe she could just wrap them in a napkin and kept them in her purse when she got it back from the front counter. Or, if all else failed, her bra. As terrible of an idea that it was.

Despite eating a good number of them already, she wanted more of the pigs in blankets. God help her, they were really good. She didn't even have to look where they were by this point, she just reached over.

And her hand hit his.

"Max!" She said

"Hey!" Max said "Shit, I wasn't even sure you made it by this point."

"Maybe I should have texted you."

"Hey, I didn't invent this party. I may have invited you, but you weren't obligated to tell me."

"I know, but, well I've been hoping for someone to talk to for a while here. Maybe if you knew when I was coming you could have said hi to me or something."

"I, well, didn't bring a date or a friend so. If you still want someone to talk to I could, do that."

"You have helped make my night Maxwell Turtle."

"Heh. Sorry just, not everyone calls me Maxwell. It's, a little refreshing I guess."

They went to the seats, Harley was lucky enough to get back into the chair she'd had earlier. It was still a little warm.

"So what did you get, anyway?" Harley said, looking over at Max's plate.

"Just these little hotdogs." Max said "Can't help it, I really like hotdogs."

"Yeah." She gave him a smile. "Me too. You have these fish yet?"

"No, but I know what they are. Sardines with alfredo sauce and a little bit of pesto. It's odd but I hear it's good."

Harley dropped one of the fish into her mouth. "Phuck, thesh are goot."

"You uh, may want to chew a little, I could barely make that out."

"Thorry." She swallowed. "Want one?"

"You, want me to eat off your plate?"

"Hey it's not the only time we've shared germs, right?"

Max ate one of Harley's fish. "Alright, not bad." He managed to talk and eat without sounding like a dolt.

"Are all of the parties here like this?" Harley said

"Yep, pretty much." Max said "We don't do the typical college parties, if those even are a real thing. Can't get too wild when the staff is catering, and, I like this anyway. It's my style."

On the subject of style, Max's apparel was just the sort of thing she knew he would be wearing. Like a lot of the other guys, he was wearing a black suit and tie. His black shoes seemed to shine brighter than everyone else's. On his left thumb was his silver spiky crown ring, and on his right middle finger was a simple silver band. She noticed him unbutton his suit jacket. Apparently he felt the need to winddown a little bit. It was nice to see him like that, compared to how stressed he could be. She didn't like seeing him worried or upset, he deserved to be happy as much as possible. It also set off this weird discomfort in her stomach to see him go through something.

And granted, a weird yet pleasant feeling was going through her stomach just now anyway.

The music kicked back up again. A slow beat, made for slow dancing and not much else.

"You know this song?" Harley said

"Nope." Max said "Do you?"

"No. But, you wanna dance to it anyway?"

521

"You and me?"

"Yeah. No one else I do want to dance with, in all seriousness."

"Alright. Let's get up and slow dance."

Harley lead Max onto the dance floor. Her leading just made sense to her. They picked a perfect spot. Not the centers of attention, and not too many other people around them to get in their way. She wanted this dance to feel like just the two of them. Just like leading, it simply felt right.

She placed her hand on his right shoulder, and their left hands interlocked. Max placed his hand on her shoulder.

"Um." Harley almost felt like blushing. "I feel like, you should hold my back."

"Oh?" Max said

"Yeah. Just, seems silly for both of us to touch shoulders."

"Alright."

Max moved his hand down her back. Harley had to admit to herself, it caused a nice sensation. He was gentle and firm as ever. Once he got to the right spot, his grip held right in place. It moved her a little closer, and she very much had nothing to complain about being closer to Max.

This was going to be nice.

She continued leading, letting the sway of the music take her away as she danced. Max followed without a complaint.

"You're a really good dancer." Max said

"You too." Harley said

The music continued, but Harley no longer paid it any attention. As she swayed side-to-side with her dance partner, he was all she could see. His warm smile, his gorgeous face. She could almost kiss him right now, just to thank him for making her evening wonderful in two seconds.

"Izzy?" She said, just barely noticing a new arrival.

"Who?" Max turned to look. "Oh yeah, Izzy Platt from the piercing store. Yeah, to help pay the fees we get some fashion folks and the like to promote. Looks like she'd giving out the business cards and talking."

Harley watched Sheena walk by where Izzy was, and then watched her stop once they noticed each other.

"Hey there." Izzy said

"Hey there yourself." Sheena said

"Where were we?" Max said, turning back to Harley. His eyes now glistening from the lights of the room.

"Um." Harley found words, hard, all of a sudden. "Dancing."

There was a loud bong, and Harley saw a large timer appear near the top of the building. She'd manage to not notice the screen through all the decorations, but now that it was on, it had her full attention.

"One minute to midnight!" Said an announcer. "If you've got someone, hold 'em tight and start counting."

"Huh?" Harley said

"Oh, guess you don't know." Max said "It's an old New Years tradition. At midnight, you kick off the year by kissing someone."

"Oh!" Harley said "That sounds fun."

Suddenly, she felt as nervous as a five-year-old on her first day of school.

"You, um." She said "Would, you like to be my New Years' kiss?"

"A-aha." Max said "I, was going to ask you the same thing. Since, we're already dancing."

Harley almost had to look down, they were in fact still dancing. They stopped in place, dancing did not feel as important as this timing. She wanted it to be perfect. Not just for her sake.

"5!"

"4!"

"3!"

"2!"

♥ - Chapter 48 - ♥

"HAPPY NEW YEAR!"

Harley and Max ended their embrace. No matter how many times she had kissed him, it was still rewarding. She looked into his eyes, and he was still beaming. This ended up being a perfect night. For once, she was feeling the same rush of blood and happiness without anything sexual. It was enough being there, with him. Normally, she would wonder why, but tonight, all that mattered was a new year had started, and she'd started it off right.

"Hey." Harley said "Before I say this, this isn't for what I usually mean. You want to head back to my room for a second?"

"Well, sure." Max said "I guess so. You phrase it like that and I have to know."

Harley opened the door to her dorm. It felt empty, it was clear nobody had been staying in it for a while now. She led Max over to something under her bed.

"What's that?" Max said

"Janie gave me this bottle of whiskey a few years ago." Harley said "It's aged the right amount since then, and I never found the right time to open it. But, I think I have now. Would you like a New Year's Day drink with me? Just one, I have to drive."

"That sounds amazing." Max said

Harley cracked open the whiskey. The strong smell hit her immediately, and judging by Max's face, it hit him just as hard.

She went for some glasses, all she found were plastic cups. They were both of age, but it still felt appropriate for dorm drinking. She poured one for Max first, then herself. They drank at the same time.

"Whoa!" Max said "That's real good."

"You said it." Harley had to wipe her mouth after. "I'm glad I kept this."

"I'm glad you thought it was worth it to share with me." Max said "I've, never told you how much I appreciate all the time we spend together. I mean, I have, just. Not, well enough."

"If it makes you feel any better. I'm not so sure I have either. I, well, I don't know what to say. Sorry, I, I feel like there's something to say. Um."

"Hey, it's alright. Want to head back?"

"Maybe. Maybe it's time to go home. Believe it or not, I'm a little tired. Wore out my cankles slow dancing with you. And I don't regret it, especially if it's easier to get to sleep tonight."

"Well, take care then. I think I should head back. If you do want to stay, I'll see you. If not, don't worry. I know this time, and I'm just glad you had a great time."

Max walked out. Harley decided, maybe she could spend another twenty minutes with him and the others. After that, she could drive home and take the nicest sleep she'd had in a very long time. Might as well catch up to him now first.

Harley arrived home at three in the morning, and despite being tired, she figured it was time to get the mail. She remembered her parents had already got it from the mailbox, and no more would arrive later now that it was officially a federal holiday, but she'd not bothered to check if anything was for her.

There was. A big, pearl white envelope, with gold decals on the side. Of all people, this came from Janie.

"What the fu-"

You are cordially invited to the wedding of

Janet Olber

and

Matthew Vruck

You and a guest of your choice must RSVP as soon as possible for the date of January 14ᵗʰ. We are looking forward to your response.

Harley immediately called Janie's number. It rang for a while, past the usual three rings.

"What do you want?!?" Janie said

"It's me." Harley said

"Oh, sorry." Janie said "What is it? Wait! Did you get the invitation?!"

"Yes!" Harley said "How did you not tell me?"

"I posted about it on-"

"I mean call me, text me, for God's sake you must have been engaged for a while and I had no idea."

"About a month and a half ago, maybe."

"But the wedding's this month!"

"We don't want to waste time and don't have a long guest list. Are you coming?"

"Yes! Of course I'm coming! Congratulations! You two are going to be so happy together!"

"Hey, we're already happy, we're just doing what we know we should do by this point. Shit, now I woke him up. Sorry Harls, I'm going to try and get me and my future husband back to sleep. Love you, see you real soon."

Janie hung up, and Harley went down to her room to explode with excitement. It was a good hour and a half before she got to sleep.

♥ - *Chapter 49* - ♥

Harley had never been invited to a wedding before. If you had to ask her before today, "which one of your friends do you think will get married first?", she would not have had an answer for you. Maybe Annie, maybe Chad, and Janie would have at least been halfway through the list considering how anti-social she was around everybody else but her.

And then of course, Matt. The man responsible for Janie being the right answer to the question.

Harley, at admittedly last-minute notice, was asked as maid of honor. There were no bridesmaids to keep charge of, so her job was simple. Regardless, her outfit was as gorgeous as it needed to be.

A full yet simple yellow dress, sparkles all over the top and bottom. Dark yellow flats, and long yellow gloves. She'd asked Max what a good solid color for bridesmaid would be before she was promoted to maid of honor, and the color still suited the position. He'd also tried to convince her to wear a tiara. He tried so hard that he was almost successful.

She did have one accessory, the onyx ring was over her right glove, on the middle finger it had started to call home. Harley expected wearing jewelry over a glove would be uncomfortable, but it fit snugly. Now she understood why it was a fashion choice.

Harley mingled with the other guests, trying to kill time until Janie needed her. It was mostly Matt's friends, almost nothing for Janie's family. Harley met a cousin by the name of Pedro, who admittedly barely looked like her, which was not true for the parents in the picture he carried in his wallet. The dad was very much an older Pedro, to the point where his name was also Pedro, but Pedro Jr.'s mother shared Janie's hair color and face structure. Harley didn't bother asking which side of the family Pedro was on, she was just happy Janie had more than one guest specifically for her. It was no secret how little friends she had before they'd met.

A text message was received, telling Harley to head back to prepare with the bride. It was a small venue, it did not take Harley long to find the location. She did her best to avoid running into Matt, Janie had warned her Matt actually believed the superstition about not seeing your bride before the altar, and was worried enough that the maid of honor would be close enough as far as legends were concerned.

Harley gave a knock on the door once she found it, and said her name so Janie would be sure. They had not seen each other yet, Harley was mentally prepared to see the dress, but now her mind was jumping through hoops in anticipation for how it was going to look.

The door slowly opened. "I'm almost ready." Janie said, in perhaps the softest and kindest voice she'd ever had before.

Her dress was big and white, she was nothing short of stunning and beautiful. As soon as Harley stepped in and closed the door, Janie slipped the veil over the top of her head. Janie's face was still visible, including her warm cheeks.

Janie was looking a little different after a few years. The warmness of her cheeks looked like a mix of aging and eating. She hadn't gained any visible pounds in her waist or her stomach, but her face was definitely fuller. It made her smile more noticeable.

She'd also clearly had work done on her breasts, just as she'd once said she'd like to do. They were now roughly C-cups, and while the silicon was obvious, there was nothing too bizarre about her figure. Harley was glad to see Janie had taken her advice about finding a good surgeon seriously.

"Excited?" Harley said

"In the weirdest way." Janie said, not even hiding her blushing. "I thought I was supposed to be second-guessing or get nervous but I'm not. I'm so, happy. So completely happy. I'm getting married today. This is the last day I'm Janet Olber, I don't even have to think about being Janet Olber. There's someone who I want to spend the rest of my life with and he doesn't feel any different. I don't know why they talk about being nervous, I've never looked forward to something so much."

"So, you are taking his name."

"Of course I am. I'm proud of the fact I'll getting a different name."

"Personally, I always liked hyphenating the two names. I know kids from divorces do that a lot, but I think it works for married people too. By the way, never knew Matt's last name is Vruck."

"I'll be very happy as Jane Vruck. Or, maybe I will start going by Janet now. I don't know, just, Janet sounds older, you know? I think I'm old enough to put Janet down when I sign legal documents."

"You'll still be Janie to me if that's okay."

"Of course, but not Janie Olber. Don't even pretend I was ever called Janie Olber, or Jane Olber, I never want to see the name Olber ever again."

"Speaking of, I met your cousin Pedro."

"Oh, hope you liked him. Pedro's about the only family I have I still like. We played together a bit when we were kids, but he moved so we just kept in contact instead. It's so good to see you again Harley."

Janie offered a hug, and Harley was more than happy to oblige. Once they embraced, it was a little hard to let go. Janie had become maybe Harley's closest friend, and this was the first time being in the same room for well over a year.

The slightly sharp pain across her chest was enough to tell her they'd hugged enough.

"Let me guess." Janie said, happily lifting her chest. "These got ya."

"A little bit." Harley said

"Yeah. They're squishy and everything, but feel them too long and they feel like they look. Still love 'em, as does Matt. When I finally decided to get them done he gave me all these little talks about how he loves the way I look and there's nothing I could or couldn't do to change that. A week after these puppies and he starts batting them like a kitten. Never let guys tell you they don't like fake boobs. Oh, wanna see the ink I got on them?"

"Of course."

The tattoos were on the cleavage, meaning Janie did not have to strip down to show anything. There were vines, clovers, little rabbits and birds.

"Wow." Harley said

"I like to consider these my good luck charms." Janie lifted her dress back up. "Now that I actually like what I see when I look down I thought I'd get as much done on them as I could. I'm thinking I could be more something, but that's not a great idea right now, you know? Sorry for asking, but, am I showing?"

"YOU'RE PREGNANT?!"

"Okay do you not use social media anymore? I got like five hundred comments when I posted that. Frigging Annie told me congratulations."

"When did this happen?!"

"About a week after Matt proposed. Well, that's when we found out. I'm three months in, sort of. It's, such a nice coincidence. We get to start a family almost right after we take our vows, and we didn't even know until after we planned. I get why I could be worried, but, I'm not. I'm making good money and I really, really do want a kid. Matt'll make such a great dad. We're hoping for a boy."

"Well, congratulations. I hope you have a healthy baby."

"So do I. Hey, Annie already knows this, but, could you tell her I'm sorry she wasn't invited. I, talked to her about it. Messaged I mean, and, she agreed that it wouldn't be a good idea, but she needs to hear sorry from somebody."

"Annie mentioned she wasn't invited. It was odd how she wasn't sour about it. She said that it would be better to just be happy for you instead of being here and pretending to get along with you."

"She's not a bad person, and neither am I. We don't get along, we can still find some way to be friends. I've been trying, and I think she is too."

Janie ended up crossing her arms, and screwed up a specific type of smile. "Alright now, tell me." Janie said "Where's your date?"

"I didn't bring one." Harley said

"You're joking." Janie said, cocking her head to the side. "How?"

"Well, you knew about Damian, but I guess I didn't tell you we broke up."

"No, you did. Come on, you have to know what I mean."

"That I would get a date this fast? Sorry, but, no. I didn't."

Janie sighed. "I guess you didn't. …. Really now? There's so much of that I can't believe."

"Janie what are you trying to say to me?"

She sighed again. "I guess either I thought wrong or, you know the other option is incredibly rude to say out loud. And, we don't even have time, because that door is starting to open."

The door did in fact open, and Janie was called to her spot at the end of the aisle.

"My dad isn't here, so." Janie said "I think you have to walk me."

"Eh, alright." Harley said "Sounds appropriate."

Harley and Janie walked away. Harley walked behind, and easily noticed just how often Janie had to stop herself from walking too fast. They took their places, and stood, waiting for their cue in the music.

Without flower girls or bridesmaids, Janie walked down the aisle just as gracefully as a bride with a million of them. Harley could not keep her eyes off her friend. She was as happy as she was proud. Unlike Janie's real father, Harley had watched Janie grow up to be a beautiful woman, had been there for her when she needed someone to confide in.

Matt was in a black tuxedo, clean and well-kept more than Harley had ever seen before. He was the same man Janie fell in love with, and now he looked as great to everyone else as he looked every day to her.

Janie reached the altar, Harley stepping back in her spot. Matt had a best man, who may as well have been featureless for as much as Harley bothered to look in his direction.

"The couple have written their own vows." Said the priest "Matthew, you may go first."

Matt stifled a cough. "Janie, I. I remember how I met you. I didn't mean to go to school that day and help out some stranger, I was just doing what I knew needed to be done. After that, I knew we'd keeping knowing each other, but. I couldn't have expected to be so in love with you. I'm proud that I was there for you, and I'm proud of everything I've ever seen you do. Janie, I know we're good for each other and that you're perfect for me. I'm going to do whatever I can to be perfect for you, and for our little baby. I love you Janie Olber, I think I always did."

Even from the angle Harley was at, she could see Janie beam.

"And now, Janet, your vow." The priest said

"Matty." Janie said "Before I even met you, I don't know what kind of person I was. I was miserable, I hated my life, I couldn't believe in anything or anybody. And I also know it wasn't just knowing you that got me out of that. I learned to love my life, I learned to believe in people. And it wasn't just from you, I know that. And in a way I'm glad it wasn't, because if I had realized I love you and just assumed everything in my life would be been fixed just by being with you, I know I would have dragged you down with me. I wouldn't have been able to forgive myself. And now, I am happy, and all I want now is to share my happiness with you. I do deserve to be happy, and you deserve someone who'll do whatever they can to keep you happy. Now that I'm happy, I know just how nice it really is to be around you. Seeing your face, hearing you speak, the way that you smile and tell me anything you can think of. There's some, warm feeling inside of me that isn't tradable and is the greatest thing I can think of. And I know I make you feel the exact same way. I love you so much,

Matty Vruck. I'm a better person now, but you are still my better half."

After a short pause, the priest began his part. "We are gathered here today."

Harley tuned out the priest, looking only at her friend and the man she was about to marry. Matt's vows had been lovely, a perfect little piece to say how he felt.

And Janie's, even, more so. While listening, Harley could only imagine how if must have felt to have been in her position. And then came the latter half.

Being so in love she was happy just to see him. So in love that anything he said felt fine. The torch that would burn even when things were boring.

Why, oh why, did that sound so familiar?

"You may now kiss the bride."

Harley had to stop her contemplating, there was no way she was going to miss this part.

The reception was absolute fun. The other guests knew how to talk without dragging on too long, which meant Harley could quickly get over to the cake.

"So who made this?" Harley said, wiping frosting from her face.

"A customer of mine is a baker." Janie said "His cakes are about as good as his taste in ink. Last year I got to put the poster to his favorite movie, wrapped around the book it's based on, right on his upper back. You can tell it's a good choice when I say 'I got to' instead of 'I had to'. I'd had some idiotic ideas as well. And a lot of motorcycle logos. Hope they enjoy those."

"He must like your work, because this cake is enormous."

"You bet it is. We figured that a smaller guest list only meant more cake for everyone, so we ordered the regular size. Have as much as you want, you're the maid of honor and every single bridesmaid, if anybody complains I can ask them to leave."

"You don't have to do that, but I am eating more of this."

Harley grabbed herself two more slices of cake. The white frosting had a delicious light crunch to it, and the fluffy inside was the fluffiest she'd ever eaten in her life.

"Hey," Harley said "so all that stuff about, just being the happiest you've ever been by seeing him and talking to him. What, uh, what does that feel like?"

"It feels like how I described it." Janie said "I already did it once, I'm not doing it again."

"Yeah, yeah. It's just, I dunno. It sounded, familiar, to me.

"That's great. It's the best feeling in the world."

Harley thought about it a moment. "It sure sounds like it."

"I think if you've felt it, you'll figure out why." Janie said "In the meantime, enjoy the party. Thank you for everything. Not just the bridesmaid thing, thank you for being my best friend and helping me be who I am. I couldn't ever replace you."

"You either." Harley said "Now go see how your husband is doing, Mrs. Vruck."

"I have every intention."

❤ - *Chapter 50* - ❤

For the past several weeks, college felt like nothing more or less than a painful and slow drag. She remembered she'd gone to classes, but there wasn't a single one that Harley could bring up instantly in her mind. She was having trouble even remembering the class's names, despite the fact she was never late to any of them so far. There was one tonight, and she had too much time to kill.

Today she wore a black flowing shirt, that ended just above her waist. Under it was a short purple shirt, that was visible for a brief second when she turned or ran. Her jeans were blue, and her shoes were black flats. Her nails were painted black, simple but still attractive. On her head was a black and red beret.

She didn't feel like putting too much effort into her clothes and overall look today. After all, it was her birthday. Twenty-three years old, and only just about to finish school in several months. Maybe that's why it was taking its time.

No, that wasn't it. Ever since the wedding, Harley felt like she was missing something. The thing she could not place her finger on was bugging her to a bigger degree than she expected. At first she thought she was over-thinking it, but that couldn't be the case by this point.

Annie walked through the door. Her hair had gone to a short brown, a thin and tiny ponytail coming out of the very back. She was wearing a white t-shirt with a pink heart and red arrow through it, and a blue jean skirt. She and Malcolm had gone on a date.

"So how did it go?" Harley said

"He's still the greatest date I've ever had." Annie said "And, well, we kind of talked about some serious things."

"Oh?"

"It's not a secret that Malcolm will graduate before I do, since I still have about five or so years left until I can get my medical license. And, Malcolm just told me that while he's not sure exactly how far the relationship will go by that point, he knows we are still going to be together and that he's going to patiently wait for me until school is out of the way."

"That's wonderful."

"I know. I knew one day I wouldn't run around anymore, and, I'm starting to think I'm really close to it."

There was a knock on the door.

"Can't be for me." Annie said "Must be you."

Harley got up, and opened the door.

The fluttering inside her gut felt so strong she was surprising the hallway didn't hear it.

"Max!" She said "What a nice surprise. Come in."

"I can't actually." Max said "I'm on my way to a class but I have about ten minutes. I, well, I've got something for you and today seemed like the right day."

Max was wearing a light purple vest over a blue-and-black dress shirt. Its pattern resembled a bowling shirt, but the fabric was clearly a higher quality, and looked far better than a typical bowling shirt too. His slacks were black with hints of white and blue. His shoes were brand new, white with a pink bottom.

He reached into his jean pocket, and retrieved a little silk bag.

"Luna finished the design you sent her." Max said, giving her a smile. "This is your last semester, and you might as well show it off as soon as you can while you're still here."

Harley needed no further instruction. She opened the jewelry bag, and found the college ring she and Max has designed. It was large, she'd chosen the style men typical chose, her finger could handle it.

It was gold and platinum, at least in color. There were little pink stones all around it, with the center ones being a slightly darker pink. This was an evolved version of her high school ring, and it was perfect for her finger.

She slipped it on, snugly onto her right ring finger. It glistened in her eyes, and she went straight over to her jewelry box.

"Tell me something." Harley said "You see, when I got older I always thought about turning into one of those middle-aged ladies who go everywhere wearing every single ring they own all at once." She slipped on her metal black heart thumb ring and her onyx and bronze middle finger ring. "How's it look at this age?"

"Excessive in a good way." Max said

"Can I say something too? Annie said

"Sure." Harley said

"Those look really nice together. If you want to be like the old ladies you're going to need more, but this is such a good start you may just want to wear those ones every day."

"I agree." Max said "Lots of finger rings aren't too hard too pull off, and you're already doing it, so all you need to do now it get used to the feeling."

"Thank you so much." Harley said "You and Luna did a perfect job on this. It's not as heavy as I thought it would be, too."

"Gold's a lighter material than you'd think. And, it's not plated so it's not as heavy." Max said

"You spend this much on me?" Harley said "Wow. I guess I'm getting out my checkbook."

"Hey, it's fine." Max said "Like I said, I felt like you should have it today considering what it is. I have to go, so Happy Valen-"

Max stopped himself. Harley felt a blood rush to her face. She wasn't wondering what the word was, she knew it. But, for some reason, she needed to hear him say it.

"I mean," Max said "Happy, Happy Birth-. No, no, I did mean Happy Valentine's day. You should have something nice for Valentine's day. You don't get one this year and you just had one last year, so, Happy Valentine's day."

".... Thank you." Harley said, and she meant it, more than she knew. "Happy Valentine's day to you too Max. Can I, call you later or-, wait, I have a night class. We'll talk soon."

"Great. Looking forward to to. Goodbye." Max left, he was already late for his class by this point, it was best to get going.

Annie closed the door, and Harley sit admiring her ring. The gesture of just giving it to her for free. So, kind. And, it wasn't out of place. Something like this from somebody else, and she'd have refused to not pay. With Max, it felt right. She could easily do something just as nice for him, and she would, somehow. It felt right to do the nicest thing for him she could think of, just in general, really.

"This really is beautiful." Harley said

"Yeah…" Anne said

"I hope when I pay him back it's with something just as lovely."

"…. Hey. Look, Harls. I need to say something to you."

Harley looked up. "Okay."

"Now, I need to be as blunt as I can be with this."

"I don't see anything wrong with blunt."

"Okay then. You're a fucking idiot."

"Alright, and you're a ho bag. Any reason we're suddenly insulting each other?"

Annie grabbed her chair, sitting down exactly across from Harley.

"What do you plan to do when school's over?" Annie said

"Become an architect, you know that." Harley said

"I do. Is there anything else you want? I don't just mean from school, or in the far future, the near future. Is there anything you want? Even if you can't think of it exactly?"

"Huh." Harley said "Yeah. And I really don't know it."

"Then think really hard about it." Annie said "Think about what you know about it, when you feel it, everything you can. Because the thing is Harley, I know what it is, and if I have to tell you, then I can't be sure you really deserve it."

Harley took a moment to reel the whole thing in. "I guess that's fair. Okay. I'll just close my eyes, and think about, whatever comes to mind. Maybe that's the best way to do it."

Close her eyes she did. At first, black, nothing at all. She then tried thinking about school. Her classes. It was still completely nothing.

Food was always a nice thought. Chocolate cake, pancakes. Hotdogs. Her mind went very quickly to hotdogs.

And hotdogs led to Max. Even without open eyes, she knew she was smiling. Even picturing Max made her happy.

She tried thinking of something else, but then, she didn't end up wanting to. Max was in her thoughts, and there were events she wanted to replay.

Him sleeping on the floor in a sleeping bag with her. Their first night together and the barbeque where they met. The fashion show she still regretted leaving. The New Years party. Being his model. The first time she told him she was born on Valentine's day. Chatting in Professor Anghula's class. The hug she got when she told him Janie was moving. The look on his face when she told him Damian asked her out. Lunch in the mall food court.

There wasn't a single minor or major event in her mind with Max Turtle that wasn't immemorable. The same feeling was in her gut, but this time, the warmness and happiness instead felt, reassuring. This time, it didn't feel like it was confusing her. It felt like the answer was right in front of her face, and she would get it.

She tried for any other memory, and all she got was Janie's weddings vows, and the discussion they tried to have.

They were related, this memory and Max Turtle. Or at least, she felt that until she said it out loud.

"What does Max have to do with being in lov-"

She opened her eyes, and took a few seconds to recover from the shock.

She had to be sure that was the answer. The exact reason, every single thing that she needed to know. Was she in love? Had she finally figured out what love was and felt like, because she'd already found the one she was supposed to be with?

She asked herself another question: "Do I want that to be the answer?"

That question was easier to figure out, and the divisiveness was completely gone. Instead of thinking or talking to herself any more, she instead began running straight out the door.

Max's classes this semester were all in the same building, she remembered him saying that before. She didn't have time to call him, and he wouldn't answer it after being late already. She had to hope to catch him before he got there.

He was about to open the door to get it.

"Max!" Harley said

"Huh?" Max did not open the door, but his hand was still on it. "Is something wrong?"

"Max, don't go to class right now." Harley said "I. I need to tell you something and I don't know if I can be quick about it."

Max let go of the door. "Okay. Shoot."

"I.….." Harley was struggling for the words. She knew it now, knew it without a doubt, and the hardest part of the realization was how to put it in coherent words.

"Max. You, you and I. I'm sorry Max, I. I'm sorry that I'm trying to say this to you but it took me so long to find out, and, and if I don't say it now I don't know if I'll ever find the right time. You mean, more to me than anyone else ever has. And I've always said that to you, and I always meant it. But I never realized exactly how much it meant to me, and what I really should have been saying. Max, you are the greatest guy I've ever met and you deserve to be happier than anybody else I know, you're too good to me and everyone else and that should come back around to you more than anyone.

"And the truth is, I didn't know what I really thought about you and everything you've done for me. You've been the best parts of my day, you've said the right things to make me smile, and I can't think of anything you could do to really make me truly mad or upset! Max, when I first came here you were the first person I made friends with and I made one of the greatest memories I could ever have, and nothing about it could have been made better, because it was with you.

"I didn't expect the first man I ever slept with to be the one I wanted to spend the rest of my life with, but you are!"

Harley could feel hot tears come down, but they could not stop her.

"I love you, Max Turtle. I didn't think I knew what love was but it's been staring me in the face practically since the first time we talked. I've grown to love you more and more every day and there's no one else I think I could be in love with other than you. And I know we're just friends, so if we can't be together, then I love you so much that I know you deserve to hear what I really, truly think of you. You complete me, and I'll always be there for you no matter what you may think of me."

Harley couldn't wipe away the tears. She could not do anything, until she got a reply. It was not long before she did.

"You have no clue how happy you've just made me." Max said

Instead of saying another word, Max and Harley ran into each other arms for a hard wet kiss.

"I love you." Harley said

"I love you too." Max said

"When did you know?"

"The morning after the photo shoot. I couldn't stop thinking about how you made me feel, and I'd already thought I may have liked you more than a friend before that. I tried so hard to say something but it couldn't not matter how badly I wanted to."

"I didn't even know it was love until now. I feel like an idiot, you were everything I wanted and my whole body was telling me. Oh God, I broke your heart when Damian came along didn't I?"

"As long as you were happy I knew I would survive."

"Oh Max."

"I'm going to cut class. I don't want to do anything today but be with you now."

"Then I guess that makes two of us."

And so, dear reader, that was their love story.

♥ - Epilogue - ♥

Harley and Max were able to graduate holding hands. The rest of their lives ahead of them, their dreams now slightly changed to more than just the careers they choose, with now a long life of loving each other.

As for everyone else;

Annie later graduated early at the top of her class, and became the top respected surgeon in the state. She and Malcolm married a year later. Eventually, they were blessed with the miracle of twins. Twice.

Janie and Matt's first child was in fact a son. Five years after, Janie gave birth to a daughter. The Vruck family became the owners of a successful tattoo parlor, and both children ended up taking up the trade from their mother.

Will and Sarah married happily the same year as Janie and Matt, with an expensive wedding that pleased both sets of parents. They later had one child, a son who took a lot after his mother in terms of hobbies.

Izzy and Sheena hit it off after meeting at the party, and later married. They adopted three sons, one of them took up the Platt family tradition.

Clyde Feathers finally struck luck with his football question, settling down with a sports reporter. They ended up raising two daughters.

Luna became closer to Victor after they had an idea to open up shop together. One half erotica, the other half jewelry. He became her second husband.

Dom ended up being Chad's true love, with Harley becoming maid of honor for the second time thanks to the both of them.

Mimi spent enough time at the bar to get the attention of the bartender. She wore him down in no time, and they married with one child, a daughter.

Damian also met someone at the bar, a laid-back woman who wore her sunglasses almost everywhere. They married with one child, a son.

Alex proved to truly be a fashion prodigy after all, and opened a successful brand of dress stores. He never married, but did adopt a son and a daughter.

Professor Bills-Brooke passed away in his sleep at the age of 87. A wing in the math department was dedicated to his memory.

Clive the dog exceeded all expectations and lived to the age of 16. He was surrounded by the humans who loved him.

Josh was arrested.

Professor Anghula quit her job to work full time on her almost-pornographic video content. It was not as successful as she convinced herself it was.

And of course, there is still more to say about those two.

Harley Millsboone-Turtle was sitting outside, admiring the house she had designed for her and her family. A secure and stylish roof, lovely white walls, a little bit of art deco in the best possible way. She felt like this was the best one she'd done, especially counting who it belonged to.

She was wearing a quite white sundress and sandals. The sun was glistening off her rings. Her college ring, the rings Annie and Janie had bought her well over ten years ago, and the set that made her happiest of all. Her wedding band and original engagement ring.

A mix of emerald, ruby, and pink diamond. Max still knew what she loved, even now.

She looked up from her patio chair, and caught her husband playing with their beautiful daughter.

Max was wearing a simple blue t-shirt and blue jeans, brown sneakers. He still dressed like he did all those years ago when they went out, but when they were home, he had to dress comfortably enough to do house chores and keep up with the little one.

Their daughter was six now, and could play as much as she could talk, it felt. Their little bundle of joy did not have an off-switch as long as she was awake.

Like her mother, she was wearing a quiet dress. White with hints of yellow and pink, designed by her loving father himself. She had short brown hair, and while her skin tone was very close to her father's, facially she looked just like her mother did at her age.

"Mommy!" She said, running over to Harley.

"Hey baby." Harley said, helping her daughter climb up into her lap.

She had to be careful, she and Max's second child was comfortably on his way. Harley was happy when the ultrasound revealed a boy. While Will had been an older brother, and the age difference between them was smaller than her own children's would be, she knew how wonderful having a brother was, and looked forward to her daughter knowing that experience too.

"Hey mommy." She said

"I know. Hey pumpkin." Harley said, rubbing her daughter's head.

"Whatcha doing?"

"Relaxing."

"Why?"

"Well, mommy works hard, so mommy is relaxing because she can now."

"Oh. That makes sense."

Max walked over to them. "How are my favorite girls doing?"

"Mommy's not a girl." Their daughter said "I'm a girl."

"Mom's are girls too sweetheart." Harley said, giving a warm smile.

"Mommy's been a girl since before I met her." Max said

"How did you meet?" Their daughter said

"Uuuuuuuuuuuh." Harley was at a loss for words.

"We met in college." Max said "At a barbeque. We became friends and later fell in love with each other."

"Can we have a barbeque?" She said

"Maybe." Harley said, composure back in place. "Sometime, okay?"

"Okay. I wanna get down and play now."

Max lifted her off of Harley's lap, and set her back on the grass. She ran off quick, but not out of her parent's sight.

"Nice save." Harley said "Just about the only person besides my mother who I can't tell that I fucked you so good I practically had to love you."

Max laughed, which led to the smile Harley still enjoyed seeing just as much all these years later.

"I love you." Max said "So much."

"I know." Harley said "I love you too. And I won't get tired of hearing it."

"Good, because I still don't think I've said it enough to make up for all I times I should have said it."

"I'll take that as a promise."

The End

Thank you

CPSIA information can be obtained
at www.ICGtesting.com
Printed in the USA
LVHW030214110520
655341LV00019B/1768